KT-404-529

A2 397 493 3

Daughter of the Downs

By the same author:

Theatre of Dreams
Portrait of a Star
Brighton Belle

Daughter of the Downs

PEGGY EATON

LITTLE BROWN & COMPANY

A Little, Brown book

First published in Great Britain by
Little, Brown in 1995

A CIP catalogue for this book
is available from the British Library.

Typeset by Solidus (Bristol) Limited
Printed and bound in Great Britain by
Clays Ltd, St. Ives plc

ISBN 0 316 87570 8

Little, Brown and Company (UK)
Brettenham House
Lancaster Place
London WC2E 7EN

FOR MARGARET RANDALL

Acknowledgements

With thanks to the following for their permission to use songs included in this book:

'La Novia' – words and music by Joaquin Prieto and sub-author Fred Jay. © 1961 Editions Fermata, Argentina. Reproduced by permission of Peter Maurice Music Co. Ltd. London WC2H 0EA.

'Room With A View' – words and music by Noel Coward. © 1928 Chappell Music Ltd. London W1Y 3FA. Reproduced by permission of International Music Publications Ltd.

'I'll See You Again' – words and music by Noel Coward. © 1929 Chappell Music Ltd. London W1Y 3FA. Reproduced by permission of International Music Publications Ltd.

'Zigeuner' – words and music by Noel Coward. © 1929 Chappell Music Ltd. London W1Y 3FA. Reproduced by permission of International Music Publications Ltd.

'My Life Belongs to You' words by Christopher Hassall, music by Ivor Novello. © 1939 Chappell Music Ltd. London W1Y 3FA. Reproduced by permission of International Music Publications Ltd.

Daughter of the Downs

CHAPTER ONE

Valley Farm, Sussex 1931

'Get out of my house, woman,' Moses Crow stormed, 'and don't come back until you've got rid of it and I can bear the sight of you.'

Edith clutched her swollen stomach as another contraction seized her 'But where can I go?' she asked helplessly.

Her husband plunged his huge hands into the stone sink and splashed cold water over his grizzled head. Then he shook himself like a dog.

'I don't know and I don't care. Go to the barn where I can't hear your wailing, or have it under a hedge like the beasts of the field.'

Obedient, as she'd been all her married life, Edith padded to the door on slippered feet. She had her pride and even in her agony tried to hold herself upright, but as she reached the step she bent over and clutched the gnarled frame.

'Moses,' she begged. 'I'm going to die.'

'Die then! But not in my kitchen. Get on with it, woman. As it is I shall have to see to the cows for you.'

Bent double like an old woman, Edith Crow stepped into the yard and disappeared from her husband's view. He pulled a rough towel from the string line and rubbed his hair so that it stood out like wire wool around his red, angry face.

'Where's Edie then?'

Matthew was standing in the inner doorway, his narrow shoulders rounded under the grey shirt he'd slept in. His innocent blue eyes stared at his brother like a trusting child's. His thick bottom lip pouted miserably.

'Gone out.'

'Gone out?' Matthew Crow tried out the words as if he didn't understand their meaning. His sister-in-law, Edie, should be getting his breakfast like she did every morning; and now Moses was telling him she'd gone out. He looked around despairingly at the unswept hearth and the cold porringer. 'But I want my breakfast, Mo.'

'Then you must get it yourself.'

Although the words were surly, the tone was gentler than the one he'd used to his wife. As the elder brother Moses Crow had protected and cared for Matt ever since the death of their parents. Matthew had always needed protecting because, although he was physically a grown man, mentally he wasn't much brighter than the animals on Valley Farm. Edie was usually kind to him too: fetching and carrying, and seeing to his needs as diligently as she did for her husband. Matt knew he was lucky, because without their care he might have been sent to an institution.

Impatient with the helpless way his brother looked around the kitchen, Moses picked up a knife and carved two slabs of bread from a loaf on the table. Smearing one generously with butter he held it out.

'Thanks, Mo.' Matt accepted the bread gratefully and took a large bite, scattering crumbs in all directions. 'Where's she gone then?'

'Who?'

'Edie. Where's Edie gone?'

'Out the front. She's got the bellyache.'

Matt's eyes widened. He knew what that meant. Hadn't he tended Star when she was in foal? Hadn't he been watching Edie's belly growing all spring, and guessed before the summer was over she'd drop it?

'Where is she, Mo?'

'I told you, she's out the front somewhere.'

'Well, shouldn't you be with her?'

'What for?'

'The baby. She'll need someone with her when she drops it.'

'What do you know about a baby, Matt?'

Moses sounded angry. Matt crammed the last of the bread into his mouth so that his cheeks bulged.

'Nothing, Mo,' he muttered, but he glanced slyly in his brother's direction.

'Listen, Matt.' Moses was kind again. 'You know Edie can't have babies – not live ones, anyroad. Aren't there four babies buried up in the churchyard? My four sons. The sons she promised me. All stillborn. I only wanted one, Matt. I'd have settled for one.'

'I know, Mo. I'm sorry. Perhaps this one'll live.'

'Which one?'

'The one she's dropping now.'

'If she drops a baby today, Matt, it's not one of mine, that's for certain. I haven't been near her since the last one was buried, and well you know it.'

'But Mo . . .'

'You know it, Matt. Go on, tell me you know it.'

'I guess I know it, Mo.'

Matthew spoke slowly and obediently as if he was reciting a lesson He saw his brother relax and knew he'd done right. But he couldn't forget, nothing could make him forget, the time Moses had got drunk.

It was just before Christmas, last year when there'd been a sudden cold spell. The grass had been white with frost, and the water in his pitcher had frozen in the night. He'd had to break it with the back of a brush before he could wash his face in the morning. The root vegetables had been solid in the ground, held hard in an iron grip, and no matter how he dug and turned the ground he couldn't loosen them.

'Pray,' Moses had ordered them. 'Pray for a thaw.' And Edie and Matthew had prayed over their fast cooling bowls of porridge for a let-up in the inclement weather, so that they could harvest the last of the year's produce.

It was Matthew who'd found the bottle of whisky hidden in the cellar. Strong drink wasn't allowed in the house since Moses had found God and taken the pledge. It was an old bottle, green with mildew and dusted with cobwebs, but when he'd wiped it on his shirt-tail he'd seen that it was full and unopened.

His thick lips and cold hands had trembled with desire, and he'd opened the bottle. The first draught had burnt his tongue so that he'd spat it out. The second mouthful had made him gag. But the third had been bliss, and he'd sat down on the straw-littered floor cradling the bottle on his lap.

'What you got there, Matt?'

He still remembered how he'd jumped guiltily at the sight of Mo's thick body standing above him on the stone stairs. He'd looked like some avenging angel outlined against the fading daylight: legs akimbo and hands on hips.

'Nothing, Mo,' he'd tried to say. He'd shoved the bottle between his legs; but his voice had given him away, the words coming out blurred.

But Moses Crow, the bible thumper, the man of God, had made him hand over the bottle. Matt had shrunk back, waiting for the lecture on the evils of the demon drink, but Moses had only chuckled.

'Don't tell Edie,' he'd whispered. 'Just one to keep out the cold.'

But the one had turned into two, and as the light in the cellar had faded the brothers had drained the bottle, smacking their lips with glee like errant schoolboys. Matt couldn't remember when he'd been so happy: probably not since they'd been children together and caught out in some naughtiness. So when Moses unloosed his belt and relieved himself against the wall Matt followed suit, more out of bravado than need.

He was already fumbling with his buttons, his unsteady hands finding it difficult, when he became aware of the silence. Moses was staring at him, such a look on his face that Matthew bit his lip in fear.

'What is it, Mo?'

'Come here, brother.'

Holding up his heavy trousers with one hand, Matt walked slowly across the floor to stand in front of Moses. The bigger man seemed to sway in front of him, but perhaps it was only himself that was swaying.

'Clap your hands.'

'No!'

Matt knew what was coming next. Wasn't it the game they

used to play when they were boys? Or at least Moses said it was a game, although Matt didn't enjoy it at all. Games were supposed to be fun, but the games Moses had played with his younger brother were never fun, particularly the one where he had to clap his hands so that his pants fell down.

'Do as I say, brother. Clap your hands.'

Matt had no option but to obey. He kept his elbows tightly to his sides to try and hold the waistband in place, but he hadn't managed to fasten the button and the heavy twill of his working trousers slid down over his thighs to land in a wrinkled pool around his bony ankles.

'Bend over.'

'I don't like this game,' Matt whispered, as he had when he was ten years old.

'You'll like it even less if you don't bend over.'

'I don't want to.'

'Stop whining, you little sod, and do as you're told.'

But Matt wasn't ten years old any more. Although he was afraid of his brother, he hadn't drunk nearly as much from the bottle so he was steadier on his feet, and his weak brain was still working in its usual sluggish fashion. He wasn't going to let Moses hurt him any more. Even the beasts in the yard didn't treat each other in this fashion. Matt didn't know anything about love, but he knew enough about sex to feel uncomfortable about the way Moses liked to use him. Never again! He wasn't going to let him do it ever again!

'No!' he screamed, and backed away, hastily pulling up his trousers. 'No!'

He'd never said no to Moses before. He'd always been as obedient as Edie, or the dog in the yard who'd learned early to keep out of the master's way.

A look of astonishment passed over Moses' puffy features. Matthew held his breath, waiting for the storm to break. But it didn't.

Moses stood there in the gloom, the empty bottle shining greeny-brown and gold in his hand, and his corduroy trousers bulging at the crotch. Then he carefully laid the bottle down on a nearby box and, using his huge hands to steady himself, he climbed the stairs into the house calling for Edie.

Matthew had remained huddled in the cellar, one ear cocked to hear what was happening overhead. He heard his brother call his wife's name twice; and her answer, soft and indistinct. Half an hour must have passed, although Matt had no means of judging the time, before he was brave enough to venture up the stairs, and then it was hunger that moved him.

He'd thought his luck was in: that Moses had come to his senses and gone about his work. Perhaps he could grab some leftovers from the larder to fill his belly.

The passage seemed to be empty and he could see the flecks of dust hovering over the grey slabs of the kitchen floor. There was a freezing draught coming from somewhere and Matt huddled his shoulders in discomfort. And then he saw them. On the floor, halfway under the deal table like two old sacks. Edith was sprawled on her back where her husband had thrown her; her hair, which was usually screwed tightly into the nape of her neck, had fallen down and was strewn around her pale face. Her lips were clenched tightly into a semblance of a grin, and her eyes were tightly closed as if she was asleep. But Matt knew she wasn't asleep because he could see the panting of her breath under her old jumper as Matt pumped into her again and again. Her woollen skirt was up around her waist like a screwed up rag, and Matt could see the whiteness of her thighs and the dark wet cavern between them.

He'd watched the mating of the animals in the farmyard too often to be surprised, but he'd never witnessed the act between human beings before, and it excited him. His arms and legs were cold as ice but his loins were burning. He was so hard his newly buttoned trousers felt tight and uncomfortable. Automatically he unbuttoned himself and was astounded at how large his member had grown. It must be the sight of the half-naked woman, who seemed to have no resemblance to his sister-in-law, that had made his head throb. And then Moses had looked up over his shoulder and seen him.

'Don't go, brother.' Moses was on all fours, but he was grinning and looked friendly again, so Matthew, who'd started to back away, stopped in his tracks. 'This filly isn't bothered who she goes with. You'd never believe who she was with last week. It's your turn now; show her you're a match for any country gentleman.'

Matthew didn't know what Moses was talking about, but like a sleepwalker he took his brother's place. He wasn't sure what was expected of him, but instinct took over and he copied what he had seen. Edie didn't seem to mind. She was like a dead thing, only the rising and falling of her chest giving away the fact that she was indeed alive.

When he was exhausted Moses led him away. They were both stone-cold sober as they faced each other in the cold passage.

'I've made a man of you, Matt,' Moses said. 'You should be grateful.'

'I am, Mo. Thanks.'

'But you got to forget what happened – right?'

'Forget?'

'That's what I said, brother. Think of it as a dream. A happy dream; but now you've woken up.'

Matthew was puzzled; he didn't understand. For the first time in his life he'd made it, or damn near made it, with a woman, and now he was to forget all about it. What about Moses? What about Edie? Surely they wouldn't forget.

'But Mo . . .'

'We won't talk about it again, Matt. It didn't happen, see? Nothing happened. Do you understand?'

He wanted to argue. He opened his mouth to argue but Moses stopped him quickly

'It was a mistake, Matt, a silly mistake. It could happen to anyone. You know I haven't slept with Edie since the last baby died. I swore I wouldn't. It was God's will. He told me not to.'

'But Moses.' Matt's voice faltered. 'Didn't God see you just now?'

'If he saw me, brother, he saw you.' Mo's voice was soft but menacing. 'If God saw you with my wife – he'd send you to hell.'

Matthew knew his brother was right. Didn't it say something like that in the Bible, in the Ten Commandments? Since he'd found God Moses Crow liked to preach in the chapel, and he'd threatened eternal damnation to anyone who made love to another man's wife.

'You're right,' he said quickly. 'I suppose I was dreaming. It never happened, did it?'

He'd almost but not quite forgotten the day he'd found the whisky bottle. He shook his head and was back in the present.

'You know I haven't been near Edie since we buried the last

baby,' Moses was saying for the second time. 'Don't you, brother?' Matthew nodded. 'If you've finished eating you can start watering the animals. I'm off to the top pasture. There's a break in the fence I noticed last night that needs mending.'

Matthew licked his fingers. He was still hungry but the last of the bread was gone. He could have made some porridge; there was a bag of oats on the shelf, but that was Edie's job and it never occurred to him to do it for himself. His job was to don the old-fashioned yoke and carry out the water for the animals. Valley Farm had never moved into the twentieth century, and the brothers went about their business as their forefathers had done.

Although it was a hot August day Matthew put on the leather vest that would protect his shoulders, and slung the yoke across. The pails containing water and grain swung unsteadily against his legs as he walked in his heavy boots across the cobbled yard.

He stumbled. 'Get away!' he yelled at the hens who followed him, pecking at the fallen grain. The black dog, Sampson, came barking loudly at the sound of his voice. He aimed a friendly kick in its direction. It rolled adoring eyes at him and attacked his dangling string laces that threatened to trip him up at every turn.

He forgot about Edie. He forgot about Moses. As he went about his daily tasks he forgot everything, until his stomach rumbled at midday and he retraced his steps to the house.

'Edie!' he called, lowering the empty pails to the ground. There was no answer. 'Edie!'

And then it came back to him. If his brother's explanation for Edie's absence was correct, surely she must have dropped the baby by now. Matt didn't know anything about babies, but surely if she'd had it she should be back at her job of getting his dinner. Meat pudding was what he fancied; or chops with plenty of vegetables and gravy.

'Edie!'

The kitchen was just as he'd left it earlier, so now that he was unencumbered Matthew went in search of his sister-in-law.

The farm was deserted, like a dead place. Even the animals were silent, either feeding or basking in the heat of the midday sun.

He tried the barn and the dairy, but there was only the

solitary donkey meditating in a corner of the cobwebby barn, and the dairy stank of sour milk and unwashed pots. The long side barn hadn't been used for years. It housed only some ancient machinery that occasionally generated electricity for the house. Most of the time it was out of action, and then they lit tallow candles or just packed up and went to bed early.

The door was standing ajar. Hesitantly Matthew pushed it wider and stepped inside.

It was a place of shadows. The giant water wheel took pride of place as it reared its ugly head and rusty spokes towards the rafters. Something moved nearby, and Matt looked up for the hanging shapes of the bats that sometimes roosted there.

The movement came again, nearer the floor, to the right, followed by a sigh that made his blood run cold. Was it a ghost? Matt could believe almost anything. But then he saw her . . .

Edith had made herself a makeshift bed in the corner, almost under the wheel. She'd arranged a couple of sacks on the floor and a bundle of straw for a pillow before stretching herself out. She looked just as she'd looked that day in the winter when he'd seen her on the kitchen floor, her legs stretched pale and her skirt wound up around her waist. But now her eyes were open, and she'd pulled another sack over the mound of her stomach. Her eyes seemed to be begging him. As Matt stared she drew her knees up and rocked from side to side in silent agony. If she'd been a cow or a mare Matthew would have known what to do; but faced with a woman he felt helpless and started to turn away.

'Matt.' Her soft voice held him and he had to say something.

'You all right, Edie?'

'Help me, Matt . . . please.'

He wanted to run. He wanted the warm kitchen and a plate of steak and kidney pie, and Edie there to wait on him. But her eyes held his in desperation and he couldn't ignore her. He sank down beside her on his haunches. He saw the pile of flesh-coloured stockinet underwear she'd folded neatly on the floor, and the rolled ball of her grey cotton stockings.

'Help me!' she begged again, and then moaned as a fresh contraction seized her.

He didn't have to be an expert. Edie was the expert and she guided him. Hadn't she already given birth to four children –

four dead children – and even if this proved to be the fifth dead child only she could expel it from her body. So she panted and groaned, biting her lips until the blood came and her front teeth were stained red.

'Hold onto my hand, Matt,' she commanded. He took her hand between his big dirty palms and didn't flinch when her fingernails dug into his flesh.

They both lost track of the time. He knew when the baby was coming because he felt her breathing change and her whole body flowed with the rhythm as she bore down. It wasn't that different from the cattle, he marvelled. Then it was over. He held the little squirming creature in his hands and automatically wiped away the blood and mucus. Then he cut the cord as Edith instructed.

They rolled the baby in Matthew's shirt and made a hollow in the straw for a bed. Then Edie smiled at Matthew for the first time.

'Do you know where Moses is?'

'He said he was going up to the top field.'

'He'll be wanting his dinner.'

She asked for a pail of water and some rags. Matthew watched as she scooped out a hole and buried the afterbirth, and then, completely unembarrassed, she cleaned herself up. She didn't glance once at the bundle in the straw. When she'd finished he tried to help her to her feet but she pushed him away.

'I'm all right, Matt.'

When she'd finished coiling up her hair she headed for the doorway. He had to run to catch up with her.

'Edie . . . the baby!'

'I expect it's dead, Matt.' There was no emotion in her voice. 'I only have dead babies.'

Matt looked back over his shoulder. He was sure he saw the bundle move.

'It's not dead, Edie. I saw it move. You can't leave it there.'

'Well, I can't take it into the house. Moses won't let me.'

'But who will look after it, Edie?'

'I suppose God will have to.' Edie laughed, but there was no humour in the sound. 'It's in his hands. There's nothing I can do about it.'

Matthew shifted nervously from one foot to the other. The

gap between them was widening and he didn't know what to do. After all, it was Edie's baby. She was responsible. So why did he feel so bad?

'Perhaps we can smuggle it into the house, Edie, without Mo knowing.'

'And what happens when it cries? He's bound to hear it. Leave it there and come away.'

'I can't, Edie.' Matthew was whimpering and there were tears on his cheek. 'And you shouldn't either. Even Tess stayed with her babies; she didn't leave them to die.' Tess was the farm cat, a half-wild tabby who regularly had litters in the barn.

Edith stopped in her tracks A bitter expression passed over her pale face but vanished as swiftly as it had come, so that only her eyes were alive, dark and gleaming like two hard pebbles.

'And what happened to Tess's last litter, Matt? Tell me that.'

'Moses made me drown them.' The words were soft, but they seemed to echo around the dusty place. Matt wished he hadn't spoken.

'And that's what he'll get you to do again if we take it into the house. It's better to leave it there.'

Edith seemed to have regained her strength. She turned away, and swinging her stockings like two long grey ropes she walked across the cobbled yard towards the farmhouse door. He wanted to follow her but the bundle half-hidden in the straw drew him. He dropped to his knees beside it. Perhaps Edie was right. It didn't stir as he put out his hand to push the shirt back from the tiny face. It must be dead.

But it wasn't dead. Its eyes were open and they were the colour of newly opened violets, pale and delicate. There was a fringe of dark hair on its head and its tiny mouth was making sucking movements. It was so frail it wouldn't survive even if they had taken it into the house. With Moses around perhaps it would be better dead.

And then it mewed, just like Tess's kittens had done just before he'd drowned them in the bucket. The violet eyes seemed to be looking straight at him.

'What you doing, brother?'

Guiltily Matthew sprang to his feet, grabbing a rake that was leaning against the wall nearby. He raked the loose straw into a heap so that it covered the pathetic bundle.

'Just tidying up a bit, Mo.'

'About time too. We should oil these ratchets before the weather sets in.'

Moses started to test the chains that held the heavy wheel in place. Matthew prayed that the baby wouldn't mew again.

'I'll see to it, Mo.'

'Why are you so nervous? What have you been up to?' Moses stared at his brother and Matthew felt his neck reddening.

'Nothing.'

'Well, get into the house and get some dinner. That gale last week had a couple of trees down. You can take a saw to them this afternoon. The log pile's getting low.'

'Yes, Mo.'

He sounded so eager that Moses stopped in the doorway as if he suspected something. But what could he suspect of a simple-minded man like Matt? With a grin he turned on his heel and stumped his way across the yard.

A savoury smell was issuing from the kitchen door. Edith was back in control. Moses wasn't interested in her morning's activities. That was women's work, and as long as she was back in harness like the beasts he owned, all was well with his life and Valley Farm.

Edith heaved the iron pan onto the range and a pain shot through her making her gasp. Perhaps she shouldn't be lifting things so soon. It felt as if her insides were falling out. But what option had she? She dropped three fat chops into the bubbling lard and some cakes of potato and cabbage. Moses loved bubble-and-squeak, and it was quick and a good way of using up yesterday's leftovers.

'Sit down. It won't be long,' she said to her husband. 'Where's Matt?'

'He's coming.'

The chair creaked under the weight of Moses' big frame. Edith silently placed three sets of knives and forks on the table and then returned to the range. The hot fat shimmered in the heat and jumped out of the pan like fire-crackers, burning her bare arm under the rolled up sleeve and making her jump back.

She wasn't hungry, but not wanting any questions she

divided the contents of the pan between the plates and carried them to the table. The smell of grease made her feel sick. She forced a forkful of food into her mouth and washed it down with a gulp of water.

But she couldn't face any more. With a clatter she dropped the fork onto the table and rose to her feet. The chair leg screeched across the worn stone slabs.

'Where you going?' Moses was chewing, his mouth opening and closing as if it was on springs.

'To get Matt. His dinner's getting cold.'

'That's his fault. Sit down, woman.'

Edith sank back into her chair. With relief she heard the ring of boots on the cobbles and saw her brother-in-law standing in the doorway. He was in his vest and his arms were clasped tightly across his chest. He was carrying his shirt. A silly grin lit his unshaven face and he licked his lips nervously as he edged into the room.

'Come and sit down,' Moses said kindly. 'Your dinner's getting cold.'

'I'm not hungry.'

'Don't mumble, Matt.' Her husband's sudden sharpness made Edith nervous as well, and she dropped the forkful of food that was halfway to her mouth. It clattered from the table to the floor. 'What's the matter with you, woman?'

'Nothing, Moses.' Edie bent down to pick up the fork and the room spun dizzily. She suddenly felt weak.

'Now, what did you say, brother?' Moses was looking around the table as if he'd lost something. 'Where's the bread, Edie?'

'There isn't any left. I didn't bake this morning.'

'You know I like bread to soak up the fat.'

'I'm sorry, Moses. I'll make another batch tomorrow.'

'Pass me a spoon, Matt.' Matthew edged across to the dresser. He almost dropped his shirt as he passed a spoon with one hand to his brother. 'Did you remember to grease Betsy's udders as the veterinary said?'

'Yes, Mo,' Matt said, proud that he'd remembered.

'And the cow with the torn ear – did you see to that?'

'Sorry, Mo . . . I forgot. I'll do it first thing this afternoon.'

'Sit down and eat, Matt, and stop hovering.' Moses turned in his chair, the spoon in his hand 'And put your shirt on for heaven's sake.' Matthew froze. Moses was staring at him and the expression on Edith's face frightened him. He was suddenly scared. 'I said put your shirt on.'

'I can't, Mo.'

'Why not? I see, you've got something hidden in it, haven't you? What is it – apples?' Moses' voice was almost jovial. 'Take as many apples as you want; they're half yours anyway.'

'It's not apples.'

'Then what is it? What do you think he's hiding, Edie?'

'I don't know.' Edith didn't know, but suddenly she guessed. Her heart missed a beat.

'Come on, let's see.'

Moses was out of his chair and across the room in two strides. He yanked at the shirt so that he almost pulled it out of his brother's arms. A mewing cry made him freeze, and he looked down at what Matt was carrying with an expressionless face.

'It's mine, Mo.' The tone of Matthew's voice would have moved a weaker man. But not Moses Crow.

'Yours?' And then Moses started to laugh. He laughed with his hands on his hips and his mouth wide, so that his brother could see pieces of green cabbage caught between his teeth. 'You fathered that?'

'Yes,' Matthew said desperately. 'It's mine and I'm going to keep it.' He looked from his brother to his sister-in-law, almost daring them to put barriers in his way. 'Think of it, Mo: a little boy to help on the farm, to take over when we've gone. Isn't that what you've always wanted?'

'A boy, eh?' Suddenly Moses was looking at the bundle in a different light. 'Let's have a look at him then.'

Edith turned away as the bundle was passed over. She busied herself at the sink.

Moses pulled the stained shirt away and looked down at the tiny naked form. Another man might have been moved to pity by what he saw; but not Moses Crow. What he saw displeased him. He rolled the baby up as if it were a parcel and thrust it back into his brother's arms.

'Get rid of it.' His voice was hard as granite. 'A boy, you said. I might have let you keep a boy – but that's a girl! Get rid of it.'

'No!'

Matthew was clutching the bundle so tightly that the cries were muffled.

'What did you say, brother?'

'I said no.' There was fire in Matthew's eyes, and the first real semblance of sanity Moses had ever seen. 'She's mine and I'm going to keep her. A girl can help Edie in the kitchen, and I'll look after her so she'll be no bother to you.' He looked down at the tiny face peeping up at him and his voice was soft, almost as if he was talking to himself. 'I'm calling her Lily because she's going to live at Valley Farm.' He turned from his brother to Edith. 'She'll be known as Lily from the Valley.'

CHAPTER TWO

Ring House December, 1938

'I want a pony for Christmas,' Betty Thomas said.

She put up her arms knowing James would pick her up and set her on his knee. He leant over, his paunch tightening, and lifted his daughter up into his arms, planting a fond kiss on top of her head.

'Whatever you want, my pet.'

'And a little red jacket – and a hat with a feather. A green feather.'

'I won't forget.'

'And boots, Daddy. Black shiny boots.'

'And boots.'

'You won't forget?'

'I promise.'

Betty sighed happily. She leant against the gold watch chain stretched across her father's waistcoat and looked up into his round red face. She loved him dearly. At fifty he was still a handsome man, although his hair was nearly all silver and his doctor insisted he was overweight. But he was nearly six foot in height and carried the extra pounds well.

His seven-year-old daughter, Betty, was a chip off the old block and the apple of his eye. She was as plump and round as a ripe peach, with dimpled cheeks and blonde curls. The dimples were genuine, but the curls were the result of the tongs which her mother applied every morning. There was a silky blue ribbon threaded through her hair, and her dress was blue wool with a white lacy collar that matched the trimming on her socks. Her shoes were black patent, and they drummed relentlessly against her father's leg to remind him of his promise. Everything was perfect in Betty Thomas's little world.

'You spoil that child.'

Elizabeth Thomas spoke from the depths of the big armchair facing the fire. She pulled a thread of pink silk through the cushion cover she was embroidering and cut the end neatly with her tiny silver scissors.

'I haven't any other children to spoil,' James said complacently.

A small frown flickered across Elizabeth's gentle features. That was the one blot on their otherwise perfect marriage: the fact that they'd only managed to produce one child, and that one in their later years.

After years of disappointment Elizabeth had become pregnant at the age of forty-one; the age when most of her friends were looking forward to becoming grandparents. James had wanted a son: someone to leave his well-earned possessions to. He was a wealthy man by the standards of Lenton village where he lived. Lenton was set in a fold of the Sussex Downs, about ten miles from the historic town of Lewes, and it was surrounded by farms and smallholdings most of which belonged to the Thomas family. They even owned several rows of cottages in the village; poor dwellings, rented out at a few shillings a week.

But James was a fair landlord and a popular man, and the small houses, although overcrowded, were well maintained. Albert Jackson, his manager and right-hand man, collected the rents, travelling around the farms and cottages on his high-saddled bicycle, or driving the old Vauxhall saloon that James had bought in the early thirties. He'd paid £530 for it, and an extra fifteen for a sliding roof. Apart from himself the only other person James would trust to drive it was Bert Jackson.

Every spring a gallon of whitewash and the same of paint was delivered to each tenant so that the fronts of their properties could be kept looking spruce. Anyone who didn't comply got a firm reminder.

The villagers thought the Thomas's lived in splendour at the top of the hill in Ring House, but although the family wanted for nothing it was in fact quite a businesslike establishment. James couldn't bear waste, and although he liked to give his wife and child everything they wanted, his own needs were small. The cellar hadn't been replenished for years, and the furniture, although sturdy and comfortable, was well worn and old. James Thomas bought to last.

'I haven't seen Jackson today,' Elizabeth said, rethreading her needle. 'I thought you wanted to get the rents in before the holiday.'

'So I do. He sent me a message last night that Emma's poorly. I told him not to leave her.'

Emma was Bert Jackson's wife, and she was expecting her third baby any day now. There were already two young male Jacksons – Michael and Peter – living in the cottage at the gates of Ring House. James knew they were hoping for a girl this time.

He sighed deeply and cuddled his plump daughter closer. He was too good-natured to be jealous, but sometimes when he saw the two sturdy Jackson boys playing on the green a sense of loss washed over him. Sons were the passport to the future; not daughters, however charming.

'Oh dear,' Elizabeth said. 'If the rents aren't collected you know what will happen.'

'What will happen, my dear?'

'Well, it is nearly Christmas. They'll be borrowing a shilling here and there to fill the children's stockings, and when the new year comes they'll be full of excuses.'

'I know. That's why I'm going to do the rounds myself.'

'You, James?' Elizabeth looked up. She was startled – she couldn't ever remember her husband collecting the rents before.

'And why not? Your old father's still got his faculties, hasn't he?' and James pinched his daughter's plump cheek like a butcher testing the weight of a plucked capon. 'He can still add up when he has to.'

'What's faculties?' Betty asked.

'Brains, my dear. Brains. That's what faculties are.'

'Have I got faculties, Daddy?'

'Of course you have. You're a Thomas, aren't you? And Thomas's are known for their good looks and their brains.'

Elizabeth looked down at her sewing and gave a secret smile. Her husband was a good business man, but he was also lucky; everything he touched turned to gold – like King Midas. But he was practical rather than intellectual. Betty took after him.

She could sew a fair seam and even do French knots. Elizabeth was teaching her to knit and she already knew the difference between plain and purl. Her fat little fingers spun the wool in and out of the bone needles so fast that they clicked together like miniature castanets. As for beauty Betty was pretty because of her pink and white skin and corkscrew curls, and the fancy clothes her mother made for her. But there was no doubt she was sturdy and built like her father. From a plump little girl she would grow into a large woman who would have to be careful if she didn't want to develop into a fat matron.

'I hope if you're going out you'll take the car, James. The sky is very overcast.'

'Nonsense. I'm going to walk. John Butler says I should leave the car at home and take more exercise.'

'Wrap up then.'

'Can I come, Daddy?' Betty was looking up at her father with what she hoped was a smile he wouldn't be able to resist. It had never let her down yet.

'Go and get your coat then.'

'Goody.'

Betty was off his lap as fast as her plump legs could manage, and her parents heard the patter of her feet across the hall and up the stairs.

James fetched his own heavy coat from the hall-stand. It kept out the cold, and smelt of the tobacco and peppermints he always carried in his pockets.

'We shouldn't be too long,' he told his wife as he draped a woollen scarf around his thick neck and tucked the ends away.

'Good,' Elizabeth replied. She brushed some invisible fluff from his shoulder. 'You don't have to go to Valley Farm, I hope?'

'Of course I have to go to Valley Farm. The Crow brothers are my tenants, and they owe me money just like everybody else. Why?'

'I don't like that place, James,' Elizabeth said. 'And I don't like the idea of your taking our Betty down there.'

'She'll be with me,' James said reassuringly. 'And they don't let anyone in the house. Moses is all right, even if he has got religion, and Edith was all right when she was younger.' In fact James could remember a time when Edith Crow had been more than all right. But he'd been younger then, and more virile, and Betty hadn't been born. 'If you're worried about Matthew you don't have to: he's harmless. And there's no one else there, more's the pity. It's about time I had a talk with them anyway, and threw out a few hints about smartening the place up a bit. They should have mains water and a proper electricity supply. Perhaps if I told them I'd pay for it . . .'

'I'm ready, Daddy.'

Betty ran down the stairs and took her father's hand, looking up into his face for approval. She was wearing her best blue coat, with a matching hood lined with white velvet. Around her neck hung a muff from a silky cord with a tassel on the end. The outfit was new and Betty was very proud of it.

'Do I look nice?' she asked coyly.

'You look quite the lady.'

Betty almost exploded with pleasure. If her daddy said she looked like a lady she was going to behave like one. She tossed her head and strutted by his side like a small fat peacock.

'Be back for tea,' Elizabeth called after them. 'It's crumpets and plum cake.'

Father and daughter found the walk between the outlying farms at first invigorating and then exhausting. They were both out of condition. So when Sydney Jones from Abbots Farm offered them a lift into Lenton they accepted gladly.

Everywhere they stopped Betty had been admired and plied with cakes and home-made lemonade, and James had drunk so much tea, and eaten so many mince pies, he feared he wouldn't be able to do justice to Elizabeth's tea when they got home to Ring House.

He'd left Valley Farm and the Crow brothers until last: partly because it was on the way home, and partly because he wasn't looking forward to the visit. Valley Farm was a gloomy place at the best of times. Set in a hollow of the Downs and surrounded by trees and thickets, it was almost invisible from the road. Even the five-bar gate was hanging from broken hinges. A muddy path wound downhill between leafless trees that reminded Betty of skeletons.

'Do we have to go down there?' she asked in a small voice, looking down at her dainty shoes.

'I'll carry you.'

James lifted the heavy child into his arms and she wound her arms around his neck fondly. He was glad when they came into the open and he could put her down on the cobblestones.

The farmhouse, a long, low, rambling building, looked like a crouching animal against the grey sky. There didn't seem to be anybody about. The only sign of life was a brown hen pecking wearily at a patch of brown earth. It cocked its head slyly at the intruders.

'I'll go and look for Mr Crow,' James said. 'You wait for me here.'

Betty was pleased to be alone. She'd drunk so much lemonade during the course of the afternoon that she badly needed to go to the lavatory. She knew enough about farms to guess that one of the ramshackle sheds would contain a privy.

The first one she tried turned out to be a henhouse. The roosting birds squawked noisily at the intrusion so she backed out again hastily. Another held barrels of potatoes. The floor was littered with half-mouldy apples and her feet slipped on the squashy fruit. Out of desperation she tried the door of a big shed, but it was only full of rubbish. A huge wheel towered over her threateningly. She quickly slammed the door and stood in the yard looking around helplessly.

The solitary hen had lost interest and was disappearing along a cinder track between some evergreens. Betty had no alternative but to follow it. Her tummy hurt, and she was terrified that she was going to wet her knickers. It wouldn't be a bit ladylike to squat on the bare earth and relieve herself, but she couldn't think what else to do.

She found a spot well hidden from the house and lifted her skirt to pull down her white frilly pants. The cold air hit her plump buttocks like a knife and Betty shivered before crouching down. What a relief it was as her muscles loosened and she could let go, but how undignified. She giggled. Her father had said she looked like a lady in her blue coat and muff, but she didn't look much like a lady now.

She was busy straightening her skirts when she heard

someone singing. The voice came from somewhere close by. Whoever it was was singing a carol in a sweet high voice.

'The holly and the ivy,' the clear voice trilled. 'When they are both well grown . . .'

Who could it be? Betty was frightened. She wanted to run away, back down the overgrown path to her father's safe arms But she was also curious. She took a step nearer the voice, pulling aside a bramble so that she could see the singer.

Betty found herself looking into a little clearing amongst the trees where a small girl was busy over a wooden cart. Or at least Betty thought it was a little girl about her own age, by the long trail of dark hair, but apart from that the child cut a strange, sexless figure.

Thin stick-like arms and legs stuck out of a tattered man's green jersey that reached to the child's knees. It was bunched around the waist by a strip of torn leather and the sleeves were rolled up to leave the arms free. On the child's feet were the remains of a pair of home-sewn slippers, but her legs were bare and blue with the cold. Her face was pale under a film of dirt, and the long mane of dark hair tangled, and stuck here and there with dry leaves and pieces of twig. As she sang the child was binding bunches of holly with string and arranging them on the wooden slats of the cart.

Betty thought the child was ugly, but her judgement was based on clothes and appearance. She didn't see the sweetness in the pale face, or the beauty in the big violet eyes fringed by thick sooty lashes. And the hair, tangled as it was, was thick and heavy as a rope, almost too heavy for the thin, childish figure.

'Of all the trees that are in the wood, the holly bears the . . .'

The sweet voice broke off as if the singer was aware of someone watching. Betty moved back letting the brambles swing into place, but she stepped on a dry twig and it snapped under her foot like a gunshot.

'Who's there?'

The unkempt child seemed to have the instincts of a wild animal. She looked around quickly and spotted the movement in the brambles. Before Betty could run away her hiding place was discovered. It was difficult to tell which child was the more frightened, but Betty recovered first.

'How do you do,' she said, in the sort of voice her mother

used to new acquaintances. 'I'm Betty Thomas.' She didn't hold out her hand. She wasn't going to soil her fingers by shaking hands with this grubby child. 'Who are you?'

'Lily,' the child answered.

Betty waited for the child to tell her her surname, and when she didn't became impatient. 'Is your name Lily Crow?' she asked, remembering the name of the family who lived at Valley Farm.

The other child screwed up her face in puzzlement. 'I don't think so,' she said. 'Matt calls me Lily from the Valley.'

'That's not a proper name,' Betty insisted.

'Isn't it?'

'No. It sounds silly. Do you go to school?'

Betty herself went to the village school. She was proud of the fact that she was the only child driven to school every morning in a motor car. The other pupils who didn't live in Lenton tramped in from the outlying farms whatever the weather. Betty didn't like them very much. Some of them were rough and poked fun at her pretty clothes and nice manners. They didn't dare go too far, because Betty's father was Mr Thomas who owned most of their homes. Although she kept herself apart, Betty knew most of the children by sight, but she didn't remember ever seeing Lily before.

'I don't go to school yet,' Lily admitted. 'But Matt's always saying I should. But you only have to go to school to learn to read and write and I can do that already.' She saw Betty's look of disbelief and continued. 'I taught myself from the newspaper, because Matt doesn't read very well.'

'Is Matt your daddy?'

Betty didn't like the way the conversation was going. This strange girl sounded almost proud of the fact that she'd had to teach herself to read and write; almost as if anyone who had to go to school to learn things was stupid.

'I don't think Matt's my father,' Lily said after thinking carefully.

'Who is he then?'

'Oh, he's just Matt.'

'Anyway, we don't only learn to read and write at school,' Betty said. 'We learn to sew, and say prayers, and play games.'

'There'd be no point in me going then. Edie could teach me to sew if she wanted to, and Mo knows ever so many prayers, and Matt plays games with me sometimes.'

Betty rubbed the toe of one patent shoe in a patch of grass to remove the dust; then she held out her skirts with both hands. 'Do you like my coat?' she asked proudly. 'It's new.'

Lily put out a finger and touched the soft material of the muff dangling across Betty's well-padded front. 'What's that?'

'It's a muff – to keep my hands warm.'

Lily spread her own hands in front of her as if she was comparing them. The nails were broken and edged with dirt, and there was the beginning of an itchy chilblain on one forefinger.

'My daddy says I look just like a lady in my new coat,' Betty said, almost daring Lily to contradict her.

'You're too fat to be a lady,' Lily said. She'd seen pictures of ladies in the newspapers Moses left lying about. They were all tall and thin and wore big hats and stylish clothes. 'I shall be a lady when I'm old enough. I shall have a hat with poppies round the brim and a coat edged with real fur.'

'You can't,' Betty insisted. 'Who would buy them for you if you haven't got a daddy?'

'Matt would. And I have got a daddy – he's out there somewhere,' and Lily looked dreamily into the distance, 'and one day he's going to come and get me. He's very rich, and he'll take Matt and me to live with him in his castle – and I'll be a lady.'

Now Betty knew Lily was pretending. Nobody lived in castles these days. Only people in stories. If Lily's daddy was rich why was she dressed in such awful old clothes?

'You're lying,' she said boldly. 'I'm not supposed to talk to children who tell lies.'

'I'm not lying!'

Betty was surprised at the anger in the other girl's voice. She'd looked harmless enough, but now her violet eyes were flashing dangerously and there was a spot of red on each cheekbone. She leapt at Betty and gave her such a push that she lost her footing, toppled backwards, and landed on her bottom. Betty sat there, dirt on her skirts and tears in her eyes.

'Why did you do that?'

'Because you called me a liar.'

The two little girls stared at each other. Betty had felt sorry for Lily at first. She liked being admired and thought her smart new clothes would be bound to impress. But after such a display Betty decided that she didn't care for Lily at all. And Lily? Lily looked at the plump bundle on the ground and thought she looked ridiculous. She turned back to the cart.

'Aren't you going to help me up?'

'No. I've got work to do.' Lily picked up some sprigs of holly and began to bind them into a bunch with a piece of string.

'Work! Little girls don't work!'

Betty sounded horrified at the very idea. In her world only the grown-ups worked. Children were petted and spoiled and didn't have to soil their hands. She scrambled to her feet and brushed down her clothes.

'Well, I have to,' Lily said solemnly. 'I make the bunches and Matt pushes the cart to the market and sells them. He gets sixpence a bundle,' she ended proudly.

'I've got sixpence,' Betty said. 'Can I buy some?'

She had a silver sixpence in her pocket her father had given her to buy sweeties with. She produced it regally and held it out as if she was doing Lily a favour.

'I don't want it,' Lily said. Money meant nothing to her. She never went anywhere to spend it, and she had no pockets to put it in. 'But I'll give you some if you want.' She handed Betty a dark green bunch liberally dotted with bright red berries. Before Betty could thank her she heard someone calling her name.

'Betty! Betty, where are you?'

'I'm over here, Daddy,' Betty called back. 'I'm coming. I have to go,' she told Lily. 'My daddy's waiting to take me home. Thank you for the holly – goodbye.'

Lily didn't answer, so Betty ran back down the cinder path. She emerged breathlessly in the yard where James was pacing up and down, an anxious expression on his face.

'There you are,' he said with relief. 'Where have you been? I told you to wait for me here.'

Betty didn't want to tell him the reason she'd wandered away, because the Crow brothers were standing only a few yards away and might hear her. She guessed the smaller one with the rounded shoulders was Matt, because the other one, huge and scary, looked just like an Old Testament prophet who would know a lot of prayers. In the background a thin woman was hovering, wiping her hands nervously on a dirty print apron. Her thin lips were pursed into a narrow line and her hair was tightly drawn back into a bun, so that her eyelids were pulled higher than nature intended. It gave her pale face a startled look.

Betty was glad she didn't live at Valley Farm. It looked a forbidding place and the people seemed unfriendly. She slipped her hand into her father's and looked up into his face.

'Where did you get that?' James asked, seeing the bunch of holly his daughter was clutching. Before she could answer he turned to Moses. 'I'm afraid she's been stealing your holly,' he said with a smile.

'I haven't,' Betty protested.

She wanted to tell him all about the strange little girl called Lily, but she had to wait because James was busy sorting out a handful of small change. He passed a florin over to Moses Crow, who stowed it away quickly in his trouser pocket and nodded in a surly fashion.

'Come along, my dear,' James said, drawing Betty away. 'It's getting dark and your tea will be waiting for you.'

Betty trotted along by her father's side. She waited until they were out of earshot before she got his attention.

'You didn't have to pay that man for my holly,' she explained. 'It was given me as a present.'

'A present!' James laughed. 'And who would give you a bunch of holly as a present?'

'The little girl.'

'What little girl, Betty? There aren't any little girls at Valley Farm.' James thought that she'd invented an imaginary playmate to explain away the bunch of greenery she'd gathered without permission.

'Yes, there is,' Betty insisted. 'I talked to her, but she wasn't a very nice little girl. She was ugly and rough and she pushed me over.' She showed her soiled coat.

James thought she was trying to make excuses for her dirty clothes. After all, she was only a child and probably scared of being told off. As if he would!

'I'm not cross with you,' he assured her, 'even if you are making things up.'

'But I'm not!'

Now Betty was cross. She'd accused Lily of being a liar, but she didn't like being thought one herself. She stopped in the middle of the path and looked back over her shoulder at Valley Farm. It was shrouded in mist now as the sky darkened; in fact she could only see the roof and top windows, and one chimney from which no comforting smoke spiralled. It was dark and gloomy and might have been deserted if she hadn't known better. Just as she was about to turn back a movement in the undergrowth caught her eye. She took hold of her father's arm excitedly.

'There she is,' she said. 'There's Lily.'

James looked in the direction of his daughter's pointing finger. A few yards behind them a figure had stepped onto the path; he could just see the silhouette against the darkening sky. A little bent figure, of indeterminate sex, hauling a ramshackle cart in its wake. For all he could make out it could be a midget or a gnome, so misshapen did it seem to him. But it was certainly there, and not a figment of his imagination. As he watched it heaved the cart onto the path and began to trundle it towards the ghostlike farmhouse, almost disappearing into the mist before his eyes.

'There!' Betty said with satisfaction. 'I told you.'

'Come away,' James said, suddenly anxious to be home. 'Mummy will be cross with us staying out so late.'

Father and daughter hurried their footsteps towards the security of Ring House. Betty chatted excitedly all the way, but for some reason James seemed to be deep in thought as if he had something on his mind.

Elizabeth Thomas was waiting impatiently. Twice she'd sent her maid, Florence, scurrying back to the kitchen with instructions on keeping the crumpets hot. She'd drunk two cups of tea out of the best silver pot, and now they'd have to make a fresh pot. James hated his tea stewed. It was nearly half past four and she liked to have tea promptly on the hour. It had become a ritual, and threw her evening out if it was even a few minutes late.

When he did come in her husband was full of excuses and apologies, and Betty's new coat was covered in dirt. Elizabeth was so pleased to see them she rang the bell loudly to alert Florence and decided to overlook the lateness of the hour.

Tea was over and the table cleared. Elizabeth settled down to play dominoes with Betty, while James dozed in his chair in front of the fire. At least he looked as if he was dozing, but instead of the gentle sighing and snorting which was usual, he kept twisting and turning against the cushions as if he had something on his mind.

The long evening seemed endless. At last the dominoes were put away in their box and Betty came to kiss her parents goodnight. Elizabeth saw her daughter safely tucked up in bed, and when she returned to the drawing room found her husband wide awake and staring into the embers of the fire. She picked up her sewing and settled down beside him. He looked at her with a smile.

'Is Betty asleep?'

'Not yet, dear. But she's tired out by the walk. I read to her for a while and she settled down without any trouble. I'll go up again in a little while to see if she's dropped off.'

They sat in companionable silence for a few minutes, and then James said, 'Did you know there was a child at Valley Farm?'

Elizabeth looked at her husband with astonishment written all over her face. 'Never! You must be joking. That's no place for a child.'

'I know.'

'Did you see a child then, James?'

'Not exactly. But Edith did have children, didn't she?'

'She had several pregnancies but they all came to nothing. Miscarriages and stillbirths, I seem to remember. I felt sorry for the poor woman at the time. I knew how she felt being childless myself; but then we had Betty and I suppose I forgot her troubles.'

'Yes. We've been lucky.' James pulled his pipe out of his waistcoat pocket and lit it slowly, sucking the stem with noisy puffs to get it going. 'I remember talking to Moses about it years ago. He was set on having a son and heir – as if he was the owner of Valley Farm and not the tenant, and wanted someone to leave it to. After that they all seemed to go a bit queer and shut themselves away.'

'Perhaps I should have put myself out to be friendlier to Edith,' Elizabeth said sadly. 'No one ever sees her in the village any more.'

'I heard Moses fancies himself as a preacher. Perhaps he thought religion was the answer. And that brother of his has certainly taken a turn for the worse. He just seemed to shuffle about and mumble. All their clothes were only fit for the ragbag.'

'Well, I'm sure you must have made a mistake about a child,' Elizabeth said complacently. She put away her sewing and got to her feet. 'I'll go in and see Edith after Christmas if I can find the time. There may be something I can do for her.'

'You do that.' James guessed she had no intention of doing any such thing.

'Are you coming up?' Elizabeth, on her way to the door, had already forgotten the Crows.

'In a minute.'

But James Thomas sat for much longer than a minute in his armchair, sucking on his pipe, and thinking.

CHAPTER THREE

Christmas

'When's Edward coming?'

'Not until tomorrow, Betty,' Elizabeth said with a smile.

'Last year he came on Christmas Eve and helped decorate the tree.'

Betty looked up into the green boughs of the fir tree standing in the corner of the drawing room. It was a fine specimen, almost six foot tall. She hoped there were enough decorations to justify its grandeur. She rifled through the box on her lap and held up some silvery baubles to catch the light.

'Doctor Butler is out on an emergency,' James said from the depths of the armchair where he was supervising the decorating. 'So they're driving down in the morning. They should be here in time for lunch.'

Betty's face had dropped a little at the news and her parents smiled indulgently. John Butler was the family physician and James's oldest and best friend. He had a large and busy practice in Lewes and lived there with his only son since his wife's death.

Edward was nine years old, two years older than Betty, but she adored him and looked forward to his visits. Doctor Butler had plans for his son, visualizing the boy taking over his reins in due course. Elizabeth and James also had plans for Edward and did everything to encourage the friendship between the two children. They thought it would be a fine thing for Betty to be a doctor's wife, and Edward was a good-looking boy and their daughter was obviously very fond of him. Of course they were still only children, but the time would soon pass. They were looking forward to a rosy future for their child.

'Can I put the fairy on top of the tree?' Betty asked.

'No,' Elizabeth said immediately, looking at the wobbly stepladder. She wasn't going to risk family limbs. 'Hand it to Florence and let her do it.'

The little maid in her print dress and apron climbed the ladder and swayed precariously on the top step. But Elizabeth wasn't worried: after all, that was what she was paid for.

The fairy was soon in its place, if a little bit crookedly. Betty handed up a bundle of tinsel, and watched in delight as Florence laced it between the branches.

'How's that, Mrs Thomas?'

'Lovely, Florence, you can come down now.'

James heaved himself to his feet and held the ladder while Florence climbed down, and then he looked around the cosy room. The cards were already displayed along the mantelshelf and on every other convenient surface, and the walls were festooned with the coloured chains Betty had made with her mother's help. James didn't feel he'd contributed much so he looked around for something else to do.

'What next?'

'It needs some holly,' Elizabeth said. 'Or mistletoe. Even ivy would be better than nothing.'

'Isn't there any in the garden?' James thought of the well-tended gardens around his house. Surely there must be a holly bush somewhere on his estate.

'We've got some holly.' Betty was jumping up and down excitedly. 'Don't you remember, Daddy, we brought some back from Valley Farm.'

Of course James remembered. It came back to him in a flash: Betty standing on the cinder path clutching her bunch of holly, and that pathetic little figure trudging away from them bent double over the handles of the cart.

'It's in the pantry,' Florence said. 'I put it in water to keep it fresh. I'll go and get it.'

The holly was as fresh and green as the day it had been picked, and when sprigs of it were tucked behind picture frames and into vases it made all the difference to the room.

'It certainly looks seasonal now,' Elizabeth said, looking around and wondering how Florence was going to dust.

Betty danced about, clapping her hands in delight, but her father had sunk back in his chair deep in thought. He was wondering what sort of celebrations the Crow brothers had planned. And that little figure: if it was a child, what sort of Christmas she was going to have?

Christmas morning dawned cold and frosty. Betty was awake early and squealed with delight when she found the little red jacket, the hat with the green feather, and the shiny boots all neatly packaged at the foot of her bed. There was the traditional stocking as well, bulging with hidden treasures and smelling enticingly of oranges and barley sugar. But that would have to wait.

Struggling into the jacket, and with the hat cocked over one eye, she padded over to the window and looked down the drive in anticipation. She need not have feared. Albert Jackson, an old tweed cap on his head and his collar turned up against the cold, was already trudging towards the house leading a little fat brown pony with a swinging tail and a child-sized saddle on its back. It might be a small animal, but it was sturdy, chosen carefully by James Thomas to carry his well-built daughter.

Betty was too excited to wait for breakfast. She ran down the stairs as fast as she could, almost colliding with her father who was just coming out of the dining room.

'What's all this then?' he asked, pretending not to understand the reason for Betty's excitement.

'It's my pony! Jackson's outside with my pony! I'm going to call him Bracken – and, oh Daddy, thank you.'

They hurried through the front door together. Warm steam was curling into the cold air from Bracken's nostrils and he was pawing the ground as if he was anxious to be off. James lifted Betty into the saddle, and she trotted the pony up and down the drive, Jackson on one side and her father on the other.

'My boys are ever so jealous,' Jackson said. 'They've been helping me look after your pony and right difficult it was to keep him out of sight.'

'They must have a ride sometime.' James turned to Betty. 'Bracken will be kept down at the cottage so Jackson can care for him. He'll be brought up to the house when you need him.'

Betty leaned over and stroked the pony's soft muzzle. 'He's my pony, and nobody must ride him but me,' she said firmly.

'Whatever you say, miss.' Jackson's face fell slightly. Pete and Mike were going to be disappointed when he told them. They'd been so sure that Betty would share.

It was the cold that sent them indoors. The grown-ups settled down in front of a roaring log fire, and cracked nuts and drank port and lemon out of tall glasses that only saw the light of day on special occasions. Betty curled up on the padded window seat to watch for Edward and his father.

The appetizing smell of roast turkey and sage and onion was wafting through the house from the kitchen before Dr Butler and his son arrived. Betty was so pleased to see them she ran out to welcome them, not bothering about the cold.

They were both muffled up in heavy coats with scarves around their necks, and John Butler wore a funny tweed hat on his balding head. It had earflaps, and was secured by a strap under his chin.

Edward was bareheaded. His straight blond hair blew away from his face, and his grey eyes fringed with long pale lashes looked solemnly at Betty. She ran forwards, her hands outstretched in welcome, and his good-looking face broke into a smile.

'Hullo, Betty. Happy Christmas.'

'Happy Christmas, Eddie.' Suddenly Betty felt shy. She hadn't seen him since the summer holidays and he seemed to have grown so tall. He looked almost grown-up compared to the boys in the village.

'Come inside out of the cold,' James said, pleased to see his old friend, and leading the way into the house.

Now the festivities could really begin. First came the exchange of presents. Betty had knitted Edward a pair of mittens with hardly any mistakes, and he insisted they were the warmest he'd ever had. He gave her a leather bookmark with her name on it in goldleaf. He'd painted it himself, and Betty promised to keep it for ever.

Seeing that the grown-ups were busy exchanging news, Betty and Edward slipped away upstairs to the attics where they could be private and talk.

It was cold under the roof but they'd carried rugs with them to drape over their shoulders. Betty settled in the depths of an old cane chair with tattered cushions, but Edward, who usually liked the attic, crossed to the dormer window and stood there looking out at the grey winter scenery. All you could see from there were fields and woods and a few chimneypots belonging to outlying cottages.

'You're very quiet,' Betty said at last. 'Is something the matter?'

'Of course not.' Edward turned to her, his face alight with its usual gentle smile. 'I've got some exciting news, that's all.'

'Oh, tell me!' Betty sat upright, all attention to hear her friend's confidences. 'I've got news, too. Daddy's given me a pony. You can ride him if you want.'

'I wanted new paints,' Edward said. 'But all I got was a set of encyclopedias.'

'Poor you.' Betty laughed at his downcast face. 'Was that your news?'

'No, of course not.' He crossed to her chair and sat down on a nearby packing case, crossing his legs casually as if he hadn't a care in the world. 'I'm going to my father's old school.'

'So? I go to school.'

'It's a boarding school – in Brighton. It's what they call a preparatory school.'

'What does that mean?'

'It prepares you for public school.'

Betty thought that one over. She didn't really know what a public school was, but it sounded impressive. 'Brighton's not far away, is it?' she said at last. 'Don't you want to go?'

'Not very much,' Edward admitted. 'I shall miss Dad; and King and Queenie.' He had two pet King Charles spaniels to whom he was devoted. Then he brightened. 'You have to wear the college blazer – and a straw hat.'

'In the winter?'

'I don't know. Dad showed me one of his old photos and all the boys were wearing straw hats.'

Betty took his hand and looked up into his face. She thought he was beautiful. Although she was only seven years old she planned one day to marry him. She had no idea that her parents already had ideas in that direction.

'It'll be all right,' she assured him. 'If you hate it I expect your father will take you away.'

'Do you think so?' His grey eyes were swimming with tears, but he swallowed them down manfully. He wasn't going to cry in front of Betty.

Just then Florence poked her head up through the trapdoor to tell them that dinner was ready and they were to come down to the dining room at once.

It was a jolly meal; everyone was hungry and did justice to the roast meat, crispy potatoes and vegetables. Then they pulled the brightly wrapped crackers while Florence and Elizabeth cleared the table. Edward and Betty giggled helplessly over the silly mottoes and swapped paper hats, so that Edward ended up with a nightcap complete with pom-pom, and Betty had a witch's head-dress.

'Here comes the pudding,' James announced, and Florence entered the room bearing the steaming plum pudding on a heavy dish. Elizabeth followed behind with the mince pies and a jug of rich yellow cream.

'Hurrah!' Betty yelled, and clapped her hands excitedly. She knew there were silver threepenny bits in the pudding and hoped she'd be lucky enough to get one.

'Wait a minute.' John Butler stayed James's hand as he polished a knife on his table napkin. 'There's something missing.'

'What's that?'

'There should be some holly on top. You must always have a sprig of holly on your Christmas pudding. It's supposed to be lucky.'

'Then we must certainly have some.' James looked around the room. There was a spray, heavy with berries, hanging over a picture. He broke a piece off and stuck it jauntily in the top of the pudding. 'There!'

Now that everything seemed to be in order Elizabeth pushed forward the plates, and Florence carried the slices of pudding around the table. It was such a large pudding that when everyone was served there was almost half still left on the plate, dark and rich with fruit, and the sprig of holly sticking out of the top.

James chewed slowly, hoping he wouldn't get indigestion. He felt stealthily in his breast pocket to make sure he had his peppermints handy. It was better to be safe than sorry.

'I've got a threepenny bit,' Betty suddenly shouted. 'Look,

everybody, I've got a threepenny bit.'

Elizabeth made sure that Edward found one as well so both the children were happy. After second helpings John Butler picked up the discarded sprig of holly from the remains of the pudding.

'I've never seen such large berries before,' he said to James. 'Is it from your garden?'

Before James could answer Betty piped up. 'It came from Valley Farm. Lily gave it to me.'

No one seemed particularly interested, but James found himself contemplating the holly and remembering the day when they'd carried it home. The memory of the little figure bent over the cart had haunted him and he hadn't been able to get it out of his mind. Sometimes he couldn't really believe it had been a child he'd seen, whatever Betty said. She was only a child herself and sometimes got things mixed up. But whoever it was had been rough and pushed his daughter over, so although small they could be dangerous. Perhaps it had been some crazy midget or madwoman escaped from a circus. In a small community like theirs people should be warned. He'd intended looking into it, but had never found the time. But the little figure had stuck in his mind like a bad dream, and he knew he wouldn't find peace of mind until he'd made enquiries.

Elizabeth took the children into the drawing room to do a jigsaw puzzle. She felt they needed quietening down after all the excitement. Doctor Butler had been up half the previous night with a patient and asked if they minded him indulging in forty winks. James settled his friend in a wing chair in front of the library fire, with a blanket over his knees and the whisky bottle close at hand.

On a sudden impulse James went into the hall and put on his overcoat. He wondered if he could slip out of the house unobserved. But it wasn't to be: Elizabeth heard his footsteps and appeared in the drawing-room door.

'Wherever are you off to, James?' she asked.

'Just need some fresh air. You know what John said.'

'Are you feeling unwell?' Elizabeth looked concerned. 'Perhaps you shouldn't have had that second portion of pudding.'

'I'm fine. John's asleep in the library so I thought I'd take a walk.'

'Do you want us to come with you? I'll call the children. It won't take a minute to get their coats.'

'No. You stay in the warm. It looks a bit overcast and you don't want to get caught if it snows.'

'Don't be long then.' Elizabeth looked worried. She knew her husband so well, and he was behaving out of character.

Assuring her that he'd be back in time to play with the children, James stepped out onto the drive and walked away purposefully. He could have asked Jackson to get the car out, but he didn't want to disturb his Christmas day with his family. Anyway it would be easier to explore Valley Farm on foot rather than drive up in a car.

The first thing that he noticed was that the gate was still broken. Perhaps he could use that as an excuse for his unheralded visit. He could say he was passing, and offer to pay to have it repaired.

His footsteps were muffled by moss growing among the cobbles, but somewhere a dog heard him and started to bark. He willed it to be quiet and it seemed to get the message. It was only a matter of weeks since he'd been here but the whole place seemed drearier than ever. He noticed a broken pane of glass in a window; someone had stuffed it with discoloured rags to keep the cold out.

There was not a movement or sound anywhere and no smoke issued from the chimney. Perhaps the Crows were away for Christmas. James smiled at the very idea. They were like a family of wild animals in some underground burrow; it would take more than Christmas to thrust them out into the normal world.

James peered through one grimy window and saw a room full of old-fashioned furniture. The curtains at the window were hanging in strips and there was dust everywhere. On the sill stood a half-dead geranium in a copper pot; one green leaf struggled bravely to reach the light.

A tide of litter lapped against the grey walls of the farm-house, and sometimes he found himself wading almost ankle deep through dead leaves. If the Crows didn't celebrate the holiday perhaps they were still working in the fields. Satisfied that the house was unoccupied, he peered through another window and found he was looking directly into the kitchen.

Edith Crow was standing only a few feet away from him

chopping carrots on the draining board. The knife was large and glittered in the light as she moved it listlessly up and down. Then she picked up an onion and sliced it expertly, the blade sliding through the skin as easily as if it were butter. She was concentrating on her task and James was sure she hadn't seen him so he stepped back slightly.

Once she'd been a fine figure of a woman with a merry laugh no one could resist. The change in her was sad and moved James unexpectedly; he thought he'd got over Edith Crow a long time ago. She was so thin and uncared for, her hair screwed back in the nape of her neck, and her mouth was set in such a tight, bitter line. He wondered how old she was now.

From where he was standing he could just see into the room, and as his eyes grew accustomed to the light he could make out the huge shape of Moses sitting in a high-backed chair by the table. The fire was unlit, and there was nothing comforting about this dreary kitchen to make it the 'heart of the house'.

There was no one else in the room. No sign of brother Matthew, or a child.

James turned away. He didn't really know what he was doing there, or what he'd expected to find. It had been a spur of the moment decision and he wished he'd stayed in the warmth of Ring House with his family.

There was a barn on his left and a huddle of outbuildings. He didn't know why he chose the barn to investigate; perhaps it was because the door was half-open.

His first impression was of darkness and the smells associated with animals, musky and earthy. Then he felt the air stir as if someone, or something, had moved. He heard a faint humming sound, like a trapped bluebottle searching for an open window.

Suddenly there was a flash of light. It was faint and lasted only a moment, but it helped his eyes to focus, and illuminated the barn enough for him to take in the interior. He saw the straw-littered floor, and the bales of animal fodder stacked high into the rafters. A donkey was tethered in the far corner, chewing patiently, and flicking its long ears backwards and forwards; and in a clear space in the centre of the floor was a small fir tree propped sideways in a broken box.

Someone had made an attempt at decoration. Strips of torn paper were draped over the branches, and a star made of cardboard, with six crazy spokes, was fastened to the top. The stubs of household candles were arranged among the foliage, and the lighting of their wicks had caused the sudden spark of light.

James could just make out a huddled figure with a mane of thick hair crouched in front of the little tree. He heard the rasp of a second match, and the flame was held waveringly towards the nearest stub, but before it ignited James stumbled and stubbed his foot against a stone. He swore under his breath, and the lighted match jumped and fell from the little hand. James saw it fall onto the dry straw littering the floor.

The tiny flame leapt a couple of inches high and the little figure jumped to its feet. A bare foot stretched out and tried to trample the flame. A cry of pain brought James to his senses. He hurried forward and stamped the fire out with the sole of his shoe; then he caught the little figure up in his arms and carried it outside into the full light. Two violet eyes stared up into his. He saw he was carrying a little girl wearing only an old man's jersey, the ragged sleeves rolled up to leave her hands free. He knew who she was at once: she was just as Betty had described her.

'You're Lily,' he said bluntly.

The child nodded and struggled to free herself. He carefully stood her on her feet on the cold stones. She immediately balanced on one leg to inspect the tender sole that had tried to put out the flame.

'It hurts,' she said sadly. It was more a statement than a complaint, as if she didn't expect James to do anything about it.

'It needs a dressing,' he said. She looked puzzled, so he added 'We must wash it and put some ointment on it, and then cover it with a bandage.'

'Why?'

'To make it better.'

This seemed to please Lily and she smiled for the first time. The smile lit up her dirty little face, and in spite of the awful jersey, and the matted hair, James realized that the child would be pretty if only she were clean; in fact she would be more than pretty. With those delicate features and amazing eyes she would be beautiful.

'You make it better,' Lily said firmly. From her childish lips it was an order and James's tender heart turned over.

'You'll have to come home with me,' he said on impulse.

'All right,' Lily said, and she slipped her hand trustingly into his. 'Have you got a Christmas tree?'

'Yes.'

'I only wanted a little tree, with candles on it,' Lily said sadly, and she looked over her shoulder at the pathetic tree she'd attempted to decorate herself.

'I've got a Christmas tree with candles on it,' James assured her. 'It's got silver balls on it as well, and a fairy on the top.'

'A fairy!' Lily said in wonder.

'Yes. Would you like to come and see it?'

'What's going on here?'

Lily backed away, a terrified look crossing her pale face, and James found himself confronting Moses Crow. James was himself a big man, but he felt small beside the huge bulk of the tenant farmer. But the child trusted him, and he turned to face the other man knowing he had right on his side.

'Who is in charge of this child?' he demanded.

'She belongs to Matt,' Moses said. 'He's ill at the moment.'

'So why aren't you and your wife looking after her?'

'She's nothing to do with us.' Moses turned away as if he'd lost interest.

'She's a child – just a little child. Damn you, Moses Crow, have you no heart?'

Lily stood between the two men looking from one angry face to the other. Then she seemed to come to a decision, and putting out one small hand tugged at James's coat.

'I want to see your Christmas tree,' she said. 'You said you'd take me home with you.'

'And so I will, little one.' James dropped down onto one knee so that he could put his arms around the child. He thought of his own daughter Betty, cared for and cosseted, and sheltered from life's hardships. His heart went out to this child who looked half-starved. He looked up at Moses, who towered over them threateningly, hands on hips like some demon king. 'I suppose you have no objection?'

Moses jutted his chin out aggressively; he was ready for a fight although it was obvious he didn't care what happened to Lily. 'She's got work to do,' he said sullenly.

'On Christmas Day!' James stood up with the Lily in his

arms. 'No one should work on Christmas Day – least of all children. I'm taking Lily home with me whether you agree or not. If you cause trouble I shall call in the police, and a doctor to examine her. She's obviously undernourished and uncared for, and probably ill-treated. You have a lot to answer for, Moses Crow.' James walked away carrying his little burden and Moses didn't try to stop him.

Lily laid her cheek against his warm red one, and her violet eyes were looking up into his kind face with such trust that he felt tears choking him.

Elizabeth looked at the clock on the mantelpiece; her husband had been gone for nearly two hours. The children had finished their puzzle and she could hear them thumping about overhead. They'd wake John Butler if they weren't careful.

'Do you want me to lay the tea yet?' Florence poked her head around the door. She'd been given the evening off to visit her family and was anxious to get the last of her duties done.

'I'll come and help you.' Elizabeth got to her feet. 'Did you remember to put the sherry in the trifle?'

'Yes, Mrs Thomas. It set really well – and there's milk jellies for the children.'

They were crossing the hall when the front door opened, letting in a draught of cold air. James filled the doorway but neither woman seemed to see him. Their eyes were drawn to the child standing holding his hand. Florence let out a little cry and put her hand to her mouth to stifle the sound. But Elizabeth looked from the child to her husband, and then stepped forward, her arms outstretched.

'You poor little thing! She's frozen, James. What's your name, my dear?'

'I'm Lily from the Valley.' The words were clear and steady from a child so young.

'Her name's Lily,' James explained. 'And she comes from Valley Farm.'

'You're welcome, I'm sure.' Elizabeth looked at her husband questioningly.

'She's come for a visit. I invited her. Perhaps she should have a bath first – and she's hurt her foot.'

Lily stood obligingly on one leg like a stork to show the

blister, but all the women could see was the dirty skin, blue with the cold.

'Haven't you any shoes?' Elizabeth asked.

'I did have some. Matt made them for me; but they fell to pieces.'

'Is there any hot water, Florence?'

'Only in the kitchen, Mrs Thomas. I can get out that old hip bath and put it in front of the fire.'

'That'll be fine.' Suddenly Elizabeth was all a-bustle. James didn't usually spring surprises – not like this one, anyway, but the child was here and they'd do their best. 'You go with Florence,' she instructed Lily, 'and I'll fetch some towels, and some of my daughter Betty's clothes for you to wear. She's bigger than you, but I expect you'll manage.'

'Is John still asleep?' James asked.

'I don't know. I haven't heard him.'

'I'll go in and see,' James said, disappearing through the library door.

Elizabeth hurried up the stairs, and Lily followed Florence nervously into the kitchen. When the maid told her to take off her clothes while the bath was being prepared she nearly argued. Hadn't the kind man brought her to his house to see his Christmas tree? Nothing had been said about washing. But Florence wouldn't take no for an answer, and Lily soon found herself sitting in the warm water watching the flames from the fire leaping up the chimney. Florence held out a cake of soap.

'What's that?'

Florence laughed 'It's soap. Anybody would think you'd never had a bath before.'

'I haven't. I swim in the brook in the summer when it's hot.' Lily took the soap gingerly and put it up to her face. 'It smells.'

'Of course it smells. Look, you rub it between your hands like this and it makes a lather.'

Lily smiled. She liked the perfumed smell of the soap and the bubbles it made. Like a baby she splashed the water with her hands, causing it to overflow onto the floor.

'None of that now!' Florence reproved. 'If you want to get out you can stand on this hand towel until Mrs Thomas comes back. I'll go and get you some ointment for that foot.'

Left alone, Lily looked around. To her Ring House was a palace. She wanted to explore the kitchen before the maid came back, so she climbed carefully out of the bath and wrapped herself in the rough hand towel. She was so small and thin it covered most of her body, leaving only her arms and legs free.

She investigated a tray on the kitchen table that contained a plate of tiny sandwiches, and a trifle in a glass dish decorated with crystallized fruits. She couldn't resist dabbing her finger in the creamy surface and licking it. It was sweeter than anything she'd ever tasted before. She ate a cherry and wondered why it had no stone. Then she tried one of the sandwiches. It was fish paste so she pulled a face and spat it out.

'What do you think you're doing?'

Betty was standing in the doorway, her curls bobbing and her pink velvet dress spotless. Her mother had told her about the unexpected visitor and she'd come down to see for herself. Edward was close behind her.

'I'm hungry,' Lily admitted. She recognized Betty immediately, but by the look on the other girl's face wasn't sure if she was welcome. 'I've come to see the Christmas tree.'

Betty smirked and swirled her skirts. She wasn't sure if she liked the intruder. She wanted Edward all to herself and couldn't help showing off.

'This is Lily,' she said by way of introduction. 'She works at one of my father's farms.' She made sure she emphasized the word *work* so that Edward would understand the other girl's lowly position.

'Hullo, Lily,' Edward said in a friendly voice. 'Would you like some chocolate?' He broke a large piece off the bar he carried in his hand and held it out. 'We're just going to have a game of hide-and-seek. Would you like to play?'

Lily didn't know what hide-and-seek was, and she'd never tasted chocolate before. But she thought the fair-haired boy was wonderful: just like a fairy-tale prince. She knew she'd play anything, and eat anything, if it pleased him.

Betty was furious with Edward's attention. She could see that he was captivated by Lily. Jealousy stirred in her heart like a knife, and she knew that from that day on Lily from the Valley was a potential enemy.

CHAPTER FOUR

September 1940

'Is there something the matter with Betty, Mrs Thomas?'

'She's had a letter from Doctor Butler's son, Florence. From his school in Brighton. You know how she dotes on him.'

Elizabeth was helping Florence in the kitchen. The maid, enveloped in a huge pinafore, was polishing silver at the table, while her mistress spring-cleaned the dresser shelves. The blue and white Willow Pattern china was Elizabeth's pride and joy and she wouldn't let anyone wash it but herself; ever since Florence had dropped the sauce boat in the sink and chipped it.

'Not much fun living in Brighton these days, so I've heard,' Florence said with a sniff. 'They say there's sandbags and barbed wire everywhere to stop the Jerries landing. The Army Sappers have even blown gaps in the piers.'

'I'm glad we don't live there,' Elizabeth agreed. 'It's safer in the country. They say it's worse in London.'

'I wouldn't know; I've never been there.'

It was true that although war had been declared the year before and Lenton had steeled itself for the worst, so far it had hardly touched the village. The occasional aircraft zoomed overhead to the excitement of the schoolchildren, and they had to abide by blackout regulations, but apart from that life went on as normal.

Florence rubbed a fork with a chamois leather and held it up to the light to make sure there was no polish left between the prongs. 'Why did Betty look so sulky then? If she had a letter from Edward she should have looked pleased.'

'Because he's allowed out of school on a Saturday and he wanted her to visit him. And Lily, of course.'

Florence smiled. She knew any invitation Edward made would include Lily. Since the child had come to live at Ring House she'd watched the friendship grow between the two children.

It was nearly two years since that fateful day when James Thomas had introduced the ragged urchin from Valley Farm into the household at Ring House. It had not been easy for any of them because Lily had not learned any of the graces normally taught to children at their mothers' knees. Matt had fed her scraps from the kitchen and given her his old clothes to wear. He'd played games with her and told her stories, but apart from that he'd treated her more like a pet dog he liked to have around than a child in need of care, and when he had tired of her she had been left to her own devices. Moses and his wife Edith had ignored her.

But Lily had proved to be a child of character. She'd taught herself to read and write in the long, lonely hours she spent by herself. There was a bookcase at Valley Farm full of old books nobody ever read; and Moses often left his newspapers lying about. Lily had mastered her letters early and by the time she was seven could read most things, although she particularly liked stories about poor girls marrying princes, and orphans finding their true fathers. She'd fallen in love with Edward Butler on that first day and immediately identified him as the handsome prince in the fairy stories – and one day, one day she was sure, she'd find her father, just like the poor orphans did.

In the meantime she was happy. She was warm, well fed, and had a little bedroom all to herself on the top landing, since Betty had refused to share.

Betty! She was the one fly in the ointment; the one person who spoilt things and made her stay at Ring House less than pleasant. Betty was always rubbing in the fact that Lily was there on sufferance, and that one day she'd be sent back to her old life at Valley Farm. So Lily made the most of every day and tried to please everybody, so that her stay would be a long one.

James Thomas would have been sad if he'd been aware of the enmity between the girls, but they hid it from him. However, he knew enough to change his original plans for Lily's welfare.

He'd intended to adopt her. Once they'd taught her the rudiments of cleanliness she wasn't any trouble, and Elizabeth had always wanted another child. They both agreed that Betty needed company of her own age. Much as James loved his daughter he was aware of her shortcomings, and put it down to her being an only child and not having anyone to share things with.

Enquiries about adoption had been made, but it was difficult when no one seemed to know anything about Lily's parentage. Someone had interviewed Moses and Edith Crow but they'd denied any involvement, saying the child belonged to Matthew. Matt himself insisted he'd found the baby in the barn and wanted to keep her. After a lot of discussion the authorities agreed that Lily could stay with the Thomas's while further enquiries were made. That was two years ago and they'd heard nothing since.

Anyway, after a few tantrums from Betty, James had dropped the adoption idea. He didn't want to upset his daughter, so until she was ready to accept Lily as a sister the idea had to be scrapped.

Florence inspected her face in the bowl of a tablespoon and patted her hair. It had a way of falling down when she wasn't looking. 'Aren't you going to let them go then?'

'Go where?' Elizabeth had been distracted by a hairline crack on a dinner plate.

'To Brighton. To visit Edward.'

'Of course not. They're far too young.'

'Brighton isn't far,' Florence said thoughtfully. 'My auntie's in the hospital there.'

'They'd have to go on the train. What if there was an air raid?'

'Couldn't your husband go with them, Mrs Thomas?'

'If you've finished the cutlery you can rinse the dusters out in this water,' Elizabeth said, taking the last plate out of the bowl and polishing it dry on a linen cloth. 'My husband isn't free that day or he would have taken them. That's why Betty's upset. Of course if I could find someone else who's going to

Brighton on Saturday I might let them go. But it would have to be someone responsible.'

Florence plunged the yellow cloths into the suds and kneaded them energetically. 'I could take them,' she said. She kept her face over the bowl so that Elizabeth wouldn't see how eager she was.

'You, Florence?' Elizabeth looked at the maid's bent shoulders.

'Yes, Mrs Thomas. You still owe me a day. There's not much doing here on a Saturday and I could leave you something cold for lunch. I could take them in on the train, and visit my auntie at the same time. Edward's a good boy and he'd look after them. Then they could meet me later and I'd bring them home.'

Elizabeth looked thoughtful. 'Well, it's an idea. But I'll have to talk it over with Mr Thomas.'

'Of course.'

James thought it was such a good idea that before the children knew it the plans were made. Betty immediately wrote a letter of acceptance to Edward, telling him how much she was looking forward to the visit and seeing him again. She finished with the brief information that Lily would be coming too.

The days passed quickly. Saturday dawned a perfect September day for an outing. The children waited excitedly in the hall for Florence and Jackson, who was going to drive them to Lewes station to catch the train.

Betty, a head taller than Lily, was wearing a red coat with a velvet collar and a matching beret on her sausage curls. Lily was dressed in a brown coat with knobbly buttons and a cap with a silky tassel. Both girls wore Clark's sandals and carried gas masks in square boxes slung over their shoulders.

The goodbyes were so emotional they might have been setting out for a world tour and not just a day's outing. Betty clung to her mother as if she was never going to see her again while Lily stood solemnly in the background.

Two years had changed Lily into a beautiful child. She was as small and delicate as a china doll, although her limbs had rounded out and no longer looked like sticks. Her mane of dark hair was shorter although it still reached below her shoulders. It shone with cleanliness and brushing, and although it was straight, tiny wisps escaped the brown cap and curled around her ears and over her pale forehead. Her face was oval with a slightly pointed chin and small nose, but the thing most people noticed first was her large violet eyes fringed with sooty lashes, that stared at the world with wonder, as if everything she saw was new and incredible. There was usually a frown on her face as if she had a secret sorrow, but when she smiled her face lit up with a luminous beauty that most people found irresistible.

Florence, small and neat, in a grey costume and sensible shoes, helped the children into the back of the car and then took her seat beside Bert Jackson. She was just as excited as they were at the prospect of a day out.

'Have a lovely day,' James instructed. He leaned through the car window and held out a silvery half-crown. 'Florence has the money for your fares, but you'd better take this for extras.'

Betty was nearest so she took the coin. The pocket of her coat bulged and Lily looked at it curiously. Betty produced a large tin of Mackintosh's toffees and waved it under Lily's nose.

'It's a present for Edward,' she said proudly. 'I've been saving up and Mummy gave me her sweet coupons.'

Lily's face fell. She hadn't thought of bringing Edward a present. The prospect of seeing him had driven all other thoughts out of her head.

At Lewes they boarded a train. It was full of men in uniforms; but they were cheerful and whistled songs like 'The White Cliffs of Dover.' Blue smoke curled upwards from their Capstan cigarettes so that Betty covered her mouth with her handkerchief and Lily had a coughing fit.

They were pleased to reach Brighton, and walked out of the station forecourt into air smelling of salt and fish and chips.

Edward was waiting for them. He'd grown taller and was wearing his school blazer and tie, long grey trousers and highly polished black shoes. He carried his straw hat proudly and his fair hair was cut short at the back, but one lock fell over his forehead and he kept pushing it away from his eyes.

'This is for you,' Betty said. She handed him the toffees and gave him a kiss on the cheek.

'Thanks.' His neck flushed pink with embarrassment. 'Hullo, Lily.'

Lily smiled and shuffled her feet. Florence felt sorry for her and said quickly, 'I'm going to visit my auntie. She's in the Sussex County Hospital. Do you know where that is, Edward?'

'Yes.' Edward straightened his shoulders, proud of being able to give directions. 'It's in Kemp Town, near my school. There's a trolley bus that goes quite near. I'll show you.'

They walked down Queen's Road towards the bus terminus at the Aquarium. Betty walked in front chatting to Edward, and Lily and Florence followed close behind.

'I was going to take you to the pictures,' Edward said. 'The Odeon is showing a film I want to see. But my headmaster would only let me have one and sixpence of my money and it costs a shilling to get in.'

'That's all right,' Betty said, her eyes sparkling. 'Daddy gave me half a crown so I can pay for myself, and I'll have plenty left over.'

'What about Lily?'

'Oh, Lily hasn't got any money, so she can't come. I don't expect she'd want to anyway.'

Florence wanted to interfere; she guessed the money had been meant for both the children, but if she argued Betty would have a tantrum. She looked at Lily who was lagging behind and staring at the ground. She suspected the child was close to tears and put a comforting arm around her shoulders.

'You can come with me to the hospital. I'd like the company, and Auntie likes children.' Lily didn't respond so she added 'If I had the money I'd pay for you myself, but I've only got enough for the bus fare.'

The fare was twopence, and Lily cheered up a bit when Edward led them up the stairs to the top deck. Florence was a bit scared, particularly when they went around corners, but the children loved the feel of the breeze blowing through their hair. The panoramic view of the town was exciting with its tall old houses and busy streets, after the small village they were used to.

The bus climbed up a steep road and Edward told them they were coming to the race-hill. Betty looked at the fenced-off open grassland with the Channel Coast in the background.

'Where are the horses?' she asked.

'They can't have races now,' Edward told her. 'Not since the war started.'

The bus took them to a stop just below the hospital. They alighted and stood in an uncomfortable group on the pavement. Edward looked from Betty to Lily.

'We don't have to go to the cinema,' he said. 'We could go for a walk instead.'

Betty pouted. 'But I want to go. I've never seen a film before.'

'But what about Lily?'

'I don't mind,' Lily said in a small voice. But her lip trembled and gave her away. They all knew just how much she minded.

'I want to see *Pinocchio*,' Betty said. 'That film about the wooden puppet. She was looking at a poster pasted to a hoarding, advertizing the Walt Disney film.

'That's only on at the Palladium,' Edward explained. 'On the seafront. But there's an Odeon Cinema just along here that has a children's matinée. I went last week and saw a Tarzan film; but they always have a Walt Disney cartoon as well.'

'Can we go there then?'

'If you want to.'

Edward didn't look very happy at the prospect of leaving Lily behind; but Betty had become the leader and he didn't want to upset her.

'Your mother wants us back before the blackout starts,' Florence told them. 'That's at seven forty-six tonight, so we'd better start back about five so that we have plenty of time.'

Sadly Lily turned away and followed Florence up the steps and into the hospital. Why hadn't Mr Thomas given her some money as well? She'd never been to the pictures and it sounded exciting. But then why should Betty's father spoil her when she wasn't even a relation?

The hospital was the most frightening place Lily had ever been in. It was so large and grey, with long, bare passages and high ceilings. Women in white uniforms and strange hats appeared and disappeared through many doors talking in low voices, their soft-soled shoes humming over the uncarpeted floors. Lily thought it was like a human beehive. They were climbing a flight of stairs to the second floor when they first heard the aeroplane.

'I didn't hear an air-raid warning,' Florence said, hurrying her footsteps. 'I expect it's one of ours, but keep away from the windows just in case.'

Lily was terrified. The noise of the plane's engine was so close. She could even see the tip of its wing as it passed the window; but then it soared higher and seemed to pass overhead.

'That was a near thing,' Florence admitted. 'Come on, Auntie's in the ward for old people along here.'

The first thing Lily was aware of was the smell. Children smelt of warmth and powder, ladies smelt of the flowery stuff they sprinkled on their handkerchiefs, and men smelt smoky and pepperminty like Mr Thomas. These old ladies, propped up in narrow beds with white painted frames, smelt of damp wool and urine. Most of them were tiny, with rounded shoulders covered with hand-made bed jackets, but the bed Florence led Lily to housed a mountain of a woman with a mass of springy white hair on her pink head, at least four chins, and a bosom like a shelf. On the bedside locker was a smeared glass containing a grinning set of false teeth.

'Hullo, Auntie,' Florence said. 'How are you?' She leaned forward and kissed the old woman on her flabby cheek.

'No one comes to see me,' Auntie complained, her loose lips flapping over her empty gums like some marine creature. 'Who's that?'

'This is Lily. I'm looking after her today.'

'Come here, child.' The old woman stretched out her hand but Lily backed away. 'Do you want your fortune told?'

'No, thank you,' Lily answered, trying to be polite.

'Go on, let her.' Florence nudged Lily and smiled reassuringly. 'She's ever so good. I think she's got second sight.'

Lily didn't know what second sight was, but she allowed her hand to be held although she hated the feel of the old woman's clammy fingers. Her tiny hand seemed to disappear in the other's grasp and she could feel a horny nail tracing her palm. But Auntie's eyes were closed, and she was rocking to and fro, her chins wobbling. When she spoke the voice was small coming from such a large body, and seemed to come from a long way away.

'I see a house. A big house in the country, with many trees behind it.'

'That must be Ring House . . .' Lily started to say, but Florence put her finger to her lips to hush her.

'I see a plump lady with a kind face, playing with a little girl with yellow curls. The little girl is laughing and calling her Mummy.'

'Betty and Mrs Thomas,' Lily said softly.

'And there's another little girl – much smaller – with dark hair.'

'Is that me?' Lily couldn't help asking.

'Don't interrupt,' Auntie snapped. 'There's a man as well: a big man with grey hair and a gold watch chain. The dark girl is holding his hand. He's . . .' Auntie rocked even more violently so that her bosoms rocked in time with her chins. 'Yes – he's her father.'

Lily pulled her hand away and turned to Florence with a disappointed look on her face. 'You said she was good.'

'She got Betty and her mum right, and Mr Thomas does wear a gold watch chain. She's only an old woman; she can't get everything right.'

'Let me have another go.' Auntie leaned her bulk towards Lily, and the child didn't know what to do. But just at that moment a shadow passed the window and they could hear the drone of another plane.

'It's coming back!' Lily cried. 'That plane's coming back!'

'It's gone past.' Florence cocked her head on one side. 'Just keep away from the windows.'

Her advice almost came too late because as she spoke there was a whining sound and a loud thud. The walls around them shook and even the solid floor vibrated under the blast. The glass in the windows held because of the criss-cross of sticky tape, but through the diamond-shaped gaps Lily could see the tail of the plane. There was a second thud, and then a third, and a spiral of smoke began to ascend into the air outside.

'They've bombed us!' A woman in the next bed set up a wail of distress. 'They've bombed the hospital!'

'No, they haven't, you silly old woman,' Auntie said. 'But it was close.'

Lily couldn't stop trembling. She'd heard Mr and Mrs Thomas talking about air raids but she never thought she'd be involved in one. It made the war seem awfully close and not just something you read about in the newspapers.

'Do you think Betty and Edward are all right?'

'I hope so.' Florence looked worried. 'Stay here a minute.' She went outside and spoke to one of the nurses. She didn't look any happier when she returned. 'We're to stay here while they try to find out what's happened. Have a boiled sweet.'

Lily took one gratefully. She was hungry because she hadn't eaten since breakfast. Even then she'd only managed a small piece of toast because of the excitement.

Cups of tea and biscuits were being wheeled in for the patients, but nobody thought to offer the visitors any. It seemed an awfully long time until the nurse came back. She was full of self-importance and her starched cap floated out behind her like a ship's full sail. She looked around solemnly before making her announcement.

'I have to tell you that a great many bombs have been dropped on our town. As many as twenty, I think. Shops and houses have been hit and there are casualties. The numbers won't be known until later. Luckily our hospital has been spared, although there's a few cracked window panes. The nearest bomb fell on a local cinema.'

Before she finished speaking Florence was on her feet. 'Do you know which cinema?'

'The one down the road. The Odeon someone said. It was full of children watching the Saturday matinée. I expect they'll bring some of the injured to us.'

'Oh, my God!' Florence put her hand up to her mouth in horror. 'Betty and Edward!' Lily started to cry but Florence was too distressed to comfort her. 'Come on,' she said. 'We must go and look for them.'

'No one must leave the hospital,' the nurse said firmly, but Florence took no notice. She hurried out of the ward dragging Lily behind her, forgetting even to say goodbye to Auntie. Nobody tried to stop them.

When they reached the road outside they were met by a scene of destruction. A pall of grey smoke hung over the town like a dirty blanket, and the pavements were littered with broken glass. Florence hurried through the wreckage looking neither to right nor left. Lily followed behind in a daze.

It reminded her of a nightmare she'd had once, where everything that was safe and reassuring suddenly changed and became distorted and threatening. The streets they'd driven through in the trolley bus had been lined with houses that had lace curtains in their windows, and window-boxes outside full of late summer flowers; but now there were gaps in the terraces as if some giant dentist had passed by and yanked out buildings as easily as human molars.

They passed one house where a bedroom wall was suspended over a heap of rubble. Torn pink wallpaper flapped in the breeze and a picture of the Sacred Heart hung drunkenly in space. In the remains of another house a cistern swung crookedly from an upper wall while the broken pan lay in the back garden. Nearby a cracked pipe oozed a steady trickle of water into the crushed flower bed. People who only an hour before had been going about their normal business were wandering the streets in a dazed condition. There seemed to be an uneasy silence covering the town.

'Where are we going?' Lily asked. She'd lost her sense of direction and clung to Florence, afraid of getting lost in this strange, threatening place.

'To the Odeon Cinema. To find Betty and Edward.'

'But is this the right way?'

'I don't know.'

Florence had been walking blindly without looking where she was going. She was in a state of shock and worry and wasn't thinking clearly.

'Shall we ask someone? Look, Florence, there's a man coming, let's ask him.'

An ARP Warden was approaching carrying a little boy in his arms. The child had lost one of his shoes and there was blood on his face; but his eyes were open and he was still alive.

'Can you tell us if were going in the right direction for the Odeon Cinema?' Florence asked.

'It's just down there.' The Warden nodded to the turning he'd just appeared from. 'But you should keep away. There's been a direct hit. All the little kids paid sixpence to see a film and the Jerry slams a bomb right through the roof. Landed in the stalls, it did; almost in the children's laps. This little one's lucky.'

'Did you see a little girl with fair hair, and a boy in a straw hat?'

'Couldn't say, Ma'am. All children look the same when a bomb drops on 'em.' He plodded off carrying his pitiful burden. Lily looked up into Florence's face.

'Do you think they're dead?'

'Don't be silly,' Florence answered briskly. 'That's a dreadful thing to say.' But Lily could see by her set expression that she suspected the worst.

They found the cinema without any problem, but weren't allowed inside. The front doors were still standing but they could see the hole in the roof. A flapping poster proclaimed to anyone who was interested that the main feature that week was called *They Came by Night.*

'That's a laugh,' a man standing near them muttered. 'Seems to me they came by day.'

They were surrounded by people in uniforms: wardens in their tin hats, ambulance men, and Salvation Army ladies in navy blue and red handing out cups of hot tea.

The sight of the devastation made Florence's knees wobble and she sat down on a wall and put her head in her hands. Whatever would Mr and Mrs Thomas do to her if anything had happened to their daughter? And Doctor Butler? Edward was all he had in the world. She shouldn't have let them go off on their own like that. Lily was pulling at her skirts but she ignored her. Lily was the least of her worries; why couldn't she have been the one to get lost? There were no anxious parents to face as far as that little person was concerned. Why oh why couldn't it have been Lily?

Then Florence felt guilty at her own feelings. She pulled herself together and looked around to see that Lily was safe.

'It's all right,' she said, crossing her fingers and praying that it was. 'We'll find them.'

'They're over there.'

'I'll go and ask that ambulance man if he's seen them. Don't worry, they'll be all right.'

'They're over there, Florence.'

'What!'

'They're over there on the other side of the road, Florence. They've just come round the corner. Look, you can see Betty's red coat and beret.'

Lily's words penetrated the fog that seemed to be surrounding Florence's brain. When she looked in the direction Lily was pointing to she saw the two children they'd been searching for nonchalantly wandering hand in hand along the pavement.

'Betty!' she called loudly. 'Edward! Over here.' And Lily joined in, yelling excitedly. 'Betty! Edward!'

Betty heard them and waved, pulling on her companion's

sleeve. Slowly, as if they had all the time in the world, they crossed the road. Florence grabbed the little girl in a bear hug, so relieved was she to find her safe and well. Lily just stood on the pavement staring at Edward with tears in her eyes. She'd begun to wonder if she was ever going to see him again.'

'Isn't it exciting?' Betty was babbling. 'There was an air raid. I heard the bombs dropping. You wait till I tell Daddy.'

'But where were you?' Florence demanded. She was beginning to feel cross now that she'd assured herself that her charges were unharmed.

'In the cinema, of course.'

'But a bomb went through the roof . . .'

'Not the Odeon. That was full up. So Edward bought me some chips because I was hungry and then we went to the other cinema. There was a serial about a sheep dog, a cowboy film, and a Mickey Mouse cartoon. It was just like a church inside, except that it was painted blue and gold.'

'It's called the King's Cliff,' Edward explained. 'I'm sorry if you've been worried, Florence, but we didn't know the Odeon had been hit until we came out. We heard the bang though.'

'I thought it was the cowboys and Indians shooting at each other,' Betty butted in. 'I didn't know at first it was bombs.'

'I thought you were dead,' Lily said, and her face was so pale Edward put his arm around her shoulders and hugged her tightly.

'Silly goose! It would take more than a lot of bombs to kill me.'

'Well, all I can say is I'm glad to see you're both safe and sound,' Florence said. 'But I've had enough of Brighton; the sooner we're back on that train the better.'

Edward insisted on escorting them back to the station, and they were relieved to find that the bombs had missed the railway line and the trains were still running.

Betty immediately flopped into a corner seat. She was tired and cross, and when Florence tried to dust her down and tidy her hair she started to cry.

But Lily stayed by the window. She couldn't take her eyes off Edward because she had no idea when she was going to see him again. As the train gathered speed she waved until he was only a dot on the platform; and then he vanished altogether. But she still wouldn't leave the window. She felt as if there was an invisible cord stretching between them like a piece of elastic, and she was afraid to break it. To her childish mind it was a silver cord, and one day it would bring them together, and they would live happily ever after just like the princes and princesses did in the very best fairy stories.

CHAPTER FIVE

The May Queen

'We're having a competition at school tomorrow to choose the May Queen,' Betty Thomas told her mother excitedly.

'That'll be nice, dear. Stand still or I might burn you by accident.' Elizabeth pulled the hot tongs out of cinders and spat on them. The spittle sizzled in a satisfactory manner so she knew they were hot enough. Carefully she combed out her daughter's ringlets and wound each one around the hot metal. When she slid the tongs out it left a fat sausage curl which she pinned close to the little girl's head. All she would have to do in the morning was comb it out.

'Ouch!' Betty protested as she felt the heat near her ear.

'Who do you think they'll choose then?'

'Me, of course.' Betty sounded surprised that her mother could have any doubt.

'It's a competition,' Edward said from his place at the table where he was doing his homework. 'Our teacher, Miss Stringer, has told all the girls to bring along their prettiest dresses. Then she's going to get them to parade around the classroom and the boys will choose the best. The one we choose will be this year's May Queen.'

'That sounds fair.' Elizabeth tied a strip of muslin around Betty's head and secured it with a bow. 'Do you want your hair curled, Lily?'

'No, thank you.'

Lily was curled up in an armchair with a book of fairy tales open on her lap. Her dark hair hung in a smooth curtain over her shoulder like the shining wing of a bird. She pushed it away with her hand and peeped at Mrs Thomas through her fingers.

'Curls are fashionable,' Betty said, pirouetting around the room in her fluffy dressing gown. 'I passed Mrs Jackson in the lane yesterday and she said I looked just like Shirley Temple.'

Edward smiled and picked up his pen again. He was glad Lily didn't want curls. He thought she was pretty enough as she was. 'How do you know they'll choose you?' he asked as Betty danced past him.

'Because I shall be the prettiest. I'm going to wear the party dress Mummy made me last year. The yellow one with the frills. You'll vote for me; and Mike and Peter Jackson if I promise them a ride on Bracken; and the other boys are sure to when they see my dress.'

'We'd better go and get it out of the wardrobe if you want to wear it tomorrow,' Elizabeth said. 'It's probably all screwed up at the back and needs ironing. Let's go and get it now.'

Betty followed her mother out of the room leaving Edward and Lily in companionable silence. The glow of the lamp fell on Lily's pale face, outlining it with a golden aura. Her dark blue dressing gown was quilted, and Edward could just see the tips of her pink toes poking out from under the hem. She sighed and turned a page of her book.

'Don't you want to be May Queen, Lily?'

'Not really.' Lily uncoiled her small body, and her hair swung forward again, almost hiding her face. She shook it back and felt with her foot for her discarded slippers.

'They're under your chair.' Edward got up from his seat at the table and dropped to his knees, pulling the slippers from their hiding place. He slid them gently onto Lily's feet. 'I think you'd make a lovely May Queen.'

Lily blushed at the praise. Even her blush was delicate; not like some girls whose faces went bright red for no reason. Lily's face remained pale as ivory, but her cheeks were lightly flushed with pink, making her prettier than ever.

'I haven't anything to wear.'

'I'm sure Aunt Lizzie would find you something if you ask her.'

'I expect she would.' Lily looked thoughtful, but then she sighed for the second time. 'Betty wouldn't like it.'

'Probably not,' Edward agreed. He knew only too well how hard Lily tried not to upset the other girl.

Edward had been living with the Thomas family, at Ring House, since September. After the children's escape from the bombs in the Brighton air raid John Butler had feared for his son's safety. The school, situated on high land overlooking the sea, had escaped without damage; but next time it might not be so lucky.

Doctor Butler drove to Brighton the next day, collected Edward and took him home to Lewes. After the first pleasure of being reunited with his dogs had passed, the boy had soon become bored. John had a busy practice and was often away from home, and he soon saw that his son was missing company of his own age.

When James and Elizabeth offered the boy a home for the duration of the war he gladly accepted. Betty and Lily were only two years younger than Edward; and although the village school was small it had crammed its tiny classrooms with evacuees and extended its age group to cater for all the children staying in Lenton. James Thomas also had the time and knowledge to give Edward extra tuition. Everyone seemed happy at the uniting of the two families. Especially Lily. It wasn't long before Edward was calling the Thomas's uncle and aunt, although they weren't related.

Having Edward living at Ring House had been beyond Lily's wildest dreams. To see him every day; to hear his soft voice and merry laugh, brought a smile of pleasure to her own face. She was happier than she'd ever been before, and tried to make light of Betty's petty jealousies.

Betty came back into the room to show off her party dress. For all her energy she hadn't slimmed down, and the frilly skirt and puffed sleeves made her look plumper than ever.

'I've grown a bit,' she admitted, 'but Mummy's going to let the seams out.' She struggled to pull the thin material over her head.

'Mind!' Elizabeth laughed, coming to her aid. 'You'll tear it if you don't look out. What are you going to wear, Lily? There isn't time to make you anything.'

'It doesn't matter,' Lily said quietly. 'Betty will make a better May Queen than me.'

'Why don't you go upstairs and look in that old army trunk in the attic? It's full of old clothes we keep for dressing up. You might find something.'

'That's an idea,' Edward said quickly, seeing the doubtful look on Lily's face. 'Come on. Even if we don't find anything it'll be fun.'

They left Betty struggling to free herself from the yellow muslin. They climbed the stairs slowly because Elizabeth had let them borrow a lamp and they had to be careful not to spill the oil. Edward set it down on the window-sill where it glowed like a beacon. Then he turned his attention to the trunks and boxes stacked in a cobwebby corner.

There were three of them: two big ones, and one a bit smaller. Edward lifted the smallest one down onto the floor and called Lily over.

'You see what's inside this one,' he said. 'I'll look in the others.'

Lily looked nervous: she'd heard about horrible things being found in trunks, like the skeleton in the song 'The mistletoe bough'. It was too small to contain a whole skeleton. But there could be spiders! While she gingerly blew the dust off the top Edward was lifting the lid from the second trunk. First there was a layer of old newspapers, brown as toast, and when he lifted them out the edges crumbled away under his fingers. Something soft and red met his eyes.

'Here, Lily! Come and look. It's velvet.'

'Is it a dress?' Lily peered over his shoulder.

'I don't know. Help me.'

Between them the children lifted the heavy material out of the trunk and unrolled it.

'Curtains!' Lily said in disgust.

'It's a lovely colour. Red really suits you.'

'I can't wear a curtain, Edward; and there isn't time for Mrs Thomas to make it up into a dress. It's May Day tomorrow.'

'Was there anything interesting in the little trunk?' Edward asked.

'Only books. Boring ones: all tiny print and no pictures. There's a box as well.'

'What sort of box?'

'A wooden box with brass bands on the sides.'

'What's inside?'

'I don't know. I haven't had time to look.'

Lily turned to her trunk and lifted out a wooden box about a foot square. There was a keyhole in the front and no key, but the lid, which had tarnished hinges on the back, lifted easily.

'It's a desk,' Lily said in surprise. 'Look, Edward! When you open it it turns into a little desk. There's a leather top to rest your paper on, and a tray for pens and pencils. There's a pen there already but its nib is broken. Oh! Isn't it lovely? I wish it was mine.'

'Let me look.' Edward admired Lily's find and then handed it back. 'If you showed it to Aunt Lizzie perhaps she'd let you keep it.'

'No, she wouldn't,' Lily said crossly. 'If Betty saw it, she'd want it.'

'This is for blotting paper, and this little bottle with the screw top is for ink,' Edward said. 'Have you looked inside?'

'Not yet.' Lily lifted the flap and disclosed a pile of jumbled paper. It looks like letters.'

'Perhaps they're love letters,' Edward said with a grin. He was busy opening the remaining trunk.

'Don't be silly.'

'They could be. Love letters from Uncle James to Auntie Lizzie.'

'This one isn't.' Lily unfolded the topmost one. 'This is a letter about one of the farms. There's lots of bills.' She delved deeper and pulled out a square of cardboard. 'Look, I've found an old photograph.'

'Who's it of?'

'I don't know. Just a lady.'

'Is it Aunt Lizzie?'

'No, it's too slim and pretty for your aunt. You have a look. Who do you think it can be?'

Edward took the picture out of Lily's hand and studied it. 'I don't know; but she reminds me of you when I've said something to make you smile. She's showing the tips of her teeth just like you do.'

'Everyone smiles like that, silly.'

'There's something written across the bottom, but it's all faded.' Edward held the picture nearer the lamp. 'Can you make out what it says?'

'There's a big L,' Lily said slowly. 'It's Love. I know – it says

Love from Eddie. Eddie!' She burst into a gay laugh. 'It's from you.'

'No, it isn't. There's only one D. It's not Eddie, its Edie: short for Edith. Do you know anyone called Edie, Lily?'

'Only Edie from the farm; but she's nothing to do with the Thomas's, so it can't be her.'

'It's probably some distant relative. Put it back and we'll have a look in this last trunk. Perhaps this is the one with the dressing up things inside.'

They soon forgot the mysterious photo. The last trunk held what they'd been searching for: dated frocks and ball gowns, men's dress clothes and sports wear, all neatly folded in tissue paper.

'Pooh!' Edward said, shaking out a pair of trousers 'What's that smell?'

'Mothballs.' Lily picked up one of the tiny white crystal balls between her finger and thumb. 'Those trousers are too big for you. They must have been made for Mr Thomas.'

'Everything's too big.' Edward picked up a black silk afternoon dress and held it against Lily. 'We could pad you out with cushions.'

'I'm supposed to look like a May Queen, not the fat woman from the circus.' Lily picked up a crushed straw hat with a wide brim, and balanced it on her dark head. 'What's that mauve thing?'

Edward pulled out a strip of violet silk. It shone in the light, all shades, from pale lavender to deep purple.

'It's a petticoat.'

'It's pretty. Can I try it on?'

Edward turned his back while Lily slipped out of her dressing gown. She slid the wisp of silk over her head, shaking her hair free. It had been made as an underslip for a tea gown and should have reached just below the wearer's knee, but on Lily it reached to her ankles. The silk was so fine it clung to the outline of her slender body like a glove, leaving shoulders and neck bare.

'What do you think?'

Edward looked up. 'It's pretty; it's exactly the same colour as your eyes. Put the hat back on.' Lily did as she was told. 'That's fine. But the hat needs some trimming on it: some flowers – some mauve flowers. Are there any in the garden?'

'There were some crocuses under the tree in the orchard, but they're dead now.'

'They'd be too small anyway. I know!' Edward grinned as an idea dawned on him. 'I'll make you some paper flowers. Shall I?'

'Yes, please,' Lily said simply. But the way her violet eyes lit up showed Edward how delighted she was with the idea.

May Day dawned, bright, sunny and warm. The sky was blue and clear with just a few fleecy clouds drifting across the horizon. Summer was still a long way away, but at least winter was well behind. Everyone in Lenton basked in a false sense of security inspired by the unseasonable weather.

Betty insisted on wearing her yellow party dress to school, but Lily carried the mauve petticoat in a brown paper bag, together with the newly decorated hat.

James and Elizabeth followed the children to the front door to see them on their way. Lily and Edward looked excited, but Betty was sulking.

'Why do we have to walk to school?' Betty demanded. 'I want to go in the car.'

'Sorry,' James said. He hated having to disappoint anyone. 'There isn't enough petrol because of the war. Anyway it's healthier to walk when the weather's good, and there's three of you to keep each other company.'

'It's not fair . . .' Betty started, but Elizabeth stopped her daughter's complaints by pushing a bag of sweets into her hand.

'Share these with Edward and Lily,' she said. 'You're a big girl now, and old enough to walk to school.'

'My legs get tired . . .'

Betty tried again but no one took any notice. Edward and Lily were already halfway down the drive. She had to run to catch up with them, her frilly yellow skirts billowing out around her knees.

'Let me carry your gas mask,' Edward said kindly. Betty cheered up when she was free from the square box that bounced uncomfortably against her side.

'Can we call for Pete and Mike?' Lily asked as they neared the cottage where the estate manager, Albert Jackson, lived with his wife and children.

'No, we can't,' Betty said firmly. Bert Jackson also acted as her father's chauffeur and drove them to school. If there wasn't enough petrol for the daily trip she was prepared to hold him responsible.

The cottage was a pretty little place, shining with new paint and sparkling window panes. The garden, behind its white fence, was a riot of spring flowers. Emma Jackson was pegging sheets onto her washing line which was slung across a strip of grassland at the side of the house. Billy, the youngest Jackson, was toddling around his mother's legs, pulling on her skirts as he exercised his baby legs. Emma, seeing the children approaching, called out to them.

'Pete's just coming. Mike went early, but Pete's still here. Pete!' she called.

'We don't want him walking with us,' Betty said under her breath. 'Come on, let's run.'

Edward and Betty ran on ahead, but Lily slowed her footsteps. She liked Peter Jackson. He was a friendly boy and was always kind to her, which was more than could be said about some of the village children who heard their parents gossiping about 'that girl from Valley Farm'.

As Betty's yellow skirts disappeared around the bend in the road Pete appeared in the roadway, still struggling into his jacket. He was a merry looking boy with a wide smile on his rosy face. He was always untidy. Today his rough brown hair stood out in wet spikes where he'd damped it but forgotten to flatten it down. His grey shirt hung unevenly because he'd fastened the buttons in the wrong holes in his haste. His knees were like bony knobs as they protruded from the gap between the bottom of his trousers and the top of his socks, and his face was reflected in the toes of his black boots. Peter Jackson might be known for his untidy appearance, but he was also known for being spotlessly clean. He ran to catch Lily up, panting slightly at the exertion.

'The others went on,' Lily explained. 'They were frightened of being late.'

'That's all right. I understand.'

Lily relaxed. She always felt comfortable with Pete. He seemed to understand most things.

'What you got in your bag?' he asked, as Lily's carrier bumped against his leg for the third time.

'My dress – for the competition.'

'You're going to make a lovely May Queen. I hope Miss Stringer lets me put the crown on your head.'

'I don't suppose I shall be chosen,' Lily said. 'Some of the girls' dresses are bound to be nicer than mine. Mine's just an old petticoat.'

'I shall vote for you anyway,' Peter promised.

Lily suddenly stopped still in the middle of the roadway. They were passing a thicket that was part of the boundary of Valley Farm. She hadn't been back since James Thomas had rescued her, not even to visit Matt, although she'd seen the Crow brothers in the village market. It seemed a lifetime ago. She still lived with the fear that the Thomas's would make her return if she didn't do as she was told. That was one of the reasons she put up with Betty's tyrannies.

'You mustn't vote for me,' she said quickly, and her violet eyes begged the boy to understand. 'You must vote for Betty.'

'Why? Don't you want to be Queen of the May?'

'Of course I'd like to,' Lily admitted. 'But Betty's set her heart on being chosen.'

'Then she's going to be disappointed, isn't she?' Pete kicked a stone with the toe of his boot and watched in satisfaction as it bounced along the path.

'Please!'

'It's time that Betty Thomas was taken down a peg or two. That's what my mum says. She's fat and nasty, and no one likes her.'

Peter took aim at another stone and kicked it angrily. It rose into the air and disappeared into the thicket at the side of the road. The children heard a smothered cry coming from the tangle of brambles. They stared at each other in dismay.

'You've hit somebody,' Lily said in a frightened voice.

'It's not my fault,' Pete said stubbornly. 'They shouldn't be hiding.'

'Perhaps it's a tramp. Shall we go and see?'

'I suppose we'd better, in case he's hurt.'

They were both scared when they pulled the branches aside and saw the figure of a man sitting on the bare earth with a bottle propped between his legs. His knees were poking through the twill of his heavy trousers, and his check shirt was ripped. There was a stubble of beard on his chin, and blood was trickling from a wound over one eye.

'It's Matt,' Lily said, and she pushed her way towards the unkempt figure. 'You're hurt, Matt.'

'He's not dead, is he?' Peter was frightened. 'I didn't know there was anybody hiding.'

'I'm not hiding,' Matthew Crow said in a reassuringly alive voice. 'What you kids want then?'

'Matt, it's me – Lily. The little girl dropped to her knees and put her arms around her old friend. 'We didn't mean to hurt you. We were just kicking stones.'

'Lily?' Matt looked up and a big smile of welcome crept across his face. 'It's my little Lily! And you look so smart and all. I knew you'd come home.'

'How are you, Matt? What are you doing here?'

The smile slipped away from Matt's face and he looked troubled at the question. 'I was only having a little drink; but Mo found me and locked me out. I thought Edie would let me in when it got dark – but she didn't.'

'Have you been out here all night?'

'Yes. It was cold and I thought I saw a ghost, but it was only an old owl out to scare me.'

Lily was dabbing the blood away from Matt's temple with her clean handkerchief. It was a small cut, and not very deep, so she reassured Peter that he hadn't really hurt her friend.

'We're on our way to school, Matt,' she said when Pete started pulling impatiently on her arm. 'Will you be all right?'

'Moses will be out in the fields by now, so I expect I'll find a door open. Edie will forgive me; she usually does. I'm glad you've come back, Lily.'

'I haven't come back. We were just passing on our way to school.'

'But you must come back to me.' Matthew grabbed Lily's sleeve and held on to her tightly. He looked so neglected and alone that her heart stirred with pity.

'I can't. But I'll come and see you – if Moses will let me.'

'Moses!' Matt laughed, but there was no mirth in the sound. 'I saved you from Moses – do you understand? If Moses had had his way you'd have died for sure, and been buried in the cemetery with the other babes. His eyes were pleading, and a single tear channelled its way down the crease in his dirty cheek. 'I looked after you good, didn't I? I took care of you.'

'Yes, you did.' Lily's heart was so full she was frightened it would break. She didn't understand all the things Matt was saying, but she remembered how kind he'd always been to her.

'You must come home to Valley Farm, Lily, where you belong. If I don't take care of you, who else will?'

Peter stepped forward. He was only eleven years old, but he stood tall. He could see how upset Lily was, and in his eyes Matthew Crow was a pathetic apology of a man. 'She can't come back, Mr Crow,' he said. 'But you don't have to worry because I shall take care of her. Come on, Lily, we don't want to be late.'

He took Lily's hand and led her away; but she couldn't get the picture of Matt's sad eyes and tear-stained face out of her mind. She didn't speak as they walked side by side into the village.

They reached the school yard just as the bell was ringing. Usually the children were expected to be quiet as they filed into their classrooms to sit at the rows of narrow wooden desks under Miss Stringer's watchful eyes. But today was a special day: it had a party feel about it. The girls were busy parading their fancy dresses under the embarrassed gaze of the boys who were herded together at the far end of the room, under the blackboard. Betty was running about in her usual excited fashion; every so often she would stop to whisper in some boy's ear. Lily guessed she was showing off for their benefit.

'Don't you want to be in the competition, Lily?' Miss Stringer asked, as she saw the little girl shuffling her feet in the doorway. 'Haven't you brought a dress to change into?'

'It's in my bag, miss,' Lily said. She knew Miss Stringer was trying to be kind, but she didn't think the mauve petticoat would stand a chance against the lace and frills of the other girls.

'Go and change in the cloakroom then; and be quick about it.'

The teacher pushed Lily through the door and then turned back to her other pupils. She was a big woman, almost manly in stature. Her brown hair was curled into earphones on either side of her head, and she had a mole on her cheek as well as the beginnings of a moustache. She wore hand-knitted suits and dresses whatever the weather, and her feet were always encased in flat crepe-soled shoes. Nevertheless she was light on her feet and didn't miss any mischief the naughtier children in her care thought up. But she was kind and fair and the children respected her. She knew quite a bit about Lily's background and tried to take a special interest in the child. The other children liked Miss Stringer; as for Lily, she loved her.

The cloakroom smelt of dust and plimsolls, and there was nowhere to put anything. In the end Lily dumped her bag in a corner and commenced her transformation.

Slipping the mauve garment over her head, and feeling its cool touch sliding down over her bare skin, made Lily feel nervous. The girls outside were adorned in pastel shades: pinks, and blues, and even bridal white. Their dresses were fussy with frills and ribbon bows, whereas hers was as simple as a shift. Her only sign of decoration was the hat, and she pulled it out of her bag reverently.

Edward had worked hard to please her. He'd pulled the wide straw brim into shape and decorated it with paper rosettes. They were all colours of mauve, from palest lavender to deep purple, and matched the changing colours of her dress. She'd forgotten to bring a comb, so she had to run her fingers through her silky hair and then shake it so that it fell back naturally into a dark curtain over her shoulders. Then she balanced the precious hat on top of her head.

There was no mirror so Lily had no way of knowing what she looked like. When she opened the door the other girls had already started to process around the room.

'Join the end of the line, Lily,' Miss Stringer called. 'And walk slowly, everybody, so the boys can see you all properly.'

The boys in their role as judges were sniggering and poking each other, particularly when one little girl in powder blue was overcome by the occasion and burst into tears. But when it was Lily's turn to walk in front of them a silence fell. Perhaps it was because she looked so different, or perhaps it was because she looked so lovely, but suddenly these rough village boys were seeing true beauty for the first time in their lives. Natural beauty, simply displayed, and the innocence of a child who was completely unaware of her charms.

Even Miss Stringer was mesmerized. The slim figure walking so confidently across the classroom swayed like a graceful reed under its covering of mauve silk. Lily's neck rose pale and white like the stem of a flower, surmounted by her small head with its delicate features and the curtain of dark hair. Her face was shaded by the nodding brim of her hat.

She had such style and grace that the teacher forgot for the moment that she was watching a child: because surely no child should display such sensuality in her movements. Fear overwhelmed Miss Stringer. Fear for this strange child and what was going to become of her. Miss Stringer could see by the stunned looks on the boys' faces that Lily from the Valley was going to be a breaker of men's hearts before she was much older. If the men didn't break hers first.

'Thank you, Lily,' the teacher said, trying to control her own emotion. 'You can sit down now.'

Holding her hat in place with one graceful hand, Lily walked slowly to the nearest chair and sat down. Miss Stringer saw that Edward Butler, the doctor's son, was busy with sketchpad and pencil. Her heart turned over. She saw him glance at the girl in the mauve dress, and then he began to draw quickly.

'He's drawing Lily!' she thought in fascinated awareness. 'He's drawing her as a man would draw his lover or mistress, every movement of his hand giving the game away. He loves her, and he's only eleven years old!'

Lily had been aware of the impact she'd made on the watchers, and she'd loved every minute of it. The feeling of power made her dizzy. She knew without a doubt that she was going to be voted May Queen. She might have grown up in poverty at Valley Farm and it was true that she had no idea of her parentage, but to be chosen out of all the girls to be their Queen would prove she was their equal. Her cheeks glowed and her violet eyes sparkled. She knew all the boys would vote for her.

'Each boy will take a slip of paper and write down the name of the girl he's chosen,' Miss Stringer said, although she was also aware that it was a foregone conclusion. 'Don't let anyone see what you've written. Then fold your papers in four and bring them to me.'

There was much shuffling of feet and chewing of pens before the boys bent to their task. The girls waited with bated breath for the verdict.

There were fourteen slips of paper on Miss Stringer's desk. She unfolded the first one and smiled. But as she worked her way through the pile the smile slipped; she even started again and did a recount, as if she couldn't believe her eyes. At last she faced the expectant class, and coughed to clear her throat and steady her voice.

'The voting was fair and I hope nobody's going to be disappointed. Everyone can have a part by joining in the procession to crown the May Queen.' She paused and looked over her glasses as if daring anyone to question the result. 'There are only two names put forward: Betty Thomas and Lily. Betty has twelve votes and Lily two – so Betty is our May Queen.'

Lily couldn't believe her ears. Her whole little world collapsed around her like a house of cards. Betty was so unpopular that she couldn't believe that twelve children would have chosen her, and yet it appeared that was just what they had done. Her face burned with shame and disappointment and the mauve petticoat suddenly seemed a poor shoddy thing. Even the hat had lost its charms and she tried to hide it under her chair.

'Come on, Lily,' Miss Stringer said kindly. 'Don't you want to come outside and watch Betty being crowned?'

Lily felt numb. She mustn't cry or show that she minded. She followed the others, and watched the girls strewing petals along the path towards the gold painted chair that served as a throne.

Edward had been chosen to crown the May Queen. He stepped forward like a little Prince Charming, and placed the crown carefully on Betty's fair curls. The other children clapped and cheered.

'I voted for you,' a small voice said at Lily's elbow. It was Peter Jackson, standing there twisting his hands together.

'I know you did, Pete. Thank you.'

'And Edward did too. I looked over his shoulder.'

'I don't mind,' Lily said desperately. 'It doesn't matter.'

'Yes, it does,' Pete went on. 'Because it wasn't fair.'

'How do you mean?'

'Betty rigged it. I heard her. All the boys live in cottages owned by her father. She threatened to get him to turn them out of their homes if they didn't vote for her. They were too frightened not to.'

Lily looked across at Betty who was smiling complacently from her seat on the golden throne. Edward was kneeling on the ground at her feet adjusting her footstool. To some people Betty Thomas might appear as a silly, spoilt little girl; but behind her childish smile was the ageless look of triumph.

For the first time Lily saw her in her true colours: as a scheming threat to all her desires.

CHAPTER SIX

Summer 1950

'I've been talking to Florence,' Elizabeth said. 'She wants to leave us.'

James lowered his newspaper slowly and blinked at his wife in a puzzled fashion. Elizabeth continued knitting, her needles clicking as she expertly turned the heel of a sock.

'Whatever for?' He was quite put out, which was unusual. Normally it took a lot to ruffle James Thomas. 'She must have been with us ten years at the least.'

'Fifteen.'

'Fifteen? Good God! Why's she leaving then?'

'She's getting married.'

'Married! Florence getting married!'

'Yes. Don't look like that James, it isn't funny.'

'Well, I think it is. I thought she'd be with us for life.'

'Then you thought wrong, didn't you?'

James recovered his dignity, folded his newspaper, and cleared his throat. Of course he was pleased if the little maid-of-all-work had found herself a husband. It was just such unexpected news.

'Who's she marrying then?'

'Someone she met last year when she went to visit her sister in Exeter. It seems they've been corresponding ever since, and now he wants to marry her.'

James thought quickly. His response was characteristically generous. 'Ask her what she wants for a present – no expense – anything she wants. And old Sam's cottage is still standing empty. I'll have it done up for them.'

'She won't want it,' Elizabeth said calmly. 'Her fiancé's got his own home in Exeter. He's a tailor, and he lives over the business.'

James rustled his paper again petulantly. 'So she really means it? She really wants to leave us?'

'That's what she says. We can hardly expect her to travel up and down from Devon every day.'

'But, damn it all, Elizabeth, what shall we do? You can't manage this big house single-handed.'

'We'll have to replace her.'

'Who by?' James's face had gone quite red. 'You have no idea how difficult it is to get staff these days. Since the war all the women want to go into factories and offices. No one goes into service. John's been searching for a housekeeper for months and he still has to make do with an elderly charwoman who's past it by what he tells me.'

'I know it's difficult.'

Elizabeth put down her knitting and folded her hands calmly in her lap. She'd thought carefully about telling her husband the idea she'd had about overcoming the servant shortage. Knowing James, she wasn't sure how he was going to take it.

Through the French window she could see Betty and Lily playing tennis. Neither of them were very good, but what they lacked in expertise they made up for in enthusiasm. They made a pretty sight in their short white tunics. Betty, nearly nineteen, had slimmed down considerably. Her new sleek hairstyle suited her; in fact she'd grown into quite an attractive girl. If it wasn't for her sulky expression and graceless movements Elizabeth would have felt quite satisfied with her. But Lily, there was no doubt about it, Lily had grown into a beauty.

As Elizabeth watched the smaller girl tossed a ball into the air and sent it skimming across the net. Betty missed, and let out a loud shriek of dismay.

'You did that on purpose!'

'Sorry.' Lily lobbed an easier one at her partner and the game continued.

Elizabeth frowned as Peter Jackson came out of the bushes wheeling a barrow. He slowed down as he passed the tennis court. Deliberately, Elizabeth thought. He slowed down on purpose so that he could watch Lily. As her slim figure stretched upwards to hit the ball he could see the clear outline of her small pointed breasts beneath the thin material. It was disgusting, Elizabeth thought angrily, disgusting that a young girl should appear so voluptuous while playing a simple game of tennis. And the worst part was that Lily herself seemed completely unaware of her charms.

Her dark hair was plaited into a heavy rope that swung between her shoulder blades. It was threaded with a white ribbon. She'd tucked a large white daisy flower behind her ear: Elizabeth considered that ostentatious.

Everywhere they went, people, particularly men and boys, swarmed around Lily, leaving poor Betty out in the cold. Elizabeth was fed up with it. After all, she was only some homeless orphan that James had felt sorry for; but now she'd settled into Ring House as if she belonged there. In Elizabeth's eyes she'd outstayed her welcome. She'd stopped feeling sorry for the girl a long time ago, and thought it was time for a change. Thank goodness they'd never actually adopted her; then things would have been far less easy.

'I admit it's difficult,' Elizabeth said again. 'But I've had an idea.'

'Come on then, let's hear it.'

Elizabeth took a deep breath before plunging in. 'I thought perhaps Lily could replace Florence.'

'Lily?' James looked astounded. 'Lily's one of the family.'

'No, she's not, James,' Elizabeth chided gently. 'She's not one of our family, or anyone else's that we know of. We've more than done our duty to that girl, and I think it's about time she started repaying our kindness.'

'Elizabeth! Elizabeth!' James sounded really upset and she hoped she hadn't gone too far. Sometimes she thought her husband was fonder of the orphan girl than he was of his own daughter. She had to tread carefully. 'We shouldn't expect kindness to be repaid,' James went on reproachfully. 'That isn't Christian. I thought you loved Lily as much as I do. She loves you. She thinks of you as her mother – the only mother she's ever known.'

'She still calls me Mrs Thomas.'

'That's just her way. She calls me Mr Thomas as well. But that's because we've never adopted her legally. Perhaps it's still not too late . . .'

'No!'

'You sound most emphatic, Elizabeth.'

'I am, James. Lily has grown up in our house and has had all the benefits of a daughter. But she isn't our daughter; and now she's nearly a woman our duty is to prepare her to face the world. She can't stay here at Ring House for ever.'

'Why not? Betty will.'

'Only until she marries Edward. You know it's only a matter of time until he proposes.'

'I know no such thing,' James said quickly. 'I know it's what we've always wanted, but last time I saw the young things together I rather thought Edward favoured Lily.'

'All the more reason why we should put a stop to it and show Lily her place.'

James put his head in his hands. He felt at a loss, and didn't know how to deal with the situation. He didn't want to hurt any of them: Edward, Betty or Lily. And there was his old friend John Butler to consider.

'I'll think about it, Elizabeth.'

'James, you must do more than think about it. Do you want to break your daughter's heart? You know she's always loved Edward.'

'Is she still that serious about him?'

'Yes, I'm afraid she is.'

James sat silently for a few minutes, but he couldn't see any happy solution. In the end he said forlornly 'Do whatever you think best, Elizabeth.'

'I knew you'd see sense, dear.' Elizabeth put down her knitting so that the needles stuck out at all angles. They looked dangerous. 'I think it would be kinder to clear the air as soon as possible.'

'You don't have to be hasty . . .'

'I'll go and have a little chat with Lily now. –'

Elizabeth got to her feet and crossed to James's side. He looked so sad that she bent down and kissed his cheek fondly.

'Be careful what you say.'

'Of course. Trust me. I wouldn't hurt Lily for the world.

Look, they've finished their game; what an opportune moment.'

Elizabeth walked through the french windows into the garden, her chiffon scarf floating out behind. The two girls turned as she approached. Betty was changing her shoes and Lily was adjusting the flower behind her ear.

'I think we're getting better, Mummy,' Betty said. 'Were you watching?'

'Of course, darling. You'll soon be able to join the tennis club. I'll treat you to a year's subscription.'

'And Lily?'

'I don't know. Lily may be too busy.'

'I wouldn't want to join on my own,' Betty insisted. 'I wouldn't know anybody.'

'It will do you good to meet fresh people and make new friends. Now, I want to have a little chat with Lily, so you can go indoors to your father. He hasn't seen you all day.'

Swinging her racket, Betty strolled over the lawn towards the house. Lily pulled at the hem of her tunic. In all the overdone glory of her afternoon frock, Mrs Thomas made her feel undressed.

'Shall we walk, Lily?'

The dark girl nodded, and her plait fell forward over her shoulder, half hiding her face. She didn't know what was coming, but expected the worst. Mrs Thomas's voice sounded too bright and cheerful. She was hiding something and Lily had no idea what it was.

They took a favourite walk towards the rose garden. Elizabeth led the way through a trellised arch, and Lily followed her. The roses were Elizabeth's pride and joy, but Lily found their perfume somewhat overwhelming. She preferred simple flowers like the daisy-headed marguerite she wore in her hair, or the buttercups and poppies that grew profusely in the fields. Elizabeth stretched up and picked an aphid from the velvet petal of a rambler, squashing it between her finger and thumb.

'Greenfly!' she said in disgust. 'I'll have to remember to tell that Jackson boy to get out his syringe when the sun goes down.'

'I'll remind him,' Lily said.

'What do you think of these new standards?' Elizabeth had

stopped in front of a riot of yellow blossoms.

'They're lovely.'

'Aren't they? A bowl full of them would look lovely on the drawing-room sideboard.'

'Shall I tell Florence?'

'Ah!' Elizabeth paused, untangling her scarf from a prickle. 'It's Florence I want to talk to you about. She's leaving us.'

'I know.' Lily's pretty face lit up in a pleased smile. 'She told me she's getting married. Isn't it grand?'

'I suppose it is for her. But it does put me in quite a spot.'

'In what way?'

'Who will do her work? It's impossible to get living-in staff since the war. I've just been talking it over with Mr Thomas.'

'What does he advise?'

'He agrees that I must have some help in the house. He thinks that you should offer,'

'Me?' Lily looked at Mrs Thomas in surprise, and then she looked pleased. 'What a good idea. I've always wanted to learn to cook and this will be my chance; and Betty's very good with her needle. I know she's only done embroidery so far, but I'm sure she'll be good at turning sheets and mending. You don't have to worry about a thing, Mrs Thomas, we'll help all we can.'

'We!' Elizabeth looked at Lily with a flush of anger staining her cheeks. 'I'm not talking about Betty – I'm talking about you.'

Lily crumpled the hem of her skirt between her fingers. Somehow she'd picked up the wrong message, and she wasn't sure how to put it right.

'I'm sure Betty would want to help.'

'I dare say.' Elizabeth picked a pink rose from a nearby bush and buried her nose in its petals. 'But Betty is being brought up for a position in life. It won't include domestic jobs. One day she will be a lady with a home of her own, and her own servants, I hope. Whereas you . . .' She paused, and when Lily didn't say anything, carried on, carefully choosing her words. 'Whereas you, Lily, will one day need a job. You can't expect us to keep you in luxury for ever; so a good grounding in domestic work would really be doing you a favour.'

'I see.'

'Look at it like this, Lily. Peter Jackson is learning his trade in the garden, and Mr Thomas is also thinking of sending him for a part-time course to a horticultural college. In the same way you can learn a trade in the house.'

'Will I get a wage?'

Lily's question took Elizabeth aback. Somehow she hadn't thought money would come into the proposed arrangement.

'What a thing to ask,' she said tartly. 'I didn't think you, of all people, would be so mercenary. After all, we've clothed and fed you all these years. And an extra mouth to feed doesn't come cheap. Think of it this way, my dear: if my husband hadn't taken pity on you, you'd still be living in poverty.'

She thought that would be the end of the matter, and half expected Lily to apologize, but she hadn't taken into consideration the girl's nature. All these years Lily had tried to conform out of gratitude to the Thomas's. She'd put up with Betty's taunts with hardly a murmur; but there was something in Mrs Thomas's tone that annoyed her. It hurt her pride to be spoken to in such a fashion. Nobody, not even Lily herself, had known how proud her nature was. Now she stood tall, and faced Elizabeth as if she was an equal and not a beneficiary.

'You didn't answer my question, Mrs Thomas. I asked if you were going to pay me a wage?'

'Well,' – Elizabeth looked decidedly uncomfortable – 'I'll have to talk it over with my husband of course, but I suppose we could pay you the same as Florence – when you're trained.'

'And how long will it take you to train me?'

There was no denying the sarcasm in Lily's voice; but anger had made her even more beautiful. There were two spots of colour on her usually pale cheeks and her violet eyes had darkened. Her beauty was another cross Mrs Thomas had to bear. Her daughter, Betty, cut a pale figure in front of this vital girl standing so proudly in front of her. She'd never been all that fond of Lily, it was James who'd been so taken with her, and now she positively disliked her.

'Florence is leaving us in October. I'm sure she'll be happy to teach you how I like things done. And then it's usual to have an unpaid period of probation while you find your feet. Shall we say the new year is a good time to start paying you? Do I make myself clear?'

'Yes, Mrs Thomas, you make yourself very clear.' There was no mistaking the mockery in Lily's voice. She found it almost a relief not to have to hide her feelings any more. Now she'd started, she didn't seem able to stop. 'I expect you'll want me to move into Florence's room, and do I inherit her apron? – or will you buy me a new one?'

'There's no need to be sarcastic, Lily. I know this has been a shock for you, but when you've had time to think it over I'm sure you'll realize it's for the best. You don't have to give me an answer right now. But I should like to know as soon as possible so that I can make arrangements.'

Even if Lily had intended answering she didn't have the chance, because Elizabeth had turned on her heel and was already walking away from her. She watched the solid back with its trailing scarf until it disappeared and then with a heavy sigh let the feelings sweep over her.

A trail of roses hung over the wall by her side. They were so perfectly formed, and their perfume so overpowering, that Lily put out her hand to touch one. Mrs Thomas's instructions were that her roses were only to be gathered when she gave the word. In deliberate defiance Lily plucked a blossom. A sharp prickle caught her finger bringing a bead of blood, as red as the flower itself. On a wave of unhappiness she began to tear the petals, scattering them around her on the grass.

'There's no need to do that, Lily. The rose hasn't done you any harm.'

She hadn't heard Peter Jackson crossing the lawn. The soft turf had deadened his footsteps. He stood in front of her: so safe, so solid, that she wasn't ashamed of the tears that were streaming unheeded down her cheeks, or the sobs that were shaking her narrow shoulders.

'Oh, Pete!' she sobbed. 'You've no idea what's happened.'

'Then you're wrong. I was weeding just behind that bush and I heard every word.'

Somehow Lily was glad that he knew. He, of all people, would understand. He handed her a spotlessly clean handkerchief and watched while she blew her nose and wiped her eyes.

'Then you heard how horrible she was to me. What am I going to do, Pete?'

'It seems to me there's only one thing you can do.'

'What's that?'

'Exactly what she asks. –'

'Oh! You don't mean that!' Lily stepped back as if he'd hit

her. For some reason she'd imagined he'd have some alternative suggestion.

'I do mean it, Lily. And I can't help thinking that she might be right.'

'Right! Never!'

'I know she didn't put it very well, but she was probably embarrassed. You didn't expect them to keep you all your life, did you?'

'I don't know. I hadn't thought.' Lily put her head in her hands in despair.

'That's it. You hadn't thought. There's nothing wrong with working for your living, you know. You've had it soft all these years. In your own sweet way you're almost as spoilt as Betty.'

'Never!' That did it. The tears stopped, and when she turned her swollen face to Pete she saw he was grinning. 'Well, perhaps a bit,' she admitted.

'That's my girl. There's nothing to be ashamed of in working for your living, Lily.'

'I know. It's just the way she put it.'

'So what are you going to do about it?'

'I don't know. I'll have to think.'

Peter was pleased to see she looked somewhat calmer. He was glad he'd been near at hand when she needed him. He'd been waiting for this moment for a long time.

She shook back her hair and adjusted the flower, and when she turned to him there was a smile on her face. 'I know,' she said, almost gaily. 'Edward is coming on Saturday because it's Betty's birthday. I'll ask him what he thinks.'

The table was laid for tea. Special birthday tea parties were a tradition at Ring House, and Florence and Elizabeth had laid the dining-room table early.

There was the best china, with its border of gold and delicate floral pattern, and the apostle spoons. Sandwiches filled with meat paste, cucumber and sardines were already arranged on plates in the cool larder, together with the trifle, topped with angelica and swirls of cream. The cake, made by Florence but iced by Elizabeth, was standing on the sideboard for everyone to admire. The topping of smooth white icing with its border of sugar flowers nestled in its paper frill. Elizabeth had wanted to have candles – after all it was a birthday cake –but Betty declared she was too grown up.

Grown up or not, she'd been as excited as a child when she'd unwrapped her presents. A gold charm bracelet, a fountain pen, and her first adult hat, all from her parents. The hat was a feast of feathers, so colourful that no bird in living memory had ever worn such bright plumage. It sat firmly on Betty's yellow head and suited her new hairstyle. Lily had given her a writing compendium with matching notepaper and envelopes, all contained in a leather zip-top folder. There would be other presents when the guests arrived.

James's sister Dorothy and her husband Walter were coming for lunch, which would be a light meal taken informally in the garden. But the vicar and his wife – Susan and Donald Plummer – and Doctor Butler and Edward were all arriving for tea.

Lily and Betty helped Florence carry out the trays of salad and biscuits, while their elders sat around in deck chairs catching up on the gossip.

Dorothy was an imposing woman. Not in stature – in fact she was as small and brittle-boned as a bird – but she had a surprisingly deep voice that spoke in dictatorial tones as if defying argument. Her husband, Walter, was a large man, but very quietly spoken on the rare occasions that he contributed to the conversation. He was probably out of practice with a domineering wife who hardly ever stopped talking.

'Haven't the girls grown?' Dorothy said to Elizabeth as Betty and Lily crossed the lawn like two bright butterflies.

Betty was wearing pink, a crisp cotton dress piped with white. It had a nipped in waist and a full, bell-like skirt. She was wearing white high-heeled shoes that made her ankles look slightly puffy; but they were her first heels and she felt very grown-up in them.

Lily was dressed in green, a colour that suited her. It was a simple dress with a pleated skirt, and a fitted bodice with a turned back collar. Her hair was loose and hung in a thick cloud over her shoulders, framing her pale face. Her sandals were flat so that she only reached her companion's shoulder. Both girls were looking their best, but there was no doubt to the onlookers who was the most attractive.

'Thank you, my dear,' Dorothy said, as Betty offered her a plate. Then, with a biscuit in each hand, she turned to her sister-in-law. 'Walter quite spoils me: he's just bought me a washing-machine.'

'A washing-machine!' Elizabeth said in amazement. 'I've never heard of such a thing.'

'It's only been on the market a couple of years; but I was fed up with that old copper. Everything gets so steamed up. This is made by Hoover and works by electricity. You just put in the clothes, fill it with water, and switch it on. It's wonderful.'

'Is it very expensive?' Elizabeth asked.

'Twenty-five pounds, but worth every penny. You should really get James to buy you one. He can afford it.'

'Did you hear what Dorothy said?' Elizabeth said loudly in her husband's ear. He was dozing in his chair and came to with a start.

'What was that? Have the Butlers arrived? Is it tea-time?'

'No, dear,' Elizabeth laughed. 'Dorothy was just telling us about a wonderful new invention called a washing-machine. Perhaps we could get one when Florence leaves. It would make Lily's work easier.'

Lily was passing behind the chair as Elizabeth spoke. She heard every word and flushed angrily. How dare she! How dare Mrs Thomas talk as if it was agreed that she'd take Florence's place! As if she hadn't a mind or will of her own. She hadn't decided, and she wasn't going to decide until she'd talked it over with Edward. Oh, why didn't he come!

'Let's go down to the gate and wait for Edward,' Lily said, and Betty agreed.

Anything was better than standing about doing nothing. They walked side by side down the drive. If they sat on the wall by the Jacksons' cottage they'd have a good view of the road.

'I hope Edward brings my present,' Betty said.

Lily looked at her companion: she seemed to be taut with expectation.

'Do you know what he's getting you?' she asked.

'Yes. I told Daddy what I wanted, and he phoned Edward's father. Doctor Butler said I was a minx, but he'd see what he could do.'

'What is it?' Lily was curious.

'I'm not telling you.'

'Why not?'

'It's a surprise. You'll know soon enough.'

'I can hear a car. Come on, Betty, let's run.'

Lily was lighter on her feet and reached the bottom of the drive first, but Betty was close behind. It was the Butlers. John was driving, with Edward at his side. As the car turned slowly into the drive Betty jumped onto the running board. She leaned in at the window on Edward's side and struggled to unfasten the door.

'Come out and walk with us,' she insisted.

Edward obediently opened the door and stepped out. He'd grown taller, but in her heels Betty could reach to kiss his cheek. He coloured slightly and didn't kiss her back, although he did slip his arm through hers.

'Happy birthday, Betty,' he said. Then he turned to the girl in the green dress who was standing in the background. 'Hullo, Lily.'

'Hullo.'

Her voice came out small and strangled because somehow he looked different. Different from the Edward she thought she knew so well. He was so tall and handsome now that he was a grown man of twenty-one. His hair was just as fair, the front lock that hung over his eyes bleached almost white by the sun. He was wearing grey flannels and an open-necked shirt, with a blue handkerchief loosely knotted at the neck. His eyes were just as clear and grey, but they looked so sad, and after briefly meeting Lily's they looked away. Whatever was the matter with him?

'Did you remember my present?' Betty broke in, guiding him up the drive towards the house.

'Of course. Do you want it now?' Edward put his hand in his trouser pocket.

'No!' Betty giggled. 'Not in front of Lily. Let's go to the summer-house where we can be alone.'

Lily watched them disappear around the side of the house: Betty so eager, and Edward being dragged along whether he wanted to or not. He looked back over his shoulder once, but although Lily smiled his expression didn't change. Then he was gone.

She wandered into the house. Florence was setting out the plates of sandwiches on the long dining table. Lily helped her, more to pass the time than anything else. There was a big bowl of yellow roses as a centrepiece; the heavy perfume made her feel dizzy.

'Move the flowers out of the way,' Florence instructed. 'Then there'll be room for the birthday cake.'

By the time they'd folded the serviettes and arranged the place mats they could hear voices approaching. Elizabeth appeared, towering over Dorothy's tiny form. They were still gossiping avidly about the merits of the Hoover washing-machine. Behind them came the vicar and his wife, with Dorothy's silent spouse. After a pause James entered with John Butler, and close behind Betty, still hanging onto Edward's arm.

'Shall we sit down,' Elizabeth said to the company. 'Florence, you can pour out now.'

'Yes, Mrs Thomas.'

As Florence busied herself with the silver teapot, Lily stared fixedly at her plate. Next year, would it be her talking in that restrained voice, saying 'Yes, Mrs Thomas' and 'No, Mrs Thomas' as if she had no right to an opinion of her own? What if she said, 'I won't pour out your tea, Mrs Thomas, because I hate you. And I won't wear this silly apron any more because I want to be a lady, like you and Betty, and I want to have servants of my own to order about.' Would she get the sack?

Everyone had taken their seats apart from James. He stood at the head of the table, his gold watch chain stretched across his paunch, and a big smile on his face. He held up his hand for silence, and when he'd got the attention of the party he began to speak.

'I know you're all here to wish my little girl a happy birthday.' Someone started to clap and he put up his hand again. 'But before we do that Betty has something to show you. Come on, Betty.'

Betty needed no encouragement. She jumped to her feet and smiled happily at her guests. Then she lifted up her left hand to show the diamond ring twinkling on her finger. For the first time in her life she seemed at a loss for words. All she could manage was: 'Edward and I are engaged.'

'Oh! My darling!' Elizabeth said, and looked as if she could easily burst into tears.

'Congratulations,' boomed her Aunt Dorothy; and even Walter mouthed something, although nobody could make out what it was.

'You must get in an early booking for the wedding,' the

Reverend Plummer advised, and everyone laughed and clapped and shouted 'Congratulations!' and 'Speech!'

All except Lily. At the announcement her usually pale cheek had turned paper-white. The room spun before her. She mustn't faint! It would be too humiliating if she fainted. But Edward, her darling Edward, her Prince Charming, was going to marry Betty Thomas, and there was absolutely nothing she could do about it.

No one seemed to notice when Lily got out of her seat and slipped from the room. She had to pass the kitchen doorway to get to the stairs and Florence heard her.

'Is that you, Lily?' she called. 'Come and carry these fruit dishes in for me.'

Lily pretended not to hear and carried on up the stairs. She wasn't going to help Florence in the kitchen ever again, because bereft of Edward's advice she'd made her own mind up about the future. As soon as the guests had departed she was going to confront Mrs Thomas and turn down her offer of a job.

Tomorrow, she'd decided, tomorrow she would be leaving Ring House. She was going home to Valley Farm.

CHAPTER SEVEN

November

'You're looking better this morning.'

'Am I, Lily?' Matthew Crow pulled himself up in the bed and grinned over the fold of bedclothes like a mischievous goblin.

'I've brought you some breakfast. Let me make you comfortable.' Lily pummelled the pillows until they were soft, and then draped a cardigan around Matthew's hunched shoulders. The room was chilly although a weak sun was shining through the window. When everything was to her satisfaction she balanced the tin tray across his knees and smiled encouragingly. 'There's a boiled egg and toast; and the tea's just the way you like it.'

'Nice and strong.'

'Strong and sweet: just what the doctor ordered.'

No doctor had been called to Valley Farm for years as the Crows believed in ignoring illness or doctoring themselves. But Lily had proved herself a good nurse, and had correctly diagnosed Matthew's illness as a cross between self-neglect and poor nourishment.

It was now November and she'd been back at the farm for three months. It hadn't been an easy time for any of them. At first Moses had refused to let her in. He'd called her a harlot, and told her to go back to her godless companions before he brought the wrath of God down on her sinful head. Edith had hovered silently in the background, her clothing flapping around her gaunt, emaciated frame like the rags on a scarecrow.

There had been no sign of Matthew.

Lily had spent the first two nights in the barn. She had nowhere else to go and at least it was warm in the straw. There was a barrel of apples which she ate to stave off the worst of the hunger pangs. It gave her plenty of time to think.

She didn't regret burning her boats at Ring House, although she missed its familiar comforts. Mr Thomas had seemed genuinely sorry to see her go; but when he saw she was adamant he hadn't tried to make her change her mind. Mrs Thomas had told her she was ungrateful, and Betty seemed positively delighted at the prospect of losing her. She hadn't seen Edward again – not even to say goodbye.

In fact the only person who seemed concerned about Lily's welfare was Peter Jackson. As she'd struggled down the drive carrying her suitcase he'd looked up from his work in the cottage garden. She'd only packed the bare necessities, but even these proved to be bulkier and heavier than she'd expected. At the gate she'd stopped to shake back her hair, and Peter had paused in his labours to lean on his spade and listen to Lily's story.

'Do you think I'm doing the right thing?' she'd finished, her violet eyes begging for her friend's approval.

'It's not for me to say. You wouldn't take my advice anyway.'

'Not if you told me to go back to Ring House and work for Mrs Thomas. I couldn't do it, Pete. Betty would gloat and I'd be really miserable.'

'How do you know that you're going to be any happier at the farm?'

'I don't, but I'll take the chance. Matt's the nearest thing to a relation that I've got. As for Moses and Edith, my biggest fear is that they won't let me in.'

Peter looked over his shoulder at the cosy little house that was his home. He could just see his mother shaking a duster out of an upper window. 'You could always come and live with us.'

'No!' Lily said vehemently. 'That would be just swapping one kind of charity for another. I want to go to Valley Farm to see that Matt's all right. Last time I saw him in the village he looked so thin and unkempt. He needs someone to look after him.'

'It'll be a hard job you're taking on.'

'I know, but at least at Valley Farm I'll be in control of my life. I won't be just a glorified skivvy, which is what Mrs Thomas has in mind for me.'

'Well, don't forget the offer's there. Mum likes you, and she could do with an extra pair of hands about the place. And we've got a spare room now that Mike's gone.'

'You're so kind. Thank you, I won't forget.' Lily leaned over the gate and kissed Pete on the cheek. It wasn't a passionate kiss, just a friendly gesture of affection. Even so Pete blushed so much that his usually rosy face turned bright red.

For two days, from the safety of the barn, Lily had watched the morning routine: Moses striding off into the fields to do a solitary day's labour, and Edith walking down the lane as if she'd an appointment to keep. Still no sign of Matthew. The haymaking should have been in progress, but most of the eighty acres of land seemed to be left uncultivated, and in the barn there was only one cow with its calf – enough to supply the household with fresh milk. There were a few chickens pecking about in the yard, and someone, probably Edith, had started a vegetable patch; but it didn't look as if any serious work had been done around the place for years.

On the third day, after Moses and his wife had gone about their business, Lily had ventured into the house.

After the warmth and homeliness of Ring House, the interior of Valley Farm semed stark and cold, bleaker than she'd remembered it. After all, she'd only been a mere seven years old when she'd left it with her rescuer, James Thomas. But she still remembered her way around. She wandered through the cheerless rooms, from kitchen to parlour, dairy to scullery, looking and calling for her old friend.

The plaster walls had not been given their customary coat of whitewash, and were now the colour of ancient ivory. She remembered the grandfather clock that stood in an alcove opposite the stairs: it used to tick away the seconds and minutes of her childhood. It now stood mute and faceless in its corner. The settle underneath the row of clothes hooks was stuffed with horsehair but the covering of pink tapestry was now in holes and looked as if it was a breeding ground for mice. There were the familiar dark pictures of biblical scenes, so beloved by the Victorians, and the faded sampler Edith had once admitted stitching. The wording was still clear: 'In the beginning, God', and another: 'God is Love'.

Lily climbed the dusty stairs that were bare of carpet, and found the bedroom she'd shared with Matt so long ago. The door was ajar. As she stood in the doorway surveying the room a feeling of despair swept over her. The smell was overwhelming: a mixture of stuffiness, old clothes and unwashed humanity. The windows were tightly closed, and the floor littered with rags and old newspapers. The cot she'd slept in as a child still stood in the same place under the window, its flock mattress bare and torn. Matt's iron bed was almost hidden under a pile of torn blankets.

At first Lily thought the room was empty, but a movement from the direction of the bed made her look closer. First she saw a foot protruding from the rags – a long, thin foot with overgrown toenails like yellowing talons – and when she pulled aside a blanket she saw Matt, skeleton thin, with hair wild about his bony skull, and eyes sunken into their sockets. He was wearing only an old pair of stained combinations.

Her first instinct was to run away in horror. She would go to Pete and the Jacksons where a kindly Emma would look after her and she would find a welcome. But then she looked down at Matt again, and knew her duty was to remain where she was and do what she could for her old friend.

'Matt,' she said softly, and put her hand on his arm. It felt cold and clammy and for one awful moment she thought he was dead. But a groan came from the emaciated body, so she said again, only louder this time, 'Matt! Are you awake?'

His eyes opened slowly so she knew that he heard her voice. At first they were dead eyes, devoid of all expression, but then they recognized the familiar face and a glimmer of hope lit up his thin features.

'Lily?' Matt said, and the voice sounded rusty as if he hadn't spoken for days. 'Is it really you?'

'Yes, Matt. It's really me.'

'You've come home. I knew you'd come home.'

'Let me help you.'

Matt was struggling to sit up, but he was too weak to manage it without help. Lily propped him up against the bedhead, and when she saw a tear coursing down his cheek a feeling of anger swept over her. Matt, her dear Matt, the only friend of her childhood, had been left here by Moses and Edith Crow. If he'd died no one would have been aware of it. But she was here now, and he wasn't going to die, because she would look after him just as once he'd looked after her.

When Edith and Moses returned they found Lily installed in the kitchen. The stone slabs had been washed of the accumulated filth of months, and the pots were clean and neatly stacked beside the sink. Lily had managed to light the range and was busy stirring porridge into a pan of boiling water.

'What's this then?' Moses growled, sinking onto the settle to remove his boots. 'Have your rich friends had enough of you and thrown you out?'

Lily didn't answer. She'd found a rusty tray and was laying it up for the invalid. She wasn't frightened of Moses any more: after all, what harm could he do her? He and Edith were almost as pathetic as the man upstairs.

'Smells good,' Edith said, her tongue running hungrily around her pale lips. 'I'm hungry.'

'Then you can make your own,' Lily said tartly. She remembered a time when she'd hungrily watched the husband and wife tucking into big platefuls of food, while she'd existed on the leftovers Matthew had saved for her. 'I found the oatmeal in a tin in the scullery, and I milked the cow myself.'

As Lily crossed the floor with the tray Edith asked, 'Are you staying?'

Two pairs of eyes stared at her, waiting for an answer. She stood on the bottom step of the staircase, silhouetted against the light from the open door, a graceful figure of youth and beauty. She looked from Edith to Moses, her violet eyes daring them to argue.

'Yes, I'm staying,' she said firmly in Edith's direction. 'And I'll take charge in the kitchen.' Then she turned to Moses who was holding his boot in his hand as if he would like to throw it at her. 'And I will look after Matt.'

Something about the way Lily spoke seemed to deter Moses. Instead of throwing the boot he placed it carefully on the floor at his feet.

But that had all happened over three months ago. Today, Matt's room, although bare and cold, was at least clean and uncluttered. There was a colourful rag-rug on the scrubbed boards and curtains at the window, and the bed linen was crisp and sweet-smelling.

Matthew himself had filled out, so that his head no longer seemed reduced to a skull. Lily had trimmed his hair herself, and helped him to shave, and now he sat tucked up under the covers like some large, pink, overgrown baby. He was even wearing striped pyjamas, although the neck was gaping open where he'd pulled off a button.

Lily stirred his tea, and handed him the cup before crossing to the window to pull the curtains back properly, so that they could make the most of the weak autumn sunlight.

'You're looking so much better, Matt. I think today you should start coming downstairs.'

Matthew froze, the cup halfway up to his mouth. 'But why, Lily? I like it up here.'

'I know you do. But you can't stay up here for ever.'

'I don't see why not,' Matt said childishly. 'You're not going away, are you, Lily?'

He asked this question every morning, as if he was afraid of losing her. Every day so far she'd reassured him, but today she felt restless herself. She had to be honest even if she hurt him.

'I'm not going away for a while, Matt. But I've been here three months already, and I can't stay for ever.'

'Why not?'

'Because you're better. I promised to stay until you were better.'

'But what will I do, Lily, about them downstairs?'

'Now you're feeling better you'll be able to cope with them.' The fear on Matt's face puzzled her. After all, Moses was Matthew's brother, and they'd lived together all their lives. And Edith was hardly an unknown quantity. They might not care about each other, but Lily couldn't understand his fear. 'Eat your breakfast,' she said. 'It's getting cold.'

'Only if you promise to stay.'

'I've told you: I'll stay as long as I can.' Suddenly Lily felt trapped. It wasn't that she regretted coming back to Valley Farm. It had been an experience for her, running the household and learning how to cook. In fact she'd found she had quite a flair for it. At least she was her own boss. She answered Moses back in kind, even when he started his eternal preaching. Edith had got quite used to her, and they'd managed to share the kitchen without falling out too often. Although the older woman didn't say much she seemed to like Lily's company.

'When it's time for me to go,' she went on, 'you'll have to stand on your own feet, and help Moses like you used to. He doesn't seem to get much done about the place these days, but two of you could make quite a difference.'

'He hurts me.'

Matthew spoke the words softly, as if he was afraid of being overheard. Lily stared at him. He wasn't bright enough to lie.

'What do you mean, Matt? Does he beat you?' She'd felt the back of Moses' hand many times in the past, but she'd never known him turn on his brother.

'No.' Matt buried his nose in his cup again as if he already regretted his confidences. 'There's worse things than beating.'

'What things?'

'Things he does when he's been drinking.'

Moses! Drinking! Lily relaxed and crossed to the window after straightening Matt's bed. A tree tapped its branch against the glass pane, as if it was calling for her to come outside. She had a longing to get into the crisp November air and run and run until she was exhausted. 'You know Moses doesn't drink,' she said. 'He's always preaching against it.'

'That doesn't stop him doing it. He thinks nobody knows. But I know. He was drunk that day.'

'What day?'

'In the cellar – oh, a long time ago. And he sometimes drinks now. That's when he hurts me – or Edie. Sometimes he hurts Edie.'

'There's Edie now,' Lily said, as the downstairs door slammed and she saw the thin form walking away from the farmhouse. Every morning Edith left at about the same time, as if on some important errand. Lily had become curious about this daily ritual. 'Where does she go every day, Matt? Do you know?'

'She goes to the churchyard.' Matt grinned, but a curtain had come down over his eyes, as if he feared he'd already said too much. 'I've finished.' He pushed the tray away, and Lily had to leap forward to stop it crashing to the ground.

'You've lost a button from your pyjama jacket,' she said. 'Do you know where Edith keeps the sewing things?'

'In her room, I expect. That's where she keeps the scissors.'

Lily carried the tray out onto the landing. She could wait until Edie returned from her mysterious outing, or she could look in the bedroom for the needlework box. She'd never been inside the master bedroom, although she'd often wondered what went on there between husband and wife. Did they kiss and make love like other married couples? Somehow Lily couldn't imagine what went on behind the closed door. But Moses was always out at this time of the day and she'd just seen Edith walking away, so the coast was clear. She opened the door and stepped into the room.

Somehow she'd expected the same sort of disorder she'd found in the rest of the house when she'd arrived, so it was almost a shock to find a room almost as bare as a hermit's cell. The huge iron bed had pride of place and filled a third of the floor. The tapestry drapes were faded and frayed at the edges, but the covers had been pulled neatly into place, and the pillows were reasonably clean. There was a pair of grey cotton stockings draped over a chair, and Lily could just see the rim of a chamber-pot sticking out from under the bedframe. There were no mirrors or pictures, or ornaments to soften the crude contours of the bare room. In fact, the only other piece of furniture was a mahogany tallboy with shiny handles. On its dusty top stood an enamel candlestick with an inch of candle wedged in the bottom.

The floor of the room was bare of covering, and Lily's shoes seemed to make a noisy tap-tap as she walked across the boards. She slid open the top drawer of the tallboy and peeped inside. It was full of old-fashioned pink underwear, worn thin in places, and stretched out of shape with much washing.

She closed it quickly and opened the next one. This contained a jumble of tins and cardboard boxes, but she was pleased to see a home-made needle-case and a reel of cotton hiding under some papers. The cotton was black but she didn't think Matt would mind.

She was replacing the papers smiling over an old birthday card with an unreadable signature, when she saw a photograph. It was stuck on a piece of card, and faded and brown with age. A young woman's face stared up at Lily: a young woman with a slim, shapely body and an attractive smile. She'd seen this photo before but couldn't remember where. All she knew was that it was a long time ago.

Carrying her find carefully Lily took it to the window so that she could see the features more clearly. Her mind went back over the years and suddenly she remembered. She'd been standing in the attic at Ring House with Edward, looking at the same picture and wondering who it could be. It was the day they'd been looking for a costume for her to wear on May Day. They'd laughed together over the signature. 'Love from Edie' had been the wording across that picture, but this one was blank. Edith was a common enough name so neither of them had thought it odd, presuming it to be a friend or distant relation of the Thomas's. But now, in the drawer at Valley Farm, it took on a different significance. Carrying the sewing things in one hand, and the photo in the other, Lily returned to Matt.

'Take off your jacket,' she instructed, 'and I'll have the button sewn on in next to no time.'

Matthew did as he was told. Then his eyes took in the picture lying on the coverlet.

'What you got there then?'

'Only an old photograph. Do you know who it's of, Matt?'

'That's our Edie.' Matthew grinned. 'Don't you recognize her?'

'She's changed. Here, you can put this back on now.'

'Where'd you find it?' Matthew was busy admiring Lily's handiwork.

'In the bedroom. In the drawer of the tallboy.'

'You'd better put it back then. Edie don't like her things touched.' Matthew picked up the photo and looked at it again. 'It was taken when she was walking out with Mo. Pretty little thing, she were. All the boys around here were after her, but Mo got her.'

'She's smiling in that picture,' Lily said. 'She looks so happy. I don't think I've ever seen her smile properly.'

'P'raps because she's got nothing to smile about.'

'What was Moses like in those days?'

'He were a fine man. He looked after me, even when we was kids. If anyone were unkind to me he hit them. Everybody liked Moses in those days.'

'What happened to change him?'

'It was when the babies died. One after another they died. Moses thought it was a punishment from God because he was an unbeliever. That's why he turned religious. Edie thought so too – she changed as well.'

'It's sad,' Lily said. 'Such a sad story. I'll put these things back before Edith finds I've taken them.' She carried the photo and needlecase to the door.

'There's no hurry,' Matthew insisted. 'She's gone to the cemetery to visit the babies. She goes there every morning and don't come home for hours. I think I will get up for a while. There's a job I need to do. I want some grease and some old rags.'

Lily replaced Edith's belongings and went downstairs to the kitchen. Clad in his wool dressing gown, with trailing cord, Matt followed her. His legs were still a bit shaky but he looked more like his old self. While Lily found him a tin of oil and some old rags he rummaged about in the cupboard under the sink. He emerged triumphantly with something rolled up in a piece of sheeting. When he unwrapped it on the table Lily saw that it was a rusty old shotgun.

'What are you going to do with that, Matt?' she asked nervously. 'I hope it's not loaded.'

'Of course not; but there should be a tin of shot somewhere. I was good with this when I was a boy. Don't know how many rabbits I didn't bag on a good day. Course, Mo was better than me, but he's out of practice now.'

'What are you going to do with it?'

'Clean it up a bit – in case I need it.'

Lily left him pulling the old gun apart and rubbing away at the rust with a greasy rag. She didn't think he'd come to any harm. Pulling on her coat she stepped out into the breezy November day. The wind caught her hair so she tucked it inside the collar of her coat, and set out at a brisk trot in the direction Edith Crow had taken an hour before. Matthew's story had made her curious, so she'd decided to go to the churchyard and see for herself.

Lenton boasted two churches. St Patrick's was a new building standing near the schoolhouse. It was large and cold with a tall spire; the villagers called it an eyesore. St Michael's, the old Norman church, stood just outside the village at the end of a tree-bordered lane where the farmers used to lead their sheep to the lush pastures on the Downs. The church itself contained an unusual font and some beautiful stained glass; but no one could enjoy the interior, as the door was kept firmly locked, and no services had been held there for many years.

Lily slipped through the gate into the churchyard. A carpet of nettles grew to the height of a foot, hiding the graves that no one bothered to tend. A few weathered stone crosses still stood among the waving greenery, and a marble angel lay across her path with one damaged wing and its hands raised in prayer.

A wailing sound, that wasn't the wind, drew her around the side of the building, where she almost fell over a kneeling figure. Edith Crow was singing tunelessly as she tore away the grass concealing four small graves. Four small squares of turf, each with a wooden cross, marking the resting places of her children. She rocked backwards and forwards as she sang, and wisps of greying hair blew around her head and over her face. The baggy cardigan she wore was hardly enough to keep her warm, and her hands were red and rough with the cold. She looked up, and didn't seem surprised to see Lily there.

'Are these the graves of your children, Edie?' Lily asked softly.

'Harry, George, Stephen and Bruce,' Edith chanted in a singsong voice. 'Harry was the first – he'd be twenty-eight now. George lived for just one hour and I nursed him until he died. Stephen was strangled by the cord and Bruce never breathed at all.'

'And you come here every day?'

'I do now. They're closer to me now than they've ever been.'

Suddenly Lily felt overwhelmed by sympathy at this woman's tragic story. She felt that now she could ask questions. Now she might get answers.

'Edith,' she said softly. 'Do you know who my mother was?'

'You! You had no mother.'

'Everybody has a mother. Who gave birth to me, Edith?'

'Matt found you – in the barn.' Edith began to rock from side to side, and her voice rose shrilly. 'Moses said you were the daughter of Eve: the fallen one. The first woman who sinned against God.'

'And you, Edie – whose daughter do you say I am?'

'You're the daughter of a harlot! That's who you are,' and Edith began to laugh. It was a harsh, painful sound, and Lily couldn't bear it.

She put her hands over her ears to deaden the sound and stumbled back over the turf, the noise of the cruel laughter ringing in her ears. When she reached the lane she began to run. The wind tore at her skirt and hair so she didn't see the figure walking towards her. It was too late to stop herself running into it.

'What's this then?' Peter Jackson said. He put out his arms to stop Lily from running past, and when he saw the expression on her face, held her fast. 'Has something frightened you?'

'Not something – someone.' Lily pulled herself away. 'Oh! You wouldn't understand.'

'I might. Why don't you try me?'

'It's just that Edith Crow's in the churchyard singing to her dead babies. She just gave me the creeps. What are you doing here, anyway?'

'Gathering herbs for mother.' Pete held out a sweet-smelling bunch for Lily's inspection. 'She's drying the last of them before the winter sets in. We always get our wild garlic from the bank below the old church; and there's a rosemary bush growing by the vestry door. Can I walk along with you? I think I've got enough here to keep mother busy.'

'If you want.'

They walked side by side towards the roadway, pausing on the kerb to let a car pass. Peter waved at the driver. It was his father driving Mr Thomas's car towards the village. As they passed Lily saw the occupants of the back seat. She could just see Betty's fair head deep in conversation with her companion: a young man with very blond hair. Lily's heart turned over. She wanted to run after the car to get a better look, but Peter put out his hand to stop her.

'What do you think you're doing?'

'That was Edward Butler, wasn't it? I didn't know he was here.'

'He's been here a week, staying with the Thomas's.'

'And he hasn't been to see me.'

'Why should he?' Pete's words were deliberately cruel. He couldn't understand what Lily saw in Doctor Butler's son. He was good-looking and pleasant enough, but Peter had always found him a rather weak person. But of course he was jealous, because he'd have given anything in the world for Lily to look at him in the same fashion she always looked at Edward. 'He's keeping himself busy painting pictures. He sets up his easel all over the garden in the most awkward places; usually just where I want to work. I would think he had better things to do: after all, I heard he's going to be a doctor like his father.'

'He draws beautifully,' Lily said. 'He always wanted to be an artist and paint pictures for a living.'

'A man who's getting married in a few days should have something better to think about.'

'Married!' Lily stopped still in the roadway, and her face turned even paler than usual.

'Of course.' Pete laughed. 'It was you who told me about his engagement to Betty Thomas.'

'I know. But I didn't think they'd get married so soon.'

'You mean you hoped they wouldn't. What were you hoping for: that they'd break it off, and then you'd be able to step into Betty's shoes?'

'Why not?' Lily looked fierce and her fists were clenched tightly at her side. 'He loves me. He always has. I'm going to get him back.' And she turned and fled down the road, leaving Pete staring unhappily after her.

CHAPTER EIGHT

The Wedding

'But I wanted to get married at St Michael's. And I wanted a dress with a train and six bridesmaids.'

If Betty had been younger she would have cried and stamped her feet. It had usually got her her own way; but nowadays it didn't work.

'I did ask Mr Plummer if he would open up the old church. He put it to the Management Committee at their last meeting, but they refused.' James spoke from his armchair by the fire. 'Something to do with subsidence and dry rot. It wouldn't be safe.'

St Patrick's is a very pretty church.' Elizabeth selected a pin from the pad on her wrist and turned another inch of hem up. Betty was trying on her mother's old wedding dress as there wasn't time to get anything made for the first week in December. 'This will suit you when I've finished the alterations.'

'It's the wrong shape,' Betty pouted. 'The waistline's all uneven.'

'Nonsense, dear. When you stand up straight it hangs perfectly.'

'And it's tiresome of cousin Sophie to let me down like this.'

Elizabeth sighed. 'She couldn't help her girls getting measles. You'll still have Aunt Mavis's daughter, and the twins. I know they're really excited about being bridesmaids.'

James let the argument wash over him and picked up his newspaper. He'd be quite relieved when the wedding was over and done with and his daughter was safely off his hands. The last few weeks had been very irritating. Now if it had been Lily getting married he was sure things would have gone much more smoothly. Lily, with her dark hair and violet eyes, would have made a beautiful bride. Any father would be proud to walk down the aisle with Lily on his arm.

Sometimes James forgot that Lily wasn't his daughter. She'd become so much a part of the family at Ring House that when she'd walked out so suddenly he'd taken a long time to get over it. Elizabeth had shown him no sympathy when he'd said that he missed her presence around the house. The girl was ungrateful, she retorted, and they were better off without her.

The door slammed open and the new maid charged into the room to clear the tea things. Her name was Mary Biggins and she was really too old for the job. By the time she'd pedalled on her bicycle from an outlying farm she was too exhausted to start work straight away. Elizabeth had to ply her with strong tea and biscuits until she was sufficiently recovered to take orders. They had to share her with the vicar and his wife, so she only came three days a week. But they hadn't been able to get anyone else. So until they found someone to live in they had to make the best of it.

'Shall I clear?' Mary didn't wait for an answer; she charged across the room and almost tripped over Elizabeth who was still kneeling in front of her daughter, her mouth full of pins.

'Watch where you're going,' Betty said petulantly. 'We're busy. Can't you come back later?'

'Only if you want to do the washing-up, Miss Hoity-Toity. I finish at four, and it's ten to already.'

'Don't be so rude,' Elizabeth said. She wasn't used to servants answering back.

'I speak as I find.' Mary started for the door, laden down by the heavy tray. 'Now that Mr Edward's a different kettle of fish. A real gentleman, he is. Always holds doors open for me, and says "Good-day, Mary. How are you," every time he sees me.'

Betty frowned. 'You should call him Doctor Butler, Mary.'

'But he's not a doctor, is he, Mrs Thomas?' Mary looked at Elizabeth for confirmation.

'Not yet. But he will be eventually.'

'When he passes his finals.' Betty gave a pleased smile and tweaked at a gather on her skirt. 'Then he's going into partnership with his father. We're going to live at his father's house in Lewes after the wedding. It's a big house, almost as big as this. Edward says I must have a live-in maid.'

'You'll be lucky,' Mary said darkly.

Betty ignored the gibe. 'Have you seen my fiancé ?' She asked loftily. 'He didn't come in to tea.'

'I saw him earlier on going out through the garden door. He was carrying his easel and his box of paints. I suppose he's gone to paint some more of those pictures of his.'

'He should be reading his medical books, not wasting his time painting,' Elizabeth said. 'The waistline looks better, Betty. I'm glad you're going to wear my dress; it was much admired on my wedding day.'

'It's a bit old-fashioned, but I suppose it'll have to do. Mary!' The maid stopped with her hand on the doorknob. 'If you see Doctor Butler, tell him I want him.'

'What do you want me for?'

The blond young man in the doorway smiled around at the assembled company. Betty gave a little shriek and tried to hide behind her mother.

'Go away, Edward. I'll join you in the library in a few minutes. You mustn't look at me.'

'Why ever not?'

'Because it's unlucky.'

'She's trying on her wedding dress,' Elizabeth explained. 'It's supposed to be unlucky for the bridegroom to see it before the day.'

'I didn't know you were superstitious.'

'I'm not usually,' Betty said. 'But I'm not going to take any chances. So go away while I change.'

'Oh, all right, if you insist.'

Snatching a biscuit from the tray as he passed Mary, Edward backed out into the hall. He'd left his painting things leaning against a wall in the passage, so he picked up the canvas he was working on and carried it into the library where the light was better.

When Betty entered a few minutes later, now wearing a grey skirt and blue twin set, he was standing in the window inspecting the half-finished picture of the autumn scene. He'd painted the Downs after the harvest, when the fields were brown and rich with loam and the trees were bare of leaves.

Edward was studying his picture thoughtfully, with his head on one side. He hadn't got the sky quite right. The indigo was good, streaked with yellow to show the sun going down. But it was too dark, too purple. He'd soften it by adding some Chinese white. What he was aiming for was the colour of Lily's eyes.

Whatever had made him think that? Edward froze with the canvas in his hand. He hadn't thought about Lily for ages, and yet a picture of her had suddenly sprung into his mind. He saw again her slim body with its crown of dark hair, and those amazing eyes the colour of newly opened violets.

'Aren't you going to kiss me then?' Betty was standing behind him looking over his shoulder, her lips, fashionably reddened, pouting childishly.

'Sorry, darling.' Edward obliged, but the kiss was only an absent-minded peck and Betty was disappointed.

'What's the matter? Don't you love me any more?'

'Of course I do. Don't be silly. Come here and I'll show you.' He put his arms out and Betty went into them willingly. He kissed her hard on the lips so that it almost took her breath away. That was more like it. Betty sighed contentedly and nestled against Edward's body, her head on his shoulder. 'Was that better?'

'Yes. I do love you, Edward.'

'And I you.'

'I haven't seen you all afternoon. There's still lots to do, you know. Some more presents arrived this morning, and I had to unpack them all by myself.'

'Anything interesting?'

'Another wall plaque, with a water-wheel on it this time. Still, it makes a change from flying ducks.'

'I suppose it's the thought that counts.'

'That's why I think we should have a serious talk, Edward.' Still holding his hand, Betty drew him towards an armchair and laughingly made him sit down. She perched on his knee in the same fashion she'd sat on her father's knee when she was a small child. 'Now I've got you trapped,' she said. 'And I'm not going to let you get up until you've made me a promise.'

'Anything.'

Edward was enchanted by her fair prettiness. She was such fun, and was so set on having a good time. He loved falling in with her whims and fancies, buying her little presents and thinking up surprise treats. He'd forgotten how tiresome he'd found her when they were children, when she sulked if she didn't get her own way.

'It's this painting nonsense.'

'What do you mean?'

Edward saw that she was staring at the canvas he'd left propped up by the window. Once again he found himself studying the sky. It was definitely much too dark. If he could only have half an hour on his own he'd be able to put it right.

'We think you spend too much time on your painting, when you should be doing other things.'

'Who's we?'

'Mother and me. I know it's only a hobby, and you are very good at it, but even so, there are more important things that you should be doing.'

'Such as?'

'Well, studying for your finals for one thing.'

'I am studying. But a fellow can't work all the time. He has to have relaxation.'

'But painting, Eddie! It's such a waste of time.' The corner of Betty's mouth twitched, almost as if she was laughing at him. 'If you need a hobby it should be something we could share.'

'What would you suggest?'

'I don't know. Collecting things? When I was a girl I used to collect butterflies.'

Edward burst out laughing. 'Butterflies! Can you imagine me collecting butterflies? They give me the creeps for one thing, when they're pinned on those trays under glass. The place for butterflies is in the fields and hedge-rows where they belong.'

Betty got up from Edward's knees huffily. 'Don't laugh at me, Edward. I don't like it.'

'Well, don't scowl like that: it spoils your pretty face.'

He got to his feet and tried to take her hand, but she twisted away from him.

'And now you don't like my face. Oh, Edward, sometimes I think you don't love me a bit,' and she allowed one tear to trickle down her cheek. She made sure Edward saw it before she dabbed it away carefully with her handkerchief. It had taken her a quarter of an hour to put on her new pancake makeup, and she didn't want to spoil it.

'I do love you, Betty,' Edward said urgently. 'You know I do.'

Betty allowed him to put his arms around her again, and turned her face so that his kiss landed on her cheek.

'Then you promise?' she asked softly.

'Anything, darling.' Edward was mesmerized by the softness of her body pressed close to his, and the perfume that she wore reminded him of walking through her mother's rose garden on a summer's day. 'What do you want me to promise?'

'I told you,' she drew away slightly so that she could straighten the collar of his shirt with her pink-tipped fingers. 'I want you to give up painting. It takes up too much of your time, and your clothes always smell of oil and turpentine.' She saw him frown so added quickly, 'You'd promise willingly if you really loved me.'

'All right,' Edward said. 'I promise to give up painting – but not until after we're married.'

'Oh, Edward! I knew you would. You really are the dearest man.' Betty's face was wreathed in smiles now that she'd got what she wanted. Edward tried to kiss her again, but she twirled away, her hand up to ward him off. 'Not again, Eddie. It takes me simply ages to make up my face, and my hair's coming down. You don't want me to look untidy like the village girls, do you?'

'I don't care how you look,' Edward said truthfully. 'I always find you perfectly lovely.'

'Flatterer. I must go and find Mummy. It was her idea to talk it over with you. She'll be so pleased that I've made you see sense.'

She was gone; out of the room and across the hall, her heels tapping on the polished boards.

Edward sighed; but he was happy. He hated disagreement, and was prepared to promise almost anything if it kept life running along smoothly. He did love Betty. He always had.

Even at her most temperamental she could still be charming and lovable.

Of course the engagement had been her idea. But once he'd got over the initial surprise he'd been almost as keen as she was. Mr and Mrs Thomas had been delighted, calling him a 'dear boy' and insisting that he was going to be the sort of son-in-law they'd always wanted, and his father had said he could now look forward to retirement. He had a son entering the medical profession who would be able to take up the reins where he left off. With a wife at his side to boost him on, John Butler felt his son would achieve much more than on his own. Everyone was happy.

And yet, sometimes Edward didn't feel comfortable. Whatever his father said, he had a dread of doctoring. Illness alarmed him, and he had to steel himself not to become a positive hypochondriac after reading symptoms in medical books. He hated the sight of blood, and once, to his shame, had been sick after a man had staggered into his father's surgery spurting blood from a severed artery on his wrist. But, as John Butler pointed out, he wasn't going to be a surgeon, and the day-to-day routine of a family doctor was made up of diagnosing ailments and doling out pills. Anybody could be a doctor with a reasonable amount of intelligence. Yet Edward still experienced niggling doubts that he wasn't cut out to be a doctor. And, more seriously, he felt real sorrow at having to give up his dreams of becoming an artist. But, as Betty had been quick to point out, they had been youthful dreams. Painting was all very well to while away the hours of a lonely bachelor's life, but what sort of future was there in it? Like writers, artists starved in garrets, and very few became famous. There wasn't anything romantic about starving.

Edward sighed again and picked up his unfinished canvas. He had two more days. He'd promised Betty that he'd stop painting when they were married. Today was Wednesday; there were still two whole days before his wedding day. Time to finish his picture to the best of his ability. Time to get it right.

The light was still good. Although there was a brisk wind blowing, he could find a sheltered spot down by the old orchard and paint until the sun went down. He could hear footsteps advancing along the passage and hoped it wasn't Betty or her parents. But it was only Mary Biggins lumbering along with a tray in her hand. He waited until she'd disappeared through the doorway into the kitchen. Then he retrieved his paints and easel and escaped through the garden door. He felt like an intruder in Ring House, and not a favoured guest.

A wonderful sense of freedom swept over Edward as he strode through the garden. Peter Jackson certainly kept everything spruce. The hedges were neatly clipped and the lawns smooth and green, the bulbs asleep in the borders waiting for the spring.

The orchard was Edward's favourite spot: out of sight of the house, but with a splendid view of the Sussex scene. The South Downs rolled away in all their glory: a pageantry of patchwork fields, with clumps of trees and the occasional chimney outlined against the sky.

Edward unfolded his easel and studied his picture. The sky still displeased him. He added a touch of gold, and then white to lighten the purple. Paler, paler, he told himself, and added more white until his painted sky was as near to violet as he could get it. Violet – that was right. The colour of Lily's eyes.

Thinking of Lily made him wonder if a figure would improve his landscape The slim figure of a girl staring out over the fields with her long hair streaming backwards in the wind. He picked up a small brush and with quick strokes began to sketch in a figure. When he glanced up the figure was there – moving towards him across the field. He wasn't dreaming: it really was Lily. She was wearing a scarlet skirt and jacket and a white scarf wound around her neck. Her hair blew about her as if it had a life of its own. It seemed a lifetime since he'd seen her. He put down his brush.

'Edward,' she said, panting slightly as she reached his side. 'Pete told me you were staying at Ring House, but I didn't expect to find you out here.'

'I wanted to finish my picture. I couldn't get the sky right.'

'Let me look.' Lily inspected the canvas with her head on one side. 'It's very good,' she said at last. 'Who's the girl?'

'You.'

'I thought so. Oh, Edward, I had to come. There's something I have to tell you. I've wanted to tell you for ages but I haven't liked to.'

'I know.' Edward grinned. 'You want to tell me that I paint

so well that one day I'm bound to be famous. That I shouldn't get married or become a doctor, but concentrate on my art.'

'How did you know?'

'I was joking, Lily.'

'So was I.' Lily coloured and looked at the ground. Her hair fell forward over her face like a dark curtain. 'Or at least I was partly joking.'

'Come on then, what is it? What is it you've wanted to tell me for so long?'

'I love you.' The wind caught her words and carried them away. They stood there, staring at each other, as if they'd never really seen each other before. 'I've always loved you, Edward, and I sort of thought you cared for me a bit.'

'I do,' Edward said in a low, thoughtful voice.

'Of course I do understand about Betty. I know she tricked you into an engagement, but I thought you'd break it off. I mean, when you realized you didn't love her you wouldn't go through with it. But then I heard that you're getting married on Saturday – I thought it was because I hadn't actually told you that I love you.'

'Lily, you' re a darling, but . . .'

Now that she'd started, Lily wasn't going to be stopped.

'You'll never be happy married to Betty. You haven't anything in common. She doesn't understand about your painting, does she?'

'She understands me better than I thought.' Edward's expression was so sad that Lily longed to put out her hand and comfort him. But she was afraid to. 'She's made me see that there are more important things in life than painting. It's a difficult profession to get into, and you have to be really good to succeed.'

'But you are good!' Lily's eyes burned with passion. 'She's a fool if she can't see that. Your pictures are beautiful, full of the most wonderful colours. You'd be wasted as a small-town doctor.'

'What do you suggest I do about it?'

For a minute Lily thought he was playing with her, but when she looked into his eyes she saw that he was serious. She'd touched some chord in him that had caused him to doubt the choice he'd made. If she played her cards right perhaps she would win after all. She was prepared to stake everything on her love for this fair-haired young man.

'You could always come away with me.'

'Where would we go?'

He wasn't looking at her; he was looking past her with a dreamy expression on his face.

'We'd go somewhere where there's an art school, and you could get a proper training. We'd get one of those studio places where you could paint all day. I would look after you. I wouldn't expect you to marry me, Edward, at least, not at first. But I love you, and we'd be together, and that would be the most important thing.'

'What about money? There'd be rent and tuition fees, and, oh! all sorts of things. I've only got about twenty pounds with me and that wouldn't last long. My father holds the reins on my money. How much have you got?'

'Hardly anything,' Lily admitted. 'But Matt might lend me something. There's a jamjar in his bedroom where he keeps his loose change. He's always telling me to help myself if I need anything – but I've never had much use for money.'

'So what do we do when my twenty pounds runs out?'

'I'd get a job.' Now was the time to touch him. Lily stepped closer and put her arm through his, drawing him to her. 'I love you so much that I wouldn't mind working for you. I just know you'll be unhappy marrying Betty and giving up your painting. Come with me, Edward. We'll go to Brighton – I think there's a good art college there. Do you remember when we came to visit you when you were at school? It was a lovely town, even though there was a war on. There's bound to be plenty of opportunities in a big town like that. It's not that far away; but it's big enough to get lost in.'

'You're sweet.' Edward bent down and dropped a kiss on the top of Lily's sleek head. 'But it's about time you grew up.'

'I am grown up.'

'No you're not.' He put his hand to his head in a helpless gesture. 'This idea of running away is the sort of thing a child might do. I'm marrying Betty on Saturday. Everything's arranged. I couldn't do that to her, Lily. It would break her heart.'

'What about my heart?'

Lily's eyes swam with tears because she knew she'd lost him. He was going to marry Betty Thomas on Saturday, and there was nothing she could do about it.

'I'm sorry, Lily.'

'Are you.' Lily pulled away. 'I'm going anyway. I'm leaving Valley Farm on Saturday. If you change your mind I'm catching the ten o'clock bus from the crossroads.'

She started to walk away, and didn't look back. She'd burned her boats, and now it was up to fate to take a hand.

'Are you awake?'

'Yes.' Betty opened her eyes sleepily and then struggled to sit up in bed.

'I thought you'd like a lie-in; but it is nearly half-past nine.' Elizabeth twitched the curtains back, letting in watery daylight. 'I'm afraid it's raining.'

'Oh, no! Everything will be spoilt – and what about the photographs?'

'Perhaps it'll clear up, dear.'

'It had better,' Betty said ominously. 'Have you brought my breakfast?'

'No. I didn't think you'd be hungry. I wasn't on my wedding day.'

'Well, I'm starving. I'll have toast, and fruit, and coffee.'

'I'll get it for you directly. The cake's arrived: it's really magnificent – much better than I could have made. Jackson's fetched the flowers, and we've put them in the cold larder until the rooms are cleaned.'

'I know something's going to go wrong. I can feel it.' Betty patted her head which was covered with a knobbly pattern of curlers.

'Nothing can go wrong,' Elizabeth said soothingly. She was determined that everything should go smoothly so that her daughter wouldn't get upset.

'Is Edward up? I want to see him.'

'Mary gave him an early breakfast in the kitchen, and you know it's unlucky for a bride to see the groom before they meet in church. He did say he wanted to see you. Something he wanted to tell you; but I said it would have to keep. I didn't want you bothered. His father's going straight to the church. Shall I get your breakfast now?'

'Yes, please.' Betty stretched lazily. 'And then you can run me a bath.'

Mrs Thomas kissed her daughter fondly. She was going to miss her. After the wedding Edward would be carrying her off to his father's house in Lewes. It wasn't far away, and they'd promised to visit often, but even so it would be different when she was only a visitor in her old home.

In the kitchen Mary Biggins was tearing about like a demented banshee. When she saw her mistress she burst into noisy sobs.

'Whatever is it?' Elizabeth asked impatiently. This was all she needed: a hysterical maid!

'That Mr Edward. He said the milk was too cold. So I boiled it up for him and then he threw it at me.' Mary was busy mopping up her tears on the corner of her apron.

'That doesn't sound like Edward. Are you sure you're not exaggerating, Mary?'

'Well, the jug was hot. I suppose it might have slipped.'

'I'm sure that's what happened. Where is he now?'

'I don't know, I'm sure. He rushed away as if he had something important to do.'

'He is getting married today. Perhaps he's forgotten something, or lost the ring. Oh, dear!' Elizabeth put her hand up to her throbbing brow. 'I shouldn't have let him stay. A man isn't supposed to sleep in the same house as a woman on the night before their wedding.'

After that the morning got steadily worse. The door knocker sounded repeatedly, and poor Mary had to trek along the passage from the kitchen to answer it. Presents and cards were still arriving. They all had to be opened, notes made of the givers' names, and then displayed. The dining-room table had been pushed to the far end of the room to hold the food for the reception. James found his wife staring in horror at the centre of the carpet.

'What's the matter, dear?'

'I hadn't realized how worn the carpet is, James. Look. It's so thin in the middle you can't see the pattern any more. Whatever will people think?'

'I hope they'll be too busy talking and eating to want to look at our carpet. You shouldn't worry so much.'

'I can't help it.' Elizabeth put her hand to her head again. 'I've got this feeling that something awful's going to happen.' She looked around. 'The bridesmaids! Have the bridesmaids arrived?'

'I saw three little girls in pink dresses. They looked like bridesmaids to me. The vicar phoned to say the best man's already at the church – so I suppose Edward's with him.'

'Thank goodness for that. At least that's one thing I won't have to worry about. Whatever's that?'

Mary Biggins was crossing the hall bearing a large wicker basket. She was holding it at arm's length as if it contained something fragile. Before Elizabeth had time to investigate Betty came rushing down the stairs dressed in her bridal finery. She almost snatched the basket out of Mary's hand.

'I'll take this,' she said. 'It's the present I've bought for Edward. He is going to be surprised.'

'Whatever is it?' Elizabeth asked.

'A puppy.' Betty opened the lid to disclose a small shivering spaniel with liquid brown eyes, and a big satin ribbon bow attached to its collar. 'He's missed King and Queenie ever since they died, so I've bought Princess as a replacement. I'm taking her to the church with me.'

'You can't do that,' James said quickly. 'Whatever will Mr Plummer say?'

Betty gathered the tiny bundle up into her arms and rained kisses down onto its soft golden head. 'I don't care. It's my wedding, and I'm taking her –.'

Elizabeth decided it was better not to argue as there were more immediate things to worry about. The smallest bridesmaid had just been sick all down her dress. She was carried away to the bathroom to be cleaned up.

Then the cars arrived. The first one was for the relations and friends, the second one for the bridesmaids and Mrs Thomas, the last one for the bride and her father. It stood waiting outside with a big white bow decorating its bonnet.

Suddenly Ring House, which had reverberated all morning with noise and action, was silent. Mary was staying behind to look after things. James could hear her thumping about in the kitchen as he waited at the front door for his daughter.

Tears came to his eyes when he saw her. The years seemed to fall away, and it was Elizabeth again: the same dress, and the same pink and white complexion under its halo of lace. Elizabeth had carried freesias on their wedding day; but Betty had chosen hothouse roses, perfectly formed but scentless. Draped over her arm was the mournful puppy.

'You look lovely,' he said. 'I'm proud of you.'

'Thanks, daddy. Come on: help me with my veil. I don't want to tear it, and we mustn't be late.'

'It's only a five-minute drive,' James reminded her. And brides are always expected to be a few minutes late. At least it's stopped raining.'

'Good. I want to be on time. Come on . . .'

Betty almost ran to the waiting car, as if she was afraid it would leave without her. James helped her into the back, and then handed her the puppy before taking his seat.

'Drive on, Bert,' he called to Jackson, and the car slid away down the drive.

As they drove through Lenton the village street was lined with people. Everybody wanted to catch a glimpse of the bride. After all, she was their landlord's daughter, and most of them had known her all their lives. When they arrived at St Patrick's James was surprised to see his wife standing in the porch with the bridesmaids and the vicar. Whatever was she doing? She should have taken her place in the pew reserved for the family.

'What's the matter?' Betty asked. 'Why are Mummy and Mr Plummer looking so worried? Help me out – I want to find out what's wrong.'

'Stay there,' James said firmly. But Betty ignored him, and father and daughter reached the porch at the same time. 'What's the matter, Elizabeth?'

'Oh, James! Edward isn't here. Mr Plummer's just told me.'

'What do you mean, Edward isn't here?' James shouted the question so loudly that the bridesmaids jumped back as if shot. 'Where is he?'

'You tell him,' Elizabeth begged the vicar. If she had to tell the story she was afraid she'd break down.

'He sent a note to the best man.' Mr Plummer held up a sheet of paper as if it was already burning his fingers. 'It just says, "Called away. Tell Betty I'm sorry. Edward." '

'Is that all?' James thundered.

'No.' Mr Plummer looked at Mrs Thomas, licked his lips nervously, and then continued. 'One of our WI ladies came to do the flowers. She said she saw Edward this morning boarding a bus at the crossroads. He was carrying a suitcase.' He paused before carrying on. 'He wasn't alone. It appears he had a young lady with him. Your protégée, Lily – the girl they call Lily from the Valley.'

Betty gave a little shriek and collapsed into her father's arms. And the little dog, frightened by the sudden noise, started to yap loudly.

CHAPTER NINE

The Runaways

'Excuse me.'

'What is it, mate?'

The conductor looked down curiously at the young fair-haired man pulling at his sleeve; and then his gaze travelled to the girl sitting next to him. He'd noticed them when they'd boarded his bus. So young, so unspoilt, so nervous. The way the dark-haired girl had clung to her companion's arm had made him suspect they were newlyweds.

'We don't know Brighton very well. Do you know of anywhere we could stay?'

'We're not going to Brighton. Brighton's in the other direction.'

'Are you sure?'

'Course I'm sure. Hey, did you hear that?' The conductor called back over his shoulder towards the driver's cab. 'He thinks we're going to Brighton – as if we don't know where we're going.'

'I'm sorry,' Edward said. 'Where exactly are you going?'

'Just coming into Pierhaven. Seaside resort. Bungalows, boarding houses, a pier, naturally. Not much different to Brighton, but smaller. Most people come here to die.'

'Die!' Lily spoke for the first time.

'Two-thirds of the population's retired. Pierhaven's quiet and friendly so it suits the elderly.'

'I see. Do you know of anyone that takes in boarders? Somewhere you can recommend.'

'There's plenty of small hotels run by families.' He considered the couple with the suggestion of a knowing twinkle in his eye. 'You on your honeymoon then?'

'Well no, not exactly.'

The young man blushed and the girl tightened her hold on his arm, pressing her fingers into his sleeve as if to reassure him.

'I understand. I'm a man of the world. The little lady must have a bed for the night.' I wouldn't mind sharing my bed with her, he thought. She had such pale, flawless skin and unusual eyes.

'I don't think we can afford a hotel,' the young man admitted.

'Well, there are plenty of boarding houses, and it's out of season so you should be lucky. If you're stuck you can always look at the adverts in the local paper.'

'Thanks.'

The couple bent their heads in consultation and the conductor called out, 'Fares please,' and started to climb to the upper deck. The bus was now travelling through a residential area, and the driver had to slow down to stop more often and pick up passengers.

'We could always get off and find a bus that goes back to Brighton,' Lily said.

'It's a bit late now we've come this far.'

'But the art school . . .'

'There must be other schools.'

'But where shall we sleep tonight?'

'Don't worry,' Edward said softly. 'We'll find somewhere.'

'I'm not worried.' Lily smiled to reassure him. 'At least it's stopped raining. If we can't find a room perhaps there'll be some shelter in a park.'

'At this time of year – we'd freeze.'

'We've both got coats. We can keep each other warm.'

Edward was worried. It was all right for Lily to take things so lightly, but he felt responsible for her. He was already beginning to regret their hasty departure. Betty would never forgive him for leaving her in the lurch, and he didn't blame her. It had been a cruel action on his part and now he had to pay for it; in fact by the inner turmoil he was experiencing he was already paying. And yet Lily was a darling and he'd always been fond of her. She believed in him and he wasn't going to let her down if he could possibly help it. But he was afraid.

'Sorry to interfere, dear, but did I hear you say you were looking for somewhere to stay?'

A fat woman in the seat in front was looking at them over her shoulder. She was wearing a black coat and a felt hat with a flower pinned to the side. On her lap was balanced a bulging shopping basket.

'It would have to be somewhere cheap,' Edward said. Lily had perked up and was smiling at the fat woman eagerly.

'Do you know of somewhere?' she asked.

'Not exactly, dear, but I have a friend who was thinking about taking in a lodger. Her son's just left home, so she's got a spare room. She asked me only the other day if I knew of anybody.'

'But there's two of us, and . . .'

'And you're not married?' The woman smiled in an understanding fashion. 'Don't worry, dear, I won't let on. Tell Doris you're husband and wife. I suppose you've no objection to sharing a room?'

'Doris?'

'Dot Miller: my friend, and her husband Arthur. Look, I'll write their address down.' She scribbled on the back of an old envelope and passed it to Edward. 'Get off at the next stop. It's a turning off of Thornton Crescent. Tell Doris that May Blunt sent you.'

'Thank you very much, Mrs Blunt,' Edward said. 'You've been very kind.'

'Not at all, dear. I was young once myself.'

'Tivoli Cinema. Who wants the Tivoli?' The conductor's voice rang out, making them jump.

'This is it, dears.' Mrs Blunt waved her hand as the bus drew to a standstill. 'Good luck.'

'Have you got everything, Lily?'

Lily nodded, passing her suitcase to Edward, and they clambered off the bus and found themselves on a main road busy with traffic. Opposite was the huge façade of a cinema, with a queue of people waiting outside for seats in the one and nines. Further down the road there was a factory and a bus depot, and a row of shops. It was a commercial area rather than residential and Lily and Edward looked at each other not too happily. The expression on Lily's face made Edward put the luggage down on the pavement so that he could put his arm around her. She looked so small and lost.

'Cheer up, Lily.'

'I'm all right. I'm just hungry, that's all. Look, there's a café over there. Can we afford something to eat?'

It was a workman's café and didn't look too clean. The tables were covered with oilcloth pitted with brown holes where customers had accidentally put down their cigarettes, and the windows were streaming with condensation. But the warm atmosphere was comforting, as were the mugs of tea and thick wedges of cheese between hunks of bread, cheap but filling. Edward paid the bill, and when he returned to the table he looked more cheerful.

'That's a bit of luck. I asked where Thornton Crescent is, where Mrs Blunt's friend lives, and it's only a five-minute walk away. Come on, Mrs Butler, let's go and find a bed for the night.'

'Mrs Butler?'

'You'd better answer to the name if I've got to pass you off as my wife.' Edward grinned. 'Don't worry, I won't take advantage of you even if we do have to share a room.'

Lily wasn't worried about that; in fact she wouldn't have minded Edward taking advantage of her. But she still wasn't sure of his feelings towards her. If she rushed him she might spoil things and live to regret it. After all, she'd won so far so she could afford to be patient. She loved him and was prepared to devote herself to his happiness. She'd got him away from Betty, and that was good enough for a start. But she didn't want to think about Betty Thomas because it made her feel guilty. She told herself that Edward's happiness must come first: she was sure she'd saved him from an unhappy marriage.

The address was easy to find. Thornton Crescent was a steep hill and the turnings branching off seemed to be balanced precariously on the side of a precipice.

'How much further?' Lily asked, panting along the pavement, trying to keep up with Edward's long stride.

'No idea.'

'Look!' Lily stopped with relief, she was getting a stitch in her side. 'There's number twenty-two.'

Edward had been studying the houses as they passed, and the feeling of depression, never far away, had returned. It wasn't a slum, but it certainly wasn't what he was used to. He looked gloomily at the rows of houses with dingy fronts and chipped paint, broken-down prams, bicycles propped against the walls, and untended gardens crammed with rubbish. A fretful baby was wailing somewhere close at hand. A woman's voice shouted loudly, 'Shut up, you!'

'Look,' Lily said again. 'This one is twenty-two.'

Edward dreaded to look, frightened of the feeling of panic that kept returning. He had to keep cheerful for Lily's sake. So he looked at number twenty-two and had the first pleasant surprise of the day.

It was a small house, wedged between its neighbours like the filling of a sandwich, but it was the neatest little house in the street. It had white walls and new green paint on the front door and window-frames, and a comforting spiral of smoke curled up from the chimney above the grey slate roof. A row of freshly planted wallflowers made a cheerful splash of colour under a neat privet hedge, and scrubbed steps led up to the door with shiny brass fittings. Through the crisp lace curtains he could just see a potted chrysanthemum in a china bowl on a table with an embroidered cloth.

'It looks nice, doesn't it?' Lily said, and ran up the steps to ring the bell.

Doris Miller must have been in the hall because the door was opened almost immediately and the homely little woman standing on the mat opened her arms as if she was welcoming them. She wore a hand-knitted jumper and skirt, with a clean print apron tied around her waist. Her hair was curled under a net and round glasses balanced on her stub of a nose.

'I'm sorry.' Her arms dropped to her sides at the sight of strangers, but the friendly smile remained and was reassuring to the cold and tired travellers. 'I thought you were Arthur – my husband. He's always forgetting his key. Can I help you?'

'We heard you have a room to rent,' Edward explained. 'A Mrs Blunt gave us your address.'

'That would be May.' Mrs Miller chuckled as if she found

her fat friend a huge joke. 'I did tell her I might be letting Ken's room, but I hadn't decided for sure.'

Lily's face dropped with disappointment. She liked this little woman and her house, and the thought of being turned away was depressing.

'It'd only be for a night or two while we look around,' Edward said coaxingly.

'But it's a single room – and it's not very big. I have got a camp bed but it wouldn't be very comfortable.'

'I don't mind,' Edward said quickly. 'Lily can have the bed and I can sleep anywhere. What do you charge?'

'Well . . .' Mrs Miller frowned with concentration before admitting, 'I've never done this before, you see. Perhaps you'd better come in and see the room.'

The house was just as cosy and spotless inside. They passed the open door of a sitting room with a solid horsehair three piece suite drawn up to a roaring fire, and a piano, its top stacked with sheet music and photograph frames. Other doors opened onto a dining room and a small kitchen. They followed Mrs Miller up a steep flight of stairs and along a narrow passage to the second bedroom.

'This is my son's room,' she said proudly, and stepped aside to let them pass. 'He always wanted to be an actor but he had to do his National Service. Then he got a job in the office of a wallpaper firm and acted in the evenings. Nothing special, just an amateur group. But someone saw him in a Bernard Shaw play and offered him a part with a touring company. Only as a walk-on – and two lines to speak – and he has to stage manage as well. But it's a start.'

'You must be proud of him,' Lily said.

'We are. He's our only son, you see. I'll leave you to have a look round. I'll be downstairs when you've finished.' She pattered over to the door and Lily and Edward were left on their own.

'It is small,' Lily said, looking around. 'But the bed looks comfy.' She sat down on the edge and bounced up and down.

'I suppose this is the camp bed.' Edward dragged an object made of metal, wood and canvas away from the wall. 'Hold the end, Lily, and I'll try and open it.'

It opened like a concertina. Lily let go and it sprang closed again, trapping Edward's thumb in its claw-like jaws.

'Ow!' He pulled his thumb free and sucked the bruised flesh. 'That hurt.'

'There's a metal bar on the side that locks it in place like a bolt.' Lily was busy experimenting, and then she stepped back to view the finished bed. 'It doesn't look very comfortable. Perhaps we could borrow some cushions.'

Edward was still inspecting the room. 'What do you think then?' he said.

It was a small room and barely furnished. The only other pieces of furniture were a chest of drawers and a marble-topped washstand. There was a tiny oil stove standing in the hearth and a framed picture of Queen Victoria hanging on the wall. A couple of bent coathangers dangling from a nail behind the door served as a wardrobe.

Lily crossed to the window that looked out from the back of the house.

'I wonder who takes care of the garden?' she said. There was a neat oblong of grass, bordered by beds that would be ablaze with colour in the spring. A square shed stood at the far end, next to a water-butt and a stone pedestal holding a birdbath. She turned to Edward and smiled. 'Let's hang up our coats and go downstairs. Then Mrs Miller will know we want to stay.'

They found the landlady rearranging the photographs on top of her piano. When they entered the room she turned to them holding in her hand the picture of a young man with a pencil-slim moustache.

'Is that your son?' Lily asked politely.

'Yes. This is Ken.' The little woman hugged the picture to her chest before replacing it carefully. 'Do you think he's good-looking?'

'Very.'

'Better looking than your husband?'

'But I haven't got . . .'

'She means me,' Edward butted in hastily. 'We're on our honeymoon, Mrs Miller. We only got married today.'

'That's what I thought. All starry-eyed you were when I opened the door. I guessed you were newlyweds as soon as I set eyes on you. You can call me Dot if you like. Everyone else does. And my husband's Arthur. Here he is now.'

Arthur was blowing on his fingers as if they were cold. He

was a short man, not much taller than his wife, but where she was thin he was well padded. The buttons of his overcoat strained over his belly and looked as if they might explode at any minute. His wife's hair was sprinkled with grey but his was still dark and glossy, although the sides had begun to recede. He looked from his wife to the two strangers as he began to unwind a hand-knitted muffler from around his neck.

'What's this then?'

'They've come about Ken's room, Arthur.'

'That's quick. We only talked about it yesterday. I didn't think we'd decided anything.'

Arthur removed his coat. He stepped back into the hall to hang it on a hook by a woman's coat and a couple of mackintoshes.

'I mentioned it to May, and she sent them. You know – May Blunt.'

'We met Mrs Blunt on the bus,' Edward explained. 'She recommended you and gave us your address. I'm Edward Butler and this is Lily.'

They shook hands and then Arthur sat down on the nearest chair and started to remove his shoes. 'Where are my slippers, Dot?'

Mrs Miller pattered over to the fireplace where a pair of check carpet slippers were warming. She slipped her hands inside each one to test them and then handed them to her husband.

'Thanks,' Arthur grunted and put them on. 'How much are they paying, Dot? We can't keep them for nothing. Money doesn't grow on trees, you know.'

'We haven't got around to money,' Dot explained. 'I thought it was best to wait for you, dear. You're better at these things than I am.'

This seemed to please Arthur Miller. He crossed to the armchair facing the fire and sat down thoughtfully, hooking his thumbs in the armholes of his waistcoat. After a few minutes' contemplation he cleared his throat and looked up.

'Five bob?'

'Pardon?' Edward wasn't sure quite what he meant.

'Five bob bed and breakfast – each, of course. Dot's breakfasts keep a man going for hours so it's cheap at the price. Eggs, sausages, fried bread and bacon, washed down by gallons of tea. Or a nice pair of kippers, with rice and hard-boiled eggs. What do you say?'

'Sounds great.' Edward looked at Lily. She was smiling at the thought of all that food.

'Say thirty bob a week each? That fair to you?'

'It's a deal.'

Edward held his hand out and they shook on it. Then he counted out three pound notes and passed them to Mrs Miller who folded them neatly and wedged them under the marble foot of the mantelpiece clock.

'That'll be a great help, and a worry off our shoulders,' she said with a smile. 'I've been working at the sweet factory. That's the big grey building behind the cinema; I expect you passed it. I had a job on the assembly line, packing boxes. I really liked it because the other women were so friendly. It was ever so fiddly, mind you; particularly sealing the boxes down. But work slacked off a bit, and as I was the oldest packer I had to go. Arthur's a fireman at a big department store.'

By now the daylight had faded and Dot switched the light on and drew the curtains. 'I'm going to make a bit of tea now,' she said. 'Will you join us?'

'You're very kind,' Lily said. 'But . . .'

'Please. After all, it is your first day. It's only a bit of bread and butter with some jam. But there's some homemade cake that needs eating up.'

They sat down to tea at the drop-leaf table in the back room. Dot was in charge of the fat brown teapot and Arthur sawed hunks of bread from a crumbling loaf. When they'd finished Lily helped with the washing-up. She was shaking the crumbs from the cloth outside the back door, watched by a hungry sparrow, when Edward joined her.

'I'm going out for an hour, Lily. I hope you don't mind.'

'Where to? Can I come?' She looked at him in surprise.

'Arthur wants me to go to the Queen's Head with him. That's his favourite pub. I thought I'd go to be friendly.'

'Oh, Edward! Do you have to?'

Lily didn't want to complain but she didn't like the idea of being left on her own. After all, the Millers thought they were newlyweds, and bridegrooms didn't usually go off and leave their brides on their wedding night.

'Don't worry, dear.' Dot had come up behind them.

'Arthur'll look after him, and bring him home safely. It'll give us a chance to have a little chat and get to know each other. Your Edward will be back before you've had a chance to miss him.'

'All right,' Lily said, trying to hide her disappointment. Edward had already fetched his coat and was putting it on.

'Can I wash my hands?' he asked.

'We haven't got a bathroom, dear,' Dot said. 'But there's some hot water left in the kettle, and you can use the washing-up bowl. You can have a jug of hot water in your room every morning if you don't mind coming down to get it. If you want the lav it's just outside the back door.'

When the men had finally gone Dot led Lily back into the front room. They sat side by side on the two-seater settee and for the first time seemed to be at a loss for something to talk about.

Lily saw the older woman looking at her left hand and suddenly realized that she, as a newly married woman, should be wearing a ring. Her landlady must think it strange that her finger was bare. She tucked her hands out of sight and tried to think of a subject for conversation.

'Do you play that piano, Dot?' she asked.

'Yes. It was left to me by my father. I've got three sisters, but I'm the only one who can play. He left me the piano in his will. Would you like me to play you a tune?'

'Yes, please.'

Mrs Miller got up and riffled through the music on top of the piano. At last she found what she was looking for, sat down on the stool, and ran her fingers over the keys. Then she looked over her shoulder at Lily. Her eyes were sparkling as if she was looking forward to the chance of performing.

'Would you mind turning the pages for me?'

'Of course.' Lily joined her. As the first notes of 'I'll Be Seeing You,' filled the room she found herself humming in time to the music.

'Do you know it?' Dot asked.

'Yes. I've heard Vera Lynn singing it on the wireless. Can you play 'Autumn Leaves'? That's my favourite.'

'Is this the one?'

The music changed and Lily couldn't help joining in. She loved singing and had a high, clear voice. Dot Miller was a good accompanist. In the middle of the song she stopped abruptly and looked up at Lily.

'You've got a lovely voice, my dear.'

'Have I?' Lily was pleased. She still wasn't used to praise.

'Yes. But you stand badly, and your breathing's all over the place.' She got up from the stool and walked around Lily, inspecting her posture. 'Now stand tall. Tummy in and shoulders back, feet slightly apart to balance your weight. Good. Now breathe in.' Lily followed the instructions and breathed in deeply, and when Dot told her to, held it. 'Good. Now push the air out slowly, and relax.' She placed the palms of her hands against Lily's diaphragm. 'Harder! Try and push my hands away. That's better. Now sing . . .'

She could feel the improvement as her voice soared out into the room, and Dot rushed back to the piano to pick up the tune. After that they had a go at most of the sheet music in Dot's collection – 'I'll Get By', followed by 'Stardust', and Lily's favourite, 'I'm in the Mood for Love'. When Dot started to play Ave Maria Lily thought it would be beyond her, but she found she could reach the high notes effortlessly. Dot nodded and smiled so enthusiastically that Lily knew she was doing well.

They were so engrossed that when they heard the scraping of a key in the lock, and the sound of male voices, they were both surprised at how quickly the evening had flown. Arthur was a bit wobbly on his feet, and his flushed face and raised voice told the women that he'd enjoyed more than one drink at the local. Even Edward had a telltale spot of colour on his cheeks. But he wasn't drunk, just happy.

'See, girls, what did I tell you?' Arthur said. 'I've brought the bridegroom back safe and sound. And if he did have a little drink, he earned the money to pay for it.'

'How did he do that?' Dot asked.

'You tell them, Eddie.'

'I drew a sketch of the barman,' Edward said proudly, 'and he liked it so much he bought it for five shillings, and pinned it up on the wall. Then I was asked to do others. Some bought me drinks and others paid me half a crown a time.' He delved deep into his trouser pocket and produced thirty shillings in loose change. He handed it to Lily. 'You'd better have it and keep it safe.'

'Tell her the rest then,' Arthur prompted.

Edward blushed with pride. 'They want me to do an oil painting of the Queen's Head.'

'Oh, Edward!' Lily's eyes were like stars. 'I hope you said you would?'

'I took a ten shilling deposit.' Edward produced a note. 'So I've got to. Mr Baines, that's the landlord, is going to pay me another four pounds ten shillings when it's finished.'

'That's wonderful.' Lily looked from Dot to Arthur. 'Isn't it?'

'It's fine,' Arthur admitted. 'You've got yourself a really clever husband.'

'I know. That's what I keep telling him.'

Dot made cups of cocoa to celebrate Edward's good fortune and then it was time for bed. Lily and Dot climbed the stairs together because Arthur insisted on showing Edward the procedure for locking up; just in case he was the last one in one night. The two women wished each other good night, and then Lily went into the little room she was going to share with Edward.

Suddenly the room seemed strange and hostile. With the curtains drawn and the lights on it seemed even smaller, and the furniture threw strange shadows. Mrs Miller had lit the little stove and the uneven wick flickered moving shapes across the ceiling. Lily wasn't cold but she hugged herself for comfort. She'd been the instigator of this adventure and she didn't know how it was going to end, or what demands were going to be made on her. Would Edward expect to sleep with her? The single bed was so narrow there was hardly room for one person, let alone two. She loved him so she wasn't really afraid – in fact deep down she wanted him.

It only took a few moments to slip out of her clothes and splash her face with cold water before pulling a nightie over her head. It was a simple affair of white cotton, with puffed sleeves and a ribbon drawstring at the neck. She felt childish standing on bare feet with her hair hanging over her shoulders. She wished she had something soft and clingy to wear, or some fluffy slippers with heels to make her look taller. But beggars can't be choosers and she had to make the best of things.

She brushed her hair until it shone, and then pulled the neckline of her gown as low as she could in the hope it would make her look more glamorous. But nothing could disguise her thin figure or the small, childish breasts that hardly showed under the thin material.

When Edward entered the room Lily was sitting in the middle of the bed with her knees drawn up to her chin. Her pretty face was white as paper and there were dark smudges under her eyes. She looked so tragic that he crossed to the bed and took her hands in his.

'What is it?' he asked.

'I was waiting for you. I was afraid you weren't going to come.'

'Well, I'm here now.'

She didn't want to release his hands, and when he pulled them away she felt bereft. Edward crossed the room and slowly began to remove his clothes. He looked afraid and Lily felt sorry for him. When his body was disclosed to her she found he was as beautiful as she'd guessed he would be. His skin looked golden under the artificial light, the blond down giving it a silky sheen. He was slender, but his muscles were as taut as an athlete's, and his movements were just as graceful. She was speechless with wonder and couldn't stop looking at him. As he buttoned the jacket of his pyjamas he became aware of her gaze and looked at her with a half smile.

'What is it?'

'Nothing.'

'You must be tired. Go to sleep.'

'All right.'

Obediently Lily slid down under the covers, stretching her toes against the cold sheets. She turned on her side, her face still towards Edward, and watched as he crossed to the door to switch off the light. Would he come to her? Or would he get into that awful concertina contraption that Mrs Miller had padded with cushions?

The little oil stove gave out a flickering light. The sight of Lily huddled like an unhappy child on the narrow bed upset Edward. Earlier in the evening, in the pub with Arthur, he'd felt impatient to get back to her. He'd thought of her as a desirable woman, passionate, and beautiful to look at. His body had yearned for her in a way it had never yearned for Betty. And now he'd got back and found only a frightened child. It would be a crime to violate that tender body. The thought of his lust disgusted him but he couldn't dampen the ardour in his loins.

Edward climbed into the camp bed; the metal joints creaked ominously as he tried to get comfortable. There was no sound from the bed; not even the sound of Lily breathing. Was she holding her breath?

'Are you asleep, Lily?' There was no answer, so after a moment he said again, 'Are you asleep?'

Lily didn't answer because she couldn't. Her chest had tightened so that she couldn't breathe, and she had to swallow the silent sobs that shook her. Eyes tightly closed and teeth biting fiercely into her lip, she lay stiff in an agony of despair.

Then, just when she thought she was going to die of unhappiness, the blanket was pulled aside. She felt Edward climb in beside her and press his warm body against hers. He put his arms around her and drew her into an embrace. But he'd managed to control the passion: he held her like a parent would hold a beloved distressed child. Lily couldn't stop the sob that escaped her before she buried her face in the hollow of his neck.

'Don't cry, Lily.'

But she couldn't stop. He was holding her like a father or brother, and not like the lover she'd dreamed of. And then she heard him crying too. So they lay together, their tears joined in misery, as were their bodies.

CHAPTER TEN

A bed for the night

'How much money have we got left?'

'Not much. You'd better count it.'

Edward put down the pad on which he'd been drawing and emptied his pockets. He passed a handful of loose change and some notes across to Lily, and then picked up his pencil again.

They were sitting on their beds in Mr and Mrs Miller's house. It was a January afternoon and bitterly cold outside although a watery sun was shining through the bedroom window. The stove glowed in the hearth, giving out fumes rather than heat. They had blankets draped over their shoulders to help keep themselves warm.

'There's three pound notes and two ten shilling ones, and seven and six in change,' Lily said. 'Is that the lot?' Edward nodded absently. 'What about the twenty pounds you brought with you?'

'We spent that a long time ago. There was the rent, and then I had to buy paint and brushes for Mr Baines's picture.'

'It was kind of him to get you that commission, wasn't it?'

After Edward had finished the painting of the Queen's Head Mr Baines had recommended him to the publican of another house. The landlord of the Seven Green Bottles had paid

Edward to paint a sign for him to hang outside his pub in Thrower Street.

'It only took me five days.' Edward tore the top sheet from his pad, screwed it into a ball, and tossed it into the cardboard box they used as a wastepaper basket. 'If I could get a commission every week we could live like royalty.'

'On five pounds a week?' Lily laughed. 'It costs us three to live here.'

'I know.'

'Surely you don't want to spend the rest of your life painting pub signs and sketching old men with pints of beer in their hands?'

'No. I'd rather sketch beautiful young women. Sit still, Lily; your hair keeps falling over your face.'

'Sorry.' Lily shook her hair back. 'Have you given up the idea of going to art school?'

'Not entirely, but it would cost money, so how can I?'

'I'll get a job,' Lily said. 'It's about time I did my share. And we ought to start looking for somewhere to live.'

'We live here.'

'We can't stay here permanently. It's not fair on Dot and Arthur. We were supposed to be on our honeymoon, and that was five weeks ago. They've been really kind, giving us a nice Christmas and everything. They didn't ask for anything extra either.'

'I know. I thought we could stay until they ask us to leave.'

'They'd never do that. But it's awkward for them – because their son's coming home.'

'Kenneth?' Edward stopped drawing and gave Lily his full attention.

'Yes.'

'How do you know?'

'I heard them talking. I'd just come in from out the back. They were sitting in the dining room with the door open, so they didn't know I was there. Dot had had a letter from Ken and was reading it out loud to Arthur. That play he's in is coming to Sussex and he wrote to tell them, and say how much he was looking forward to seeing them. He told them to keep his bed aired because he'd be needing it soon.'

Edward bit the end of his pencil thoughtfully. 'Why haven't they said anything?'

'Because they don't want to upset us. They're so kind hearted they'd probably give us their own beds if we had nowhere else to go.'

'That's all right then.' Edward started drawing again.

'It's not all right!' Lily sounded angry and Edward looked up at her in surprise. 'We can't take advantage of them like that. It's not fair.'

'What do you suggest we do then? Give them a week's notice while we go house-hunting?'

'No. That would put them in a terribly embarrassing position. They'd feel guilty. I think we should just pack up our things and move out.'

'What, now?'

'Why not?' Lily got up gracefully, folded her blanket, and began to pace about the room restlessly. 'They've gone to the pictures and won't be back for at least an hour. I know because Dot asked me to lay up the tea things for her. I can do that while you pack; we can be out in half an hour. We'll leave them a note so they won't worry.'

'But where shall we go?'

Lily could tell by the tone of his voice that Edward wasn't keen on the idea of becoming homeless again. Over the last few weeks she'd come to realize that she was the strong one, and Edward was quite happy to drift along without worrying about the future. Of course it was the result of their different upbringings. Edward had always lived a sheltered life at home with his father, whereas she'd had to fight for as long as she could remember. She felt responsible for him, because without her encouragement he'd never have left Ring House in the first place. But the last thing Lily wanted was to see him run back to Betty Thomas's arms. Edward belonged to her now – and she intended to keep him.

'First we'll have to find somewhere to live,' she said. 'And then I'll get myself a job. I don't mind what I do as long as they pay me.'

'You're amazing,' Edward said. And he meant it.

'So are you.'

Lily danced across the room to drop a kiss on the top of Edward's head. She took the pad and pencil out of his hand and pulled him to his feet. He soon caught her enthusiasm and began to throw their few belongings into the suitcases they'd stored under the bed. They seemed to have collected an awful lot of rubbish during their stay and without looking too closely he dumped it all in the waste box.

Tearing the top sheet from the sketch pad Lily sucked the pencil thoughtfully before writing in a neat hand: 'Dear Dot and Arthur. Thank you for looking after us so well. We've been called away suddenly and didn't have time to wait and say goodbye. Don't worry, we'll be all right. Love from Lily and Edward.'

They left the note together with the key on the tea-table, and then let themselves out of the front door. It closed behind them with a final click, and they walked side by side along the pavement towards the main road carrying their cases. They were lucky not to bump into Dot and Arthur who'd already left the cinema, but had decided to go home via the nearest fish and chip shop which was in the opposite direction.

Neither of them knew the layout of Pierhaven very well. For the few weeks they'd lived there they'd hardly left the friendly neighbourhood of the Millers' house. But there seemed to be plenty of red buses rolling down the road that looked as if it led to the town centre.

'Come on,' Edward said as they neared a bus stop. 'Let's get a ride into town.'

Lily's arms were already aching and she was tempted. It was so cold that she'd knotted a scarf gipsy fashion over her head, and Edward had pulled the collar of his coat up to protect his ears. They both had gloves – hand-knitted ones that Dot had made them for Christmas – but Lily's shoes had thin soles and her feet were numb. She put down her case to rub her fingers and watched an approaching bus longingly.

'We can't afford it,' she said.

'Yes, we can,' Edward insisted. 'We've got four pounds seven shillings and sixpence.'

'No, we haven't.'

'You added up the money. That's how much you said we had.'

'I know,' Lily said quietly. 'But I left three pounds for the Millers. It only seemed right when we were leaving so suddenly to pay a week's notice.'

Edward stood still on the pavement and stared at Lily in astonishment. The bus drew up behind them, picked up its passengers, and drove away. He couldn't be cross: it was the sort of unexpected thing Lily was liable to do.

'So that means we've only got thirty bob,' he said with a sigh.

'One pound seven and six, actually. Don't worry Edward, I'll get a job tomorrow.'

But Edward was already walking away from her and she had to run to catch up, the case banging against her leg. She thought he was angry, but after a while he slowed down and took the suitcase from her with his free hand.

'Are you cross?' she asked.

Edward looked down at her. There was no point in being cross: the deed was done. Lily looked so fragile and young in her brown winter coat. Her face was a pale oval and there were dark shadows under her violet eyes. Whenever she spoke her breath left white spirals on the cold air. He suddenly felt very tender and protective towards her.

'No,' he said. 'I'm not cross. But we'd better walk and save on the fare. At least it will help us keep warm.'

Edward was right. The brisk walk did help, and they both had rosy cheeks by the time they reached the main centre of Pierhaven. The pavements were still busy with housewives carrying shopping baskets, and schoolchildren with satchels hurrying home for their teas.

Lily stopped in the middle of the pavement. 'I'm tired,' she said. 'I can't walk any further.'

'Don't be silly.' Edward looked around helplessly. 'We're in everybody's way. You can't stop here.'

'I need a rest. Let's buy a newspaper and see if there are any rooms to let.'

'We'd better save the pennies,' Edward said pettishly. 'If you hadn't left that money for the Millers we could have bought tea as well as newspapers.'

'Don't be horrid.' Lily felt tears pricking her eyes and swallowed quickly. 'Look at that building over there. It says museum and library. Don't libraries have reading rooms where you can look at newspapers for nothing?'

'Clever girl.' Swinging the cases Edward led the way. 'Let's go and see.'

At least it was warm inside. The heavy doors swung to behind them and Lily's spirits lifted. They were in a grand entrance hall with heavy dark pictures frowning down at them and a floor laid out like a Roman mosaic. Passages led away to their right and left lined with roped off antique furniture. There were glass cases full of old and interesting exhibits.

They followed the general crowd and found themselves in a long room with polished boards that creaked as they walked over them. Lily paused at a cabinet that was full of brightly coloured china.

'Look,' she said, pointing to a dark blue fan-shaped dish. 'I wonder what you'd use that for?'

'No idea,' Edward answered. 'All it says is it's a Japanese ceramic, and it was made at the end of the eighteenth century. What's that one? The little pot with the figure on the top?'

Lily peered through the glass and read from the label. 'It says it's a water bottle. Funny shape for a bottle, isn't it? Now you can see that the one next to it is a cup.'

'A mug,' Edward corrected. 'They don't make cups that large. And those things, like big pennies, are medals, made of bronze and silver.'

There were many interesting things to look at. Now that she was warm Lily delighted in wandering through the rooms inspecting everything. At last they reached a staircase that curved upwards, and a sign hanging from the newel post said it led to the library and art galleries. So they climbed up to the higher floor and found the gloomy library with its notice demanding silence. It seemed to be full of serious students in duffle coats leafing through heavy volumes.

'Come on,' Lily said gaily. 'I'll ask where the newspapers are.'

'Sh!' A tall thin woman looked up from behind a dark wood counter and put her finger to her lips with a warning gesture.

Lily and Edward crept past and found the table of newspapers themselves. From their dog-eared appearance it was obvious that they'd been well read, but they were current issues and Lily settled in a high-backed chair to study the pages of adverts.

'There are lots of flats and houses to let,' she said excitedly. 'And they're all unfurnished.'

Edward soon brought her down to earth. 'We can't afford a flat, let alone a house,' he told her firmly. 'And we haven't got any furniture, remember.'

'I told you I'd look for a job tomorrow.'

'Aren't there any rooms, or bed and breakfast accommodation?'

'Seven and six is the cheapest.'

'Write down the address then. We can afford one night in comfort.'

Lily wrote down the address and slipped the piece of paper into her pocket for safety. The money they had left would just about see them through until the next day. She wasn't going to look further ahead than that. She wandered over to a shelf of books and picked one out at random, flicking through the pages idly.

'Come on,' Edward said. 'There's an exhibition on in the art gallery. I'd like to have a look.'

Lily was immersed in her book. 'This is by someone called J.B. Priestley. I read a book by him once; it was all about actors and actresses. This one is called *Let the People Sing*. I wonder if it's about opera singers?'

'I don't know.'

'Do you think they'll let me borrow it?'

'I don't see why not. Ask that woman at the counter. Its supposed to be a free library so it shouldn't cost us anything.'

Lily carried the precious book over to the counter and waited patiently for the librarian's attention. At last two steely eyes looked at her questioningly.

'Ticket, please.'

'Pardon?'

'I asked for your library ticket.'

'I haven't got one.'

'You can't borrow a book without a ticket.'

'Well, how can I get a ticket?' Lily didn't like the woman, or the way she was being looked up and down as if she was of no consequence. She tossed her hair back and tried to stare the other out.

'Are you a resident?'

'You mean, do I live in Pierhaven?'

'Yes.' The librarian sighed, and picked up a pen to fill in Lily's details on the appropriate card.

'Not exactly.' The pen dropped back on the counter with an impatient click. 'At least, we may stay if we can find somewhere to live.'

'You'd better come back when you have a permanent address.'

'I only want to borrow a book, for heaven's sake!' Suddenly Lily felt tired and cross. Why did she have to fight for everything she wanted – even the loan of a book? 'I'm not going to steal it.'

'Please keep your voice down.' The librarian was looking again at the notice requesting silence. 'You're creating a disturbance.'

'I can create a bigger disturbance than this,' Lily said. She raised the book as if she was about to throw it, but on second thoughts slammed it down on the counter. 'But I doubt if J.B. Priestley is worth it.'

'Come on,' Edward said. His face was red with embarrassment. He put his hand under Lily's elbow and guided her firmly in the direction of the art gallery. 'Let's go and look at the pictures.'

'It's probably a rotten story anyway,' Lily said loudly over her shoulder as a parting shot.

The gallery seemed to be deserted so they took their time wandering down the length of the room studying the pictures. Most of them seemed to be water-colours in the style Edward favoured. There were country scenes with animals and windmills, and coastal studies of sailing ships. Although Edward liked them there was nothing particularly striking about the artist's technique. Lily thought they were pretty, but was sure Edward could do as well, if not better.

'Lily, come and look at these.'

Edward had wandered away and was standing in front of some black and white paintings. They were large pictures composed of black strokes on a white background: figures leaping and stretching, giving a feeling of life and energy. Lily didn't understand them at all and was puzzled by Edward's look of excitement.

'I wouldn't want one of those hanging on my wall,' she said firmly.

'I think they're wonderful,' Edward said. 'I wish I could paint with such power. Look, they're signed by someone called David Titmus. I wonder who he is?'

'He's an idiot.'

'Pardon?'

Edward and Lily jumped. They'd been so sure that they

were alone, but now they saw that there was a figure sitting on the floor in the corner of the gallery: a man who looked not much better than a tramp, wearing paint-splashed overalls and an old army jacket. His features were ugly: a full sensual mouth, broad flattened nose, and the brightest blue eyes almost hidden under thick untidy brows. To top it all he wore a knitted woollen hat pulled well down on his head. Lily didn't care for the way he was staring at her.

'I said, he's an idiot,' the strange man said again.

'Who is?'

'That Titmus fellow. The one who painted those pictures.'

'Do you know him?' Edward didn't care if the man was a vagrant or not; the fact that he seemed to know the artist excited him.

'I should do – it's me.'

'You! You're David Titmus?'

'Yes. I'll sell you one if you like. Would you like to make me an offer, young man?' The artist clambered to his feet and stretched lazily, scratching his nose with a paint-encrusted finger. 'If you don't care for any of these I've got plenty of others at home. Girls with clothes on – girls with no clothes at all – but none of them as pretty as this young lady.'

He was looking straight at Lily, and she had the grace to blush. She wasn't sure if she liked being spoken of in the same sentence as naked girls. She looked at Edward to see how he was taking it; but he just seemed thrilled to be in the company of a real artist.

'I can't buy anything,' he admitted. 'We're broke – or nearly broke.'

'Are you on holiday?' David Titmus was looking pointedly at the suitcases. 'Funny time of year to take a holiday.'

'Not exactly,' Lily said. 'My name's Lily, and this is Edward. He's an artist, like you. He paints wonderful pictures.'

'Where are you staying?'

'We haven't found anywhere yet. I don't suppose you know of anything? The thing is, it'll have to be cheap.'

'I might.' David pulled his hat off and ran his fingers through his untidy hair. Suddenly Lily realized that he was almost handsome in a rugged, buccaneer fashion, and his smile was warm and friendly. 'What sort of place are you looking for?'

'Anything,' Edward said eagerly. 'Just a room with a bed would do.'

'What about the bed without the room?'

'We're desperate. We'd even settle for that.' Lily was half-joking, but when she looked again at the friendly artist she could see that he wasn't.

'Chris and I have a studio in Monkey Walk,' David said slowly. 'It's the loft over a deserted bakery about ten minutes' walk from here. We often put people up. There's a spare bed but not much privacy. I paint there, and Chris makes clothes and does the cooking, and anything else that needs doing.'

'Is Chris your wife?' Lily asked the question more out of politeness than anything else, but as soon as the words were out she wished she hadn't spoken. David's blue eyes had glazed over and he looked away, the smile fading slightly from his friendly face. She guessed at once that he was only living with Chris. After all, artists were known for living a bohemian lifestyle. But then she and Edward weren't married either and they had nothing to be ashamed of. She put her hand out impulsively and pulled David's grubby sleeve. 'I'm sorry. I didn't mean to be nosy. Edward and I aren't married.'

Suddenly the artist began to laugh. It was a loud, cheery sound that made Edward smile and Lily relax. He grabbed Lily's case in one hand, and gesturing to Edward to follow, led the way out of the gallery and down the stairs to the street.

The January air was still as cold, and a bitter wind was blowing, whipping the skirts of their coats around their legs and making Lily's hair stream out behind her as she hurried to keep up with their guide. The road was darker and quieter now that the shops were closing for the night, but they were surprised when David suddenly dived into a dark alleyway.

'Where do you think he's taking us?' Lily whispered, slipping her arm through Edward's for reassurance. 'I didn't know they had twittens in towns.'

David must have heard her muttered words because he looked over his shoulder with a smile. 'It's not a twitten – it's what we call a cat's-creep. I hope you can both climb.'

They soon understood what he meant. A flight of stone steps climbed upwards, and then there was a stretch of flat paving lined with garden walls, back doors and dustbins, before a second flight of steps made them climb again once they'd got their breath back. The rows of prowling figures, staring at the intruders from the tops of the walls, told them how the word cat's-creep had entered the town's vocabulary.

When they reached Monkey Walk it turned out to be a narrow road lined with empty buildings and warehouses. Once it had probably housed a busy community high on the hillside overlooking the sea, but gradually the population had left. The attraction would be for larger seaside towns; there were many dotted along the coast. Even changing its name and building a pier hadn't put Pierhaven back on the map. Now it was a popular place for retired people, who brought money into the area and could afford to build their own homes, and didn't need jobs.

'We're here,' David said.

He'd stopped by a broken brick facade, where double doors were swinging in the wind. Lily could just make out the words 'Grubbs Bakery' painted in faded letters over the door before following her companions inside.

It was dark but their eyes soon got accustomed to the gloom.

'Watch your step,' David instructed as dim shapes loomed up in front of them.

There were crates and boxes, piles of rusty tins, and rounded shapes like boulders.

'Ouch!' Lily stubbed her toe on one of them. 'Whatever are they – stones?'

'Sacks of flour,' David said, and laughed at her expression of disbelief. 'Left behind when the bakery closed down. First the mice got at them, and then the damp. There are beetles and cockroaches as well – but only down here. Follow me.'

He led the way through the obstacles, pointing out the huge brick ovens in the walls, unused now and crumbling, and a flat spade-like object with a long handle that had been used to carry the loaves on and off the coals. A square of light fell through an open trap-door in the ceiling. A ladder, which looked as precarious as everything else in the building, was propped up against the opening.

Edward and Lily exchanged looks. Whatever had they let themselves in for? David mounted the ladder with Lily's suitcase on his shoulder. He pushed it through the opening before pulling himself up effortlessly.

'It's only me, Chris,' they heard him say. 'I've brought some friends who need a bed for the night.'

'You go first,' Lily said to Edward. She waited below until he'd disappeared and then climbed up after him.

They found themselves in a surprisingly warm and airy loft. It stretched the whole length and breadth of the building, like an enormous room with odd corners and alcoves. There was no ceiling, just a vast sloping space that reached up into the rafters: a dark, high place, where a heavy curtain of dusty cobwebs swayed in the draught. The floor was uncarpeted, just bare boards with cracks between them, and knot-holes smooth and worn with age. There was an odd assortment of furniture: chairs with broken seats and tables with wobbly legs; the sort of pieces most people would have thrown away a long time ago.

Edward was immediately interested in the space under a skylight which David was using as a studio. There was an easel on which a half-finished canvas was propped, and a raised block for a model to pose on. The surrounding floor was covered by old sacks and newspapers on which stood jars full of brushes, tubes of paint like small squashed snakes, and all the other paraphernalia that an artist needed. Against the nearest wall leaned stacks of canvases, huge sketch blocks, and folders bursting with finished drawings.

Lily was drawn to a treadle sewing machine around which was heaped piles of coloured fabrics. Close by stood a tailor's dummy wearing a yellow satin petticoat stuck with pins.

'Come and meet Chris,' David said.

Lily and Edward had been so busy studying their surroundings that they'd forgotten the other occupant of the studio. But now they followed David over to an alcove and looked down at a tattered Victorian couch. It was heaped with brightly coloured cushions, and draped with a fringed shawl and a shaggy fur rug. There was such a tender expression on the artist's face that they both looked with curiosity at the strange figure reclining on the makeshift bed in the golden light from an oil lamp.

A foot hung over the end of the couch – a long, narrow foot from which dangled a fluffy pink slipper – and above that a bony ankle laced with blue veins. Lily's eyes travelled slowly upwards, taking in the emaciated body wrapped in a loose black silk robe. It was an oriental dressing-gown with wide sleeves and a wrap-around skirt, heavily embroidered with scarlet and gold chrysanthemums. The hands crossed almost innocently on the flat chest were as bony as the ankles, with long, thin fingers tipped with curved nails painted blood red. A head of long golden hair rested on the cushions, and the air was full of the smell of a heavy cloying perfume.

'Chris,' David said again. His voice was low and as gentle as a caress, leaving no doubt in Lily and Edward's mind. Even if they weren't married, David and Chris were certainly lovers.

The fair head moved and a pale face was turned towards them. Lily hadn't been sure what she was going to see, but she certainly wasn't prepared for the sight that met her eyes: a face as white as paper, with cheek bones from which the flesh seemed to have wasted away; faded eyes the colour of putty, ringed with black paint; and a large mouth the same colour as the fingernails.

'Let me help you.' David leaned over and lifted Chris into a sitting position. Then he pummelled the cushions into more comfortable shapes, and smoothed a pale lock of hair away from the creased forehead. 'Is that better?'

'Thanks.'

The voice was gritty, as if it was an effort to talk. Then Chris coughed, and the strain seemed to exhaust the thin body. The eyes closed and the body became rigid.

'Chris isn't feeling very well,' David said, stating the obvious. 'So I'll get the supper. There's some soup somewhere, and it won't take a minute to heat it up.'

The soup was tinned, but heated over a paraffin stove and served with lots of bread it was filling. There was also wine, even if it did taste of vinegar, and a splendid cake full of dried fruit and nuts. Lily found she was hungry, even eating in such strange company. She ate everything she was offered. She saw Edward screw his nose up in distaste at the watery soup and refuse a second helping. David ate with relish. Chris managed a few spoonfuls but then pushed the bowl away.

'I've had enough.'

David frowned. 'Some cake? It's Italian. I bought it in that special foreign shop.'

'Perhaps later.'

'Have you managed to work today?'

'I was too tired. I'll be better tomorrow.'

Lily helped David to clear the dishes and took the opportunity to talk to him in a low voice.

'Your friend is ill. Perhaps it would be better for Edward and I to find somewhere else.'

'No.' David carried a screen over to the far corner of the loft. Lily could see the outline of a brass bed piled with folded blankets. When opened out, the screen just fitted around the bed-frame. 'Chris can't do much, just a bit of sewing on good days. We need the company. Please stay.'

'All right. If you're sure.'

David smiled and his ugly face lit up with pleasure. 'The bed is comfortable; I'll leave you to make it up. Then you can be private.'

The frame sagged and the mattress was lumpy but Lily soon made the corner snug. She looked forward to crawling under the heavy blankets and curling up against Edward. At least the bed was a double so there was plenty of room for the two of them.

When Edward joined her he found her bouncing about in the middle of the mattress. She put out her arms to welcome him so he slipped out of his clothes and joined her. At last, Lily thought, at last the time seemed right for Edward to show his love. Surely, seeing the affection between the tragic couple whose home they were sharing would make him aware that she was a woman – a woman who loved him.

'Edward,' she said softly, stroking his bare arm. 'I love you.'

'I know you do.'

Those weren't the words of a lover but Lily wouldn't be put off.

'I love you,' she said again, dreamily, 'as much as David loves Chris.'

'Be quiet!' Edward said roughly. Lily thought it was because he was afraid her words would carry across the room.

'I'm not ashamed of loving you,' she said firmly. 'If I was Chris, wouldn't you still love and care for me like David does?'

'Be quiet, Lily,' Edward hissed in her ear. 'Haven't you realized yet that Chris is a man?'

CHAPTER ELEVEN

Follow the dream

Lily couldn't sleep. She stretched out on her back in the bed and wriggled her toes impatiently. She was warm, the mattress was reasonably comfortable, and Edward was sleeping peacefully beside her, she could hear his even breathing, and yet sleep eluded her. She couldn't forget the words he'd spoken – the words that had shocked her into wakefulness – 'Haven't you realized that Chris is a man?'

How could he expect her to understand? She'd lived a sheltered life in the village of Lenton: first at Valley Farm, and then at Ring House under the protection of James and Elizabeth Thomas. Her visions of love had been learned from the books she'd read. The prince in love with the princess, the hero in love with the heroine, and everybody living happily ever after. She'd never heard of two men falling in love with each other or heard of the word homosexual; but although she was frightened by what she was imagining, she needed to know.

'Edward,' she said softly, and turned on her side to shake his arm. 'Are you awake?'

'What is it?' He groaned and pulled away from her, leaving a gap in the blankets down which the cold air tunnelled.

'I want to ask you something.'

'Can't it wait until the morning? Go to sleep, Lily.'

Love, Lily thought, wasn't as straightforward, or as easy as she'd imagined. Love had made her persuade Edward to run away with her. She had him now; he was all hers. And yet the back turned towards her seemed suddenly that of a stranger. At Dot and Arthur's house he'd behaved towards her like a big brother, caring and protective. Although they'd introduced themselves as newlyweds it would have been impossible to consummate their pretend marriage, even if Edward had wanted to. The beds had made it impracticable.

Tonight Lily had hoped things were going to be different. She wasn't ugly, was she? And she'd tried to make herself as attractive as possible. Lily knew she was better looking than Betty Thomas, and Edward had been prepared to marry her. But now everything was spoiled.

Lily's spirits had lifted at David Titmus's friendship towards them. After all, he was an artist, and they were renowned for living unconventional lifestyles. She'd even been prepared to accept Chris, feeling sorry for the frail figure, and admiring David for his love and devotion. It had seemed romantic.

It was true that Chris had made her feel slightly uncomfortable. Now Lily knew why. Chris was short for Christopher, not Christine. David's lover was a man and their feelings for each other were unnatural. The revelation had killed Lily's desire. If Edward had tried to make love to her, the new knowledge would have made her sick.

She turned away and curled up on the very edge of the bed, screwing her eyes tightly shut and willing sleep to bring her temporary relief. But the loft was bright with moonlight. The skylight was uncovered and the beams illuminated every detail of her surroundings, outlining everything with silver. She could bear it no longer. Pushing the covers away Lily slid onto the floor, wrapping her arms across her chest for warmth.

'What's the matter?'

She'd disturbed Edward. He was propped on one elbow, his hair shining almost white in the moonlight, and his eyes heavy with sleep.

'I need the lav.' It was the only explanation Lily could think of.

'Mind you don't fall down the ladder.' Edward buried his face back in the pillow.

'I'll be careful. I won't be long.'

But she was talking to herself. A faint snore followed her as she pushed the protecting screen aside and stepped out into the vast expanse of the loft.

It seemed less spacious to Lily now that she had to pick her way around the furniture. She was afraid of disturbing the sleepers, but luckily her bare feet made no sound on the floor. Although there was plenty of light there were also plenty of shadows, and when she bumped into the yellow-clad tailor's dummy she jumped back in fear, thinking for one moment that it was the ghost of a human being.

She'd forgotten the exact location of the trapdoor, and found herself stepping carefully through the cluttered portion of the loft which David used as his studio.

Lily knew next to nothing about art. She liked a pretty picture, and admired the water-colours that Edward painted. But then, loving him as she did, she would have admired anything he created. But David Titmus was a recognized artist. His pictures were exhibited in the town's gallery, so must be considered good by the experts, although Lily hadn't cared at all for the leaping black and white figures. Now, confronted by David's easel, she was curious to see what else he was capable of. She positioned herself in front of the canvas and studied the half-finished painting.

It was a large picture about five feet by four. The background was the loft, because Lily recognized the painted red drape as a faded chenille curtain hanging across one corner. The figure stretched on the fur rug in the foreground was nude. She wasn't surprised as David had told them in the gallery that he painted girls with clothes on, and also without. The head was Chris: the long, thin face with its sunken cheeks, the faded blue eye-sockets outlined with black, and the unnaturally fair hair. Chris might be a man, but the painted body was undoubtedly female. The torso was thin; but the artist had ignored the male genitals and had rounded the hips and buttocks, and given the model generous breasts. Although the painting wasn't finished, Lily could see that the artist was trying to portray what he wanted to see, rather than the truth. Or had Edward made a mistake?

Lily turned away, feeling uncomfortable. She felt as if she'd been looking at something private, something that should be hidden and not put on public display. She backed away and almost stumbled against the corner of the couch on which the lovers were sleeping. Although it was in a shadowy corner she was now used to the light, and her eyes were drawn to the couch and its occupants.

They lay side by side with the fur rug drawn over them. David's ugly face looked younger in repose, his rough hair tousled against the cushions. One strong arm was around his companion's shoulder, and the fair head was resting trustingly in the crook of David's arm. They looked so peaceful: like grown-up versions of the Babes in the Wood. Lily made no sound, but her presence must have disturbed Chris, who sighed, stretched, and turned over. Lily stepped back quickly.

For a moment she thought she was falling. Her right foot was waving in space feeling for a foothold, and the heel of her left foot had nothing to rest on. Alice must have felt like this just before she fell down the rabbit-hole. But in Lily's case it was only the trap door. Losing her sense of direction, she'd almost tumbled down it by mistake.

The lavatory was in a yard behind the bakehouse, she remembered from an earlier visit. But would she be able to find it in the middle of the night? She gripped the top of the ladder with both hands and lowered herself carefully down into the darkness. Her foot found a rung, but she wished she'd stopped to put on her shoes, or slip a coat on over her nightdress. There were goose-pimples on her bare arms, and her feet were so cold she could hardly feel them.

She was halfway down the ladder when she thought she heard a sound below. It was a thud, as if someone had blundered into something, or knocked something over. Was someone lurking down there waiting to pounce on her?

'Who's there?'

Lily spoke softly, and clung to the ladder as if her very life depended on it. No answer; just the swirling darkness she was suspended in. She was just about to continue her descent when she heard the quick scampering of feet and immediately thought of rats.

Rats! There'd been rats at Valley Farm when she was a child. They'd lived in the barn and outhouses, and sometimes Moses had put poison down or set the dogs on them. Lily hadn't been afraid then: they'd been part and parcel of her life. But the years at Ring House had softened her, and now the thought of those rough grey bodies and evil bloodshot eyes terrified her.

But perhaps it wasn't a rat. Perhaps it was only one of the stray cats she'd seen sitting like statues on the garden walls of the cat's-creep. There was no reason to be frightened of a cat.

How could she tell? Cat or rat, they both seemed equally terrifying to Lily as she clung halfway down the ladder, suspended between the trapdoor and the ground. A decision had to be made and she made it. She decided to return to the warmth and safety of her bed, and the comfort of Edward's sleeping body. Better to lie in discomfort, with a full bladder for the rest of the night, than face the unknown waiting down below.

Just a few steps upwards and her shoulders were through the trapdoor. Then her body was through, and she was kneeling on all fours on the floor. She stood up and a hand came out of the shadows and gripped her arm.

Lily jumped. She was too frightened to scream, but her heart pounded and for a moment she thought she was going to faint. The hand was like a vice and she couldn't pull free. Then in the moonlight she saw the scarlet talons and looked up into Chris's ashen face.

For one so ill the grip was surprisingly strong. The pale eyes had taken on a new life as they stared into Lily's. Now is the moment, she thought: now she could find out for sure. Was Chris a man or a woman?

The thin body was still wrapped in the black silk robe, but the top had slipped over one shoulder pulling the neck open to the waist. Lily saw a bare chest and the outline of sharp bones through the papery skin. But there was no hair; although that wasn't proof because Edward's upper body was also hairless. The nipples were pale, almost colourless, and flat against the surrounding flesh. Even an emaciated female would have some form of swelling to indicate breasts. David's painting had been generous to this part of his lover's anatomy.

'Where have you been?' The voice was faint, the breathing laboured.

'To the lavatory. Let me go. I'm cold, I want to go back to bed.'

'Let me warm you.'

Two thin arms slid around Lily's shoulders and pulled her into an embrace. She thought she would faint because of the heavy aroma of perfume. Chris's face was only a few inches from her own.

'No!'

Lily struggled. The long switch of fair hair hanging to Chris's shoulders slipped sideways showing that the scalp was as good as bald. Lily had suspected that it was a wig. But was it worn to disguise the fact that illness had robbed Chris of a normal head of hair, or was it part of a female impersonator's costume? The face came towards her again and Lily knew the truth. No woman would have that dark shadow on her upper lip and around her chin. No man could truly hide the fact that he needed a shave.

Shock gave Lily added courage. She pushed Chris away. Careless of her passage she stumbled across the floor of the loft, narrowly escaping furniture standing in her way, and threw herself onto the bed. Without waking, Edward flung his arm out; Lily slid her cold body under the blankets and snuggled against his warmth. But it was a long time before she stopped trembling and her breathing became normal.

Lily woke to a feeling of peace and the delicious smell of bacon frying. For a moment she thought she was back at the Millers' house, and waited for the thump of Arthur's newspaper dropping through the letter-box or Dot calling up the stairs that breakfast was ready. But then she opened her eyes and saw the vast expanse of the raftered ceiling and memory came flooding back.

The nightmares of the night before quickly dwindled in the daylight, particularly when she turned and saw Edward's face so close beside hers on the pillow. His grey eyes were open and he was looking at her, a smile on his lips. Lily found herself smiling in return. She felt closer to him than at any time since they'd run away.

'Where did you disappear to in the night, Lily? I woke up and found I was alone.'

'I had to go out the back. Did you miss me?'

'Of course. I always miss you, Lily.'

She was reassured by his words. Everything was going to be all right. He needed her; now all she had to do was find a job so she could earn enough money for them to live on. David Titmus would advise them. He would recognize Edward's talent and tell him how to go about forging a career for himself as an artist.

'Come on,' she said. 'Let's get up.'

Pushing back the blankets Lily looked about for her clothes. She'd undressed hurriedly the night before and they were in a tangled heap by the side of the bed. The strap of her petticoat snapped as she pulled it over her head, and she sat on the edge of the bed holding the bodice of the garment over her bare breast.

'Bother! I've broken a strap. Have you got a safety pin?'

'Sorry. Come nearer. Perhaps I can fix it for you.'

Lily leaned towards him, and shivered as his hands touched the skin of her shoulder.

'Keep still. I'm trying to knot it.'

His voice was low and there was a tone in it Lily had never heard before. A husky tone, serious, almost pleading. She looked up and couldn't believe the passion she saw in the grey eyes staring into hers. Then she felt his hands trembling, and knew that he was seeing her as a woman for the first time.

'Don't you want any breakfast?' she asked, for something to say. 'Aren't you hungry?'

'Yes. But not for food.'

Lily knew what he meant and her heart leapt with joy. Instead of tying the strap he pulled the bodice down, so that her left breast sprang free and hung small and perfect before him. He put out his artist's finger and touched the pink nipple with wonder, and watched it harden into a bud. Then, as if mesmerized, his lips brushed the tip as if he was afraid of hurting her.

Lily's body ached with longing. She felt something deep inside growing like a seed planted in fertile ground, ready to open its petals and blossom like a flower whose time is right. She waited breathlessly, her lips impatient for the pleasure of his lips pressed to hers. But before her patience could be rewarded there came the rattle of plates from the other side of the screen, and David's cheerful voice calling to them.

'Come on, you young lovers. Hurry up if you want any breakfast.'

The spell was broken. Edward turned away reaching for his clothes, leaving Lily trembling on the bed. Ignoring the broken strap she pulled on a blouse and cardigan, tugging a button off in her haste. She felt embarrassed and her cheeks burned, as if David must have known what was going on behind the privacy of the sheltering screen.

Not daring to look at each other they left their corner. The artist, in his paint-daubed overalls, with his woolly hat still pulled well down over his hair, was crouching over the stove from which the tantalizing smells were drifting. He looked up and grinned at the sight of them.

'There's a folding table in the corner – but there's no cloth. I used the last one as a paint-rag. I'm afraid we rough it.'

Lily fetched the table, just managing to avoid a chair in her path. It was only at the last minute that she saw that it was occupied and thought David had an early morning visitor. She could see a grey trousered leg and masculine shoe resting on the floor.

'I'm sorry,' she said. 'I didn't know there was anyone there.'

The man in the chair turned to look at her and Lily started back. It was Chris without a doubt – but what a changed Chris. Lily had to bite her lip to stop herself uttering an exclamation of surprise.

He'd changed from the feminine garb of the night before and was dressed in a suit over a white shirt. Knotted loosely in the open neck was a silky blue scarf. Gone was the golden wig. He wasn't bald as Lily had thought; but his hair, almost as pale as Edward's, was cut very short and slicked down. His face without the paint and powder was almost handsome, although it was gaunt and sunken. He was the picture of some latter-day poet or composer, in the last stages of consumption.

'It's ready,' David said again. 'And getting cold.'

No explanation was made about Chris's change of attire. David seemed to take the transformation as perfectly natural. In fact the only evidence that she hadn't imagined things was the way Chris was peeling the false red nails from his fingers. He laid them carefully in a row on the arm of the chair before joining his companions.

'I shall work this morning,' he announced, refusing bacon, but accepting a cup of sweet coffee made from a bottle of flavoured essence.

'It's one of his good days,' David explained.

He watched with a tolerant smile as the thin figure sat itself at the sewing-machine. The footplate clanked up and down rhythmically, and the needle purred, eating its way into the cloth as a strip of green material was fed into the machine. Lily was mesmerized by the strange apparition and had to tear her eyes away when David spoke.

'I beg your pardon?'

'I was just asking Edward about his plans.'

'He hasn't got any. At least nothing definite.' Lily wiped the grease from her plate with a piece of bread and popped the tasty morsel into her mouth. 'But he paints lovely pictures. He's really clever.'

'I'm sure you think so.' There was a faint emphasis on the 'you' and Lily felt she'd spoken out of turn. She buried her nose quickly in her cup and let her dark hair swing forward to hide her confusion. 'But I was asking Edward.'

'I just want to earn a living by painting,' Edward said simply. 'It's all I've ever wanted to do. But I don't know if I'm any good.'

'Of course you're good,' Lily burst out. Then she quickly covered her mouth with her hand. 'I'm sorry,' she said. 'But he really is. He painted a picture of the Queen's Head: that's a public house. The landlord paid him for it.'

'And would you be happy spending your life painting public houses, Edward?'

'I don't know,' Edward admitted. 'I've mostly only painted country scenes before. You see, I've never had any lessons. My father wants me to concentrate on medicine, but I hate the idea of being a doctor.'

'Well, the first thing we have to find out is if you have any talent.'

'Of course he has,' Lily said. 'I told you, Edward's very clever.'

'Lily!' Edward said in a gentle reproving voice. 'Don't keep interrupting.'

'I'm sorry. But David must see how important it is to us.'

'I do see.' David was smiling and didn't look at all cross, so she continued.

'You've no idea what I've made him give up to follow his dream.'

'I think I can imagine – you must both tell me sometime.' He rubbed his forehead thoughtfully before adding, 'Have you brought any pictures with you?'

'We left a lot of things behind; but I've got my sketch book. I carry it with me everywhere.'

'Can I see it?'

'Of course.'

Edward put down his plate before fetching the book of sketches from his suitcase. He handed it to David who flipped through the pages idly. Lily waited impatiently for a verdict. She knew the book by heart: there were drawings of her as well as buildings and country scenes. But she was no judge of quality and just hoped that David would be as impressed by them as she was.

'Is that all?' David closed the book and handed it back. His face gave nothing away.

'Yes.' Even Edward had expected some comment and looked disappointed.

'I need to see how you work with a brush. There's everything you need over there.' The artist indicated the jars of brushes and half-used tubes of paint jumbled around the easel. 'I have to go out. Help yourself.'

'Thanks. What shall I paint?'

David jumped up from his chair so sharply that he almost overturned it. 'I shouldn't have to tell you that. An artist should see a picture in everything. Even a dirty plate can be an inspiration.' He waved a greasy plate around as if he was about to throw it at Edward. 'Find your subject – something you feel passionate about – and then paint it.'

Edward still looked uncertain so Lily put her hand on his arm as if to reassure him. 'You can do it,' she said softly.

David was busy pulling on his army jacket and yanking the woolly hat further down over his ears. 'He needs to be left alone,' he said to Lily curtly. 'No one can work with a woman leaning over them.'

'I won't disturb . . .' Lily started to say.

'No, you won't! Because you're coming with me. Get your coat.'

He gave Lily no time to argue because he was already lowering his bulk through the trapdoor. Grabbing her coat and whispering a quick 'Good luck' in Edward's direction, she followed. But she didn't catch David up until he was halfway down the first flight of steps known as the cat's-creep.

'Where are we going?' Lily tried to match her stride to his, but had to take two steps to his every one.

'Shopping'

'What for?'

'Food. We have to eat, you know.' David stopped suddenly and swung round. Lily had to move quickly to prevent herself running into him. 'Can you cook?'

'Of course.'

At least she knew she was on safe ground as far as that was concerned. They couldn't expect elaborate fare cooked on the top of a paraffin stove, and that was the only cooking appliance she'd seen in the loft. Unless one of the bakers ovens on the ground floor was still in working order. But Lily wasn't going to worry about that; she'd cooked for Matthew in pretty primitive conditions at Valley Farm, so she was sure she'd be able to cope.

David stopped at a row of comfortable looking shops, the sort of small businesses that the elderly favoured. First he bought bread, crisp and still warm, and then paused outside a butcher's.

'What do you fancy – mince or steak?'

Luxury indeed; but Lily was still a bit wary of the cooking and decided to play safe. 'How about some mutton? I could make a stew; and if you buy some suet we could have dumplings.'

'Sounds wonderful.'

So they bought the meat and a lump of suet; and then potatoes, onions and carrots in a greengrocer's. Lily was a bit worried about the amount of money David was spending. After all, they'd paid nothing yet for board and lodging and couldn't expect to be kept for nothing. But when she broached the subject David waved her aside.

'Don't worry,' he said. 'I'm banking on you making it worth my while.'

Lily didn't like to ask what he meant. She hoped he was thinking about Edward, and his reward would be the discovery of a gifted painter.

'You're very kind,' she said. 'Let me carry something.'

But David wouldn't hear of it. He filled his coat pockets with the vegetables and the rest of the shopping was packed into a carrier bag which he swung from his hand.

He saw Lily shiver as they turned a corner and the bitter east wind whipped around their legs. 'You look cold,' he said. 'I think you deserve a coffee.'

He led the way to a coffee house by the railway station. It was a small, cosy place and his rugged frame looked out of place in the dainty interior.

'Come on,' he ordered, as Lily paused to read a card propped in the window. 'It's my treat.'

But Lily hadn't been reading the prices. The card was an advertisement for a waitress and she needed a job. Her heart lifted, but then it sunk as she read the small print underneath: it said Experience Preferred. Even so, when Lily watched the young woman in the black dress and crisp white apron carrying trays to the tables, it looked so easy that she knew she'd be able to do it if only they'd let her try. Before she had a chance to discuss it with David he was giving the girl their order.

'Two coffees, please. Would you like a cake, Lily?'

'Can I have a doughnut?'

The coffee was the real thing, not from a jar of essence, and the doughnuts were oozing with red jam and sprinkled liberally with sugar. Lily tried to eat daintily but it was impossible. When David bit into his doughnut and a blob of jam trickled down his chin he put out his tongue to catch it, and winked when he met Lily's eye.

She relaxed. Warm, and full of sweet stickiness, she licked the last crystal of sugar from her fingers and smiled at her companion.

'I've finished,' she told him childishly. 'Shall we go?'

'In a minute. I want to talk to you.'

'What about?'

'Edward.'

Lily looked up quickly. The smile had gone from David's ugly face and his thick lips were set in a determined line. She guessed that he was going to tell her something that she wasn't going to like. She steeled herself for the worst.

'What about Edward?' David didn't answer so she continued nervously. 'I wonder how he's getting on? It's kind of you to let him use your things. He won't let you down. He works very hard when he gets the chance.'

'Lily . . .' David put his big rough hand over hers and squeezed it slightly to soften the blow. He knew he was going to hurt her but didn't know how to make it easier. 'Hard work isn't enough.'

'What do you mean?'

'I mean that Edward isn't going to make it as an artist.'

'But he's very talented – everybody says so.'

'And who is everybody?'

'Well, me – and his father – and . . .'

'Edward told me his father wants him to be a doctor. Perhaps he understands him better than you do.'

'Edward paints lovely pictures,' Lily said firmly. Her eyes had turned a deeper colour with annoyance, and their sooty lashes were moist with unshed tears. 'He painted one of a cornfield that was really pretty.'

'Real art isn't about painting pretty pictures.' David was studying Lily across the table and there was pity in his eyes. He hated to be the one to disillusion her. 'Did you like those pictures of mine in the gallery? The black and white ones.'

'No!' Lily said passionately. David had torn her to the quick by daring to criticize Edward's work: the work that she believed in, and he'd given up so much for. 'I thought they were horrible. All angry lines, and no colour anywhere.'

'An American collector has offered me two hundred pounds for one of them.'

'Two hundred . . .'

'I'm not boasting, Lily. I just want you to see that art isn't just about painting pretty pictures. Oh, Edward's competent enough to enjoy a lucrative hobby. To earn a few pounds here and there painting pubs and cornfields. But I could tell by looking through his sketch book that that is about all he will ever be able to do.'

'And yet you egged him on. You asked him to paint a picture while we were out. What were you going to do – have a good laugh at the result?'

'Lily, don't sound so bitter. I didn't want to hurt him. Can't you see? I wanted to tell you first – to explain. You will know how to break it to him.'

'What do you want me to do – destroy his life? You have no idea what I've made him give up to follow his dream.' Lily got up from her seat so quickly that the cups rattled noisily in their saucers. 'Anyway, I don't believe you. You haven't given Edward a chance. If what you say is true why did you encourage him? Why did you let us stay?'

'It was you I was interested in, Lily,' David admitted in a small voice. 'I was never interested in Edward. As soon as I saw you – your white skin and wonderful hair, and your eyes – I knew I wouldn't rest until I'd painted your picture.'

'Never!' Lily ignored the pleading look on David's face and headed for the door. She flung it open, and let it crash to behind her.

CHAPTER TWELVE

Harry

'Mind how you go, young lady!'

'Sorry.'

Lily had been running along the pavement, not looking where she was going. She was so angry she thought she would burst. How could David not share her opinion of Edward's talent? She'd taken it for granted that the reason he'd offered them a temporary home was because he really thought it would be worth while helping Edward achieve his dream.

It was a shock to find that his motive had been a purely selfish one. He needed a model to pose for his horrible pictures and thought she wouldn't be able to refuse. Well, she had refused. If he wouldn't help Edward, she wouldn't help him. He could throw them out into the street for all she cared. They'd manage somehow. She was a survivor, wasn't she? She'd get a proper job and keep them both – anything to prove David Titmus wrong.

The burst of anger carried Lily away from the railway station and past the shops, until she found herself in a different part of the town. She leaned on a low wall to get her breath back and shivered. Her scarf and gloves were back on the café table and her fingers felt numb. Even blowing on them didn't bring them back to life. She turned the collar of her coat up.

The wall surrounded a small park which, in the summer,

would be quite attractive. There were bare stumps of bushes sticking out of the soil that would be covered in roses at the right time of the year. The grass was well kept, although on this January day it was covered by a film of hoar-frost. A bed of wallflowers had survived the winter and some were even trying to bud. In a few weeks' time they might even open and give the park its first hint of rusty colour.

Thinking it might be more sheltered on the other side of the wall, Lily jumped over. She ignored a notice telling the public that they were not allowed to walk on the grass and began to stroll around the garden.

It was quiet and deserted and soon she felt better, as long as she didn't think too deeply about her problems. But Lily wasn't a brooder, she was a fighter. When she reached a brick well under a crab apple-tree she stopped and looked down into the water. Another notice told her that it was a wishing well. If she threw a penny into the water she could make a wish. It didn't say if the wish would be granted.

A penny was all she had. A lucky penny she carried in her pocket and had polished to a high brilliance. She pulled it out and looked at it. It was worn and smooth with age and had the old queen's head stamped on one side. Matt had given it to her years ago and she'd never had any reason to spend it. But today she needed luck and was prepared to gamble with fate for it.

I wish – I wish . . .' she said softly, and bent over the water, staring at her reflection in the dark recess of the well.

She saw a pale face looking up at her, with a cloud of dark hair. Why on earth did the artist want her to model for him? She didn't even consider herself pretty. The face she saw was that of a child: young and serious, with straight hair hanging in an unfashionable style. Lily couldn't see anything about herself that was worth painting. Of course, Edward had drawn her many times, but that was different.

The coin dropped from her fingers and Lily listened for the plop as it met the water. But the well was deep and muffled the sound; all she could see was the ripples it made and the way it distorted her reflection.

'I wish . . .' she started again. 'I wish . . .'

'I think I know what you're going to wish for.'

Lily jumped round. She'd been so sure she was on her own

and hadn't heard David's footsteps on the gravel path. He was standing behind her, a gentle smile on his big ugly face.

'Go away,' Lily said. 'I don't want to listen to you any more.'

'Because you don't want to hear the truth.'

Lily turned back to the well and looked over the rim sadly. 'You've made me waste my penny – and it was a lucky one.'

'Here, have one of mine.'

David felt around in his pocket and selected another penny. He spat on it and rubbed it on his sleeve before holding it out. Lily paused only a moment before accepting it and tossing it into the water boldly.

'I wish,' she said in a loud clear voice. 'I wish that David Titmus was wrong.'

'So do I,' David said, and dropped a second coin into the well. 'But I wish that Lily would be brave enough to admit it if he's proved right.'

'Never!' Lily said, but she didn't sound quite so confident. Although she was still upset, she couldn't keep up the feelings of anger that David had aroused, and he looked so truly sorry as he held out the scarf and gloves he'd rescued from the café.

'You'd better put these on before you catch cold.' Lily did as she was told and even managed a grateful smile. 'Come on, let's walk.'

They walked side by side through the deserted park and out onto the road. They were both deep in their own private thoughts and it was Lily who eventually broke the silence.

'I have to believe in Edward, you know.'

'Because you love him?'

'Yes. And because I've made him give up so much. He was going to get married to this girl who wanted to be a doctor's wife. But he'd never have been happy.'

'How can you be so sure of that?'

'Because I know Edward. I've loved him for years – ever since we were children together.'

'This other girl – the one he was going to marry. Have you ever thought how she must be feeling?'

'Oh, Betty will get over it.'

'I hope so.'

'Whose side are you on?'

Lily's eyes flashed again, and David put his hand gently on

her arm to calm her. He was only just beginning to get used to her quick changes of mood.

'Why, yours, of course. I don't know this Betty, do I? So how can I side with her?'

'Everyone else will. Her parents and Edward's father. It must be awful being jilted at the altar; and I made him do it.'

Suddenly Lily was crying, big sobs that shook her slender frame, so that David had to take her in his arms to console her. He handed her his own handkerchief, which was none too clean, and watched as she mopped her eyes and blew her nose. With his keen artist's eye he couldn't help appreciating the beauty of her violet eyes when they were swimming with tears.

'Better?'

'Yes.' Lily sniffed, but managed a watery smile. 'I only did it because I love him.'

'I know.'

'What do you mean: you know? What do you know about love?' Lily had stopped in the middle of the pavement. David took the opportunity to fish a crumpled packet of Craven A cigarettes out of his pocket and light one. It gave him time to think. 'Well?' Lily asked impatiently, waving away the smoke that was blowing in her face.

'I love Chris,' David said at last. He started to walk again, so fast that Lily had to run to keep up.

'That's not proper love.'

'So, Miss Know-It-All – and what is proper love?'

'Love between a man and a woman.'

'There are other kinds of love; and they can be just as strong and important.'

'What you're talking about isn't natural.'

'It's natural to us.'

Lily fell silent. A man and a woman could fall in love with each other and show it by physical union; something two men could never do. They couldn't have children either, and surely that was the ultimate proof of two people's love for each other. She glanced at David sideways and the half-smile on his face annoyed her. She suspected him of being amused.

'You're laughing at me.'

'No, I'm not. Oh, Lily, you're so young and innocent. How can I make you understand?'

'You can try.'

'All right.' David lit a second cigarette from the stub of the first one. 'Tell me how you fell in love with Edward.'

'It was at first sight. I just saw this boy with the fair hair and grey eyes and knew I would love him for ever.'

'The same thing happened to me,' David said softly. 'I'd been married, but she left me for another man. I was very unhappy and came down south to start a new life. A friend took me to this bar in Brighton. It was run by homosexuals, but I wasn't one. Like you I thought it was unnatural. I walked into this room and saw a young man sitting on a high stool at the counter; he had a glass in his hand and he was laughing. He wasn't particularly good-looking, but he turned and smiled and I fell in love with him there and then.'

'And it was Chris?'

'Yes.'

'But he dresses up in women's clothes.'

'Only sometimes. So do lots of men. But you don't fall in love with someone because of their clothes.'

'That's true,' Lily said thoughtfully. 'I'd still love Edward if he was wearing sackcloth and ashes.'

'That's exactly how I feel about Chris.'

'And does he feel the same way about you?'

'No.' David paused. He wasn't sure how much Lily would be able to understand. How could he expect her to? A young, inexperienced girl, on the threshold of life. He would try and explain, open her eyes gently. 'He has other lovers as well as me. He's never promised to be faithful.'

Lily didn't understand. She looked up at David, a puzzled expression on her pretty face. 'I can see how two men could perhaps fall in love with each other – but not how they can be lovers.'

David smiled: he was glad Lily hadn't asked a direct question. He changed the subject quickly. 'Come on. Here's the cat's-creep. Race you to the top of the first flight.'

Lily beat him easily; but then she had the advantage of nimble feet and free arms, while David was loaded down by the morning's shopping. They both paused for breath on the first landing.

'Chris and I used to race each other to the top before he became ill.'

'What's the matter with him?'

'Cancer. He's dying.' David spoke simply, as if it was a fact of life and not something to make a fuss about. 'Oh, he knows, and he's accepted it. He's passed the stage of being angry. He has his good days and his bad days, as you saw – but there are more bad ones than good these days.'

'But can't the doctors do anything?'

'He doesn't want them to. It would change our lives.'

They took the next flight of steps easily and were nearly at the top before Lily spoke again.

'Why on earth do you live right up here? I mean, if you can earn all that money with your pictures you could afford to live somewhere nice down in the town. It would be better for Chris, surely? He must feel cut off and out of things in Monkey Walk.'

'And just how long do you think a couple of homosexuals would survive down in Pierhaven amongst the retired population? They have conservative views and ideas.'

'They're human beings. They'd want to help.'

'Help to shut us away, you mean.'

'Why would they want to do that?'

Lily had stopped to stroke a beautiful ginger cat sitting like a statue on a garden wall. His big golden eyes glazed over with delight. Perhaps he'd been the intruder of the night before; padding on silent paws around the bakery, looking for mice.

'Don't you realize, Lily, that what we're doing, and the way we live, is against the law? We'd be sent to prison if we were reported.'

'Oh!' Now Lily did understand and her heart turned over with sympathy. 'I see now.'

'I don't care about myself; it's Chris that matters. I have to look after him for as long as I can – or as long as he wants me to. Up here we can live undisturbed – everybody here has something to hide. Until they drive us out, or bulldoze the buildings, we can live our lives in peace.'

'And then?'

'And then it's in the lap of the gods – which is a funny remark for a lifelong atheist to make.'

By now they'd reached the top of the steps and were walking side by side along Monkey Walk towards the bakery. They passed empty houses with planks nailed over their windows, and walls with broken plasterwork. Dead houses that nobody wanted any more, that had once been people's homes. Lily slowed down outside a particularly dirty fronted house and put her head on one side.

'What's the matter?' David enquired.

'I can hear music. Someone's playing the piano.'

'Oh, that'll be Harry.'

'Harry?' Lily looked around. Surely they didn't have a neighbour; and if they did, where did he live?

'Harry Smith – or the Last Noel. Don't look so puzzled, he lives in there.'

'But it's so dirty. Nobody could live in a place like that.'

'I expect lots of people wouldn't believe you if you told them we live in the loft over a bakery. Don't you see, that's exactly what we want them to think. In this way they'll leave us alone.'

'Who is this Harry? What did you call him – the something Noel?'

'That's just a joke.' David drew Lily aside, and dropped his voice as if he didn't want to be overheard. 'He plays the piano in clubs and bars along the coast and tries to ape Noël Coward: you know, he uses a cigarette holder and tries to speak with a clipped accent. Someone said he tried to change his name once but it wasn't allowed.'

'But why the Last Noel?'

'You've heard the carol "The First Noel"? Well, we call him the Last Noel. Not in his hearing, of course.'

'Is he any good?' Lily was thinking about Dot Miller tinkling out 'I'll Get By' on her parlour piano.

'He gets plenty of work so he must be. Here we are.' David pushed open the double doors of the bakery and stood aside for Lily to go first. 'Are you going to tell him, or shall I?'

'Tell who what?' Lily was still thinking about their next door neighbour Harry Smith, and hadn't realized that David had changed the subject.

'Tell Edward that he'd better go back to doctoring.'

'We mustn't, David.' Lily grabbed hold of the artist's sleeve. 'It would break his heart.'

'Then the sooner he knows the sooner it'll start to mend.'

'I can't do it.'

'All right, I'll do it for you.' David could see by the expression on Lily's face how worried she was, so he said, 'Perhaps you'd better keep out of the way.'

'I think that would be best.'

'You can console him later.'

'Yes.' Lily still looked worried. Edward would need more than consoling after David had dealt the blow to his dreams. She had no idea how he was going to take it.

'You can run an errand for me while I talk to him,' David said. 'I was telling you about Harry.'

'The pianist?'

'That's the one – Harry Smith. Well, he borrowed our big saucepan weeks ago, and you'll need it if you're going to make that stew. It'll give you a chance to meet him and introduce yourself.'

Lily looked at the blank facade of the house from where she could still hear the faint tinkling of the piano. 'There doesn't seem to be a bell,' she said.

'He doesn't need one. The door's never locked. You just walk in. Don't look so worried, Lily, he's harmless – he won't bite.' And David left her there standing in the middle of Monkey Walk, braving herself to invade the uninviting house next door to the bakery.

David was right: the door wasn't locked, in fact it wasn't even properly latched. It swung forwards at the slightest pressure and Lily stepped inside.

She found herself standing in a gloomy passage. The wallpaper had once been pale green and decorated with bunches of flowers, but it was now peeling and stained with damp. There was no proper floor-covering, only a strip of torn linoleum, giving further impression that the house was unoccupied. But Lily knew better. The music was louder now and seemed to be coming from a room at the back of the house: a room whose door stood slightly ajar.

Lily found herself walking on tiptoe so as not to interrupt the musician. Overcome by curiosity, she held her breath and tapped lightly on the door. The lilting melody didn't stop, it just slowed slightly before picking up the rhythm again.

'Come in, Evie.'

Lily pushed the door open and stepped into a room so bright and warm that she was dazzled and found herself looking around in wonder. After the passage the room, though small, was sumptuously furnished. A thick brown carpet covered the floor and matching curtains hung at the window, which was screened by frilled ivory coloured lace. There were armchairs padded with soft cushions and dainty china ornaments. The walls were covered with pictures, and mirrors that reflected the light from a central mantle that was switched on although it was still daylight. But what dominated the room was the piano: a dark wood grand at which the musician sat.

Harry was a small man in his forties, with receding hair and fat jowls. What hair remained was cut short and slicked back with brilliantine so that it looked black and wet. From the corner of a slack pink mouth hung a cigarette from a short stubby holder. A wisp of grey smoke spiralled gently upwards. He wore a velvet smoking jacket with silk lapels. His fingers continued to dance over the keys: fat fingers with carefully manicured nails. A lazy smile played around his lips as he glanced at the girl standing in the doorway.

'Do you recognize this tune?' he asked.

'No, Mr Smith.'

'Call me Harry.'

'No, Harry. And my name's not Evie.'

Harry Smith stopped playing. He removed the holder from his mouth and contemplated the end of the cigarette before tapping the dead ash into a brass ashtray on top of the piano.

'George said he was going to send me a girl called Evie Marshall. Of course we would have had to change her name to something more memorable; but George said she had a remarkable voice.'

'I'm sorry,' Lily said, although she didn't know why she was apologizing. She was just about to back out of the room when Harry stopped her.

'Don't be sorry, young lady. You're a looker anyway. If you can sing you might do. What's your name?'

'Lily.'

'Nice, but a bit tame, You need something a bit more romantic. Lilith – what do think about that? Lilith Fortune.'

'My name's Lily, Mr Smith,' Lily said firmly. 'And I'm not changing it. Anyway, I've only come to collect the saucepan.'

Harry almost dropped his cigarette. But he was known for not letting events shake him, so he gripped the holder firmly and stubbed out the glowing end. Then he turned to Lily, a carefully posed smile on his face.

'Saucepan! What's all this about a saucepan?'

'I need it to make a mutton stew. David said he lent you his saucepan and you haven't returned it. David Titmus, the artist, who lives over the bakery next door.'

Light seemed to dawn at last on Harry's puzzled features. 'Oh, that David!' he said. 'That saucepan!'

'Can I have it please?' Lily tried not to sound too impatient. 'Only it's going to take hours cooking a stew over an oil stove – particularly with suet dumplings.'

'Particularly with suet dumplings!' Harry mused. 'Of course you can have the saucepan, young lady. I expect it's in the kitchen somewhere. I seem to recall using it only yesterday to boil some fish. Through there – help yourself.'

Lily followed his pointing finger and found herself in a most insanitary kitchen. The oven was covered with splashes of black burnt grease, and the draining board was piled with unwashed crockery. In the sink were some dirty saucepans. The largest, a chipped enamel vessel, smelled of fish, and a few transparent scales were stuck to the bottom.

Guessing this must be the pan she'd come to collect, Lily rinsed it out as best she could under the cold tap, and then, as she didn't like the look of the tea towel, shook it dry. She could hear Harry playing the piano again; a soft romantic tune that she'd heard on the wireless but couldn't put a name to.

'This must be the one,' she said, holding out the pan so that Harry could see. 'I'll go now.'

'Back to the attic to make your mutton stew?'

'Yes.'

'Go on then. If you can't sing you're no use to me.'

That was a challenge and Lily knew it. She was always ready for a challenge. Dot Miller had seemed to think her voice was all right, otherwise she wouldn't have taken so much trouble. Brandishing the saucepan and shaking back her hair, Lily walked to the piano and looked steadily at Harry.

'But I can sing.'

'Come on then, show me what you can do.' He began to play again, a soft enchanting melody that Lily didn't know. To encourage her he sang a few bars in a low husky baritone. 'A room with a view . . . and you . . . What's the matter?'

'I don't know it.'

Lily felt foolish and tears were filling her eyes. She had no idea how attractive she looked at that moment, even to a worldly man like Harry Smith.

'How about this then?' He changed the tune to something she did know.

After a tremulous start Lily started to sing: 'I'll see you again . . .'

When they reached the end of the song Harry stopped abruptly. He inserted another cigarette into the holder and lit it thoughtfully. His eyes never left Lily's face.

'Well?' she asked at last.

'Put down that saucepan. Take off your coat and we'll do it all over again.'

They did it twice more and still Harry didn't seem satisfied. Lily tried to remember everything Dot had taught her: standing properly, taking deep breaths, and trying to relax. After all, it was worth doing her best. Hadn't David told her that Harry played in clubs and bars? If he was looking for a soloist, and Evie Marshall didn't turn up, he might offer her a job.

But Lily was disappointed. After getting her to sing 'I'll See You Again' for the third time, Harry suddenly got up from the piano stool, stubbed out his cigarette, and seemed to forget Lily was still in the room.

'Would you like me to sing something else?' she ventured. 'I know "Ave Maria" and "The White Cliffs of Dover".'

'I'm sure you do,' Harry said. 'But if you sing them in the same fashion you sing Coward you're wasting my time.'

'I'm sorry. Won't you tell me what I'm doing wrong?'

'Won't you tell me what I'm doing wrong?' He mimicked her cruelly, and now Lily couldn't prevent a tear escaping although she wiped it away quickly. She wasn't going to cry in front of this horrible man. 'You're doing everything wrong. Look at you for a start! You stand there like an innocent choir girl. You've got about as much passion as a nun. Of course, there are some men who are turned on by childish innocence – but not the sort of men I play to. Go home, little girl, you're wasting my time.'

'No!' Lily snapped out the word so that Harry had to look at her again. Suddenly he saw that the young girl standing in front of him had potential, hidden depths that would stir a male audience. It was something about the way she held herself: proud and tall, with eyes like liquid violets, and beautiful dark hair falling over her face. 'How dare you talk to me like that! You asked me to sing in the first place, and if you don't like my voice you only have to say so.'

'But I do like your voice, Lilith,' Harry said. He crossed the room and stood in front of Lily looking her up and down in a professional way. She felt like a slab of meat in a butcher's shop; any moment she expected him to pinch her to see how much flesh there was on her bones. 'But you've got a lot to learn. How to move – how to dress – and how to wear your hair. When you've mastered all those things come back, and I might have a job for you.'

'No, thank you,' Lily said proudly. 'I wouldn't work for you if you begged me. And I've got a job.' Her voice faltered slightly at the deliberate lie. 'I've got a job as a waitress at the café by the station. I start tomorrow. And once and for all my name is Lily, not Lilith' And grabbing her coat and the saucepan she swept from the room.

'You'll be back, my dear,' Harry said softly. He resumed his seat at the piano and began to play 'I'll See You Again' as if he meant it.

Lily had mastered the climb into the loft and now found it easy, even carrying the saucepan. She half-expected to see a downcast Edward, disappointed at the news David must by now have broken to him. Instead she found him at the easel painting steadily, with a look of concentration on his handsome face.

Chris was sitting in a chair, his head bowed in his hands. He didn't look up at Lily's entrance. David was unpacking the shopping in the corner by the stove. Lily felt nervous. She could feel something in the atmosphere that foretold trouble. She walked across the room and spoke to David softly.

'I've got the saucepan.'

'Good.'

'What's the matter?'

'Nothing.'

Lily picked up an onion and began to pull the brittle peel from the dry bulb. 'Did you tell Edward?' she said at last.

'No.'

'Why not?'

'I couldn't.' David guided Lily away out of earshot. 'I'm afraid there's been a bit of an upset while we were out.'

'You'd better tell me.' Lily perched on the edge of a table and steeled herself for the worst.

'It was Chris's fault. I told you what he's like. And your Edward's a very good-looking young man.'

'You don't mean . . .?' Lily turned a horrified face to David.

'He made a pass. The sort of pass Edward couldn't pretend not to understand. Edward hit him. I don't blame him; I expect he was just as shocked as you were when I told you. Luckily Chris is pretty weak these days so nothing came of it. But Edward was in such a state that I couldn't tell him the bad news about his painting.'

Lily got down from the table. She felt calmer than she would have thought possible in the circumstances. 'We'll leave tomorrow,' she said.

'No.'

'Edward will insist.' Lily began to tear the onion to pieces almost as if she wasn't aware of what she was doing.

'No, he won't. Stop doing that.' David took Lily's hands and turned her to face him. 'I felt responsible and didn't know how to make amends. So I admired his painting, and said if you both stayed on I'd give him a few lessons.'

'But David, you said he's no good.'

'I know.' The artist smiled wryly. 'But he doesn't know that, does he?'

CHAPTER THIRTEEN

Doctor Butler gets a letter

'Put the tray down on the table, Mary.'

'How many times do I have to tell you, James, that Mary has left us?'

'So she has. Sorry, dear; I keep forgetting.'

'And I suppose you also keep forgetting to get around to replacing her?'

There was something in the tone of Elizabeth's voice that made James Thomas look up from his paper. It was unusual for his wife to speak so sharply, at least to him, but he'd detected a certain impatience in her tone several times lately.

'I haven't forgotten, but nobody wants to go into service any more. Perhaps you could do your bit and ask around the village.'

'I have.'

'Nobody interested, I suppose?'

James didn't like being involved in domestic matters: it usually ended in trouble. He always got the blame if anything went wrong. Of course Ring House was a big place for one woman to care for. It was also old-fashioned, with none of the newfangled labour-saving devices that were coming onto the market; but that wasn't his fault. Money was tight these days. He'd lost a packet on his last gamble on the Stock Exchange, and in consequence had had to sell some land. If things didn't improve he might have to sell something else. The row of cottages in Lenton came to mind; but the occupants were farm workers he'd known for years and they wouldn't take kindly to a new landlord. The answer would be for the tenants to buy their own homes, but on their small wages he didn't think that would be possible. Of course, there was always Valley Farm . . .

Elizabeth handed her husband a cup of tea and brought his attention back to the matter in hand.

'There was a woman who came making enquiries.'

'Oh!' James looked up with interest. 'You should have snapped her up. We can't afford to be fussy.'

'But James, she was completely unsuitable.'

'One of the village women, I suppose. Do I know her?'

'Edith Crow.'

'Oh!'

'She came right up to the front door, and had the effrontery to ask for you. When I found out what she wanted I soon sent her about her business.'

'How is she?' James returned to his newspaper. His head was bent over the crossword so Elizabeth couldn't see his face.

'She looked terrible, James: so thin, not much better than a skeleton. And although there was a cold wind blowing she was wearing an old cotton frock and no coat. Things must be awful at Valley Farm.'

'I heard things got a bit better when Lily was there last year.'

'Don't mention that girl's name in my presence, James. You know how it upsets me.'

'We can't ignore the facts.'

'And what are the facts? Tell me that. You bring that girl into my house, she gets every care and attention, and how does she repay us? She breaks our daughter's heart.'

'Hearts mend with time.'

'Well, Betty's won't. She spends most of her time upstairs crying over that wretched dog she bought Edward. And when she does come down all she seems interested in is food.'

'I did notice how much weight she's put on.'

'She must have some consolation until she meets someone else.'

James sipped his tea, a wry look on his face. 'How will she meet anyone else if she won't go out?'

'Give her time, James. Unless you can suggest an alternative.'

'Well, there's Peter Jackson.'

'James!' Elizabeth slammed her cup down on the tray so fiercely that the teaspoon jumped out of the saucer. 'The Jackson boy is our gardener!'

'All to the good, I should have thought,' James said calmly. 'He's a clean-living, hard-working young man, who Betty's known all her life.'

'You said the same about Edward.'

'Edward was different. His father was a family friend and we took things for granted. I think we were partly to blame.'

'So it's my fault now, I suppose?' Elizabeth began to stack the cups onto the tray a little bit too energetically.

'Not yours, Elizabeth: ours. Love can play strange tricks on young people, and it's not for us to judge. Perhaps Lily and Edward are really suited? Perhaps she really loves him?'

'Nonsense! She's a common little slut, and she was jealous of Betty's good fortune. No one even knows who her parents are, although I've always suspected it was some gipsy woman passing through who abandoned her at Valley Farm. If you hadn't interfered none of this would have happened. Betty would be a doctor's wife now, living in the Butlers' house in Lewes, and we'd be looking forward to becoming grandparents.'

Elizabeth sounded near to tears and James felt sorry for her. Funnily enough he felt sorrier for his wife than he did for his deserted daughter. After all, Betty was young – not quite twenty – and she still had plenty of time to look around and choose another man for a husband. But she wasn't likely to if she didn't pull herself together.

James folded his paper carefully and got to his feet, brushing an imaginary speck of dust from the shoulder of his jacket.

'Are you going out?' Elizabeth asked, recognizing the signs.

'Just for a walk.'

'If you're going into the village you could call at the vicarage. Mr Plummer has some magazines he's promised to lend me.'

'I thought I'd walk as far as Valley Farm. See if Moses is about. Sound him out as to his financial position. Offer to sell him the farm. Of course I'll have to talk it over with the solicitor first, but I can see how the land lies.'

'By the look of Edith they haven't got two halfpennies to rub together,' Elizabeth said ominously.

'That doesn't mean anything. I was reading in the paper about an old man who was found dead. He was a sort of recluse and everyone thought he was penniless; but when they searched his house they found the mattress on his bed stuffed with five pound notes.'

'I doubt if they'll find one five pound note at Valley Farm,' Elizabeth said. 'Probably no mattresses either.'

Promising to be no longer than an hour, James set off. It was a spring day, early in May, and the countryside had just woken up after its long winter sleep. Now that he was getting older James found he had more time to appreciate the changes in the seasons. Where once he'd depended on Bert Jackson to ferry him everywhere, he now liked to drive himself, or more often walk and look around him.

Jackson had died suddenly just after Christmas: a premature death that had hit his family hard. But his son Peter was all ready to step into his father's shoes, and James was happy to allow the widow and her sons to remain in the cottage at the gate of Ring House.

As he walked down the drive James spotted Peter Jackson busy trimming the lawn around the edge of a herbaceous border. There were still late daffodils waving their wrinkled golden trumpets, but they would soon have to give way to summer bedding plants.

The young man got up from his knees, and pulled his cap off in a gesture of old-fashioned courtesy learned from his father.

'Good afternoon, Peter.'

'Afternoon, Mr Thomas.'

'Everything all right?'

'Just a few moles.' Peter indicated some little hummocks in the smooth turf. He scratched his head so that his unruly hair stood on end. 'They're always a nuisance at this time of year.'

James tapped the ground with the tip of his cane. 'Noise, that's what they can't stand. My father used to sing to them. Tone deaf, he was, and the moles couldn't stand it.'

Peter grinned. 'I might try it if I can't think of anything else.'

'I think Mrs Thomas would like some flowers for the house.

A few daffs and catkins would do.'

'I'll see to it.'

James began to walk away, and then turned back as another thought struck him. 'How's your mother, Peter?'

'Coming along nicely. Of course we all miss Dad, but she doesn't let it get her down. She says she has to keep cheerful for Billy's sake.'

'Sensible woman. How old is your brother now?'

'Billy's twelve. We heard from Mike yesterday. His wife's expecting a baby later in the year.'

'So you'll be an uncle?'

'Yes. And how's your Betty, if you don't mind me asking?'

'She'll live.' James frowned. 'Your mother could teach her a thing or two. I'll tell her you asked.'

'There are bluebells down in the bottom field. Perhaps she'd like some for her room?'

'I'll ask her.'

James continued on his way, a thoughtful expression on his face. The Jackson boy would make some girl a fine husband, but he supposed Elizabeth was right about his unsuitability for Betty. Pity, though: it might have been the answer.

He pushed the problem of his daughter to the back of his mind and strode along, swinging his cane, in the direction of the farm. He'd partly misled his wife about the reason for his visit, and felt slightly guilty. He did want to get rid of the place, and the ideal solution would be for the Crows to take it off his hands. Then if it fell down around their heads it wouldn't be his responsibility. But he couldn't see Moses Crow paying out the money. The man always behaved as if the property and land belonged to him – his right for living there so long – and he would expect to get the place as a gift. James might be generous, but he wasn't stupid.

The other reason for his visit was that he hoped to see Matthew, or even Edith. One of them might have heard news of Lily.

Lily! His Lily from the Valley. He'd never forgotten his first sight of the grotesque little figure pushing the cart full of holly; and then the frail waif he'd discovered in the barn, with the awful clothes, matted hair, and burned foot.

Pity had been his first emotion. But even then he'd been aware of the child's attraction; particularly when she'd looked at him with her beautiful eyes. Brave, trusting eyes – the colour of violets. Once when he was a boy he'd found a clump of violets hidden away in a damp ditch. He'd been searching for a lost marble at the time. He'd lifted up a rotting branch and seen the delicate flowers looking up at him. Their petals were heavy with moisture, but they were almost unbearably beautiful. In the same way he'd rescued the dirty little child from Valley Farm, and to his astonishment found she was a jewel.

James had never told anybody how he felt about Lily. How could he? Elizabeth wouldn't have understood and Betty would have been understandably jealous. Once he'd discussed it with his friend John Butler, Edward's father. John had agreed that Lily was an attractive little thing who would turn men's hearts when she was older.

'Send her away,' John had advised. 'Isn't there some orphanage that would take her? Train her for a position in service. You've done more than enough for her, and girls like that are never grateful.'

James couldn't help wondering if John was remembering his words now that Lily had run away with the doctor's own son. You couldn't blame him if he felt the Thomas's were responsible. But he'd never said a word, although his sad face was a constant reminder. He, as well as Elizabeth and James, had looked forward to a marriage between the two families. But James's protégée had put an end to that.

The gate across the entrance to the farm was still broken, and James stepped through the gap onto a path that was riddled with muddy ruts. He picked his way carefully, trying not to splash the toes of his highly polished shoes. The path was narrower than he remembered, but perhaps that was an illusion, because the undergrowth on either side had been allowed to run wild.

Perhaps he should go back. This was a place where visitors weren't encouraged, and he had no idea what sort of reception he would receive.

James was still trying to make up his mind when he had the feeling that he wasn't alone. He looked around but there was only waving greenery. But then he saw a figure walking towards him, coming from the direction of the farmhouse. He couldn't make out the features because the figure was still a long way away, but it was certainly a man. A large man – Moses Crow.

He put up his hand, partly to shade his face against the sun to enable him to see better, and partly to hail the oncomer. He wouldn't broach Moses about Lily, but he would bring up the subject of the farm.

But James had no opportunity to do either because at that moment a single scream rang out from somewhere close by among the trees, a shrill sound that was enough to chill the blood of the bravest.

Both men froze; but the farmer came to life first. Instead of continuing in James's direction he branched off to the left towards the sudden noise, and it was only then that James saw that under his arm Moses was carrying a shotgun.

James had no idea what was going on, but suspecting that someone might be hurt he followed the burly figure thrashing through the undergrowth.

He soon lost him. Moses knew the woods around Valley Farm like the back of his hand, whereas James Thomas felt like a stranger on his own property. But the noise Moses made striding along, his huge boots kicking aside debris and snapping branches, made him easy to follow. It was only a few minutes before he found himself standing at the edge of a clearing.

In front of him Moses stood blocking his view, legs apart, and head thrown back like an Old Testament prophet. The back of his neck was red and rough, the skin bulging over the collar of his twill shirt. His hair was almost white and unkempt, as was the beard on his jutting chin. He seemed to be looking at something on the ground. James moved sideways to get a better view.

'Move aside and I'll finish him off.'

'No, brother. His leg's broken – I'm going to set him free.'

And then James saw Matthew Crow kneeling on the ground beside a rusty old trap. It was an ancient contraption made of metal: a cage holding a spring that released a deadly pair of jaws that would catch small animals in its teeth. If the teeth caught the animal's neck it would be killed instantly, but if a limb was trapped it would suffer a lingering death, either from its wounds or more often starvation. James had never seen anything like it before, and guessed it was a home-made invention. A rabbit was lying in the cage, its back foot caught between the cruel teeth. It was motionless; the scream its last wild protest.

'Stand aside, Matt,' Moses said again.

'He's not dead. He's still breathing.'

'All the more reason to finish him off. Stand aside.'

But Matthew didn't move. His fingers fumbled wildly at the trap, but they either weren't strong enough to open the jaws or didn't know the secret of the mechanism. While he was still struggling to release the animal two shots rang out.

The first was a warning. It hit a boulder by the side of the trap and split it in two. Fragments flew through the air like shrapnel, making Matthew shriek almost as loudly as the rabbit. The second shot hit the beast between the eyes, making it jerk like a marionette before it fell back motionless.

Matthew was lucky not to be badly wounded. As it was there was blood as well as dirt on his hand where he'd been hit by a fragment of stone. He looked dazed, shell-shocked. His eyes stared at his brother, and James thought he was going to say something. But seeing the onlooker Matthew turned and slunk away into the bushes, bent almost double like an old man, cradling his injured hand against his chest.

'Why did you do that?'

Moses looked at James as if he was seeing him for the first time. His face was red, and purple veins stood out upon his forehead.

'Vermin are best dead,' he said expressionlessly.

'Rabbits aren't vermin.'

James remembered the little white animal Betty had kept in a hutch years before. It had been a pretty little thing with long ears and a wrinkled nose like pink velvet. To him rats and mice were vermin – but then he wasn't a farmer.

'They damage the crops and breed too easily.'

'I suppose you're right,' James said sadly. 'But there must be easier ways of getting rid of them.'

'Short and sharp, that's the way we've always done it at Valley Farm.' Moses lifted the gun to his shoulder and aimed at a magpie flying overhead. 'Bad luck,' he said. 'Bang!' and then, without pulling the trigger he swung the barrel round so that it was pointing directly at James. 'I've also been known to fire at trespassers.'

'I'm hardly a trespasser,' James said, trying to keep his voice even. He's mad, a little voice inside was saying. I'd better humour him or I might end up stretched out beside the wretched rabbit.

'This is my farm. Anyone coming on my land without permission is a trespasser.'

'That's what I want to talk to you about: Valley Farm.' James waited, but as Moses didn't speak, although he seemed to have caught the big man's attention, he carried on. 'We're not young men any more; and I don't know about you but I'm beginning to feel my age. Of course, I hope I'll be spared for a good few years yet. But if anything should happen to me I don't want Elizabeth to have any muddles to sort out.'

'What's that to me?'

Moses had relaxed slightly, and although the toe of his boot was prodding the bloody head of his victim, at least the gun was now safely tucked away under his arm.

'Well, I thought you might be feeling the same. Matthew's a bit of a responsibility, I'm sure – and then there's Edith . . .'

'What about Edie?'

'Elizabeth says she's not looking too well. I have a proposition to put to you that might set your mind at rest about the future.'

For a moment it looked as if Moses was going to turn on his heel and walk away, but then he seemed to change his mind. 'Let's hear it then,' he said roughly.

'I'll sell you and yours the farm and then you'll have security for life. Of course I'll need to get advice, but I was thinking about something in the region of five thousand. But I'm open to offers. I can't be fairer than that.'

'Fairer! What do you mean, fairer?' With giant strides Moses was closing in on his companion, and the look on his face was one of rage. 'What's fair about putting a price on a man's home and livelihood?' The shotgun was beginning to point in James's direction again, and Moses was steadying his finger on the trigger. 'Get off my land before I blow your head off!'

'Do you want anything, Betty?'

'No. Go away.'

Elizabeth stood outside her daughter's closed bedroom door

and sighed. Then she turned the handle and slowly pushed it open. Princess, the little dog, immediately jumped down from the foot of the bed and ran towards her, yelping frantically.

'She wants to go out.' Elizabeth picked the creature up and dangled it at arm's length. She wasn't a dog lover and only put up with Princess to please Betty.

'Can you do it, Mummy? I don't feel well.'

Betty was lying fully dressed on the bed. Her navy skirt and pink blouse were creased, and her stockings were wrinkled around her ankles. She'd undone the skirt because it was uncomfortably tight: she'd put on a lot of weight since Christmas. On the bedside table was a half-eaten bar of chocolate and a scattering of biscuit crumbs. She leaned over and broke off a square of chocolate and popped it into her mouth. Then she lay back licking her fingers.

'Staying in bed and eating sweets won't make you feel any better.'

Betty pouted. 'I'm not in bed; I'm just resting. Do you begrudge me a few crumbs of comfort?'

'More like half a pound,' Elizabeth said darkly. 'It's a beautiful day: why don't you take Princess for a walk?'

'Walking tires me – and I might meet someone I know.'

'You can't hide away from the world for the rest of your life.' Betty frowned at the tone of her mother's voice. Up until now she'd been treated with sympathy and understanding. In fact she'd been quite enjoying the fuss. 'People will think you've got something to hide.'

'You mean, they'll think that it's my fault? Oh, Mummy!'

Betty burst into noisy sobs. No one looks their best when they're crying, and it certainly did nothing for her. She hiccupped as she groped under her pillow for a handkerchief.

'I didn't say that; but you know what people are.'

'It was all Lily's fault. I never liked her.' Betty blew her nose and wiped her eyes.

'I know, darling. I did warn your father but he wouldn't listen. You know what a soft heart he has. But Edward's a sensible boy, and I'm sure he'll see the error of his ways in time.'

'You mean, you think he'll come back to me?'

'I'm sure he will. When he sees Lily in her true colours he'll realize what he's missing.'

'I hope so.' Elizabeth's words had cheered Betty up and she looked slightly more hopeful.

'In the meantime you must be a brave girl. Just remember that you've done nothing wrong, and when he comes back you can tell him so.'

'You mean I shouldn't forgive him?'

'Not too quickly. Then you'll be building strong foundations for the future. Nicely brought up young women know the potential of guilt in a relationship. If they use it wisely it can turn out to their advantage.'

Betty wasn't sure that she quite understood the logic behind her mother's words. All she knew was that if Edward came back she might decide to forgive him – but she'd also see that he paid for it for the rest of his life. After all, that was only justice.

'I think I will get up,' she said, not too enthusiastically.

'Good. It doesn't do any good sitting around feeling sorry for yourself.' Elizabeth made for the door, the little dog still dangling over her arm. 'I could do with some help downstairs if you feel like it. The jobs are endless now we've no servants. You could start by washing up the tea things: that isn't too strenuous.'

Betty frowned and almost changed her mind. Her idea of getting up had been to change from her bed to the sitting-room sofa and have her mother wait on her; not start doing housework like a village girl.

Slowly she got up from the bed and sat at the dressing-table, inspecting her face in the mirror. She didn't like what she saw, and started to look for a pot of rouge and choose a lipstick. If she took long enough repairing her face her mother might have done the washing-up herself.

Elizabeth opened the garden door for the little dog and watched it waddle its way across the lawn, sniffing excitedly. There were so many new smells that it took ages, and in the end she had to call it back into the house quite sharply. In the front hall she found James unbuttoning his jacket and propping his cane in the umbrella stand.

'You haven't been long, dear,' she said, holding out her cheek for a kiss. 'I didn't hear you come in.'

'I met John outside. I've put him in the library.'

'Oh, dear.' Once upon a time Elizabeth would have been

delighted at a visit from Doctor Butler, but not since his son had jilted Betty so cruelly. 'What does he want?'

'I think he's had some news. I'll call you if it's important.'

James closed the library door in his wife's face. She felt slightly indignant. If the news was to do with the runaways surely she had a right to know. She pressed her ear to the panel of the door but it was too solid for any sound to escape. When her husband opened it from the inside she almost fell into the room.

'Sorry, James,' she said quickly, regaining her usual composure. 'I wondered if you wanted any tea?'

'I've given John a whisky. But you'd better come in: he wants to talk to both of us.'

John Butler was sitting in a hard-backed chair with his drink on the table beside him. He'd taken off his trilby hat and gloves, but still wore his coat, as if he had no intention of staying long. He looked older and was almost bald now, but his pink face was kindly, and the Thomas's had never held his son's behaviour against their friendship. They waited patiently.

As he didn't speak Elizabeth prompted him. 'Have you some news?' she asked.

'I've had a letter.' John fumbled in his pocket and produced a cheap envelope.

'From Edward?'

'No.' Taking a piece of paper from the envelope he unfolded it slowly. 'It's from someone signing themselves D. Miller, from an address in Pierhaven. Perhaps you'd care to read it.'

James took the letter from his friend and glanced at it with interest.

'Read it aloud,' Elizabeth said.

'"To whom it may concern,"' James started. '"Last December I let a room in my house to a young couple who said their names were Edward and Lily Butler. They said they'd just got married and were on their honeymoon." Be quiet, Elizabeth,' he said quickly as his wife let out an exclamation. '"My husband and I liked them very much, and as I missed my son who's away from home they became part of the family. They stayed with us for several weeks and I grew fond of them, but one day while my husband and I were at the pictures they packed their things and left. They didn't owe us any money, or anything like that. In fact they were very generous. But the reason I'm writing is because they seemed so young and I'm worried about them. I would have contacted you before but didn't want to interfere. I know Edward wanted to be a painter, in fact he sold some pictures while he was here, but they didn't tell us anything else about themselves. I found this address on some paper they'd thrown away before they left. Of course it might be nothing to do with them. But if it is, if you're a relative or friend of theirs, I thought you might like to know their whereabouts. Hoping you don't think I'm poking my nose into someone's business that I shouldn't. Yours, D. Miller (Mrs)" That's all,' James ended. 'So they did get married.'

'They only told this Mrs Miller that they were married,' Elizabeth said sharply. 'Knowing Lily, she could have been lying. She was a dishonest little thing.'

'Don't exaggerate, dear,' James said mildly. 'Well, at least we now know where they went from here.'

'The thing is,' Doctor Butler said, 'what do you want me to do about it?'

'It is rather vague, you must admit. They stayed at this address at Pierhaven, but they aren't there now. We're no better off really.'

'I don't know about that. I feel it needs following up; but I wanted to talk it over with you two first.' John took the letter back, folded it, and returned it to the envelope.

'My advice is to leave things alone.' James looked from his wife to his friend. 'I can't see any good coming from going after them. And if we did find them and forced them home I can't see it helping matters. Let them come to terms with their actions in their own good time. That's my opinion for what it's worth.'

'James, how can you!' Elizabeth burst out. 'Upstairs your only daughter is breaking her heart and you want to leave things alone!' She turned to Doctor Butler. 'What do you want to do, John?'

'I want to find out if my son is all right. If he's well and happy. So I'm going to take a trip to Pierhaven to look for him.'

CHAPTER FOURTEEN

Where's my son?

'Two plates of sandwiches, Lily. One cucumber and one sardine and tomato.'

'Yes, Mrs Gunn.'

'And cut the bread thin, and don't forget to remove the crusts. You know how fussy the Women's Institute ladies are.'

'I know, Mrs Gunn.'

Lily bent to her task in the little kitchen behind the café. It was a difficult job. If she sliced the bread too thin it broke into holes as she spread the butter, and if she cut it thick the ladies complained. The only way was a sort of compromise: not too thick, not too thin.

She'd been working at the café by Pierhaven's railway station for three months now. The advertisement had been for a waitress with experience, but Lily had got the job by lying. She'd been desperate, and lying seemed a small price to pay. So she'd made up an elaborate story about helping her imaginary mother at a tearoom in Lenton. As the Gunns had never been there they couldn't prove her a liar.

Anyway, Mr Gunn had interviewed her and he had an eye for a pretty face. He didn't even ask for cards or references. His wife was a bit of a tartar so the girls didn't stay long, and he paid their wages in cash straight from the till.

Lily had proved herself to be a good worker. She learned

quickly, was popular with the customers, and was always cheerful. Mrs Gunn thought she was a bit too cheerful, particularly towards the men, and kept a beady eye on her. But Lily didn't mind dirty jobs and seemed to like washing up and scrubbing the kitchen floor. Not many of the girls welcomed that, preferring to preen themselves around the tables in their uniforms. But Lily was game for any job that paid her.

Another thing Mrs Gunn didn't care for about Lily was her appearance. She looked too good. The black dress became her, showing off the whiteness of her skin, and the frilly apron accentuated the smallness of her waist. Under the full skirt she always wore two crisp petticoats so that her dress swung like a bell around her shapely legs as she walked. On her dark hair perched a little starched cap. Mrs Gunn made her tie her hair back but it did nothing to detract from her looks, in fact it made her neck appear longer. People stopped to admire the proud way she carried her head.

Mr Gunn thought Lily was charming and hoped she'd stay with them for a long time. His wife wasn't so sure. In the meantime Mrs Gunn kept a watchful eye on the situation and waited for Lily to make a mistake.

'Shall I do the cakes now?' Lily asked.

'No. I'll do them. You watch at the window, and give me a call when you see them coming.'

Mrs Gunn chose one of her best plates. She lined it with a paper doily before arranging on it a tempting selection of cakes. First there were triangles of Victoria sponge with a filling of her own home-made lemon curd, the darker yellow flecks of yolk showing that she hadn't beaten the mixture long enough, but sandwiched in the cake no one would notice. Then there were wedges of swiss roll, and biscuits to give the customers a choice.

While her employer was busy Lily took up her position in the window. Her job was to watch for the four Women's Institute members who always called in for tea after their weekly meeting.

There were plants hanging inside the glass obscuring her view, as well as a piece of lace curtain which she pulled partly aside. The church hall was in a turning that ran beside the station entrance and the ladies should appear at any moment. Then Mrs Gunn would fill the teapot, while Lily carried the cakes and sandwiches over to the table in the corner that had a reserved card propped on it. It wasn't necessary that afternoon as there were no other customers but they always reserved the table from habit.

A train must have just arrived because a few passengers were spilling out onto the forecourt. One was a dapper little man in a dark coat and hat, who looked up and down as if he was a stranger in Pierhaven. He started to walk across the road in the direction of the café, and there was something about his walk that Lily found vaguely familiar. But at that moment the four ladies she was watching for came bustling into view and in their eagerness almost knocked the visitor over.

'They're coming,' Lily called.

She left her position in the window to help Mrs Gunn who knew the ladies by name. To Lily they were just numbers: starting with the tall thin one who was Number One, down to little fat jolly Number Four.

'Have you got any ham?' Number Three – who had hair of an unnatural colour set off by large hats – asked, peering under the corner of a cucumber sandwich.

'I'll ask Mrs Gunn.'

But Mrs Gunn said she hadn't, although Lily had seen some wrapped in greaseproof paper in the larder.

'Pity.' Number Three pouted, as if her afternoon was spoiled by the lack of ham sandwiches. 'I suppose I'll have to make do with sardine.'

Four cups of tea were poured: one black, one strong and sweet, one medium strength with one sugar, and the last so weak it resembled washing-up water. The cucumber sandwiches weren't very popular and Lily was glad because often Mr Gunn would let her take leftovers home with her. Mrs Gunn wasn't quite so generous, but as she complained that cucumber gave her heartburn she might be glad for Lily to have them. The cakes were handed round and were a great success.

'This sponge is delicious,' trilled Number Two. 'I must ask Mrs Gunn for a list of ingredients.'

'It's not the ingredients that count,' Number One said. 'It's how you beat it. Most people don't beat it long enough.'

'Why bother to bake cakes when these are so delicious,' giggled Number Four, cramming half a piece of swiss roll into her mouth and washing it down with a mouthful of tea. 'More tea, Lily dear.' She held out her cup. 'We've all finished.'

Lily loaded the four cups and saucers onto a tray and carried it into the kitchen where Mrs Gunn was refilling the pot. Behind her she heard the door open and the warning bell tinkle.

'We've got another customer,' she said.

'Go and see what they want,' Mrs Gunn instructed. 'I'll see to these.'

Groping for the order-pad and pencil that swung from the belt of her apron on a ribbon, Lily glanced around the café. The Women's Institute ladies were deep in conversation about the merits of a knitting pattern. At a side table a man was seated. He'd removed his hat, showing a balding head, and unbuttoned his coat. The hat, with a pair of gloves neatly folded over the top, was placed on the table in front of him.

'Is there any more of that delicious swiss roll?' Number Two called out as Lily passed by.

'I'll ask Mrs Gunn after I've taken this gentleman's order.'

'Or Victoria sponge. I've such a sweet tooth, you know.'

'Tea or coffee?' Lily asked. Her pencil was poised over the pad as she reached the gentleman's table. There was no reply so she repeated, 'Do you want tea or coffee, sir?' and found herself looking into Doctor Butler's eyes.

'Hullo, Lily,' he said quietly. 'I thought it was you when I looked in the window. Where's Edward? Where's my son?'

Lily was so surprised and startled that she stepped back suddenly. Unfortunately Mrs Gunn chose that moment to carry the tray of tea to the Institute ladies. Lily not only stepped on her toe but jogged her arm so that the tray and its contents shot sideways. The hot tea poured down Mrs Gunn's floral dress, and the cups and saucers landed on the floor.

'Now look what you've made me do,' Mrs Gunn said angrily.

'Sorry,' Lily muttered.

'Don't just stand there, girl, get a cloth and dustpan. You've broken at least one cup. And hurry up – what must this gentleman think of you?'

Lily had a pretty good idea what Doctor Butler was thinking. She fled to the safety of the kitchen, where her employer found her five minutes later.

'Lily, I told you to get a cloth. What has come over you?'

'Nothing.'

'I suppose I'll have to do it myself. Did you get the gentleman's order?'

'No.'

'Do it now – and look sharp about it.'

'No.'

Mrs Gunn's voice had been sharp but Lily's was even sharper. She needed time to pull herself together. She couldn't face Edward's father until she'd decided how much to tell him.

They were still sharing David and Chris's home over the bakery. As promised, the artist was giving Edward lessons, but neither of them had been brave enough to disillusion him about his future. He'd had a couple of commissions to design posters and had been proud of the few shillings the work had earned him.

Lily had been happy about Edward's successes, small though they were, thinking that they proved David was wrong. But lately she'd begun to compare the work of the two painters, and although she hated to admit it even to herself, Edward's work looked amateurish beside David's.

But it was not only the painting. Something else was wrong and Lily didn't know what it was. She just had a feeling that Edward wasn't happy. He seemed to have lost his earlier enthusiasm, and spent long hours brooding or going for lonely walks. Lily had tried to talk to him, to find out what was the matter, but he pushed her aside almost roughly, and declared that she was imagining things. At least there'd been no further trouble from Chris, and they were now used to the strange man and his occasional need to wear women's clothes.

Sometimes in bed at night Lily listened with curiosity to the two men on the other side of the screen. The noises they made frightened her. One night she heard Chris cry out 'Stop it, you're hurting me!' For some reason she couldn't understand Lily thought of her old friend Matthew Crow. Once when she'd been nursing him at Valley Farm he'd complained that his brother Moses sometimes hurt him. She hadn't understood and had asked if Moses beat him. She'd never forgotten his reply. 'There are worse things than beating,' he'd said, and when she'd asked what, he'd said,

'Things he does when he's been drinking.'

She didn't know why his words should spring to the forefront of her mind now. What connection could there be between Chris and David to remind her of Matthew and Moses Crow? There were still so many things she didn't understand.

'I told you to go and get the gentleman's order, Lily,' Mrs Gunn said again.

'I heard you.'

But instead of going back into the café Lily unhooked her jacket from the back of the door. It was no good, she couldn't face Doctor Butler. She would escape by slipping out the back way.

'Where do you think you're going?' Mrs Gunn stepped in front of the back door just in time. It's only half-past three. You're paid to work until five.'

'I'm sorry but I can't explain. I must go. I promise to make up the time.'

'You'll do no such thing.' Mrs Gunn's beady eyes were standing out from her head in anger. She'd employed some badly behaved girls in her time, but this was the first time one of them had taken it into her head to walk out in the middle of the afternoon without any explanation. It just showed how right she'd been not to trust Lily. Next time she'd insist on doing the interviewing. 'Take your coat off,' she snapped, 'and do as you're told, girl.'

It was the way Mrs Gunn said 'girl' that spurred Lily to action. All right, so she couldn't slip out the back way, but nobody could stop her walking out of the front door. Not even Doctor Butler. Lily turned on her heel, and buttoning her jacket and keeping her head down strode between the tables.

'And don't bother to come back,' Mrs Gunn called after her.

'We're still waiting for our second cups,' Number Three complained as she passed. Lily ignored her.

The bell in the doorway gave a warning jingle as Lily hurried into the street. She didn't hear John Butler call her name, or see him get up from his chair, pick up his hat and gloves, and give chase.

By the time she reached the corner of the road Lily had to stop to get her breath back, and it was only then that she realized she was still wearing her cap and apron. The black dress was her own: she'd bought it out of her first week's wages. But Mrs Gunn had loaned her the cap and apron.

She tore the cap savagely from her head, releasing her hair and scattering grips, and thrust it into her coat pocket together with the white apron. She'd think about returning them at a later date; the important thing now was to put as much distance as she could between herself and Doctor Butler.

Lily hadn't been walking for more than a few minutes when she heard footsteps behind her. Was she imagining things or was the doctor following her? At the next corner she broke into a run and dodged into a shop doorway. After a pause she saw a dark-coated and hatted figure pass by. It was Edward's father in pursuit.

By now Lily knew this area of Pierhaven quite well, so it was easy to double back and head for home via the backstreets. Even so she didn't relax until her foot was on the first step of the cat's-creep.

'Not so fast, Lily,' a voice behind her said. Lily spun round to find the doctor directly behind her. 'Did you think you'd given me the slip?'

'I don't know what you're talking about,' Lily said, wishing she could control the beating of her heart.

'Yes, you do – but I guessed I wouldn't be welcome. You were quite easy to follow, you know. I may not be as young as I was but I can still walk fast when I've a mind to, and my eyesight's good for a man of my age.'

'What do you want?'

'You know what I want, Lily. I want my son. I want you to take me to Edward.'

'Why can't you leave us alone?' Lily said with feeling. 'We've done nothing wrong.'

'Haven't you? What about poor Betty Thomas? She thinks you've done a lot of things wrong. Stealing her fiancé for one thing; and making him run away with you.'

'That's nonsense,' Lily snapped. She mustn't lose her temper, she told herself. Nothing good would come from losing her temper. 'Edward's a man, Doctor Butler, not a little boy. I didn't make him do anything. He came away with me because he loves me.'

'Oh, love! Betty loves him, but she was left at the altar. Can you imagine how she felt?'

'She deserved to lose him. She wasn't worthy of him and neither are you. Edward was unhappy, stifled, and you were forcing him into a career he dreaded.'

'He didn't give it a chance, Lily. If you'd kept your hands off him he'd have settled down quite quickly. He would have learned to conform, as I have over the years, and got this painting nonsense out of his head.'

'It's not nonsense.' Lily was almost in tears.

'No? So what is he doing now? Earning his living with his brush? If he's so successful why do you have to work as a waitress?'

'I wanted to work. I wanted to help him.'

John Butler looked sadly at the young girl poised like a wild animal before him. She looked so pretty with her hair blowing in the wind and a flush of colour staining her pale cheeks. She was twice as attractive as the Thomas girl and always had been. He could understand how his son had fallen for her. But he had to harden his heart; he mustn't start to feel sorry for Lily. He was here to find Edward and bring him home, and he mustn't forget that.

'Is he happy?' he asked.

'Of course. We both are. How did you find us?'

'Someone sent me a letter.'

Doctor Butler felt in his breast pocket and produced a crumpled sheet of paper which he held out. Lily took it gingerly and read what Dot Miller had written. Silently she handed it back.

'So you came to Pierhaven to look for us?'

'I came to Pierhaven to find Edward. To tell you the truth, Lily, I couldn't care less about you, although you seem to have charmed this Mrs Miller with your lies and evasions.'

'I didn't lie to Dot,' Lily burst out.

'You told her you were married. You told her you were on your honeymoon. I hope that that was a lie. It is, isn't it, Lily? You and Edward aren't married?'

'Not yet,' Lily admitted. 'But we will be.'

'We'll see about that. I showed this letter to my friend James Thomas, and he agreed that I should visit Pierhaven and rescue my son.'

'Rescue!' Lily laughed, but there wasn't much humour in the sound. 'You make me sound like an evil woman.'

'That's exactly what Mr and Mrs Thomas think you are.'

Doctor Butler had dealt Lily a blow and he knew it. She didn't care about Mrs Thomas's opinion of her, but James Thomas was different. He'd always been so kind, so generous, treating her like a daughter. Lily had always thought of him as the father she'd never had. She couldn't bear her old friend to think of her as evil.

'What do they want me to do?' she asked.

'The same as I want. Let Edward go. If you do that the Thomas's will forgive you. They might even offer you a home again.'

'If you think they'd do that you don't know them very well.' Lily faced Doctor Butler, and he couldn't help but admire the way she held herself proudly, even now. 'Betty will never forgive me, and her mother only wants me for a servant.'

'Now you're exaggerating.'

'I'm not. That's why I left in the first place and went back to the farm.'

'That's all in the past.' Doctor Butler smiled and put out his hand. Lily felt tearful but she wasn't going to cry in front of him. Perhaps later, when she was on her own. 'If you don't take me to Edward, or tell me where he is, I can soon find out for myself.'

'How?'

'This isn't a very big town and Edward isn't invisible. I shall find him eventually, so you may as well save me the time and trouble.'

'And if I do?' Lily almost choked on the words. 'What will you say to him?'

'I shall ask him to come home.'

'He won't.'

'I shall tell him I forgive him, and so does Betty.'

'He won't listen to you.'

'If you're so sure, Lily, why are you afraid?'

'I'm not afraid. Edward loves me, and if he has to make a choice – he'll choose to stay with me.'

They were brave words and Lily wanted to believe them. She pushed away her fears, and the image of Edward's face the last time she'd seen it: sad and a bit disappointed.

'Then we'll let him make the choice, shall we?'

Doctor Butler smiled again, and Lily allowed him to take her hand. There was nothing more she could do. She had to take the doctor to his son, and then it was up to Edward.

The climb would have daunted many a man younger than John Butler, but he took it in his stride. When they reached Monkey Walk he looked around with interest, and tried not to show his distaste at the dirty street and broken-down houses.

'We're here,' Lily said, stopping outside the double doors.

'It's a bakery,' Doctor Butler said in surprise, looking up at the faded lettering on the wall.

'Not any more. We live upstairs, but you'll have to climb a ladder.'

'Thank you, Lily, for bringing me,' John said. 'I know how difficult it was for you. Now, will you go first and show me the way?'

'I'd rather not.' Lily didn't want to witness the reunion between father and son. 'I'll stay out here if you don't mind. Can you find your own way?'

'I'll manage.' Doctor Butler pushed open the door and disappeared into the bakery leaving Lily standing helplessly in the street.

The ginger cat came strolling towards her, tail in air and golden eyes gleaming. Lily bent down to fondle him and he seemed pleased by her attention. She felt a tear trickling down the side of her nose. Needing reassurance, and the cat being the only living thing in sight, she hugged him tightly. He didn't seem to mind when a tear dropped on the top of his furry head.

'Edward would never leave me, would he, cat?' she whispered desperately in his ear. 'What do you think?' But the cat refused to give an opinion.

Lily lost count of time. She had no watch, and even if she had every minute would have felt like an hour because she didn't know what was happening in the loft. Once she even crept into the bakery and looked upwards at the open trapdoor. There was no sound. For all she knew there could be nobody up there.

Should she go up and find out what was going on? Perhaps Edward would expect her to. He might even think she was leaving him in the lurch; deserting him when he needed her most.

No, Lily decided. She mustn't come between father and son.

Whatever happened she must be patient, and in the end Edward would come to her. She would know immediately, by the expression on his face, what he'd decided to do. In the meantime she'd go for a walk. She hadn't had time to explore the other streets around Monkey Walk. Now would be as good a time as any.

'Come on, puss,' she said to the ginger tom. 'Let's walk.'

He accompanied Lily to the end of the road but refused to go any further so she left him behind. She soon lost her way because all the streets in that part of the town looked alike. They were all as deserted as Monkey Walk. It was like a ghost town: neglected and forgotten. One day soon the bulldozers would come to demolish the houses, brick by brick.

Trying not to think about Edward, Lily began to explore, poking her head through broken windows and opening doors. To her surprise she found that some of the houses had been occupied not so long ago. There were discarded bottles and food, and the empty beds of tramps or gipsies, but not a sign of life now that the wanderers had moved on.

It was nearly an hour before Lily found herself back in Monkey Walk. As she walked across the dark, littered bakery floor towards the ladder she could hear movement over her head. Not voices, just the sound of something being dragged across the floor.

'Edward!' she called, suddenly anxious to see him. She wanted to be put out of her misery quickly. 'Edward.'

There were only two people in the loft: David and Chris, and they were so occupied with their own concerns that they didn't seem aware of Lily's arrival.

The artist had dragged a rusty trunk into the centre of the floor. He was busy gathering up his paints and brushes, and was throwing them into the empty trunk any old how. Chris was slumped in a nearby chair, his head in his hands. He was wearing a deep red velvet ball gown, with a diamanté clip fastened to the bodice. His bony shoulders reared upwards like coat-hangers, and on his head was perched the blond wig. The wig was always a sign that Chris was troubled, and the fact that it was tilted on one side was an extra bad omen.

'I told you there'd be trouble,' Chris moaned, rocking backwards and forwards in his chair. 'I warned you from the start.'

'It's not their fault.' David tossed some paint-daubed palettes on top of the other things. 'I felt sorry for them. Someone had to take them in.'

'Everything was fine until they came. The boy was all right, but I never trusted the girl.'

'Lily's been no trouble. You can't blame her.'

The way they were talking about her made Lily feel that she'd suddenly become invisible. She stepped forward and asked, 'Where's Edward?'

Two faces turned towards her at the same time; their frozen expressions made her want to laugh.

'Where's Edward?' she asked for the second time.

'Gone,' Chris said, and he put up his hands to straighten his wig.

'Gone! Where?' But Lily knew the answer before David could enlighten her.

'His father came. They had a talk and Edward decided to go with him.'

'When is he coming back?'

'Never.' Chris started to laugh, although the sudden exertion made him cough. His usually pale cheeks turned an unhealthy red. 'He's left you, Lily. His father persuaded him to go back home with him.'

'No,' Lily said weakly, but she knew what she'd just been told was the truth. She pushed aside the screen that stood in front of their private corner. Edward's suitcase was gone and all his things. Her own small pile of belongings looked lonely on the foot of the bed. She turned to David, a grief-stricken look on her face. 'It's true?'

'Yes, Lily,' David said softly. 'It's true.'

'Did he leave me a note?'

'No. He just said to tell you he was sorry.' David looked away. He couldn't bear to see the pain in Lily's eyes. She looked so frail and brittle he was afraid she would break. 'He knew, you know.'

'You mean about his painting?'

'Yes. He never said anything but he knew he wasn't good enough.'

'And yet he let me go on believing in him; he let you go on giving him lessons.'

'Yes. We were all acting parts.' While David spoke he was

busy rolling a length of canvas prior to packing it into the trunk. Lily took one end to help him.

'What do you think he'll do?'

'I think he'll become a doctor, Lily.'

'You may be right.' Suddenly Lily came to life and became aware of what they were doing. 'What's happening?' she asked in a shaky voice.

'We're moving out. I'm packing our things.'

'Why?'

'We have to. Edward's father is a doctor.'

'So?' Lily looked puzzled. 'You knew that, but what has it got to do with you?'

'He saw Chris,' David said. 'He could see at once how ill he is. He said he should be in hospital and he's going to alert the authorities.'

'He can't make Chris go against his will, can he?'

'No, but he's got something worse up his sleeve. He summed up the situation here at a glance.' Chris's shoulders started to shake and David put a steadying arm around him. 'I told you the way we live is against the law. If he reports us Chris will end up in a hospital – and I could end up in prison.'

'He wouldn't do it,' Lily protested.

'Maybe not – but we can't chance it.'

'What are you going to do?'

'Move on. We knew it was only a matter of time. These houses are long overdue for demolition, so our days here were numbered anyway.'

'Where will you go?'

'Brighton, probably. It's not far to travel and we have friends there. People like ourselves. There's a thriving population of homosexuals in Brighton. Pubs and clubs and boarding houses where we can be among people of our own kind. Don't look so sad, Lily. We don't mind, do we Chris?'

'We don't mind anything,' Chris answered in an oddly proud voice, 'as long as they don't separate us.'

David's arm slid again around his lover's shoulder. The two men clung together: one so rough and masculine, the other grotesque in his female attire. Lily almost envied them their closeness, while she was now all alone in the world.

'What about me?' she asked in a sad little voice.

'You could come with us,' David said.

But Lily knew he was just being kind. He'd done enough for her, and now it was up to her to sort her own life out. She'd done it before, she could do it again.

'No,' she said bravely. 'I shall stay here.'

'You'll be all right for tonight,' David said. 'But then they may come looking for us, asking questions. If I were you I'd move down into the town. You have a job so you can easily get yourself a room.' Lily didn't answer. She was too proud to admit that she'd lost her job at the café, and all she had to her name was her few possessions and about a pound in loose change. 'If you want to come with us to Brighton the offer's still open.'

'No,' Lily said. 'I must stay in Pierhaven – in case Edward comes back to get me.'

CHAPTER FIFTEEN

Down but not out

Lily stayed for two more nights at Grubbs Bakery. On the first night she cried for several hours before falling into an exhausted sleep, but the second night she hardly slept at all. The bed felt enormous with her as the only occupant. She kept forgetting that Edward had gone. When she put out her hand to touch him she remembered that she was alone.

There were also noises she hadn't noticed before. The roof above her head creaked with every gust of wind, threatening to bring the timbers and slates down around her ears, and down below the pattering footsteps started again. Lily tried to persuade herself that it was only a cat – probably the ginger tom she'd made friends with come looking for her. But perhaps it wasn't a cat – perhaps it was a tramp, or a rat!

On the third day she decided that David had been right. His advice for her to move down into the town now seemed sensible. She felt too vulnerable up there in Monkey Walk, and when the demolition men arrived she'd have to move out anyway.

But what if Edward came back? In her dreams he did. In her dreams he promised her everlasting love and devotion, but in reality she wasn't so sure. But if she didn't hang onto her dreams she'd have nothing left to live for. So Lily chose fiction rather than fact and pinned a note to the bakery door when she left.

'Dear Edward,' she wrote. 'I've had to move out but am staying in Pierhaven and haven't got a permanent address yet. I shall be on the promenade every afternoon at five so when you come you'll know where to find me. You know how much I love you. Lily.'

She walked away with sadness in her heart; but mixed with it was excitement. She had three silver shillings in her purse and no idea where she was going; but it was a beautiful spring day and she was free.

For the last time Lily ran down the stone steps towards the town. The first time she'd ascended the cat's-creep all her belongings had been packed in a cardboard suitcase, and she'd been burdened under the weight of her heavy winter coat. But now it was spring and she wanted to travel light.

She was wearing a red jacket over a navy blue blouse and skirt, and her hair was hanging loose, streaming over her shoulders. She'd found a capacious canvas bag in the loft, and had packed it with a change of clothes and other necessities. The rest of her belongings she'd left behind. She had been through too much, and was too young, to have fears for the future.

Luck must have been shining on her that day in May, because she found a job and a room without any trouble. She was pretty, looked willing, and people trusted her. The room wasn't very big, and was at the back of a small house, but it was clean. The landlady was very trusting and agreed to her paying her first week's rent when she'd received her wages. The job was as a chambermaid at a seafront hotel. Lily lasted three days.

Her duties started at seven o'clock in the morning when she had to carry morning tea up to the top floors. A Colonel Brown was a permanent resident in room number seven, and Lily was allotted to him because no one else would go.

'What's the matter with him?' she asked the other chambermaid, a girl called Shirley. 'Is he difficult?'

Shirley giggled. 'You'll find out,' she said mysteriously. 'But I warn you, put the tray down on his bedside table and run.'

Not knowing what to expect, Lily tapped on the door of room number seven and waited. She heard a man's voice telling her to enter. Turning the handle and balancing the tray at the same time, she pushed open the door and stepped into the room.

The curtains were still closed but the room was full of light, and Lily could see clearly the man in the bed. He was about seventy and shrivelled like a gnome. His head was pink and shining, with a frizz of white hair curling onto the collar of his striped pyjamas. His eyes were black and beady and his pink mouth toothless.

'Good morning, Colonel Brown,' Lily said politely. 'I've brought your tea.'

The old man didn't answer, but he licked his lips and chomped his gums as she walked towards him. A glass tumbler containing a grinning set of false teeth stood on the bedside table. Lily had to move it before she could put down the tray.

'Nearer – nearer,' Colonel Brown mumbled in a voice like a dry leaf. He put out his hand for the cup. Lily had to lean across the bed to do as she was bid, and as she put the cup and saucer into his hand she felt something rubbing against the right side of her chest. At first she wasn't sure exactly what was happening; after all, he was an old man, and a colonel. But then she felt a cold hand under her blouse and bony fingers squeezing her breast and playing with the nipple. Looking down she saw the colonel's pale eyes fixed on her own. A dribble of spittle was running down his chin. She remembered Shirley telling her to put down the tray and run, and now she knew why.

On the second morning when Lily entered room number seven she found the colonel lying under the bedclothes. He looked like an innocent baby with the pink silk eiderdown, the same colour as his head, tucked under his chin. His eyes were closed and Lily hoped he was safely asleep. Even so she approached the bed warily.

As she put down the tray he suddenly said in quite a sprightly voice, 'Good morning, my dear,' and sat bolt upright. Lily saw with a shock that he was as naked as the day he was born, his skin wrinkled and transparent as tracing paper. She turned and ran out of the room.

But the third morning was the last straw. When she opened the door she saw that the bed was empty, the covers neatly drawn back – smooth and virginal. She let out a sigh of relief. He'd probably gone to the bathroom, and if she put down the tea quickly she could get out of the room before he returned.

No such luck. As Lily straightened from the table a figure jumped out from behind the door and started to advance towards her, a maniacal grin on its face. Colonel Brown had been lying in wait for her and his intentions were obvious. Stark naked and hairless as a plucked chicken he came nearer, his penis standing to attention and pointing at Lily. She didn't stop to think; she ran straight out of the bedroom, down the stairs and out of the front door, not even pausing to hand in her notice.

Lily's next position was in a small lending library. She found it a great disappointment and lasted just under a week.

She'd imagined a library as a friendly place full of gossiping wives, although she should have known better from her visit to the free library. The customers who visited this place turned out to be boring middle-aged professional men, and instead of modern novels and love stories the shelves were full of scientific and technical books that Lily couldn't make head or tail of. She wasn't even allowed to deal with the public herself, but spent her working day replacing heavy volumes in alphabetical order on the shelves. It was so boring that she left one lunchtime and didn't return.

Lily's third job was the shortest. It lasted two days, and she didn't leave this one of her own accord – she was sacked.

The job was for a counter assistant at a cake shop, and she was sacked for picking the cherries from the top of the coconut squares and eating them. They didn't even pay her, which meant that at the end of three weeks on her own Lily had under a pound in her pocket. She owed more than that to her landlady.

She walked along the promenade deep in thought. It was just after five o'clock on a Tuesday afternoon and she was taking her daily walk as she'd promised Edward in her note. It had become more of a habit than anything, and if Lily had seen Edward's fair head coming towards her she would have been more than surprised. But she still lived in hope; and something inside her refused to acknowledge the fact that he'd abandoned her for good.

There was a low wall overlooking a sandy beach and Lily sat down to watch the passers-by. A small boy was digging in the sand with a tin shovel under the watchful eye of a middle-aged woman: probably his grandmother. It wasn't yet warm enough for bathing, although the sea was blue and silver and looked enticing as little waves wriggled their way across the sand pushing strings of weed inland.

Lily turned her face to catch the last of the sun and closed her eyes. The warmth caressed her lids and she could see gold even though she kept her eyes tightly shut. When she opened them she could still see gold. Below her on the sand a couple were walking: a man and a girl. At first Lily thought they were father and daughter because the man was short and stout, with greying hair, and the girl was so young, at least a couple of years younger than Lily herself. But she was outstandingly pretty. A rosy beauty, with a pink and white complexion, and golden curls blowing around her face in the breeze. It was the golden curls Lily had seen when she opened her eyes. The girl was wearing a shabby blue dress made of some sort of woollen material that clung to her full, shapely figure, hugging her hips. A short grey jacket was belted tightly at her waist; and her black shoes had high heels and had once been smart, but were now worn and scuffed at the toes.

Lily couldn't take her eyes from the couple. Their relationship puzzled her. The way the man had his arm about his companion's waist, and the way the golden girl was laughing teasingly into his eyes, disproved her earlier thoughts about them being related.

As they came level with Lily they stopped, and the man drew the girl into a close embrace. She felt embarrassed and tried to avert her eyes, particularly when they kissed. The kiss was long and lingering and neither of them seemed to mind who was watching their exploits. They certainly didn't behave as if they were doing anything to be ashamed of.

Lily was just trying to decide whether it would look too pointed if she moved away, when something the girl was doing froze her to attention. The man was holding her tightly in his arms with his back half-turned towards Lily, but she clearly saw the girl's free hand slide nimbly into his pocket and come out holding a leather wallet.

The girl was just a common pickpocket and Lily felt she should intervene. She jumped down from her seat on the wall; but at that moment the man pushed the girl roughly away and smoothed down his hair with a carefully manicured hand. Now that she could see him properly Lily didn't care for him at all. His eyes were small and beady and he was looking at his companion with a calculating expression on his face. Even if the girl was a thief Lily's sympathies turned towards her instinctively.

'Thank you for a nice time,' the girl said in a cheerful voice.

'We must do it again sometime.' The man spoke abruptly; then without looking at the girl again he turned and started to walk away.

'So long,' the girl called. She waved at her departing companion with her right hand because her left one was still holding the wallet behind her back.

Lily still didn't know whether she should interfere or not. After all, she was only an innocent bystander, and it wasn't really any of her business. The girl was young and shabbily dressed, and probably as poor as Lily was herself. The man on the other hand looked as if he could afford to lose his wallet.

But what if he missed it and called the police? Then the girl would really be in trouble. Lily decided to confront the thief; then it would be up to her conscience whether she kept or returned the stolen property. She crossed the few yards of sand dividing them.

'I saw what you did,' she said.

The girl spun round and her face flushed guiltily. She was even prettier at close quarters, with big blue eyes and a dimple in her chin. But it was the sort of prettiness that wouldn't last. Like a flower the bloom would be short-lived, and when it faded heads would cease to turn in her direction.

'What are you talking about?' She tossed her head so that the golden curls danced.

'You stole that man's wallet. I was watching you. It's in your hand now.'

'Oh, this?' The girl brought her hand forward from behind her back. She opened the wallet and peered inside. 'Only five pounds: it was hardly worth it.' She extracted the money, folded it into a square and thrust it into her jacket pocket before tossing the empty wallet over a nearby wall.

Lily was flabbergasted: she'd never seen such cold- blooded dishonesty before. 'If I call a policeman,' she threatened, 'they'll arrest you.'

'But you won't?'

There was a challenge in the blue eyes, and Lily knew she

was right. Although she didn't approve of theft, she wasn't going to call the police.

'Not this time – but why did you do it? Do you need the money that much?'

'Of course I do. I wouldn't do it otherwise. I'm not stupid.'

'I didn't say you were. Come and sit down and tell me what you wanted it for.' Lily started to move back to the wall where she'd been sitting earlier, but the other girl stopped her.

'We'd better move along a bit,' she said, looking over her shoulder. 'Just in case he misses his wallet and comes back looking for me.'

This seemed a good idea. They started to walk in the opposite direction.

'My name's Brenda,' the blonde girl volunteered. 'I've seen you down here before, always at the same time. Are you on the game?'

'On the game?' Lily had never heard the term before.

'A prostitute? Because if you are there are other girls who use this bit of the prom. They might think you're trying to steal their trade.'

Lily wanted to laugh at the idea of her being a prostitute, but it made her look at her companion in a new light. 'No,' she said. 'Are you one?'

'Not exactly,' Brenda admitted. 'I just lead them on with a harmless bit of fun.'

'And then steal their money.'

'That's the first time I've done that. I usually don't have to. Most of them just want a bit of company, and are happy to pay for it with a drink or a present that I sell later in the market. But that bloke was mean: not even an ice-cream. That's why I did it.' She looked sideways at Lily. 'What's your name?'

'Lily.'

'Well, Lily, perhaps you're one of the lucky ones. Perhaps you don't know what it's like to be down on your luck. To have no proper home, and hardly enough to buy a decent meal.'

'I've got seventeen and sixpence,' Lily said. 'And I can't go back to the room I rent because I owe my landlady more than that. You don't have to tell me what it's like to be poor.'

'Sorry,' Brenda said. 'I didn't realize you were one of us.'

'What do you mean – us?'

'Homeless – out of work – people with no money.'

'I had a job,' Lily admitted. 'But they sacked me. Do you live nearby?'

'I live wherever I can get a place for the night.' Brenda sounded almost proud of this admission. 'When I've got the money I go to a cheap boarding house. If the weather gets warmer I shall find a sheltered spot on the beach. Sometimes I go to St Jude's.'

'Where's that?'

'St Jude is the saint of hopeless cases, and the nuns run a place for homeless women at their convent. They give you an evening meal and a bed for the night. And it's free.'

'Where is it?' Lily asked. She didn't know anything about nuns. She'd seen pictures of them in books and magazines and they always looked like black crows, old and ugly. But the sound of free lodging was certainly attractive. 'Do you think they'd take me in?'

'Are you a Catholic?'

'No.' Lily didn't know what she was. Never having known her parents she didn't know what sort of religious background she'd come from. It seemed safer to say no.

'There's usually a waiting list for places, and they give priority to Catholic women.'

'I could always say I am one.' Lily was getting used to lying although it still made her feel guilty. But telling a falsehood couldn't be as bad as stealing, could it?

'You wouldn't get away with it. They make you go to morning mass at the convent and you wouldn't know what to do.'

'I could just stay at the back, and kneel when everyone else does.'

Brenda laughed at Lily's ignorance. 'There's more to it than that,' she said. 'You have to make the right responses and know when to make the sign of the cross. It took me ages to pick it up.'

'You mean – you're not a Catholic?'

'Heavens no,' Brenda said airily. 'But the nuns don't know that.'

'You could teach me,' Lily said.

If Brenda could fool a lot of silly old nuns she was sure she could. Anyway, it wouldn't be the end of the world if they did guess she was lying. All they could do was turn her out into the street, so she'd be no worse off than she was now.

Brenda changed the subject. 'How much money have you got?' she asked.

'I told you – seventeen shillings and six pence. I owe my landlady two pounds.'

'And I've got five. That should be enough.'

'What for?'

Brenda turned to Lily, and her eyes were twinkling mischievously. 'Let's go and get your things and settle with your landlady. We'll still have nearly four pounds left. That's enough to pay for a room at a cheap hotel and we'll get a meal thrown in if we're lucky. Then tomorrow I'll show you the ropes.'

'Ropes?'

'Don't look so puzzled, Lily. You don't want to starve, do you? I'm only going back to St Jude's as a last resort; and there's lots of other ways of surviving on the streets with no money. I'll show you.'

Lily wasn't sure if she trusted Brenda. But she needed a friend and nobody could make her do anything she didn't want to. Anyway, if things didn't work out she could always look for another job. Perhaps someone in Pierhaven wanted a domestic servant and they'd let her live in. It mustn't be permanent because when Edward came back everything was going to be fine.

'All right,' she agreed. 'But nothing dishonest, like picking pockets.' They shook hands on the deal.

Lily's landlady didn't seem a bit sorry to lose her tenant. She just seemed relieved to get the back rent that was owing.

They found a room just off the seafront. Lily had never stayed at a hotel before and thought it was a splendid place. Brenda took it in her stride. There was a bar, and a dining room, and a lounge with deep leather armchairs; but they were ushered upstairs by a maid in a uniform and shown their room.

It was the cheapest room because it was at the back of the house and had a view of chimneypots and roofs, but they could just afford it. There wasn't much space to move about because the two beds filled the centre of the room and there was a tiny wardrobe and dressing table as well.

Lily thought it was lovely. She admired the dainty floral

curtains and bedspreads, and the frilled lampshades. It reminded her of her pretty bedroom at Ring House and for a moment she felt homesick.

They ordered cocoa which was left on a tray outside their door. The two girls cuddled down in their comfortable beds, sipping their hot drinks and chatting contentedly.

Lily was so happy she didn't want to remember the past or look into the future: the present was good enough. Even so she wouldn't sleep well until she knew Brenda's plans.

'What shall we do tomorrow?' she asked, reaching out to put her empty cup down on the bedside table. 'Shall we look for jobs?'

'No need.' Brenda stretched lazily. 'I told you I'd show you the ropes. If the weather's fine I know a way to earn enough to get by, and if not there's always St Jude's as a last resort.'

'Tell me?' Lily begged. She was curious.

'Wait and see.' Brenda grinned. 'Just trust me and do as I say. I've been in Pierhaven for almost a year and I've managed to survive.'

Lily didn't like the word survive: she wanted a life that promised her more than that. All her life so far had been one long fight for survival.

'Haven't you ever had a proper home?' she asked.

'0f course I have; everybody's got a home. But my home means my mum and dad, and they don't approve of me.'

'Why? What did you do?'

'Nothing – that was the trouble. They were always on at me to *do* something. To pass exams or read books. Boring things like that. So I ran away.'

'I'd have given anything for a family like that,' Lily said longingly. 'I haven't got a mum or a dad. You don't know how I envy you.'

'Don't be so daft.' Brenda turned over so that her cheek rested on the pillow; her face was half-obscured by her tangle of curls. She wasn't wearing a nightgown so pulled the sheet up to cover her plump shoulder. 'Everybody's got a mum or a dad somewhere, even if they don't get on with them.'

'Well, I haven't.' Lily spoke softly, her voice trembling slightly. 'I don't know who my parents are. I'd give anything to find them – particularly my father.'

Now Brenda was curious and wanted to hear the whole

story. Lily told her as much as she knew herself, beginning with her memories of Valley Farm, then the happenings at Ring House, and culminating in her elopement with Edward.

'But it's such a romantic story,' Brenda said when she'd finished. 'Like something out of a fairy tale. And your Edward is the handsome prince.'

'Who left the princess so that she didn't live happily ever after,' Lily said sadly.

'Oh, well. There must be other young men in your life.'

Lily couldn't think of any. Edward Butler seemed to have filled her life for as long as she could remember. She'd never wanted anyone else. But then she thought of a rough-headed boy, with a cheerful smile and a kind voice.

'There was one called Peter.'

'There you are, you see,' Brenda said contentedly. 'Let's go to sleep now.'

'All right.'

They lay side by side in the darkness after the light was switched out. Lily thought Brenda was already asleep until she heard a sleepy voice.

'By the way, can you sing?'

Lily thought of Dot Miller's encouragement and the session she'd had with Harry Smith.

'A bit,' she said.

'Good. See you in the morning then.'

By the even breathing Lily knew that her friend was fast asleep. I must ask her in the morning why she wants to know if I can sing, Lily thought. But she was so tired that she drifted away into slumber as soon as she closed her eyes without dwelling on the question.

'Come on, lazybones – it's morning.'

Lily snuggled deeper into her comfortable bed. She was warm and contented and felt she could go on sleeping for ever. But someone jogged the bed up and down and yanked the bedclothes off her, so she had to open her eyes. The room was full of light, and Brenda was leaning over her.

'Go away,' she protested sleepily. Then she looked at her friend again and was immediately alert. 'Why are you wearing my clothes?' she demanded.

A second look assured Lily that she wasn't dreaming.

Brenda was wearing her navy blouse and skirt, and because she was bigger than Lily they didn't fit very well. She was wrestling with the button on the skirt which didn't meet properly.

'I'll explain later. You can wear my dress.' Lily got out of bed slowly and picked up the blue garment Brenda had been wearing the day before. It was faded and the hem was torn. Brenda saw the doubt in Lily's eyes. 'Trust me,' she said. 'I told you last night to trust me and do as I tell you.'

Lily didn't like to ask any more questions. She slipped the dress over her head thinking it would be too large for her, but because it was made of soft wool it slid down over her body like a second skin. She looked at her reflection in the mirror in surprise because it really flattered her, and made her look older.

'That's better,' Brenda said critically. 'Come on.' She picked up a parcel that she certainly hadn't had the day before, but Lily didn't have a chance to ask what it was because she was already out of the door and half-way down the stairs. 'Bring everything with you,' she said over her shoulder, 'and eat a big breakfast. We'll leave as soon as I've paid the bill.'

Lily enjoyed the novelty of being waited on in the dining room. They had toast and boiled eggs, and a pot of tea all to themselves, and ate everything that was put in front of them. Lily was almost sorry when it was all over and she had to follow Brenda down the steps into the street.

'Carry this for me,' Brenda said, handing Lily the parcel. It was roughly wrapped in a sheet of newspaper and felt soft to the touch. 'Mind!' she said as she passed it over.

But Lily wasn't quick enough. It fell to the ground, spilling its contents for all to see. A towel that Lily recognized from the hotel bathroom, a pair of pillowcases, and some small tablets of scented soap were strewn around their feet.

'Help me.' Brenda dropped to her knees; but Lily stood firmly, looking down at her.

'Those pillowcases were on our beds,' she accused. 'And that towel was in the bathroom. You've stolen them.'

'Keep your voice down,' Brenda said. She looked annoyed rather than embarrassed at being caught out. People in the street were looking at them curiously.

'You're a thief. You've got to take them back.'

'If I do they'll call the police,' Brenda said slyly. 'They'll arrest you as well.'

'It was nothing to do with me.'

'Wasn't it?' Brenda tilted her golden head on one side. 'We shared a room, didn't we? And we paid for it out of the money in that old boy's wallet.'

'You did.'

'But you knew it was stolen. Come off it, Lily, we have to survive out here. It's us against them, and they won't miss a towel and a tablet of soap. They've got more than we have anyway.'

What Brenda was saying was true; but Lily still didn't feel comfortable. There must be some way of living, she thought, that didn't involve being dishonest.

By now they were back on the promenade. The good weather had attracted more people out to take the air. Couples were strolling along the sands, and a few had even braved the deckchairs although it was still early in the season. Brenda suddenly stopped walking, slipped off her shoes, and sat down on the ground.

'What on earth are you doing?' Lily asked.

Brenda didn't reply. She pulled a silvery object out of her pocket, polished the end on the hem of her skirt, and putting it to her mouth started to play a tune. A popular melody drifted across the sands. Passers-by stopped to watch the pretty musician and tap their feet in time to the music. Someone threw a silver sixpence onto the ground, and others followed with pennies and threepenny bits. One tune followed another and the crowd grew larger. Catching Lily's eyes, Brenda raised her brows in encouragement. Although no words were spoken Lily knew what was expected of her. She waited until she heard a tune she knew, and then stepped forward to face the crowd. To the accompaniment of the silver flute she began to sing, 'I'll see you again . . .'

Lily had never sung in front of an audience before and she was very nervous. But the applause that followed her first song, and the shower of coins rattling to the ground, gave her confidence. She knew now why Brenda had wanted her to wear the dress. It was much more flattering than the blouse and skirt. The soft material clung to her figure and moved seductively.

The men found the dark-haired girl with the violet eyes so beguiling that they couldn't take their eyes off her, and Lily found she enjoyed their admiring glances. She'd discovered something she could do, and she was doing it well. She wasn't aware of the figure of a man in an astrakhan coat, with a cigarette holder clenched in the side of his mouth, who was standing at the edge of the crowd watching her with interest.

When he'd seen as much as he needed Harry Smith flicked the ash from the end of his cigarette and walked away. He'd seen a policeman walking along the promenade and had something he wanted to say to him.

Lily felt she could go on singing for ever. Her eyes shone and her hair tumbled over her shoulders; but her voice sang out as clear as a bell. She was into her fourth song when she was aware of a distraction amongst the onlookers. Some of them had even started to hurry away. If Brenda could play it she would sing the Ave Maria next: that would get their attention back. But before she could begin there was an interruption.

'Move along,' a deep male voice instructed.

Lily looked up into a face full of authority. A uniformed policeman was standing in front of them. Brenda, guessing what was coming, began to gather up the coins scattered on the ground.

'Don't you know it's against the law to beg in Pierhaven?' the policeman said sternly. 'You'd better come along to the station and explain yourselves.'

CHAPTER SIXTEEN

St Jude's

Lily had never been inside a police station before and she was frightened. The men and women in their dark uniforms seemed to be figures out of another world and she didn't know what to expect. When they were marched past the reception desk and down a flight of uncarpeted stairs she thought they were going to be thrown into a cell. It was a bit like going down into the bowels of the earth. If they locked her in and there were bars at the window, like the prisons she'd read about in books, Lily knew she wouldn't be able to stand it.

In the basement they were led past a cell door. Through a little window Lily could just see the form of a man stretched out on a narrow bed. By the smell that pervaded the corridor he was a drunk, and Lily averted her face in disgust. She was glad when they were led well away from the cells and told to sit down on a bench outside an interview room.

A young policewoman smiled at them in a friendly fashion. 'Would you like a cup of tea?' she asked.

Neither of the girls had had anything to drink since breakfast, and the singing had made Lily thirsty. A cup of tea was what she longed for most. But before she had a chance to answer Brenda spoke up for them both.

'No thanks,' she said. 'But I could do with a cigarette.'

Lily was surprised when a packet of Capstan cigarettes was

produced and offered around. Brenda took one gratefully and waited for the policewoman to light it for her, but Lily shook her head. She'd never experimented with cigarettes, and wasn't going to start now when her mouth was so dry.

'The inspector will see you in a few minutes,' the young woman assured them, and disappeared through an adjoining door.

Lily sat on the end of the bench wishing the time would pass quickly. She wanted to know the worst. Brenda, however, seemed unconcerned. She lounged with her legs crossed against the whitewashed wall, puffing away expertly.

'What will they do to us?' Lily asked at last.

'I don't know. But they can't fine us because we've got no money.'

Lily thought about the pennies and sixpences she'd seen Brenda scooping up from the ground and pocketing. If they'd earned that by doing something illegal they'd probably have to forfeit it. She didn't like to mention it now in case Brenda had handed it over when she wasn't looking.

'Perhaps they'll send us to prison,' she said dolefully.

'No.' Brenda assured her. 'They'll just tell us off and then let us go.'

But Lily's imagination had started to work overtime. She could already see headlines and photographs on the front page of tomorrow's newspaper, with her name in large print. She couldn't bear the thought of Edward reading about her. What would he think? Luckily at that moment they were called into the interview room.

It was a bare little room, with walls painted a sickly shade of green, and the only furniture a wooden table and four chairs. A middle-aged man sat behind the table doodling with a pencil on a blank sheet of paper. Another policewoman, sterner looking than the first, was seated on a chair by the door as if she was on guard. The man beckoned Lily and Brenda forward.

Brenda marched across the room and stubbed out her cigarette in a glass ashtray on the corner of the table. 'Hullo, Inspector Marchant,' she said brazenly.

'Hullo, Brenda.' The inspector smiled in a fatherly fashion. 'Come and sit down.' The blonde girl did as she was told, but when she saw the inspector looking curiously at her newspaper parcel she tucked it under her arm nonchalantly. 'I see you're still up to your old tricks.'

'I don't know what you're talking about.'

'No? What have you got there then?'

'It's mine. You can't prove that it's not.'

'Then you won't mind me having a look, will you?' The inspector held out his hand. Brenda sighed and then passed the parcel over. After he'd unrolled it, disclosing the towel and pillowcases, he asked, 'And where did you steal these from?'

'I didn't steal them. I found them – didn't I, Lily?'

Lily didn't know what to do. She didn't want to get Brenda into trouble, but she didn't want to have to tell any more lies. She stood in front of the table nervously rubbing her hands together.

'So you're Lily?' Lily nodded. 'I haven't seen you before. Are you a stranger in Pierhaven? Speak up,' he said when Lily mumbled a reply.

'I've been here a few months.'

'On your own?'

'Yes,' Lily said firmly. She wasn't going to tell him about Edward; and she didn't want to tell him about the domestic arrangements at Grubbs Bakery because of David and Chris. Inspector Marchant could think whatever he liked: Lily wasn't saying anything.

'How old are you?'

'Nearly twenty.'

The inspector was surprised at this piece of news. He'd have sworn that the girl standing before him was no more than seventeen or eighteen. But she didn't look like a liar. Her friend, Brenda Williams, on the other hand, had been in and out of the station on a number of occasions. Petty theft, soliciting; she was on a downward slope and if she didn't watch out she'd end up in serious trouble. Perhaps a girl like Lily would be good for her. He thought quickly before speaking.

'You were brought in for begging. What have you got to say for yourselves?'

'We weren't begging,' Lily answered firmly. 'Begging's asking for money and not doing anything in return. I was singing and Brenda was playing her flute. The people were really enjoying it. I could see by their faces they liked us.'

'And yet one of them put in a complaint. We might have

turned a blind eye, or just given you both a warning, but when somebody complains we have to follow it up.'

'So what are you going to do?' Brenda swung her legs as if she hadn't got a care in the world and stared at the ceiling.

'You won't send us to prison, will you?' Lily's eyes swam with tears and Inspector Marchant was moved by her distress, but he had a job to do. The two girls in front of him had to be deterred from getting into further trouble. He thought carefully before answering Lily's question.

'That's not in my power, and begging's only a minor offence. Even so, it is serious when two girls of your ages are living without anyone to care for you. I need to make a few telephone calls so I suggest you wait upstairs. Are you hungry?'

'A bit,' Lily admitted, although Brenda grudgingly said she'd prefer another cigarette.

'I'll show you where the canteen is, and order you both a meal.'

He noticed the way their eyes lit up at the mention of food. They were obviously hungry but not prepared to admit it. After a conversation with the canteen staff he arranged for them to be served with plates of fried sausages and mashed potato, and left them tucking in. Afterwards they had wedges of apple pie covered with piping hot custard, and they washed it down with mugs of dark brown tea.

'That was lovely,' sighed Lily, scraping the last of the custard from her plate. 'I didn't realize I was so hungry.'

'Neither did I,' Brenda grinned. 'Here comes Inspector Marchant; let's see what he has in store for us.'

The inspector looked as if his telephone calls had satisfied him. He joined the girls at their table and smiled at them both.

'Are you feeling better now?' he asked.

'Yes,' Lily said. 'Sausages are my favourite.'

'Good. Now I've been a bit worried about you: it isn't safe to be wandering around Pierhaven on your own.'

'You haven't phoned my dad, have you?' Brenda demanded. The inspector shook his head to reassure her.

'No. I wouldn't have done that without asking your permission first. But I've been talking about you to Sister Clare.'

'Not Sister Clare from St Jude's?'

'Yes.'

'You didn't have to do that, you know.' Brenda sounded angry, as if she was about to accuse the inspector of interference. 'Sister Clare doesn't like me. She won't help us. Last time I was there she called me a troublemaker.'

'Well, she didn't tell me that. In fact she agreed to my request that you should live at St Jude's for a few weeks. You and Lily.'

Lily took this piece of news in slowly. Brenda had told her about the convent and its home for women, and the only advantage as far as she could make out was that it didn't cost anything. But she wasn't sure if she liked the idea of being supervised by nuns. Her freedom suddenly seemed very important. She turned to Inspector Marchant and spoke firmly.

'Brenda can go if she wants to. But they won't want me because I'm not a Catholic.'

'Sister Clare's already agreed to take you both,' he said. 'She has two spare beds and has already talked it over with Reverend Mother.'

'Do we have to go?'

'Yes, I'm afraid you do. I think it will do you both good to have a settled life for a few weeks. St Jude's is a quiet place and that's what you need. A place to reflect and think about what you want out of life. A place to make changes.'

'I don't want to make any changes,' Brenda muttered. 'I'm happy the way I am.'

'Lily?'

'I don't mind going,' Lily said, knowing she hadn't really got any choice in the matter. 'As long as they don't make me join.'

'Join?'

'Become a nun. They won't, will they?'

Inspector Marchant laughed. 'I shouldn't think so. You have to have a vocation for one thing.'

Lily wasn't sure what a vocation was, but didn't like to show her ignorance by asking. 'Thank you, inspector,' she said politely, getting up from her seat and holding out her hand. 'You've been very kind, and the sausages were wonderful. I don't mind going to St Jude's as long as it's only for a short while.'

'Come along then I'll drive you over. I told the sisters you'd be there within the hour. Have you got everything?'

Lily had her canvas bag and Brenda her parcel. Inspector Marchant hadn't confiscated it although he guessed the contents were stolen. He had a soft heart and wanted to make things as easy as possible for the two girls. Brenda would know what to expect at the convent, but the pretty dark-haired girl might find the place grim, and the black-robed nuns daunting.

Lily's first impression of St Jude's wasn't very encouraging. The police car crested a rise and a building of grey brick rose in front of them. It looked more like a castle than a convent, with a clock tower at one end and a turret at the other. It was a grim, fairy-tale sort of place, where a sleeping princess might have been locked up for a hundred years. It was surrounded by a high wall: either to keep the nuns in, or the public out. Set in the wall was a barred iron gate with spikes all along the top.

'I'll set you down here.' Inspector Marchant leaned over and opened the passenger door so the girls could climb out. 'Sister Clare is expecting you. Remember to behave yourselves – I told her you wouldn't give her any trouble.'

He smiled as he spoke, to lighten the words, and drove off in a spray of gravel back towards Pierhaven.

Lily's immediate thought was that they were free. The inspector hadn't stayed to watch them enter the gate, so all they had to do was walk away. But where to? Lily liked Inspector Marchant, and he trusted them, and they had nowhere else to go.'

'Come on,' Brenda said. 'That gate's always kept locked; but there's a little one round the side that everybody uses.'

The smaller gate led into a garden, and immediately Lily's spirits rose. Spread before her were green lawns and well-tended flower-beds, crazy paved paths edged with sweet-smelling herbs, and a dovecot from which she could hear the gentle cooing of the birds. She felt as if she'd been transported to another world: a quiet, peaceful, beautiful world.

'Here comes Sister Clare,' Brenda said. 'I expect she's been looking out for us.'

Coming towards them across the grass was the figure of a nun; but not the sort of nun Lily had expected. This nun wasn't small and ugly, she wasn't even particularly old. She was tall and rosy, with broad shoulders, and a round red face under her wimple. Her eyes twinkled and her skin was smooth and shining, and she was smiling a welcome as if she was genuinely pleased to see them. But most surprising to Lily was the way her black skirts were hitched up, leaving her ankles free: ankles covered by woollen stockings and large feet in flat black shoes with shiny buckles. She was holding out a hand in greeting. Then she laughed and rubbed the palm down her skirt because it was covered in loose brown earth.

'There now,' she said in a loud, girlish voice. 'Don't touch me until I've washed. I'm all over dirt from the flower-beds. You must be Lily?'

'Yes,' Lily said in a small nervous voice.

'Brenda knows my ways of old. Can't bear to stand around doing nothing. Saw some weeds and had to pull them up. Reverend Mother always says the devil finds work for idle hands to do. Do you like gardening?'

'I don't know.' Lily thought back to Valley Farm. There'd been no time for flower gardening there: only trying to force a living from the soil. Mrs Thomas had a beautiful rose garden at Ring House, but Lily hated the huge scented blooms, and had preferred the wild flowers she'd discovered in the hedgerows. But she liked the convent garden which was neat but informal, and where the plants were left to grow and seed themselves as they wished. It probably took a lot of work to give it the appearance of naturalness. 'Do you do all the gardening?' she asked.

'Goodness, no. I'd be out here all day and there'd be no time for praying. But I'm in charge, and I get the girls to help. Some help indoors, in the kitchen or laundry, and some give me a hand in the vegetable garden. I like to tend the flowers myself.'

'Perhaps I could help,' Lily said. It was so peaceful in this sheltered spot that she thought it would be a pleasure working beside this cheerful nun.

'We must see what Reverend Mother says,' Sister Clare said gaily. 'But now you must get settled in. I'll show you your beds, and then Brenda can explain everything else. I'm sure you'll have lots of questions to ask, if you haven't asked them already.'

She loosened her skirts and shook them like a large black bird ruffling its plumage, and then set off at a steady trot towards the convent. Instead of taking them in through the big front door which was studded with nails like a fortress, she led them along a cinder path to a long low extension at the back.

Lily found herself in a bright lobby. A statue in a blue gown, with a gold halo behind its painted head, smiled down at them from an alcove in the wall. As they passed Sister Clare stopped to kiss the plaster feet, and Lily hoped she wasn't expected to do the same. She would feel foolish. But Brenda walked straight past so Lily copied her. There didn't seem to be anyone else about and she wondered where the other homeless women were. She didn't like to ask, and guessed she'd meet them soon enough.

They passed the open door of a dining room. Long pine tables stretched the length of the floor, with hard ladder-backed chairs standing to attention at each place. Another life-sized statue smiled meekly from a pedestal, with a vase of lilies at its foot and a rosary draped over its prayerful hands.

Sister Clare hurried them along and they followed her up a flight of stairs to the upper floor. It seemed to be one enormous space under a gently sloping roof and reminded Lily of the loft over Grubbs Bakery, apart from the fact that everything was in such good order. It was divided into open sections with wooden walls but no doors. In each section stood two beds covered by spotless white quilts. Behind each pair of beds was a narrow chest, and a plain wooden cross hung on the bare wall. There were no carpets or pictures, or any sign of ornamentation. Everything was neat, white, and spotlessly clean.

'This is where you will sleep,' Sister Clare said, leading them to a section at the far end of the room. 'You've got the window so you'll be able to look at the garden.'

This was true and Lily was pleased. From the window by her bed she could see, not only the convent grounds, but also the roofs of the town over the protecting wall, and in the distance the sea.

'It's lovely,' she said. 'Thank you.'

And so are you lovely, Sister Clare thought to herself. She wondered what sad story this delicate young woman could tell to explain why she should be homeless on the streets of Pierhaven and in a girl like Brenda's company. She was glad her old friend Inspector Marchant had brought them to her. She would give advice and protection for as long as she was able, in the hope that when they left St Jude's they would have some plans for the future.

Many girls and women passed through Sister Clare's hands. Some were pathetic cases of abuse or neglect; some restless souls who hadn't learnt to put down roots; and a few really bad eggs.

She tried to treat them all alike, providing food, peace and a listening ear. But occasionally someone like Lily came before her: a lovely young woman untouched by the world. Sister Clare's kind heart went out to girls like Lily. They brought joy to her heart, and sadness when she had to let them go, because she never saw them again. They never came back to thank her.

'Now you can settle yourselves in,' she instructed. 'And then get your parcels from the washroom. Brenda knows the way. Then you'll be free until dinnertime. It's shepherd's pie and jelly tonight so I hope you've both got good appetites.' She turned to leave and they didn't see the tear she brushed away: the tear she always shed at the arrival of new guests.

'Come on,' Brenda said. 'Let's go and get our parcels.'

Lily followed her friend down a flight of cold stone steps into the basement where the washroom was housed. She wanted to enquire about the parcels but Brenda was walking so fast she had difficulty keeping up with her, let alone holding a conversation.

They had to pass the open door of the laundry. Lily caught a glimpse of boilers emitting steam into the already cloudy atmosphere. There were two huge mangles with wooden rollers, and rows of unbleached sheets hanging from expanding rails across the ceiling. Everlasting streams of condensation ran down the walls, adding to the pools of water on the paved flagstones. The heat was overpowering, a moist heat that tickled Lily's throat and made her eyes run.

'In here,' Brenda said, and led Lily into the washroom.

If the laundry had been overbearingly hot the washroom, in comparison, was icy cold. It was a bare, cheerless place, with a row of six baths under a grilled window, and lavatories at the far end.

The baths reminded Lily of the troughs they'd used at Valley Farm to feed and water the animals. They were the same shape, only deeper. Once they'd been painted white, but the insides were now chipped with many years of use, and dripping taps had left brown stains on the sides and around the drainage holes.

The lavatories were just as antiquated: stained bowls smelling of disinfectant, rusting cisterns, and crinkly yellow toilet paper with Bronco printed on the corners. The dormitories upstairs had felt luxurious when compared with the washroom. But perhaps that was how the nuns intended it to be: a place where you weren't encouraged to dawdle but got on with the job at hand.

Brenda twiddled with a tap on the nearest bath; after a gurgle and shudder a trickle of brownish water started to dribble out of the spout.

'What are you doing that for?' Lily asked.

'We have to take a bath. Reverend Mother's orders.'

'But we both had a bath this morning,' Lily protested. She recalled the sensuous pleasure of the warm bathroom at the hotel; the soft water and white towels.

'I know,' Brenda said with a grin. 'But it's one of the rules. Everyone has to take a bath on arrival, and leave their clothes outside the door for Sister Gabriel to take away and fumigate. Don't look like that.' The expression of horror on Lily's face seemed to amuse her. 'You should see the state some of the women turn up in. Most of them have been walking the streets and can't remember when they last changed their clothes or had a wash, let alone a bath. Come and get your parcel while the bath's filling.

The parcels were kept in a big cupboard in the corner of the room. They turned out to be rolls of unbleached linen about the size and shape of a pillow. Brenda lifted the nearest two down and handed one to Lily, while she unrolled the other one. The outer layer was a tent-like object, with a hole cut in the middle of the coarse fabric and a drawstring tape threaded through.

'What's this for?' Lily asked, inspecting her own parcel and finding it was exactly the same.

'You have to wear that in the bath.'

'What on earth for?' Lily held the shapeless garment at arm's length.

'Modesty.' Brenda screwed her face into a comical expression so that Lily had to smile. 'You're in a convent now, my girl, and the first rule you have to learn is that nakedness is a sin. You put your head through the hole, like this.' She demonstrated. 'Then you tie the string so that it fits snugly around your neck, and then drape the ends of the gown over the rim of the bath. That way no one can see you.'

The other items in the parcel turned out to be a rough towel with the texture of a nutmeg grater, and a blue and white gingham dress with a Peter Pan collar and puffed sleeves. The style was childlike, but the size voluminous. Lily held hers up to her shoulders in dismay.

'It's awful,' she said. 'I'm not going to wear this.'

'You'll have to,' Brenda replied. 'Everybody has to. It doesn't matter what you wear while you're at St Jude's because there are no men to see. At least we're allowed our own underclothing. My dress looks a bit on the small size so we could do a swop. Come on, the bath's full now – we can share it.'

They carried their bath-gowns into the lavatories to undress. Lily felt a fool in her heavy tent and crept out cautiously, dragging the hem of the gown across the floor. She was surprised to find her friend had beaten her to it and was already in the bath. Lily could see her golden curls bobbing about over the rim.

'Come on, Lily, it's lovely and hot.'

Before Lily could join her she stopped in surprise. Brenda was floating in the water with not a stitch on. Her plump pink body was languid and her blue eyes sleepy.

'Where's your gown?' Lily demanded. 'You said we have to wear them. You said it was the rule.'

'So it is,' Brenda said lazily. 'But I never keep rules; you should know that by now. Take the horrible thing off and hop in before you freeze.'

Lily was glad to strip off the restricting folds of rough fabric. She felt embarrassed standing on the cold floor with her hands crossed over her breasts and the dark sweep of hair hanging over her face. But it took more than that to embarrass Brenda. The fair girl sat up suddenly, making the water swell around her body; her smooth, swollen breasts bobbed on the surface like two ripe apples. A delicate fragrance came from the tablet of soap she was lathering herself with. It was the soap she'd taken from the hotel that morning, and her waiting towel was the soft fluffy one from the same place.

Lily climbed over the rim of the bath and lowered herself into the water. She allowed Brenda to soap her, and they giggled together like naughty schoolchildren.

They stayed in the water until it was nearly cold and their skins were wrinkled and crinkly. With their wet hair plastered to their foreheads they resembled two beached mermaids. At last they were towelled dry and buttoned into their uniform dresses. They'd been in the washroom so long that as they ventured out the bell rang summoning them to dinner.

'We mustn't be late,' Brenda said. 'Let's hurry.'

'But I'm not hungry,' Lily insisted. 'We've already had two meals today, and those sausages were filling.'

'Never turn down free food,' Brenda said over her shoulder. 'Anyway, if you don't turn up they send out a search party for you.'

They made it to the dining-room just in time. As Lily slipped into an empty chair she looked around with interest. There were about fifteen girls and women sitting expectantly in their places: the eldest looked as if she was well into her seventies, and the youngest about sixteen. They were all wearing identical gingham dresses that suited the young better than the elderly, but no one seemed to mind. The younger women chatted and laughed as they scraped the legs of their chairs on the floor; but the older ones sat silent, with expressionless faces, as if they were dwelling on their troubles.

As if on cue everyone fell silent and all eyes turned to the door. Accompanied by the swishing of skirts the nuns filed into the room in a double black crocodile.

Lily guessed that the leading nun was the Reverend Mother. Not only was she the oldest but the ugliest, with a hook nose and a jutting chin. She bore a startling resemblance to Punch's wife, Judy.

Her eyes were sharp and restless and when they fell on Lily they seemed to see through her, making her feel guilty, although she couldn't think of anything she'd done wrong. Six other black figures glided behind their leader, and Lily was relieved to see that one of them was the reassuring figure of Sister Clare.

They took their seats at the head of the table. One nun, who was the tallest and thinnest, rose to her feet to say Grace, and no sooner was it over than the door swung open with a crash. A convoy of trolleys on wheels appeared and dinner commenced.

The shepherd's pie, served with carrots and cabbage, was very good, and Lily found her appetite had returned. But the sweet that followed defeated her although it was only jelly. Brenda, however, seemed to have a bottomless stomach and cleared Lily's plate as well as her own.

There was a young woman sitting on Lily's left and she would have liked to talk to her, and be friendly, but under the intimidating eye of the Reverend Mother she didn't like to. The way the nun stared around the table, her pale eyes darting from face to face, made her nervous. On the Reverend Mother rested her immediate future so Lily decided to behave herself.

At last the meal was over, but no one dared leave the table until the nuns had risen from their seats.

'We have to go into the chapel for evening prayers,' Brenda whispered. 'Wait for the black crows to go first.'

Everyone stood by their chairs while the nuns filed past. Reverend Mother walked silently, her shoes making no sound on the floor, and her stern eyes inspecting each face. Occasionally she paused and spoke softly to one of the women, but Lily couldn't hear what she said. When she reached Lily she stopped. Lily's heart missed a beat.

'What's your name, girl?'

'Lily, Reverend Mother.'

'Ah! So you're Lily – the girl with the voice?'

'I can sing a bit,' Lily said, feeling her cheeks flushing crimson.

'Then you can lead the hymns at evening prayers. Choose something you know.'

Reverend Mother moved on with her six acolytes following behind, leaving Lily clutching the back of her chair. The old nun who looked like Punch's Judy wanted her to sing for them. The eyes, that at a distance had appeared cold and hard, at close quarters twinkled with kindness. All at once Lily knew she had nothing to fear from St Jude's, or the nuns who passed their sheltered lives within its walls. She was among friends.

That evening in the beautiful convent chapel Lily sang as if her heart would burst with joy. She hadn't been able to find a hymn she knew. Dispensing with the hymnal she stood proudly, looking out at the small congregation of nuns and homeless women, and opened her mouth and sang. The chapel had never heard or seen anything like it before: a pretty, dark-haired girl with eyes the colour of newly opened violets, singing the Ave Maria in a clear soprano voice.

CHAPTER SEVENTEEN

The singer

'I hope you're going to behave yourself tonight, Rosa?' Harry said. He climbed off the bed and pulled his trousers on quickly, as if he was ashamed of his plump white legs.

'Of course I shall, Harry. Don't I always?'

Rosemary Lane studied her lover from under her lashes. She pushed back the covers to show her figure clad in black lace French knickers and matching camisole. Sliding her legs over the edge of the bed she reached for her suspender belt and stockings and commenced dressing. She seemed to be concentrating on making sure the seams were straight, but actually she was pondering on Harry Smith's question. It had sounded like a criticism. When a man started that sort of thing it usually meant, and Rosemary knew from experience, that the end of a relationship was in sight.

'You weren't at your best last night,' Harry, now fully dressed and in control of things, continued. 'You sang flat at least twice. I was counting.'

'I never sing flat!' Rosemary snapped. What did Harry know about singing anyway? He was only an accompanist She was the artiste: Rosa Lamour, as the credits billed her.

'Well, you did last night. And you'd been drinking.'

'There's no law against having a little drink.'

'Not if it doesn't affect your performance. I suggest you

stay sober until after you've sung.'

'Sober! How can you say such cruel things to me?' Rosemary walked around the end of the bed and tried to put her arms around Harry's shoulders. He shook her off, gently but firmly. 'I wasn't drunk.'

'I didn't say you were drunk, darling. I just said you'd been drinking.' Harry didn't want to go too far. Rosemary had a good voice and a nice body, and he admired and needed both these things in a woman. She also had spirit, and he couldn't afford to lose her until he'd found a replacement. 'Just a little warning because I love you.'

'Do you?' Rosemary sounded doubtful, but she clung onto every word of affection Harry spoke.

'You know that I do. Haven't I just shown you?'

'Oh, sex? Yes, I suppose so.'

Harry tied his tie and slicked back his thinning hair. Damn the girl, what was she after? If it was marriage he'd have to put her straight. Harry Smith wasn't the marrying kind. One trip to the altar had been enough for him. He'd soon fled from that encumbrance and promised himself never to make the same mistake again.

'Get yourself tarted up while I have a warm-up.' Harry was buttoning his jacket. 'I didn't like that pink thing you wore last night; it looked like the icing from a cake. Haven't you got anything new? Something you haven't worn before.'

'Actually I have. Wait a minute and I'll show you. Turn your back.'

Harry tried to keep his patience. He did as he was told to humour her. 'Hurry up then.'

Rosemary swung the wardrobe door open and unhooked a garment hanging inside. She pulled it over her tousled head and slid it down over her slim body, smoothing her hands over her hips to remove the creases, and slipping her feet into high-heeled shoes.

'Ready,' she said playfully. Harry turned round.

'What the hell's that supposed to be, Rosa?'

Rosemary was covered from shoulder to knee in black. The plain black dress clung to her figure cancelling out all signs of femininity. Even the neckline was modest and the sleeves were narrow and tightly buttoned at the wrists.

'Don't call me Rosa! My name's Rosemary.'

'I'll call you whatever I like.' Harry's face was stormy. 'I hope this is your idea of a joke?'

'A pretty expensive joke. It cost me fifteen guineas.'

'You actually paid fifteen guineas for that?'

'Yes.' Rosemary plucked at the neckline as if she wasn't used to covering up so much flesh.

'You can't sing "London Pride" in that. You look as if you're in mourning.'

'I don't want to sing London bloody Pride. I'm sick to death of Noël Coward. I want to try something different.' Harry didn't answer, so she went on bravely while she had the chance. 'I thought I'd like to try that song Edith Piaf sings, you know – "*La Vie en Rose*". It's a lovely number. Piaf always wears a little black dress when she's performing it.'

'So you thought you'd like to be a second Little Sparrow?' Harry started to laugh and Rosemary tried to keep her temper. She couldn't bear being laughed at.

'Why not? You think you're a second Noël Coward.'

'At least I can play the piano.'

'And I can sing.'

They faced each other across the room, Harry's pale eyes meeting Rosemary's brown ones. He knew he'd met his match for now and decided that the best way out was to compromise. He knew his Rosa Lamour well, and a little flattery would convince her.

'Of course you can sing, Rosa.'

'Rosemary.'

'All right – Rosemary. Your voice is as good as that little slut Piaf's, if not better. And you look like a dream when you put your mind to it. Why didn't you say you were fed up with Coward? But there are plenty of numbers that would suit your voice better than "*La Vie en Rose*".'

Rosemary had softened as Harry knew she would. She couldn't help herself, although she guessed he was trying to keep her sweet on purpose. But at least it would be nice to sing something different for a change. She was fed up with always trying to look like Gertrude Lawrence.

'What would you suggest, Harry?' she asked coyly.

'How about "Stormy Weather" or "Smoke gets in your Eyes"?' Harry shrugged his shoulders. 'Something popular that everyone knows from the wireless. But for God's sake change out of that dress.'

'I could wear my yellow; the last time I wore that was at that nightclub in Crawley. They've never seen it at Spinners.' Rosemary delved into the depths of her wardrobe, pulling garments aside carelessly until she found the dress she was searching for almost at the back. 'Here it is,' she panted, pulling it out triumphantly. But Harry had gone. She stood there helplessly, the limp yellow garment dangling from her hand. 'Oh well, Rosemary,' she said aloud as she often did when she was alone. 'You'd better pull yourself together and make the most of yourself. Yellow's not your colour: makes you look really sallow. But with a bit of rouge and powder it shouldn't be too bad.'

She stripped off the black dress and dropped it onto the floor. It would stay there gathering dust until she had a tidy up. The yellow dress had a shiny satin underslip, tight and figure-hugging, covered by a fine, almost transparent overdress, that floated like a mist around her figure as she moved.

Rosemary stood in front of the mirror adjusting the shoulder straps and surveying herself carefully. She was a slim girl, almost thin, and wore her twenty-five years badly. Her shoulders were bony and the skin of her upper arms already loose. Her face was pert and lively with a thin mouth and tiny pointed teeth, and her hair was short, brown and curly. But her best feature was her eyes: big brown eyes flecked with hazel, under heavy sensuous lids. It was the laziness of the eyes that men, including Harry Smith, found attractive. The brittle little body and greedy mouth put them off; but one inviting look from Rosemary's brown eyes was enough to draw men closer, like moths to a candle flame.

With great care she gave her nails a fresh coat of varnish, not bothering to remove the old chipped layer. Then she paid attention to her face: outlining her lips to make them appear fuller, pinching and patting colour into her cheeks, and powdering her nose. Finishing with a few hasty strokes of the brush to smooth the rough curls into a wavy cap, she fastened butterfly-shaped clips into the lobes of her ears and dabbed on perfume.

At last she was satisfied with her appearance and slipped a fur coat, a present from Harry, around her shoulders. As she was just about to let herself out of the door Rosemary had second thoughts.

'One little drink won't do me any harm,' she said to herself, and reached under the bed for the gin bottle she kept hidden there. 'Harry will never know.' Unscrewing the cap she took a mouthful and rolled the liquid around her mouth to get the full benefit, before swallowing. Carefully she replaced the bottle under the bed.

Spinners was only a five-minute walk away, but it took Rosemary ten because of the height of her heels. Rows of coloured bulbs illuminated the façade and she stopped to admire the photograph of herself, touched up to perfection, and with a sticker across her stomach telling the world that Rosa Lamour was singing there that night.

The ground floor of Spinners was a cinema and there was a queue of people waiting to see a Gary Cooper film. Nobody took any notice of Rosemary. She pushed her way through a side door and up some narrow stairs, past the the bar and restaurant floor until she reached the club room.

George, the manager, was bustling about as usual: twitching a curtain into place, or running a finger over the polished surface of a table before inspecting a glass ashtray.

Rosemary looked around. 'Where's Harry?' she asked.

'Haven't seen him.' George grinned. 'I thought he was with you.'

'He left a quarter of an hour ago. Said he wanted to practise.'

George flapped at some imaginary dust with his handkerchief. 'He'll turn up – you know Harry.'

'Yes,' Rosemary said. 'I know Harry. Who's on the bill tonight?'

'A ventriloquist who's really good; and a young violinist. A Frenchman – just your cup of tea, my dear. So handsome; makes poor old Harry look like a grandfather. What are you giving them tonight? Not "London Pride" again?'

'No.' Rosemary laughed. 'I put my foot down. Thought I'd start with "Smoke Gets in Your Eyes".'

'That'll make a nice change. Want a drink?'

Rosemary hesitated. She not only wanted a drink, she needed one. But Harry had given her a warning and she mustn't cross him – not yet.

'No,' she said quickly, and when George looked at her in surprise, 'thanks all the same.'

At that moment Harry came in and called Rosemary over to the piano for a run-through. Before they were finished people began to crowd into the room carrying glasses and smoking cigarettes.

Suddenly Rosemary felt nervous. She'd sung the Coward numbers so many times she knew them like the back of her hand; but now, eager as she'd been for a change, she felt underrehearsed. In fact she wasn't sure if she could remember all the words of "Stormy Weather". She needed a drink now to give her confidence; but she'd already turned down George's offer, and there wasn't time to go down to the bar. Anyway, Harry would be furious.

There was a small ante room for the artists to rest as they waited their turns, and Rosemary went there now to compose herself and run through the lyrics. But it wasn't empty. A young man with curling black hair and tawny skin was standing in the centre of the floor, a silver hip-flask tilted to his mouth. He was slender but muscular, and Rosemary fell in love with him at first sight. He removed the flask from his mouth and smiled at her disarmingly.

'I didn't know there was anyone here,' Rosemary said nervously. 'I'm the vocalist.'

'Rosa Lamour?'

'Actually it's Rosemary – Rosemary Lane. Are you the ventriloquist?'

'Do I look like a ventriloquist?' The accent gave him away. Rosemary guessed who he was before he enlightened her. 'I play the violin. Would you like a drink?' He held the flask out and she took it gratefully.

'Thanks.' The golden liquid burned her mouth but it steadied her. She'd never tasted whisky before but it acted quicker than gin and was more palatable. She took a longer sip.

At that moment they heard George announcing the next act. 'Ladies and gentlemen,' he bellowed. 'We have a surprise for all you music devotees tonight. I am delighted to welcome Maurice Dupont, the young violinist, for his first performance in England. Maurice Dupont!'

There was applause, and the Frenchman raised his expressive eyebrows at the introduction and strode onto the floor, leaving Rosemary with the flask.

She moved into a better position so that she could watch him play. She couldn't take her eyes from him. He stood there showing his profile for her delight and admiration. He was tall and lithe as a young sapling: legs balanced apart and violin tucked under his chin, and the dark curls falling over the tawny forehead as he bent his head over his instrument. The music he played was wild and sensuous, stirring the listeners' blood and sending tingles up their spines. Rosemary's heart beat faster, and she raised the flask to her lips again.

And then it was over. Maurice was bowing to the audience: a curt little continental bow from the waist. Then he stood upright and flung his head back and spread his arms wide. He was playing to an invisible gallery, but especially to a girl called Rosa – or was it Rosemary? A girl who so obviously adored him. Maurice Dupont was the sort of man who would do anything for admiration.

Now it was Rosemary's turn. Without any introduction Harry started to play. Twitching her flimsy skirt into place she stepped out onto the floor, remembering just in time to hand the Frenchman his flask as they passed. She felt brave and confident as she walked across the polished boards towards the piano, and it wasn't her fault entirely that her sharp heel skidded on the slippery surface. She suddenly found herself falling. But the alcohol had blunted her senses and she didn't hurt herself, just landed in a yellow heap on the floor in a clumsy, undignified posture.

The audience, who had started to applaud the appearance of the soloist, froze. Harry stopped playing.

'Get up!' he hissed out of the side of his mouth.

Rosemary did try, but her heel was caught in the hem of her dress, and she had to struggle on hands and knees to free it without anyone coming to her aid. Suddenly there was a rip and she was free, but at the expense of the skirt that now had a split seam in an embarrassing place.

Someone sniggered, and called out 'Cor! Didn't know this was going to be a strip-tease.'

Someone else said in a loud voice, 'Hush, the little lady's hurt herself.'

'No, she hasn't,' some bright spark at the back of the room said. 'She's drunk.'

Steadying herself on the edge of the piano Rosemary rose to her feet. The mixture of gin and whisky had addled her wits and she was near to tears. But she wasn't billed as Rosa Lamour for nothing. She was a trouper and was going to sing whether they laughed at her or not.

'Play "Smoke Gets in Your Eyes", Harry,' she said softly, patting her hair into place. Harry didn't answer, and when she glanced down at him she saw that the pianist had taken his hands from the keyboard. He was staring at her with no expression on his face. 'Play, Harry,' she said again. 'I'm ready now.'

When he spoke Rosemary didn't recognize his voice; and his eyes were narrowed and full of loathing. 'I'll never play for you again,' he said softly, for her ears alone. 'Get off the floor.'

Rosemary had no option but to comply. She couldn't argue the matter out in front of an audience; and she couldn't sing without an accompanist. But she kept her dignity. Holding the torn seam together with one hand she walked from the room, her head high, although her gait was rather unsteady. A single tear channelled down through the carefully applied make-up on her face.

As if nothing had happened Harry began to play. He played number after number with gusto. The romantic melodies rippled effortlessly from his dancing fingers, so that the listeners soon forgot Rosa Lamour and began to tap their feet and hum an accompaniment. Harry didn't have to concentrate: he could play the piano with his eyes shut. Rain, storm or flood, he could play through anything. Even so, his mind was far away.

He'd known for some time that Rosemary's days were numbered. She'd served her turn but her bloom was going, and like a flower she was withering and past her best. The voice that had so enamoured him in the early days now grated with false sentimentality. The body that had once enchanted him in bed, now repelled him. Rosemary's frail bone structure had once seemed delicate, but was now reptilian, bony and fleshless. Her eyes were still beautiful, but they were full of false promises. It was time for her to go. He'd get himself a new soloist.

Harry started to play 'I'll See You Again', and a picture sprang into his mind's eye: a young, pale-skinned girl with long dark hair hanging like a veil over her shoulders, and eyes the colour of violets. The girl's voice had been promising, but not outstanding.

The last time he'd seen her she'd been singing to an entranced audience on the promenade at Pierhaven. Knowing the town's bylaws he'd reported her to the police. Her voice had improved without a doubt. She'd obviously listened to the advice he'd given her; or perhaps it was just that she performed better in front of an audience.

After that first time, when she'd sung to him in his room in Monkey Walk, he'd expected her to come back begging for a job. But she hadn't. She'd learned by his teaching and then decided to do it by herself. For that she had to be punished. So Harry, out of spite, had reported her and her friend the flute player.

What had happened to them? Suddenly Harry wanted to know. Her name was Lily, but if he could find her and train her as he'd trained Rosemary Lane, he could turn her into a real artiste. He would call the new Lily – Lilith Fortune.

And then it dawned on him how he could trace her. The police at Pierhaven would know her whereabouts; and there was one policewoman who still owed him a favour.

Harry Smith's face broke into a happy smile, and he started to play again the opening bars of 'I'll See You Again'.

'Don't dig that up, Lily.'

Lily was on her hands and knees among the lettuces. With the aid of a small fork, and a determined expression on her face, she had been about to uproot a large healthy dandelion.

'But it's a weed, Sister Clare,' she said, looking up at the jolly nun who was snipping sideshoots from a young mulberry tree.

'A weed is just a plant growing in the wrong place. That dandelion is growing amongst the lettuces, and the young leaves add a pleasing taste to a mixed salad.'

'I'm sorry, I didn't know. What are you doing?'

'Just a bit of early pruning. It won't spoil the fruit, and it looks as though we're going to get a good crop this year. They're fine for baking and preserving. In the old days the monks used to add elderberries and make wine with them.'

Lily looked at the hard green fruit and wondered what they would taste like when they were ripe. She'd probably never know as she couldn't expect still to be a guest at St Jude's when the fruit was being harvested. And yet she was happier than she ever remembered being in her life before. Summer was being kind to the south coast, and the long hot days made her forget everything else. She'd been living at the convent with Brenda for nearly a month now.

Brenda had got a job working in the kitchen. The nun who was in charge of the cooking was very generous and allowed the girls working there to help themselves to any leftovers. Chicken legs and wedges of pie found their way up to the dormitories to be consumed under the bedclothes by hungry residents.

Lily had asked to work there as well, and had been disappointed when she was allotted instead to Sister Clare and the garden. But she soon got used to being separated from her friend, and found a great joy in caring for the growing things, and feeling the fertile soil trickling through her fingers.

Although the convent was built on the side of a hill, the walls sheltered it from the winds blowing in from the sea and trapped the sun so that the gardens were always warm and still. Everything that was planted grew apace, almost changing overnight.

Lily had changed as well. Getting up and retiring early, regularly eating three good meals a day and having no worries, had changed her from a shy girl with a permanently worried frown between her brows into a calm and dignified young lady. She'd put on weight, and the new roundness of her limbs suited her; even her face was plumper and tanned a golden brown by the sun. Her thick hair was plaited, and her blue and white gingham dress was protected by a calico apron.

Inspector Marchant had been correct about Lily's needs. The quiet peaceful life had given her time to reflect and plan. The pain of Edward's abandonment was still there, but she was now strong enough to accept it. Her love for him remained strong, but had to be set aside while she got on with the important business of living from day to day.

But she had to look to the future. Lily looked around at all the green growing things and she suddenly knew she never wanted to leave – not even – not even for Edward.

'What's the matter, Lily?'

'Matter? Nothing, Sister. I was just thinking.'

'I won't ask what you were thinking about.' And then Sister Clare saw the tears in Lily's eyes and asked kindly, 'Perhaps you're feeling homesick?'

'I told you: I have no home. At least, not one I can go back to. If I'm homesick it's for the open countryside where I was brought up. For the woods and the fields and the wind blowing over the Downs.'

'And St Jude's is too sheltered?'

'Oh no. I love it here; and I can see the sea from my window. My fear is of losing it.'

'I think I know what you mean, Lily. When I became a nun I thought I was going to miss the world outside, but instead I discovered a richness I'd never believed possible. Instead of loss I'd found something infinitely more precious. Where are you going?'

On impulse Lily had jumped to her feet and was sprinting in the direction of a wattle fence that enclosed the herb garden. 'I must talk to Reverend Mother. I know where she is,' she called back over her shoulder.

Every afternoon if the weather was agreeable the old nun would sit amongst the sweet-smelling plants to recite the rosary. No one dared intrude on her privacy and Lily was breaking an unwritten law. But she wanted to ask Reverend Mother a question, and it couldn't wait.

She slowed her step as she approached the bent figure sitting on a bench, the hooked nose protruding from the headdress, and the beads sliding through knotted fingers. She didn't look up and Lily's bravery slipped away. But it had to be now or never so she squared her shoulders and held her ground.

'Reverend Mother . . .'

'What is it? What do you want?'

The hooded eyes looked up at the young girl confronting her and she sighed. Why was it that young girls were always so impatient?

'To talk to you.'

'Not now. You'll have to wait. Come to my study after evening prayers.' The fingers moved again, running the beads slowly backwards and forwards. She'd lost count and would have to start all over again. One of the penances of growing old.

'I'm sorry, it can't wait. I must talk to you now.'

Now the fingers were still and Reverend Mother was all attention. No one said can't and must to her. Everyone always obeyed her instructions: when she told them to wait – they waited.

'Your name's Lily, isn't it?'

'Yes, Reverend Mother.'

'Then you'd better sit down where I can see you and tell me what you want.'

Lily sank down on the bench. 'I want to become a nun,' she said.

If Reverend Mother was startled she didn't show it; she fixed her sharp eyes on Lily and asked, 'Why?'

'Because I've thought it all out and it's the answer to everything.' Lily's face was flushed with enthusiasm. 'I love it here so much, because it reminds me of the countryside I lived in when I was a child, surrounded by green fields and growing things. And Sister Clare is teaching me about plants. She says I'm becoming very useful to her. She said only the other day she was going to miss me.'

'Is that the only reason?'

'No. It's the singing: it's the only thing I'm really good at. I love singing in the chapel and leading the nuns in the responses. If I was a nun I would be able to do it for ever.'

'Sing, you mean?'

'And grow things.'

'What about prayer?'

'I can learn to do that. Can't you see, Reverend Mother, that it's the answer? I can start by becoming a Catholic.'

'You make it sound so easy, my dear.'

'But it is easy. If only you'll let me – please.'

The old nun smiled and Lily thought she'd won. But then Reverend Mother spoke sharply, 'You have to have a vocation to take the veil.' Back to that word vocation. Lily showed her puzzlement so the nun tried to explain. 'A vocation is a divine call, or spiritual guidance from God, to enter the life of the cloister. It is a revelation when God intervenes in people's lives and shows them what he wants them to do. Your voice is a gift from God.'

'There then,' Lily said, as if that was the end of the matter.

'But everyone has gifts. Some can sing like you, and some can dance or work with their hands. Your voice will glorify

God more widely in the outside world.'

'Do you think so?' Lily said, trying not to sound too disappointed.

'Before I became a nun,' Reverend Mother reminisced, her fading eyes seeing back down through the years, 'I travelled the world with my father. He was an operatic singer and wanted me to follow in his footsteps – but my voice wasn't good enough. But I had a good ear, and I listened to voices whose qualities were far less than yours – and yet they were classed as professional entertainers. The gift that God in his goodness has given you will be appreciated by more people in the world outside these walls.'

'But Reverend Mother,' Lily was staring into the nun's wise old eyes, her face alight with hope, 'I don't know what to do. How do I start?'

'God will find a way if you let him guide you. If he wants you to sing he will open a door. If he has other things in store for you he will show you the way if you trust him. What is it, Sister Teresa?'

So occupied had they been with their conversation that neither of them heard the scrunch of feet on the path, or saw the approach of the sister whose duty it was to supervise visitors and carry messages. Sister Teresa was the youngest nun at St Jude's and was always in a hurry and breathless. Now she was panting and red-faced, with her hands fluttering with excitement.

'There's a visitor,' she announced when she'd regained her breath. 'A man.'

'Show him into the library,' Reverend Mother instructed. 'I'll be there in a few minutes.'

'But he hasn't come to see you, Reverend Mother.' Sister Teresa waited for the words to sink in. A male visitor was an unusual occurrence at the best of times, and the homeless women weren't encouraged to have followers. 'He asked for Lily.'

'Me?' Lily looked at the nun in disbelief, and then her heart began to beat quickly. Edward – it must be Edward come back for her at last.

'Did he give his name?' Reverend Mother was also curious.

'No. But he says he's Lily's uncle.'

'But I haven't got any uncles, not that I know of.' Could it be Matthew posing as an uncle, or Mr Thomas, or even Doctor Butler come back to hunt her down?

'You'd better go and find out. You mustn't keep the poor man waiting.'

The poor man was standing looking out of the library window. He'd watched Lily crossing the lawn and admired the proud lift of her head and the new grace in her step. She was even lovelier than when he'd seen her last. And then she was standing in the doorway, one hand trembling on the knob, like a wild animal poised to take flight.

'Hullo, Lily,' Harry Smith said. 'I've come to offer you a job. I'm going to make you into a star, and the first thing we have to do is change your name to Lilith Fortune.'

CHAPTER EIGHTEEN

Lilith Fortune

'Would you mind keeping quiet, young lady? I'm trying to concentrate.'

'Sorry.' Lily pushed the opened packet of Smith's crisps into her handbag and slid down in her seat with embarrassment. All around her in the cinema mesmerized viewers were glued to the screen.

'Cor! Look, Mum,' a child's voice piped up in the row behind. 'It's in colour.'

Lily turned her attention back to the brightly lit screen. Her trips to the local cinema were pure escapism, and helped her to relax before she had to pick up the pressures of life again in this lousy south coast town.

Today she'd had a choice. One picture house was showing *The African Queen*, and Lily was a fan of Humphrey Bogart; but she'd chosen *A Queen is Crowned* because no one she knew had a television set and the radio programme had whetted her appetite. The wonderful music of Benjamin Britten's *Gloriana*, specially written for the coronation, had stirred her; and now she was not only listening to it but also seeing the twenty-six-year-old Queen crowned in Westminster Abbey, and then drive with her handsome husband by her side through the London Streets in her golden coach. The thousands of sightseers thronging the pavements were huddled under umbrellas, and buttoned into mackintoshs against the rain, but the joy and enthusiasm showed in their faces. Lily was glad that she'd chosen to watch the coronation of Queen Elizabeth II rather than a fictitious story, however good.

And then it was all over and she was pushing her way out of the crowded cinema, blinking in the sunlight. Her afternoon of freedom was over and she now had to return to the hotel – and Harry.

It was now two years since Harry Smith had traced Lily to St Jude's and, posing as her uncle, had persuaded her to leave the convent. He'd promised her fame and fortune, and told her that she had the qualities to become a star. If she put her life in his hands she would have money, beautiful clothes, and the sort of future any young woman might only dream of.

Lily hadn't felt she had any choice. St Jude's had given her sanctuary and a breathing space, and she dreaded the idea of leaving, but Reverend Mother had already explained that she hadn't the necessary qualities to take the veil, and her vocation was probably in the outside world. So she had the choice of going with Harry or trying her luck back on the streets. She'd chosen Harry.

He'd been good to her and he'd kept his promises, but it hadn't been easy. She'd had to work harder than she'd ever done before. The breathing exercises, the singing lessons, and the undignified way she was inspected by beauticians and hairdressers made her wonder who her body belonged to. When they'd finished with her she'd stood in front of the hotel mirror and felt as if she was looking at a stranger. Who was this smart woman in the fashionable green cocktail dress, with a double row of pearls around her throat, and hair cut shorter and teased into unnatural curls and waves?

Harry had come up behind her and put his plump hands on her shoulders while he studied her new reflection in the glass.

'Hullo, Lilith,' he'd said softly in her ear.

'Lily,' she'd corrected firmly. 'My name's Lily.'

'Not any more. From now on you're Lilith Fortune.'

So she was now Lilith Fortune, Harry's protégée, who sang in the best night-spots along the south coast. Her voice held listeners spellbound, whether she was singing Noël Coward, Ivor Novello, or one of the popular songs of the Fifties. Men sent her flowers and tried to take her out to dinner, but Harry protected her. He'd made her, and she was his property. Except for the occasional afternoon like this one. Then she would steal away and hide her face in the darkness of a cinema, and become again the girl Lily whose early years had been spent in poverty at Valley Farm.

'Isn't she lovely?'

'Pardon?'

'I said, isn't she beautiful? Princess Elizabeth – I mean the Queen. Don't you think she's lovely?'

An elderly woman was standing at Lily's elbow, a rapt expression on her face as she tried to relive the film she'd just seen.

'Yes,' Lily agreed.

'And those little children of hers. Did you see that bit on the balcony? They were so small they could hardly see over the rail. I read in the newspaper that they let the little prince stand on a box. Don't you envy her a husband and children like that?'

'Yes,' Lily said again, so emphatically that the woman wondered if she'd said something out of place. But her listener was smiling so it must be all right. She carried on relentlessly.

'Don't you wish you were her? All those pretty clothes and the lovely houses she lives in.'

'I don't think pretty clothes or lovely houses can make people happy,' Lily said. 'I'd give it all up for a loving husband.'

'Would you, dear?' The woman turned to survey her companion, but Lily was already hurrying away, her head high and her heels tapping on the pavement. 'It's all right for you,' she told Lily's retreating back. 'You look as if you're doing all right. I wonder who does your hair for you? And that dress wasn't bought off the peg at the Co-op.'

What she said was true. Lily's hair had been cut and set in a fashionable style by one of the town's best and most expensive hairdressers; and the dress had been designed in Paris. It was made of black and white cotton, with a tight bodice, and a full skirt that billowed out over a double layer of stiff petticoats. The scooped neck was trimmed with braid, and a wide scarlet belt emphasized the narrowness of her waist. She wore matching red high-heeled shoes that showed off her small feet and high arches. Everything about her looked, smelled, and was expensive.

The Hotel Victoria was only a few streets away. It was an imposing building with marble pillars supporting a Georgian porch. A liveried doorman was standing to attention on the front steps, waiting to welcome visitors and residents. He smiled and touched his hat as Lily approached.

'Good afternoon, miss.'

'Hullo, Gilbert.'

They'd only been staying at the Victoria for a week but Lily was already popular with the staff. She was always polite and friendly, which was more than could be said for some of the guests. The richer they were the ruder they seemed to be, that's what Gilbert Alcott found. He should know: he'd been in the hotel business for over twenty years.

'Lovely weather, miss. You been out enjoying the sun?'

Lily nodded. 'Is Mr Smith in? Have you seen him?'

'He's in the lounge. Came in about a quarter of an hour ago and asked if I'd seen you.'

'I'll go straight in then.' Lily started to walk past but stopped because Gilbert was clearing his throat noisily as if he was about to say something more. 'What is it?'

'My brother heard you sing last night, Miss Fortune.' His face flushed a deep red at the liberty he was taking. 'He said he'd never heard anything like it.'

Lily laughed. 'I hope that's meant to be a compliment?'

'Oh yes, miss. He thought you were wonderful, and when I told him you were staying here he begged me to ask for your autograph. I told him the management wouldn't like it, but he said you looked such a kind young lady he was sure you wouldn't mind me asking.'

'Of course not. Have you got something I can write on? An album, or a piece of paper would do.'

Gilbert produced a paper napkin and a fountain pen as if he'd come on duty ready prepared. Lily signed the name Lilith Fortune with a flourish.

'If your brother would like it,' she said, 'I'll send him down a photograph. I have some in my room.'

Gilbert's face flushed even darker and Lily guessed, correctly, that the brother was a fictitious invention and he wanted her autograph for himself.

'Thank you, miss,' he said. 'He'll be so pleased.'

Leaving a very happy man behind her, Lily entered the hotel. She would have liked to have gone straight to her room to rest and refresh herself, but played safe and headed for the lounge. Harry didn't like being kept waiting and she didn't want any questions asked about her afternoon's innocent activities.

He was sitting in the window sipping tea from a porcelain cup. The table in front of him was set for two. Lily sank into the opposite chair and poured out a cup for herself. As she put the rim to her lips she was aware of Harry's eyes upon her. They were small eyes, hard as marbles, and took in her shiny nose and the fact that she'd been hurrying. Harry never hurried anywhere and he hated to see her with even one hair out of place. He expected perfection.

'Your nose needs powdering,' he said.

'I know. I'll see to it as soon as I've drunk my tea.'

'You'll do it now.' His plump hand shot out and grasped hers so that she had to replace the cup on the saucer.

Obediently she reached with her other hand for her handbag. It was only then that he released her. Lily opened the enamel-topped compact and powdered her nose; then she studied her face and tweaked a stray curl into place.

'If you've finished your tea I'd like to run through tonight's numbers,' Harry said.

'Do we have to? I'm tired.'

'You can rest afterwards; there will still be time before dinner. I've written you a new song.'

Lily followed Harry out of the lounge, and waited while he collected the key to the bar and unlocked the door. He always needed access to a piano, and if there wasn't one at the hotel where they were staying he got the management to hire him one. This week he was lucky: there was a well-tuned upright in the bar and he was allowed to use it whenever he wanted.

Harry closed the door behind them and strolled across the floor to the instrument, manipulating his fingers with a clicking sound, a habit that Lily found irritating. While he made himself comfortable and ran his hands expertly over the keys Lily took up her position facing an imaginary audience.

'What songs are we doing tonight?' she asked, although she could guess the answer.

'I thought Ivor Novello for a change.' He started to play the opening chords of 'My Dearest Dear' and Lily hummed an accompaniment. At least it wasn't going to be Coward tonight. She was getting fed up with singing 'A Room with a View' and 'London Pride'. 'Someone's asked for "Zigeuner", so we'll do that first.'

Lily sighed, but started to sing 'Once upon a time, many years ago . . .' in the voice that audiences found so hauntingly beautiful.

After that they ran through the Novello numbers. Some of them were rather high even for Lily's soprano voice, and she needed the practice to help her reach the notes effortlessly. They always finished their act with a selection of popular songs that were currently at the top of the charts. This week it had to be the number one song, 'I Believe', followed by 'Hold Me, Thrill Me', which was something the audience could join in with if they felt like it.

'Surely that's enough?' Lily was feeling tired and didn't want to strain her voice.

'Just one more.' Harry began to play a pretty little tune she'd never heard before. 'Do you like it?' He paused just long enough to insert a cigarette into his holder and light it.

'It's got a lovely melody,' Lily admitted. 'What is it?'

'A new song I've composed just for you. I haven't written the words yet but it will tell the story of a young girl who comes up to town from the country and falls in love with an older man.'

Lily froze; she didn't want to hear any more. She knew exactly what Harry was getting at; she'd seen that look in his eyes before. He'd never actually tried to force her into anything, but if she'd ever given him an invitation she knew he'd have jumped at the chance of sharing her bed.

But she wasn't attracted to him – not one little bit. She would be twenty-two on her next birthday in August, and he must be nearer fifty than forty: old enough to be her father. Anyway, she still loved Edward Butler – didn't she? One day fate would intervene to make their paths cross again, and then she would be able to drop the Lilith Fortune disguise and be Lily from the Valley again. She had to hang onto her dreams or nothing in her present life would be worthwhile.

'I'm tired,' Lily said. 'I'm going up to my room to rest.'

She got up from her chair and walked out of the room. She

could feel Harry's eyes on her back and found that she was trembling, but she wouldn't look back; she didn't want him to see the panic she was feeling.

But Harry knew how she felt. He knew Lily so well by now that she was an open book to him and he could read every page. Since his affair with Rosemary Lane Lily had been the only woman he'd wanted, and he'd played her like a fish on the end of a line until he was ready to land her. He'd waited so patiently, hoping that it would all be worthwhile, and the time was ripe.

He'd taken her literally from the gutter and made her into a star. He'd got her used to good food and beautiful clothes, and most of all the applause of an audience. In return she'd earned him a lot of money. The managers of the twilight clubs knew that if they had Lilith Fortune heading the bill they would have a full house. Men particularly adored her, although there was never anything remotely sordid about her performance. She was every man's dream and that was why they flocked to see her. She looked like a queen and sang like an angel, and that made her into a figure of fantasy. She was immaculate, untouchable, and as remote as the Virgin Mary. No one had ever tried to breach her defences, knowing that if they did they would have Harry Smith to answer to. Lilith Fortune was Harry's sole property, so she was as safe as if she was wearing a placard around her neck saying 'Look, but don't touch.'

But she wasn't safe from Harry. After she left the lounge he poured himself another cup of tea, and smoked another cigarette, while he made his plans. The smile on his face was secret and sly, and he rubbed his plump hands together in anticipation. He waited a good half an hour before pushing his chair back and leaving the room to mount the stairs slowly.

In her room Lily had taken a bath, and then draping herself in a silk dressing-gown stretched herself out on the bed. But she couldn't sleep. Every time she felt sleepy and her lids drooped she saw Harry's eyes and the lecherous look that seemed to strip her naked. She'd turned the key in the door, but then, knowing that it was a futile action, had unlocked it again. If Harry wanted to gain admission he had only to knock – what reason could she give for not admitting him? He was her manager, her mentor, and he was responsible for her well-being.

She heard footsteps outside in the passage. They were approaching her door and Lily tensed as they seemed to pause; but whoever it was walked on and she relaxed again. Perhaps it was all in her imagination and Harry had no designs on her. After all, during the two years since they'd commenced working together he'd had many opportunities, and never taken any of them. So why should she fear him now?

There came a knock on the door, so sudden and unexpected that Lily sat up in alarm.

'Who is it?' she called nervously.

'Harry. Can I come in?'

'Of course.'

She was standing by the window when he entered the room. Her dressing gown was turquoise and silver, and the frilled drapes behind her were peach coloured. Harry caught his breath at the picture she made: the proud set of her head on the white neck was like the stem of an exotic flower. Her breath panted slightly under the thin silky fabric, and a pulse in her throat flickered. The violet eyes fringed with sooty lashes stared at him as if asking a question.

'I came to see if you wanted anything. I can get them to send you up something light on a tray if you're hungry.'

'No.' Lily walked across to the dressing table, and picking up a brush pretended to tidy her hair. She could see Harry's face in the glass. 'I was just feeling tired, but I'm better now.'

'Good. What are you wearing tonight?'

'I thought the blue gown with the bolero.'

'A good choice, and my favourite. Blue suits you.'

Harry was walking across the carpet towards her; she could see his reflection in the mirror. She tried to concentrate on what she was doing but his hands came down suddenly on her shoulders, making her jump although she'd been half expecting it.

'Why are you so nervous, Lilith?'

'I'm not nervous,' she said lightly, playing for time. 'Should I be?'

'I hope not. After all, we're old friends, aren't we?'

'Of course. It's your hands – they're cold.' Lily could feel the chill of his hands through the thin material of her gown.

'And you're warm, Lilith. I can feel your warmth – let me warm my hands on you.' Suddenly bold, Harry pushed the turquoise material away, leaving her shoulder bare. Then he bent over and kissed her skin with his full podgy lips while his hands slipped under Lily's armpits and cupped her breasts. They were small, but heavy, and shock hardened the nipples. She was surprised at her body's bold reactions. Her brain was repelled by what Harry was doing, and yet her body was sending out the wrong messages. 'You're warm,' he said again. 'So warm, and so beautiful.'

'Please . . .' Lily started to say. She wanted to say please stop but Harry seemed to take the word as a sign of encouragement. With horror she felt his fingers, that were so nimble on the keys of the piano, pull aside the folds of silk covering her breasts, and begin greedily to squeeze and tease the pointed nipples.

'No! Please stop!' Lily pushed him away, and stood up pulling the dressing gown into place.

'What's the matter? Why so modest? I could have sworn you liked it.'

'Well, I don't.'

'Come on.' Harry's voice was bantering but his eyes were angry. Like two pale stones they stared at Lily. She'd never been actually afraid of him before, but now suddenly a tremor of fear and revulsion crept up her spine. 'You're not a virgin, are you?'

She was, but she didn't intend discussing such intimate things with Harry Smith. She'd shared the same room with Edward at the Millers' home, even the same bed at Grubbs Bakery, but never had their intimacy exended beyond a friendly kiss or a reassuring cuddle – except for that brief, wondering moment when he'd kissed her breast. She'd seen his lean body naked and felt a warm stirring of desire in the pit of her stomach, and once she'd seen desire in Edward's eyes, but the time had never seemed ripe for them to go any further. Even so, the thought of allowing Harry to make love to her filled her with disgust; even the thought of his plump little body without clothes made her feel sick.

'I asked if you're a virgin?' Harry said again. 'You're not, are you?'

'Yes,' Lily finally admitted in a frightened little voice.

To her shame he began to laugh, his shoulders shaking with merriment, and his eyes watering so that he had to grope for a handkerchief. 'And I thought I knew you – and you've just turned out to be a liar. Haven't you realized yet that you can't lie to me?'

'I'm not lying. I am a virgin.'

Something in her voice made him stop laughing. For one moment Harry almost believed that Lily was telling the truth. But how could she be? At loose in Pierhaven, living among artists whose morals were always suspect, and then singing on the streets under the lecherous eyes of men. How could she have kept her virtue even if she'd wanted to?

But what if she had? What a gift she would be to the man who captured her – what a prize. To be the one – the only one – it would almost be worth marrying her. Harry licked his lips and decided to change tactics.

'Don't get upset, Lily,' he said softly. 'If you say so of course I believe you. You didn't think I'd force myself on you, did you?'

'I don't know. You scared me.'

'I'm so sorry, I wouldn't have done that for the world. It's just that I'm so fond of you, and I don't want to lose you to some silly boy who won't appreciate you.'

'That won't happen, I'm waiting for Edward.'

'Edward?'

'The artist – I told you about him.'

'Oh, yes.' Harry looked serious as he recalled the fair-haired young man he'd glimpsed once or twice going in and out of the bakery. 'Didn't he want to become a doctor?'

'That was his father's idea; the only thing Edward wanted to be was a painter.'

'Well, I think it's time you put him out of your mind.' Harry's voice was light, almost disinterested, but he knew Lily was listening to every word. 'Look to the future, my dear. You've worked so hard and gained so much: you deserve success. You wouldn't want to throw it up and go back on the streets, would you?'

'I'd never do that,' Lily said emphatically.

'If you left me you might have to.' Harry was putting his cards on the table and he could see by Lily's wide eyes that he'd made a point. 'Without me you might not find it so easy to find work. With me you could conquer the world.'

'What do you want from me, Harry?' Her question sounded childish, as if she really didn't know. He couldn't believe that she could be that innocent.

'I want you to come to me of your own free will. I want you to show your gratitude. What do you say?'

Lily's head was spinning. She knew he wanted to bed her – but how many times? Would he be satisfied with once – could she bear it? And yet what else could she do? Inside she was crying for Edward, but sometimes she doubted whether she would ever see him again. So would it be such a big price to pay to let Harry satisfy himself in exchange for her future?

'I'll do whatever you want,' she said, but her voice trembled and the words were almost incoherent.

'Do you promise?'

'I promise.'

'That's my girl. That's my Lilith Fortune. You'll never regret it, my dear.'

Lily was already regretting it, but as Harry was already leaving the room, after making her promise yet again that she would do whatever he wanted and be guided by him, she hadn't time to argue. She had to change for her evening performance and he would expect her to look her best.

She decided against the blue dress and instead chose a gown of silver grey and lavender. The bodice was tight and off the shoulder, and the waist nipped in and then flowed out into a skirt hanging in loose folds. Harry had given her a double row of pearls and she hung these around her neck to please him, and clipped on matching single pearl earrings. Their moonlit lustre suited her pale skin and dark hair, and the colour of her dress reflected her eyes.

As she entered the club Lily knew she was looking her best, and Harry's admiring glance reassured her. The room was filling up, and when he played the opening bars of 'Zigeuner' and she joined him at the piano there was rapturous applause. Most of the men in the audience were regulars who liked nothing more than being entertained by a pretty young woman with a lovely voice.

She followed 'Zigeuner' with 'My Dearest Dear', and then someone requested 'We'll Gather Lilacs' so she sang that. As it was such a popular song the audience joined in, humming the tune and singing the refrain. Usually they performed three or four numbers and then took a break, followed by a selection of modern songs to round things off.

But this evening Harry seemed to be in a particularly

expansive mood and he started to play the opening bars of 'My Life Belongs To You', which Lily hadn't rehearsed. She didn't like singing it very much because it was written for a man. When she didn't join in he played the opening again, and then started to sing himself.

'When first we met, I heard a voice within.

The scene is set, and here's my heroine.'

Lily had never heard Harry sing before. She was surprised because his voice was quite good, although he had changed the words of the song from 'your heroine' to 'my heroine'. Thinking that he was waiting for her, and hoping that she was recalling the words properly, Lily started to sing. But her voice faded when she realized that Harry was still changing the words. He was making the song more personal, as if he was sending her a message.

He sang: 'Your life belongs to me. Your dreams, your songs. All that you do.'

Lily started to sing again, trying to correct the words. Her mind was in a turmoil. He was reminding her with every word that he owned her; that he'd taken her from the convent and groomed her into what she was today. Without him she was nothing, and she'd promised to do whatever he wanted. She knew only too well what that was.

'And now at last the skies are fine: your tears are past and you are mine.'

The audience was applauding wildly. The tremor in Lily's voice, and the tears in her eyes, made her performance more touching than usual. And when Harry got up from the piano stool and took Lily's hand so they could make a bow they clapped until their hands ached. But when he put up his hand requesting silence they composed themselves and waited to hear what the musician had to say.

Lily waited too. Harry was departing from his usual behaviour, and although she looked calm her smile was fixed, and she held her hands together almost as if she was praying.

'Thank you for your kind appreciation,' Harry began. Before he could carry on someone called 'encore' and he had to put up his hand again. 'I know that Lilith will be pleased to sing some more; but first I have an announcement. Tonight I am a very proud man, because Lilith Fortune has consented to be my wife.'

Everyone went wild. There were cheers and congratulations and glasses were raised in their direction. So many hands were extended to be shaken, so many greetings called out to be acknowledged. Harry took her hand and led her down among the tables to be feted and admired.

Lily followed in a dream, and like a puppet on a string nodded and smiled and thanked people, saying how happy she was. But although she walked proudly with her head held high, she couldn't feel anything. All she knew was that Harry had tricked her. He'd asked her to promise to do whatever he wanted – and she'd agreed. But she hadn't dared to think he might want to marry her. Marriage was for life, between two people who loved each other. Marriage was the end of the fairy tale when the prince married the princess and they lived happily ever after.

Harry Smith was an old man and she didn't love him. She didn't even like him very much. But what could she do? What could she say, here among the crowds of excited people who were smiling their congratulations? Edward – where was Edward? He should be at her side, protecting her, wanting her. But she hadn't seen him, or had news of him, for over two years.

'Sing, Lilith,' Harry commanded, and he resumed his seat at the piano. He started to play slowly 'La Novia', and Lily sang mechanically, as if he'd wound up her spring and she was an automaton.

'Oh my love, my love, this can really be,
That someday you'll walk down the aisle with me.
Let it be . . .'

Nothing could spoil Lily's voice, not even the shock she'd sustained. It was only when she reached the words of the Ave Maria that she suddenly came to life. Her voice broke, and she looked about her as if she'd forgotten where she was.

She saw Harry at the piano, and the sea of faces, and then nothing. Her hand reached out as if for support, and then like a beautiful silver and mauve butterfly she fainted.

CHAPTER NINETEEN

A trip to the country

'Can you hear me, Mrs Smith?'

Lily tried to open her eyes to see who was talking, but her lids felt heavy, and she was tired and couldn't be bothered. Where was she anyway, and who was this Mrs Smith?

'Are you awake?'

Someone was talking to her. It was the same man's voice that had been talking to the mysterious Mrs Smith. Perhaps she was in hospital and Mrs Smith was in the next bed.

Lily decided that she was dreaming: because if she was awake she would surely remember if she'd been ill. But her brain felt sluggish, as if it was full of fog, and she couldn't remember anything.

When had she last felt so lazy and comfortable? Of course, her memory was coming back and she was in the big sagging bed over Grubbs Bakery; David and Chris would be asleep only a few yards away, the other side of the dividing screen. But why couldn't she hear Edward's breathing, the soft, even sound that always reassured her? She stretched out her hand to touch him, to stroke the smooth downy flesh of his arm; but there was nothing there. The sudden realization dragged her from the dark depths into the light of day.

'That's better,' the same voice said. 'How are you feeling?'

Lily looked around the room and then she remembered.

She'd passed out after singing at the club and Harry had brought her back to the hotel and put her to bed. He'd been surprisingly gentle and kind, although she'd hated the familiar touch of his pudgy hands doing the intimate things for her she was too weak to do for herself. Sleep had been her escape, and she'd begged to be left alone. But she'd been woken to eat the invalid meals the kitchen prepared specially for her: custards and soups that she had no appetite for. And the washing of her body and the brushing of her hair – Harry had done all that too. Harry – where was Harry?

'Don't try to sit up, Mrs Smith. You've been ill, and your husband has been very worried about you. But you're mending slowly.'

The man bending over her was a stranger. A stout middle-aged man with crisp grey hair and spectacles.

'Who are you?' Lily asked. Her voice sounded gravelly even to her own ears, as if she hadn't used it for a long time.

'I'm a doctor. Ian Banner. Your husband called me in after you collapsed. Don't you remember?'

Yes, she did remember: the bright lights, the applause of the audience, and Harry pulling her forward and telling everybody that she was going to marry him. A wedding – why couldn't she remember the wedding? Doctor Banner was calling her Mrs Smith, but she had no memory of a church or a wedding or anything like that. Surely she'd be able to recall an event that would tie her to Harry for life, and push Edward Butler even further into the past.

'Where is Harry?' she managed to say, although her throat hurt and every word came out slurred.

'I'm here, Lilith.'

The other person in the room stepped forward. Harry had been there all the time; waiting in the background for the doctor to finish his visit.

'There, you see how devoted your husband is, Mrs Smith. He's hardly left your side since you were taken ill.'

Harry smiled, and his smile disturbed Lily more than anything. It was such a self-satisfied smile: so patronising, so possessive. She turned her face away to hide the tears of dismay that were filling her eyes.

'There, there, my dear,' and Harry patted her hand. 'I'm glad to see you looking better at last.'

'How long have I been ill?' Lily asked weakly.

'A few weeks. I've been so worried, but Doctor Banner here assured me it was only exhaustion. He said a good rest would soon put you on the road to recovery. You see, you were right, doctor.'

'But it's early days yet.' The doctor was packing his bag as if he was anxious to be on his way. 'You must take it very slowly if you want to make a full recovery. But you're young and in good hands. I would suggest a change of air – a holiday,' and after patting Lily's shoulder and shaking hands with Harry he was gone, calling briskly over his shoulder 'Goodbye, Mrs Smith.'

Harry closed the door behind him and then came to sit on the edge of the bed. Lily was still troubled and stirred restlessly. What was the matter with her? Why couldn't she remember things clearly? Surely she should remember an important event like getting married; and why did her throat hurt so badly? Perhaps she was dreaming. If she wasn't – and the pain in her throat was real enough – Harry would be able to give her the answers.

'Harry.'

'Yes, my dear.'

'My throat hurts.'

'There's some orange squash on the locker. That should help.' He pulled the pillows up, and helped Lily into a sitting position before handing her the glass. But her hand shook so badly he had to hold it while she took a sip. It was cool and soothing. 'Is that better?'

'Yes. Harry – why did that doctor call me Mrs Smith?'

Harry didn't answer immediately although Lily's eyes were begging for an explanation. As if he was thinking carefully he put down the glass and took her hand again.

'You did agree to marry me: surely you remember that? And we did announce it just before you were taken ill.'

'You announced it! I only agreed to do whatever you wanted.'

Why did her words sound so feeble? Why did she feel so weak? She needed to be strong and in full possession of her faculties, not lying in bed at a disadvantage, to cope with Harry.

'But surely you knew what I had in mind?'

'No. I thought you were talking about the singing – about my career – not my life.'

'But singing is your life; and I'm your manager. As husband and wife we would be the perfect partnership.'

'Would? Do you mean we're not married?' Lily's spirits rose slightly as she turned questioning eyes on Harry.

'No. Not yet.'

'But if we're not married, why did that doctor call me Mrs Smith?'

'Just a formality, my dear. He presumed you were my wife, and I didn't disillusion him. He'd have wanted to call in a nurse or send you to a hospital, and I wanted to take care of you myself. Anyhow, it's only a matter of time. As soon as you're better we'll fix a date. I'm sure you'll want a white wedding; I'll take you over to Paris to choose a gown.'

But Lily had stopped listening. She was so full of relief to find that she wasn't married after all; that she wasn't Mrs Harry Smith, but still the girl they used to call Lily from the Valley. She was feeling stronger by the minute, as if a weight had been lifted from her heart.

Harry lit a cigarette and walked across the room to the window. He had his back turned to her and his head was wreathed in smoke. His short stocky figure looked comical outlined against the light.

'You must concentrate on getting your strength back,' he said without looking round. 'I think Doctor Banner was right about that holiday. As soon as you're well enough I'll take you away.'

'Where to?'

'London. We'll stay at the finest hotel; and you can have a new dress – two if you like.'

'I've got plenty of clothes and I'm sick of hotels,' Lily said, hoping she didn't sound ungrateful.

'I'll take you to a musical: you'll enjoy that. There's *Call Me Madam* at the Coliseum, or *The King And I* at Drury Lane, with Valerie Hobson and Herbert Lom. You can choose – what do you say?'

'Won't it be very hot in London?' Lily asked. The hotel room was stuffy and airless, and if she'd been ill for several weeks it must now be August.

'I expect so, but we'll take taxis everywhere so you won't get tired. I'll look after you. Trust me.'

He turned to face her and she knew she had to say something quickly, or she'd find herself in the noise and bustle of the big city. The very idea depressed her.

'I do trust you,' she said slowly. 'But I don't want to go to London.'

'All right,' Harry said indulgently. 'You choose; I'll take you wherever you want to go. Where shall it be: Glasgow – Liverpool?'

'I don't want to go to a big city: they're too smelly and noisy. I'd like to go somewhere where I can walk through fields and pick flowers.'

Harry's face fell. He hated the countryside: it was just somewhere to drive through on the way to somewhere else. He'd always lived in towns, and wouldn't know how to pass the time in the country.

'You'd soon be bored,' he said.

'No, I wouldn't.' Lily's face lit up at the thought of the sunshine and the fresh air. 'I was brought up in the country. I'll get better quickly if you'll only take me there. You'll like it when you get there, Harry. I promise.'

Harry hated it. He hired a car, and sat behind the wheel with a glum look on his face even before they'd left the roofs and chimneys of the town far behind.

But Lily was glowing. She was wearing a simple blue skirt and white blouse, with sandals on her feet and a cardigan slung loosely around her shoulders. Although she felt well she was thinner since her illness, and her face looked delicate, the skin almost transparent. Her hair had grown, and without the regular attention of a hairdresser hung almost to her shoulders; and her violet eyes looked even larger and stared out of the car window with excitement.

'Put your cardigan on. You'll get cold,' Harry said.

'No, I won't.'

'Wind up the window then.'

But Lily wouldn't. The warm air blowing into the car caressed her skin, making it tingle with life. She was going back to her beloved Sussex countryside, and she envisaged long sleepy days dozing in the sun, or wandering with Harry through flower-filled meadows. He'd been so kind, and she was going to do everything in her power to see that he enjoyed himself. He needed a holiday as much as she did. Of course he wasn't Edward, but she must try to be grateful, and make the best of things.

Despite it being the height of the season Harry had refused to book in advance, although Lily had said they might have difficulty finding vacant rooms. But he was banking on Lily getting quickly bored and begging him to take her back to town. A few days at the most, he hoped, and then he'd be able to take bookings again: as soon as Lily felt well enough to sing.

'Look,' Lily said, bouncing up and down in her seat like a schoolgirl on her first outing. She'd spotted a field of golden corn out of the window and it reminded her of Valley Farm.

'It's only a cornfield,' Harry said sulkily.

'But there are poppies. I can see their scarlet heads dancing in the wind. Let's get out and pick some.'

'We can't stop here. Anyway, they'll only die before you can put them in water.'

Of course he was right. But Lily was sad to see the nodding golden and red heads fading away in the distance.

The roads became quieter and narrower and they passed little traffic, just the occasional car or tractor. They passed through villages with cobbled streets, and cottages with gardens full of bright flowers and washing blowing in the wind. Lily was reminded of Peter's mother: there had always been crisp linen pegged on Mrs Jackson's washing line, and since his father had died Peter had tended their cottage garden, as well as the grounds around Ring House.

On the first night they booked into a hotel. It was set in attractive gardens, but was on the edge of a main road and just like any of the town hotels Lily was used to staying in.

Harry seemed contented but Lily was restless. This wasn't what she wanted.

'We could stay here for a few days,' Harry said over breakfast the following morning. 'The food and service are both good.'

'Oh, please let's go on,' Lily begged. 'This isn't the real country.'

Harry sighed, but he wanted to humour her. He needed her voice, and he wanted her body, and the only way he was going to get and keep both was to marry her. Until the ring was safely on her finger he had to give her her head. After that things were going to be very different. But sometimes he did wonder if it was all worth it.

'Go and pack your things then. I'll pay the bill and meet you by the car,' he said.

They loaded the cases into the boot and were soon on their way. They spent the morning sightseeing. Whenever they came to the top of a hill Lily wanted to stop and admire the view, and every village they passed through she wanted to get out and explore. She made him accompany her on walks because she said she needed to stretch her legs. By lunchtime they were passing through the town of Uckfield and Harry was feeling hungry.

'Look out for a restaurant,' he said. 'It's time we stopped to eat.'

'Surprise!' Lily said with a grin. 'I asked at the hotel for a picnic, and it's in the boot with the cases. So we can drive on and find a pleasant place to stop.'

Harry hated picnics. He didn't say anything although his face was beginning to look thundery. But Lily didn't seem to notice; she was feeling happy and enjoying herself immensely. They'd just passed through Maresfield when she spotted a grassy bank. It was just off the main road, and there was a sheltering clump of trees if the sun became unbearably hot.

She grabbed Harry's arm. 'Let's stop here. It's a perfect place for a picnic.'

'Don't do that! You'll make us have an accident.'

'Sorry.'

Harry slowed the car down, and after bumping over a ridge managed to park on a stretch of turf. But Lily was already out of the car and running up the bank. The grass was smooth and dotted with daisies, and she sank to her knees and turned her face up to the sun, feeling its rays caressing the skin of her face and the breeze playing with her hair. She laughed gaily as Harry plodded awkwardly towards her, carrying the food and a blanket to sit on.

'I'm starving,' she said. 'Let's see what they've given us.'

'I hope it's smoked salmon.' Harry was busy unwrapping a packet of sandwiches covered in greaseproof paper. 'No, it's egg. I hate egg sandwiches.'

'I love them.' Lily reached out her hand and took a big bite out of a sandwich. 'Delicious.'

'Cheese – and mustard and cress. Why didn't you ask for sausage rolls or potted meat?'

'But I love cheese and I hate sausage rolls. Look, there are sponge cakes and chocolate biscuits, and there's jelly in these little pots – and this bottle is full of lemonade.'

'They must have thought we were having a children's party,' Harry said, holding a sandwich disdainfully in the air.

'Well, I think it's lovely, and if you don't like it I'll eat your share.'

But Harry was hungry, so he ate some sandwiches and washed them down with lemonade straight from the bottle as there weren't any glasses.

'I'd like to stay here for ever,' Lily said.

Harry looked at her and frowned. There were grass stains on her skirt and her hair was a mess, her make-up had almost worn off and her hands were dirty. It was time he took her in hand.

'I've got something for you,' he said, and feeling in his pocket produced a small leather case.

'But it's not my birthday yet.'

'That doesn't matter. I thought you'd like it early.' He opened the lid and revealed a small gold ring lying on a bed of velvet. The stone was an amethyst – the colour of Lily's eyes.

'It's pretty,' she said. But she didn't take it although Harry was holding it out to her.

'Here, try it on. Give me your hand.'

Lily didn't move, so he reached out and picked up her left hand and tried to slip the ring onto her fourth finger. It went on as far as the joint and then stuck, although he tried to force it over the bone.

'You're hurting me.' Lily tried to pull away.

'Sorry. I'll have to have it made larger.'

'Perhaps my finger has swollen in the heat.' Lily rubbed her sore finger, but she looked relieved. She didn't want to wear Harry's ring until she had to. She was still hoping that fate would take a hand and she would be released from any permanent commitment. She jumped to her feet saying, 'Come on, Harry, time to move on.'

They drove further into the countryside, past farms and

cottages; but the earlier excitement seemed to have drained from Lily and she was feeling tired.

'Can we stop soon?' she asked, as the road ahead seemed to wind on endlessly. 'It'll be evening before long.'

'There's a pub ahead. We'll stop there and see if they have any rooms.'

The pub was called the Piltdown Man after the discovery in 1912 of a coconut-shaped skull reputed to be the most ancient human remain yet found in England. Archaeologists were still arguing about its authenticity, but it had brought fame to the small country village of Piltdown, and the one public house was named after the fossilized skull. There was a swinging sign outside that creaked in the wind, but it looked fairly clean and popular. But Lily didn't want to stay there for even one night. She'd heard that pubs attracted rats as well as drunks, and staying in one wasn't her idea of a country holiday.

'You go in,' she said. 'I'll stay in the car.'

She watched as Harry strolled across the gravelled forecourt and disappeared through the door leading to the saloon bar; then she leaned back in her seat and wound down the window as far as it would go.

It was still too hot. Her head ached and the skin under her hair felt damp and sticky. The road ahead was deserted, and although there was no pavement the grass was smooth and bordered with hedges of evergreen. On impulse she opened the car door and stepped out. One of her sandals slipped off, and the turf felt so deliciously cool under her bare foot she removed the other one, and dropped them back through the open window. She would take a little walk, just as far as the bend in the road, and then perhaps she would feel calmer when Harry returned and be nice to him.

She hadn't noticed the row of cottages ahead, so it came as a pleasant surprise when she saw a white fence, grey stone walls, and red roofs set back from the road. There were five cottages in all, all joined together, with patches of garden like floral aprons in front, lacy curtains, and dormer windows set in ivy-covered eaves. The only sound was the humming of insects and a dog barking, and far off the mutter of a tractor's engine.

'Boo!'

The unexpected sound came from somewhere close by. Lily

saw that the nearest gate was swinging from its hinges, and behind the white bars a face was peeping. It belonged to a tiny child, not much bigger than a baby, who had pulled itself up on unsteady legs. Wearing blue rompers and with short cropped brown curls, it was a boy child, she guessed. And a very appealing one at that.

Lily smiled and walked on; but when she heard the infant babbling his baby talk behind her she turned to wave. The weight of his solid body had pushed open the gate, and dropping to all fours he'd crawled out of the safety of the garden and was following Lily at a surprising pace for one so young.

'Where's your mummy?' she asked, bending over the little figure.

The child put up his hands as if he wanted to be picked up, so she reached down and lifted him into her arms. He quickly wriggled himself into a comfortable position and pressed his sticky face to her cheek. Lily wasn't used to children, particularly ones as young as this, but there was something so trusting about the way he was looking up into her face out of big brown eyes, that she fell in love with him there and then.

'Timmy!' a voice suddenly shrieked, and a figure came running around the side of the house, and exploded through the gate onto the grass verge 'Oh, there you are, my darling,' and the child was grabbed out of Lily's arms and covered with kisses.

'He crawled out of the gate,' Lily explained. 'It was lucky I was passing.'

'He's a little devil, aren't you, my darling? But Mummy loves you.'

Timmy's mummy turned out to be a girl of about Lily's age. A country girl, with rosy cheeks and a freckled nose, eyes as deep a brown as her son's, and hair as curly, only longer and more untidy. She was wearing a cheap cotton frock with damp patches under the arms, and a pinafore tied around her waist. Her legs were long and brown, and on her feet she wore shabby white plimsolls.

'He's a lovely child,' Lily said shyly. 'You must be proud of him.'

'Oh, I am. I'd have died if anything had happened to him, and Jake would never have forgiven me.' At Lily's questioning look she explained. 'Jake's my husband. He's a cowman at Thatcher's Farm. Timmy's our first child – so he's precious.'

'What's happening, Grace?'

Another woman had appeared round the corner of the house and was leaning over the gate watching them. An older woman, with white hair knotted into a bun, and twinkling eyes set in a plump homely face.

'Timmy got out,' Grace informed her; and then she turned again to Lily. 'This is my gran – Granny Langridge.'

'Mrs Langridge,' the older woman said reprovingly. 'I like to be called by my proper name.'

'Everyone calls her Granny Langridge,' Grace said with a grin. 'She loves it really. But she really is my gran.'

'I'm Lily.'

'Lily rescued our Timmy. Someone left the gate open and he got out.'

'Then you must come in and have some tea,' Granny Langridge invited. 'I've just brewed a fresh pot.'

Lily followed her new friends around the side of the house, past a vast vegetable garden, and up a cobbled path to the kitchen door. Tea was laid on a scrubbed table, but the room was so small they overflowed out of the back door. Lily found herself seated on the step, with a mug of tea in one hand and a buttered crust in the other. Grace sat beside her on a three-legged stool with Timmy on her lap, feeding him biscuits and orange juice. Her grandmother sat just inside the doorway guarding the teapot.

'Are you a visitor in these parts, my dear?' Mrs Langridge asked, spreading a thick layer of golden butter onto another slice of bread.

'I'm looking for somewhere to stay,' Lily told her. 'For a short holiday. I've been ill, you see, and my doctor thought a change of air would do me good. My friend is at the public house down the road, the Piltdown Man. He thought they might have a room to let for a few days.'

'I have a room,' Mrs Langridge said. 'These are only small cottages but Grace lives next door with Jake and Timmy, so I'm alone here now that I'm a widow. I don't usually let, but you're very welcome as long as you're not fussy.'

Lily liked the old lady so much that she didn't intend being fussy. This was the sort of cottage she'd dreamed about, and

Piltdown and its surroundings the sort of countryside she'd been yearning for. She liked Grace and her little son as well, and felt that in their company she would soon recover her spirits.

The tiny bedroom under the eaves that they showed her was charming. There were rag-rugs spread on the uneven boards, sprigged curtains at the window, and a patchwork quilt on the white painted bed. Lily felt as if she'd come home and hoped Harry wouldn't make any difficulties.

But Harry seemed delighted with the arrangements, and paid a generous two weeks' rent for Lily's board and keep. The Piltdown Man had only one empty room and he'd secured that for himself, as well as the use of a piano to practise on.

And so began an idyllic time for Lily. Her day started early, with the sun streaming into her little chamber and the birds twittering in the trees outside. Breakfast was soft-boiled eggs with speckled brown shells, toast and tea, eaten at the kitchen table, with the door wide open and a black cat purring on the step.

After the dishes were washed Lily sat in a deck chair under an apple tree and watched Mrs Langridge pottering about in the garden. It reminded her of St Jude's. She soon found herself carrying a basket on her arm and wearing a shady old straw hat on her head as she helped to strip the dark fruit from the currant bushes. Her legs and arms quickly turned a golden bronze in the sun.

Grace worked at the big house in the afternoons. It was called Piltdown Manor, and was the home of a wealthy couple called Mr and Mrs Sayer. Granny Langridge looked after Timmy while his mother was at work, and soon Lily was taking her turn at baby-minding. She watched over him while he played with his coloured bricks on the grass, and laughed with him while he built towers and then tumbled them down. Sometimes she strapped him into his push-chair and wheeled him across the common to the lakeside, where he liked to dabble his hands in the cool water and startle the fishes.

At tea-time he sat in his high chair and banged his spoon on the tray while they took it in turns to feed him. Then Grace, or his father, would collect him and take him next door to bed, and Lily would listen for the soft murmur of Grace's voice crooning to him as she rocked him to sleep.

Then the long languid evening was before her. She'd watch the sun go down, and the sky deepen, as she waited for Harry to take her for a drive or a drink; before she climbed the steep stairs to her own little room that fitted her as snuggly as a glove.

Every day Harry asked about her health. How was she feeling? Did her throat still hurt? When did she think she'd be well enough to sing again?

'The piano's quite good at the pub,' he assured her. 'They have it tuned regularly, and we can use it whenever we want.'

'Soon,' Lily promised. 'I don't want to rush things. I might damage my voice for good.'

'Well, don't leave it too long, Lilith, or you'll lose everything you've worked for.'

One evening during the second week Lily was waiting for Harry to collect her as usual. She'd spent the day helping her landlady make jam, and had delighted in the rich fruity smell as the currants and plums had bubbled on the stove. She'd arranged the heated jars for Mrs Langridge to pour in the hot jam with her steady, experienced hand, and then helped her to seal and label them and store them away in a dark cupboard for winter use.

But she wouldn't be here in the winter, Lily thought sadly. In fact she didn't know where she'd be and tried not to look too far into the future. Marriage to Harry and a lifetime of applause was all the future seemed to hold for her. She loved singing and couldn't imagine life without it, but watching Grace and Jake together, and their child Timmy, turned her heart over sometimes. Deep inside she was longing for a different way of life.

Lily made up her face carefully to please Harry, and brushed her hair until it shone. Without a professional hairdresser's attention it seemed sleeker and shinier, like the pelt of a wild animal. It hung to her shoulders in wings as it had in the old days. She was wearing a green dress with patch-pockets and a low-cut back. Her arms were bare, apart from a gold bangle that swung from one wrist.

Behind her the kitchen window was wide open. Mrs Langridge had the radio on and it was playing popular music. Suddenly Lily's attention was caught. They were playing a recording of one of her songs: an Ivor Novello number from *The Dancing Years*.

Lily hummed the opening bars, testing her throat. It didn't hurt any more than usual so she started to sing the words softly to herself. Her voice felt strange and croaky with disuse, but she persevered. When the music soared she tried to follow. The first time her voice cracked so she tried again.

'How slight the shadow that is holding us apart.'

The top notes broke again and even the lower register was unsteady. For the third time she sang the line, and this time she broke off in despair: she couldn't even hold the middle notes steady.

'Lilith.' She hadn't heard the gate open or Harry's steps on the path. 'What's the matter?'

Lily's face was wet with tears. 'I can't sing,' she said sadly. 'I've lost my voice.'

She wanted Harry to reassure her, to tell her that it didn't matter. Her eyes pleaded silently, but he turned on his heel and walked away. She heard the final click of the latch as he closed the gate firmly behind him.

CHAPTER TWENTY

A family gathering

Peter Jackson pushed the mower over the green lawn in front of Ring House under the late afternoon sun. He'd overhauled it and greased the mechanism but it still rattled noisily. He had to push it with all his strength to make even lines on the grass.

But he liked the job. The hard work had strengthened the muscles of his arms and legs, and the long hours spent labouring in the fresh air had weathered his skin to a dark brown. His check shirt had worked loose and flapped about his waist, and his rough hair stood up in spikes like the spines of a hedgehog. He whistled cheerfully as he bent his shoulders over the mower.

What with the whistling and the rattling he wasn't aware of someone approaching him until a shadow fell across his path. He let the blades run to a standstill before looking up.

'Afternoon, Mr Thomas.' Peter stood upright to ease his back. 'Two more strips and then I've finished for the day.'

'You're a good worker, Peter,' James said approvingly. 'Your father would have been proud of you.'

Peter smiled at the words of praise and bent over the machine again. But his employer was in no hurry and wanted to chat.

'And how's your mother? Keeping well, I hope.'

'She never complains; even when her legs are bothering her.

I try to make her rest but she says she's not used to it. She's worked hard all her life and finds it difficult to stop.'

'I know. A good woman, your mother is, Peter. You must make her take it more easy; none of us are as young as we were. I feel it myself, particularly when the weather's damp.'

'Screws, Mother calls it,' Peter said with a grin. 'Says she's got the screws in her joints.'

'And your brothers – how are they?'

'Mike's little'un will be two soon, and Amy's expecting again in the new year. Mother's hoping for a granddaughter this time – says it's about time there was a girl in the Jackson family. But Mike and Amy don't seem to mind. As long as it's healthy, they say, that's all that matters.'

'That's the right way to look at it,' James said, hooking his thumbs in his pockets and rocking backwards and forwards on his heels. 'I used to envy your parents with all you boys – and us with only the one girl.'

They were both silent. James was thinking about the other girl: the one called Lily that he'd wanted to adopt, and still thought of as part of his family. But it wasn't to be. He didn't even know what had become of her. Perhaps she was married now, and settled down to raise her own family. He hoped wherever she was she was happy. He owed her that.

Peter was also thinking about Lily. If she hadn't been so pigheaded and wayward, and run off like that with the doctor's son, he would have married her himself. She might have given his mother a granddaughter by now.

'There's plenty of time,' Peter said, as if he was trying to convince himself.

'That's what I used to say when I was your age. But you'll be surprised how quickly the years will pass.'

'That's what Mother's always saying, Mr Thomas. That reminds me: she was wondering if you had any news about Betty. We haven't seen her lately.'

'You wouldn't: she doesn't go about much at the minute. She's expecting any day now.'

'I did hear something.' Peter blushed at the woman's talk. 'Perhaps she'll give you the son you want.'

'I hope so. At least she's in good hands being married to a medical man. He's so devoted to her, and they live in such a fine house. Edward's proved himself to be a model husband.'

Again the two men fell silent, each dwelling on their own thoughts. The scandal of Betty Thomas being left at the altar, while her fiancé, Edward Butler, ran off with James' protégée, nicknamed Lily from the Valley, had been a seven-day wonder. But Doctor Butler had gone in pursuit of his wayward son and brought him home with his tail between his legs. Within weeks the wedding had gone ahead for the second time and it was an unqualified success. Everyone who saw them together remarked on how happy they looked. Betty was blooming, and Edward seemed to have got Lily out of his system. He'd returned to his studies and when he qualified would join his father in the Lewes practice.

Nobody mentioned Lily these days, and no one seemed to care what had become of her. But Peter often wondered about the dark-haired girl with the violet eyes; every girl he'd met since knowing Lily had seemed lacking in beauty and charm. She'd spoiled his life, just as she'd nearly spoiled Edward's.

'I'd better get on,' Peter said. 'Mother's expecting me home for tea. Mike and Amy are coming, and bringing little Alec, of course.'

'Then you mustn't be late. Remember me to them, won't you?'

'I will. And give Betty my best wishes.'

With a roar and a rattle Peter pushed the mower on, leaving even stripes on the lawn, and filling the air with the sweet scent of newly cut grass.

James sighed and walked back slowly towards the house. What wouldn't he have given for a son like that. A bit rough maybe, but a steady worker, who was going to make some lucky girl a good husband.

Peter finished his work and packed away his tools, after cleaning them carefully. He wanted to get home early to break the news to his mother that he'd invited a guest to the family tea party. Wasn't she always saying that it was about time he brought a girl home? Wasn't she always complaining that he'd end up a lonely old bachelor if he didn't hurry up? Well, he was going to surprise her. Not only had he invited a girl – but she'd accepted. And the girl in question was no other than the new village schoolteacher, Eleanor Clark. Peter was a bit surprised himself: surprised that he'd had the audacity to approach her, he who was usually so shy.

'Hey, Peter – they're here!'

Billy, Peter's younger brother, was running up the drive to meet him, shirt-tails flying in the wind and rosy cheeks aglow. He was fourteen and showed signs of being as untidy and energetic as his brother. They linked arms in a friendly fashion and strode side by side towards home.

'Mike's brought me a football,' Billy said. Peter was unlatching the gate, but Billy didn't bother with such mundane things. He vaulted over the fence and just missed landing in a flower-bed.

'It's not your birthday.'

'Not a new football. Someone kicked it over his garden wall, and as no one's claimed it he's given it to me.'

'We'll take it for a kickabout on the green later if you want.'

'Great!' Billy crashed open the front door and roared into the house closely followed by Peter.

Their noise was nothing to the row going on in the kitchen. The clatter of plates, the chatter of voices, the childish squeals of Peter's nephew Alec all rent the air. You would have thought there were ten families inside – not just one.

Family tea was always an occasion, and the table was laid with a crisp white cloth. There were plates of bread and butter, scones, and both fruit and plain cakes, bowls of salad as well as cold meats and pickles. Emma Jackson believed in feeding her loved ones well.

Amy, her daughter-in-law, was helping her. She was a small childlike person, with a sweet smile. She carried plates and utensils to the table, and only the small neat bulge under her cotton frock showed her second pregnancy. Her husband Mike, tall and broad as a bull, with a loud voice and a jovial manner, thundered around the small room getting in everybody's way. Meanwhile tiny Alec, thumb in mouth and cotton knickers sliding down over his bare bottom, toddled about, bumping painlessly into chair legs and table corners. Such a hullabaloo he made when he was lifted out of people's way that he was immediately administered a friendly cuff and put down again. At once he would resume his rackety exploration.

'Just in time, boys,' Emma said, beaming a welcome. 'Is the kettle on the stove, Amy?'

'I've just put it on, Mother.' Amy whisked the corner of the cloth out of her son's hand before he could tug it crooked.

'Don't do that, Alec. You'll have everything off the table.'

'It won't be long then.'

'There's no hurry,' Peter said. 'We're not all here yet. We need to set another place.'

Everyone was welcome at Emma's table and they often had unexpected guests, so Amy immediately laid another plate and knife and pulled up another chair. 'Who for?' she asked quietly.

'Eleanor Clark. I've invited her to tea. I hope you don't mind?'

'Eleanor Clark!' Emma Jackson looked at her son in surprise. 'The new schoolteacher?'

'That's the one.'

'I didn't know you knew her.'

'I met her by accident in the post office. She doesn't know many people in Lenton so I thought it would be friendly.'

He didn't tell his mother that he'd taken Eleanor Clark for several walks since their first meeting, and during these walks they'd exchanged confidences and got to know each other really well. Only yesterday they'd stopped to admire a view and he'd kissed her for the first time. It was a chaste kiss as Peter hadn't had much experience, but even so she'd seemed to like it.

Emma didn't let on that she'd seen the new schoolmistress walking through the village on several occasions with her head high; as if she thought she was too good for Lenton. Hoity-toity, Emma had decided she was.

'Whatever happened to Miss Stringer?' Mike asked, tweaking a cherry from the top of a sponge cake and popping it into his mouth quickly, hoping his mother wouldn't notice. He was still in awe of her although he was nearly twice her size, and a father himself. But Alec saw him and pulled at his trouser leg.

'Want one. Alec wants a cherry.'

'You're a bad example,' Emma said, smacking Mike's hand playfully. 'Miss Stringer left because her brother was ill. She's gone to Wales to look after him.'

'I liked Miss Stringer,' Mike said absently. He helped himself to a second cake, popped the cherry into his son's open mouth to stop him bawling, and the rest into his own.

'We all liked her,' Peter said. 'But Eleanor's just as nice. You'll love her when you get to know her. Here she comes now;

I can see her coming up the path.' He hurried to open the door to the new arrival.

Emma and Mike had raised their eyebrows at the word *love*, but when Peter ushered the visitor into the room they were all friendly smiles.

'How nice of you to come, Miss Clark,' Emma said. 'I'm Peter's mother. I've seen you in the village but haven't had a chance to introduce myself. Make the tea, Amy, the kettle's boiling.'

'Please call me Eleanor,' the young woman said in a refined voice. Peter pulled out a chair and she sat down at the table.

Miss Clark was a good-looking young woman a few years older than Peter. Her permed russet-coloured hair was held in place by a tortoiseshell comb, and her face was carefully made up. She was wearing a smart linen dress in a pale shade of green. It had a turned back collar and cuffs and brass buttons down the front, and a matching brass buckle securing the belt. She looked very neat, very clean, and rather out of place in the Jacksons' friendly kitchen. Emma wished Peter had warned her; then she would have opened up the parlour and she could have served tea out of the best tea service.

Peter, however, didn't seem put out. With a cheery grin he passed a plate to his guest.

'Bread and butter, Eleanor?' he asked. 'And there's ham and salad, or Mother's home-made jam?'

'I'll just have salad,' the young lady said. 'I don't want to get fat.'

Emma looked up from a plate that she'd piled with cold meats and pickles. 'I like people to have a healthy appetite,' she said.

'That's all right if you don't care how you look,' Eleanor said. She picked up a minute triangle of bread and nibbled the corner daintily.

Emma looked down at her own ample bosom and smiled. 'It's difficult to keep your shape as you get older,' she said. 'Particularly after having children.'

'That's all right.' Eleanor reached for the salad bowl and turned over the lettuce leaves as if she was expecting a caterpillar to poke its head out. 'I don't intend having any.'

'You'll change your mind when you're married,' Emma assured her. 'Won't she, Amy?'

Mike's wife patted her stomach. 'I won't regret it. Look at little Alec; I wouldn't change him for a perfect figure.'

Hearing his name mentioned the little boy leant his head against his mother's shoulder, leaving sticky stains on her sleeve. She didn't seem to mind.

'I thought teachers were supposed to like children,' Mike said, joining in the discussion 'Miss Stringer always did.'

'Of course I like children,' Eleanor said. 'It's my job. But it doesn't mean I want any of my own. Other people's are much better: you can get rid of them at the end of the day.'

'You wait; you'll fall in love like I did, and then you'll feel quite different.' Amy gave her husband a tender smile and gathered her son into her arms.

'Who wants more tea?' Emma asked, thinking it was time to change the subject. Miss Clark had turned out to be an uncomfortable visitor, and seemed an unlikely friend for Peter. But her son was ploughing through the plate of cakes as if he hadn't heard the conversation, and when he glanced at Eleanor his face reddened and he looked smitten. Emma couldn't imagine what he saw in the girl.

When tea was over the women cleared the table, but the teacher didn't join in. She sat in her chair smoothing her green skirts over her knees, and pulling them out of the way every time Alec ventured near.

'Why don't you show Eleanor the garden?' Emma suggested to Peter. He looked as if he didn't know what to do with himself.

'That's a good idea,' Peter said, leading the way. 'I've got some fine tomatoes in the greenhouse, and the roses are at their most colourful. They're a bit blown so I'd better not pick them – they drop their petals as soon as you bring them into the house.'

Eleanor followed him outside, and Mike covered his mouth to stop himself laughing out loud. Amy nudged him with her elbow.

'Don't you dare say anything,' she said with a smile 'I expect your mother had doubts about me.'

'But you're not prickly – and you don't worry about your figure.'

'Not much chance with you about.'

'Shh!' Mike said as Emma passed with a tray of crocks. 'I

expect he felt sorry for her; you know how soft he is.'

'Soft in the head if you ask me,' his mother said. 'There's me trying to get him to court a girl – and who does he choose but a schoolteacher.'

In the garden Peter showed off his tomatoes and wondered why Eleanor didn't share his enthusiasm. But she brightened up when he found one solitary yellow bud on a rose bush and tucked it into the buttonhole of her dress.

'Shall we go for a walk?' Peter felt Eleanor would feel more comfortable away from the house. 'We could go as far as the village shop: I need some laces.'

'And I need stamps and envelopes.'

She seemed to relax as they strolled down the lane, and Peter couldn't help taking half-glances of admiration in her direction. Her hair was the colour of autumn leaves and she walked with a swaying motion, her legs outlined against the fabric of her skirt that blew backwards like a sail. She was so handsome that he was a little bit in awe of her. She'd been quite compliant on the other occasions when she'd walked out with him so he reached out and took her hand in his. She didn't seem to mind, and her cool fingers curled around his, gently squeezing.

'Eleanor – let's stop a minute.'

'What for?'

She turned to face him, and there was a smile on her painted lips as if she was thinking of something amusing. The way his mother smiled at Billy sometimes.

'You know what for. I want to kiss you.'

She stood still on the path and Peter put his arms around her. Close together like this she was the taller of the two, and her hair tickled his cheek. He pulled her close, wishing she'd bend a little, but Eleanor stood almost uninterestedly in his embrace, her eyes closed and her lips pouting. Peter could smell flowers and thought it was her perfume, until he saw they were standing in front of a bank of yellow honeysuckle and the air was full of its scent.

'Don't mess my hair. I only had it permed yesterday.'

Peter had thought the curls and waves were natural, and wished Eleanor hadn't disillusioned him. If he'd also been aware that the colour was out of a bottle he'd have been even more disappointed. Her lips, and her coldness, excited him. He pushed her up against the bank, his body pressed to hers so that she could feel his hardness.

'I love you, Eleanor,' he said huskily.

It didn't sound like a lie, but he couldn't have told her the truth. He wanted her; his body was on fire and longed for release. He wanted to plunge himself up to the hilt in her womanhood. To explore her femininity, and break down the cold shell that enclosed her.

'Do you, Peter?' she said. Her eyes were open now, regarding him quizzically. Then she said, 'I don't think we should be doing this.'

'Why not? We're not doing anything wrong. We're only kissing.'

'But kissing can lead to other things – and only married people should do them,' she said demurely. She sounded like a sixteen-year-old, instead of a woman in her mid-twenties.

'Let's get married then.'

It was out; he'd said it and there was no going back. He wanted a wife and children, like his brother Mike. He wanted to care for his mother in her advancing years and he needed a wife to help him . . . share things.

Eleanor had said she didn't want children, but that would change if she married him. Whoever heard of a woman not loving their children after they'd carried and given birth to them? And Eleanor knew all about children, being a schoolteacher. It would be all right. If they didn't love each other now, they'd soon learn to.

'Are you proposing to me, Peter Jackson? Do you mean it? Or are you joking?'

'Of course I mean it.' Peter's knees had turned to jelly, as had the rest of him. 'What do you say?'

'Well . . .' Eleanor started to walk again, swaying her hips so that Peter had difficulty concentrating. 'I've come from a good family, you know. My parents wouldn't want me to marry just anyone.'

'You mean I'm not good enough for you?' Peter felt cross as well as disappointed. Who did she think she was anyway? His family was as good as anybody's around here; she should think herself lucky. 'I've got a job and everything – and I'd look after you.'

'I'd want a house and nice furniture, and I'm used to having good clothes. My father gives me an allowance for extras I can't afford on my teacher's salary, but he'd stop it if I had a husband to provide for me.'

'Of course. I'd see to everything. Say yes.'

Peter was having to run to keep up with Eleanor's long strides. He'd never proposed to a girl before and didn't like being put off. Why didn't she say yes or no, and put him out of his misery?

They reached the village and she still hadn't said anything and his ardour was waning fast. Lily wouldn't have teased a fellow like this. Lily had known what she wanted so he'd never asked her to marry him. Lily had wanted Edward Butler and run off with him; and then Edward had come back and married Betty Thomas after all. But no one knew, or seemed to care, what had happened to Lily. But if she was here now it would be her he'd be proposing to, and she wouldn't have kept him waiting even if she was going to turn him down.

Eleanor was speaking again, and Peter had to switch back quickly to the present.

'I'm sorry, Eleanor – what did you say?'

'I said, here's the shop. I thought you wanted some laces.'

They entered together. While Eleanor was buying stamps and choosing stationery Peter rummaged in a cardboard box for bootlaces of the right colour and length. He couldn't find what he wanted so passed over half-a-crown and asked for twenty cigarettes instead. He didn't often smoke, but thought that it might impress Eleanor and make her think him more manly. He had to buy matches as well, and lounged in the shop doorway puffing in an amateur fashion and trying not to cough.

'Can I have one?'

Peter looked at Eleanor in surprise. He'd never seen a lady smoking before although he'd read in magazines that they did. But here in Lenton it would certainly be frowned upon, particularly in public.

'If you want.'

He watched in fascination as Eleanor screwed up her eyes and drew in the smoke as if she'd been doing it all her life. Then she walked out into the village street, the cigarette dangling from her bottom lip and a stream of grey smoke trailing in her wake.

'Hullo, Peter.'

Peter hadn't noticed the approaching figure, but now he recognized the stout man with the swinging cane as his employer, James Thomas.

'Sorry, Mr Thomas – I didn't see you.' He grinned sheepishly, and dropping the cigarette, ground it out with his heel.

'I hope you weren't late for your tea party?'

'No.'

'And who is your friend?' James smiled at the russet-haired young woman. He was surprised. He wouldn't have thought she was the sort of person Peter Jackson would be attracted to.

'This is Eleanor Clark. Eleanor – this is my employer, Mr Thomas of Ring House.'

'Delighted to meet you, Miss Clark.' James shook the girl's hand warmly, noting the painted nails and the false curls. 'Any friend of Peter's is a friend of mine.'

'I'm the new schoolteacher,' Eleanor said proudly. 'I hope to make some changes.'

'For the good, I hope?'

'Of course. Everything is so old-fashioned, and I hear my predecessor wasn't up to the job.'

'Miss Stringer was a wonderful woman.' James frowned at Eleanor's criticism. 'The children loved her.'

'I'm here to do a job, and I intend doing it to the best of my ability. I don't expect to be loved.'

She walked past Mr Thomas and Peter hoped he didn't think her rude. He started to follow, but an idea struck him and he turned back.

'Mr Thomas.'

'Yes, Peter.'

'Can I ask you something? It won't take more than a minute.'

'Of course – but you mustn't keep your ladyfriend waiting.' James glanced at Eleanor, but she seemed quite happy. She was sitting on a low wall by the side of the road, inspecting her purchases. Occasionally she put the cigarette to her mouth and attempted to blow a smoke-ring. 'What is it?'

'I'm thinking of settling down.'

'Getting married, you mean?'

'I hope so.' Peter paused, and then carried on before he could change his mind. 'The thing is – I need a house.'

'None of the cottages are empty, I'm sorry to say. I've sold a lot of them off. I'd have helped if I could; you'd be a good tenant.'

'That's just it, Mr Thomas.' Peter faced his employer proudly. 'I don't want to be a tenant. When I wed I want my bride to have her own house, paid for by me. I want you to sell me our cottage.'

'What about your mother? I hope you don't intend turning her out?'

'Of course not. Wherever I go Mother will go. I promised Dad that. It's not a very big place, but there's room for a wife and a family.'

'Can you afford to buy it, Peter?'

'It depends what you'd be asking,' Peter said hopefully.

James thought quickly. He liked the young man and wanted to help him. But money was tight and he couldn't afford to be too generous. On the other hand the Jackson family had lived in their cottage for as long as he could remember. Bert Jackson, Peter's father, had been his chauffeur and gardener, collected his rents and helped manage the estate. Peter had taken over many of the jobs after his death and had proved to be just as reliable.

'Could you manage twelve hundred? There's not only the cottage, there's the garden as well. It's quite a sizable property and the price would be much higher if it was offered to a stranger.'

Peter was busy doing sums in his head. 'That's very generous of you, Mr Thomas,' he said at last. 'I've got savings, and Mother's still got the money from Dad's insurance. If it falls short I know Mike will lend me something. He's got a good job.'

'Perhaps you'd like to think about it?'

'No.' Peter put out his hand: the matter was settled as far as he was concerned. 'I'll be pleased to accept your offer.'

'I'll have the papers drawn up then.' They shook hands on the deal, and were just about to go their separate ways when James Thomas had an afterthought. 'By the way, Peter,' he said amiably, 'I can't remember when I last gave you a rise. How would an extra threepence an hour suit you?'

'Thank you, Mr Thomas.' Peter beamed. For a forty-hour week threepence an hour would boost his weekly earnings considerably.

'And isn't it time you had a holiday? I don't remember you ever asking for one.'

'Dad didn't believe in holidays ' Peter said. 'He liked his work too much.'

'You could take the young lady for a change of air.' James nodded in Eleanor's direction. 'I'm sure she'd be willing.'

'I'll think about it. Thank you anyway.'

They parted amicably and Peter joined Eleanor. She got to her feet and took his arm. 'What was all that about?' she asked. 'You look pleased with yourself.'

'I am. Come on – let's walk.'

They walked arm in arm out of the village and back up the leafy lane. It was quiet and cool now with the branches of the trees almost meeting overhead. Peter waited until they reached a spot where a tree had blown down after a gale many years before. The top had been levelled to make a seat, and it was so wide there was room for two people to sit side by side as long as they sat close. It was a popular place for courting couples.

Peter sat down, and taking Eleanor's hand said solemnly, 'You didn't answer my question.'

'Which question was that?'

'The one when I asked you to marry me.'

'Oh, that one.' Eleanor pulled her hand away and looked thoughtfully into the distance. 'I told you my terms.'

'I know.' Peter tried not to sound too eager. 'You said you wanted a house – well, I've got you one.'

That startled Eleanor. 'A house!' she said incredulously, and then, 'I hope it's a nice one.'

'It is.' Peter beamed with pride.

'What's it like? Where is it?'

'One question at a time, please.' He was delighted at her interest. 'It's a cottage, and it's not far from here. In fact you had tea there this afternoon.'

There was a pause, and then Eleanor pulled her hand away. 'You don't mean your mother's cottage?'

'Yes. Mr Thomas has just agreed to sell it to me.'

'It's a bit small, isn't it? And where is your mother going to live?'

'With us, of course. You didn't think I'd turn her out, did you?'

'But she's an old woman . . .'

'Not that old.' He tried to take Eleanor into his arms, but she was so stiff that he didn't press it. Perhaps she needed time to get used to the idea. He tried to explain. 'I promised Dad I'd look after her, and as she gets older she'll need more care. Anyway, I think it's nice for two generations to live together and share things. And when we have children she'll be able to help. She loves being a grandmother: you saw how good she was with Alec.'

Eleanor got up abruptly from the tree-stump and walked a few paces away. Then she turned and he was surprised by the cold expression on her face.

'I never said I'd marry you, Peter,' she said. 'A few kisses doesn't mean anything. When I decide to get married I shall have a house of my own, in a nice town where there are shops and things. I'm not going to bury myself in the country in a poky little cottage, with a horrible old woman to look after. And as for children, I see enough of them in my job without having any of my own. You need to marry some country bumpkin, Peter Jackson, because you'll never wed me,' and turning on her heel and swishing her green skirts she walked away, up the lane and under the nodding boughs, without even saying goodbye.

Peter sat for a long time without moving. He was thinking things over, but his heart wasn't broken. Eleanor Clark obviously wasn't the girl for him and he was glad he'd found out in time.

But if he couldn't have Eleanor – who could he have? He bent down to pull a blade of grass and suck the sweetness from its stem. Hiding in the shadows was a clump of mauve flowers with petals like stars. The blossoms seemed to be looking up at him and he was reminded of a girl with eyes the same colour, and hair as dark as the surrounding shadows. A girl he always thought of as Lily from the Valley.

Lily had always loved his mother. She'd never have spoken about her in such an unpleasant way. That was who he needed to find – a girl like Lily. Suddenly he felt pleased that Eleanor Clark had shown herself in her true colours, because now he was free.

Peter got up from the tree-stump, brushed down his trousers, and began to retrace his steps. As he walked home he whistled a merry tune as if all was right with his world.

CHAPTER TWENTY-ONE

On the trail

'Have you seen Eleanor Clark recently, Peter?'

That young man was sitting on a bench outside his mother's kitchen cleaning his boots. He took a pride in buffing the leather until he could see his face reflected in the toe-caps. He didn't answer immediately; just bent over his work. Emma Jackson tried again to get her son's attention.

'I asked if you'd seen Miss Clark?'

'No – I haven't.'

'I passed her in Lenton the other morning. I think she was on her way to school. I waved, but I don't think she saw me.'

'I expect she was in a hurry.'

'I expect she was.'

They were silent again. It wasn't the usual comfortable silence between mother and son; it was the sort of silence when both were aware of the other's thoughts but afraid to put their own into words.

'Mike and Amy will be coming on Saturday; perhaps you'd like to ask Eleanor.'

'I don't think so, Mother.'

The words were out and they could look at each other again. Emma saw the pain in her son's face and Peter saw the relief on his mother's. She hadn't taken to Eleanor, although if the schoolteacher had been Peter's choice, she'd have welcomed her into the family and tried to make the best of things.

'I'm sorry,' she said, and patted his shoulder briefly as she passed to peg a sheet onto the washing-line.

'There's no need.' Peter continued rubbing vigorously. 'She wouldn't have been happy living here. She's a handsome girl, but I didn't love her although I tried. I found I was always comparing her with . . .' He stopped as if he was afraid of saying too much.

'You mean you were always comparing her with Lily?' She'd said it, and when Peter looked up into her eyes he saw nothing but understanding there. She knew more about him than he'd imagined.

'You knew?' he said softly.

'Yes, I've always known. When you were small you were besotted with her; but even then she was always chasing after that boy: Edward, the doctor's son. I felt sorry for the poor little thing but I could never dislike her. She just had ideas above her station. I'm sure whatever happened wasn't her fault entirely.'

'Eleanor seems to think that the way we live is beneath her. Lily would never behave like that.'

'No, son. You still love her, don't you?'

'Yes. It's funny but nobody will talk about her any more, as if they're all pleased she's gone. I think they all want to forget her, but I want to find out where she is – what happened. But how can I when no one will even mention her name?'

'I suppose Edward Butler would be the one to ask – but it would be difficult.'

'I couldn't ask him,' Peter said emphatically. 'He's married now. He wouldn't want to talk to me about things that happened in the past.'

'He might if you could get him alone,' Emma said. 'He might be feeling guilty, and worried about Lily himself. He might be pleased that someone wants to do something about it.'

'What do you suggest I do, Mother? Take a trip over to Lewes and make an appointment at his father's consulting rooms; or maybe I should knock on his front door and have a chat with Betty?' He sounded bitter, and that wasn't like Peter. It just proved to Emma how deep his feelings were.

'Don't talk like that, son,' she said. 'I was only trying to help.'

'I know.'

'What about Lily's friends? Do you know of anybody in Lenton she might have kept in touch with?'

Peter thought, but had to shake his head. 'Lily wasn't a mixer, not like some of the kids. I think she was ashamed of her background, although she loved old Matthew Crow and wouldn't hear a word against him. But apart from the Thomas's there was only us as far as I know.'

'Well, that's a start anyway.' Emma made another trip to the washing-line and pegged out a row of towels. 'If you can't ask Edward you could always start with Mr Thomas or the Crows. Someone must have heard from her. She hasn't disappeared from the face of the earth.'

But as far as Peter was concerned Lily might well have done. He brooded on her whereabouts until his work suffered, and he nearly jammed a fork into his foot when he was raking over a flower-bed at Ring House. He'd have to pull himself together before someone noticed his absent-mindedness; and the only way to do that was to set his enquiries into action. The following day he packed away his tools at noon, and as it was his half-day, set out.

'Hullo, Peter. Where you off to?'

It was his brother, Billy, wheeling his bicycle up the hill towards home. Peter had been so preoccupied he hadn't noticed the boy. He grinned warmly. He could still remember what it was like to be fourteen: untidy, easily embarrassed, and all arms and legs. Billy took after his brother, but he also had an unattractive crop of pimples around his mouth that he was very conscious of.

'Just dropping by Valley Farm. Can I borrow your bike?'

'Of course.' Billy handed his precious machine over. It was old and wobbly, but he was proud of it and kept it in good condition. He knew Peter would look after it. 'What do you want to go to the farm for?'

'A private matter.' Peter steadied the machine and cocked his leg over the bar.

'One of the boys in my class lost his dog and thought it might have strayed that way. The old man saw him and chased him off. Threatened to shoot him and all – and he said it looked as if he would, too.'

'Was that Moses or Matthew?'

'Moses, I think. The older brother. He's wicked, and his wife's mad.'

'You shouldn't repeat things,' Peter reproved.

'But it's true. I've seen Mrs Crow in the churchyard. She was lying over a grave and wailing, and her hair was down and her skirts torn. It was frightening. I thought at first she was a ghost.'

'Her babies all died,' Peter said. 'That's enough to turn any woman's brain.'

'Well, if you're going to Valley Farm you'd better watch out. Do you want me to come with you?'

'Thanks, Billy, but no. I can manage,' and Peter pushed off with his foot and pedalled away.

The first part of the way was downhill so it was easy going, and he enjoyed the ride through the country lanes which were almost deserted. He crested a rise and saw a panorama spread out below. Fields bordered by hedges looked like multi-coloured patchwork quilts, and from a distance the men busy working resembled ants. But the land belonging to Valley Farm was deserted and overgrown with brambles, and when he reached a gap in a hedge where once a gate had stood no one would have guessed it led to a once prosperous farm.

Peter dismounted and pushed his machine through; but the path was so uneven, and the trees grew so close together, that he decided to abandon it. He pushed the bicycle carefully out of sight behind a holly bush.

On foot the going was easier. He had no plans, just thought he'd look the place over. If he met one of the brothers he'd pretend that he'd lost his way and strike up a conversation. Eventually he'd try and bring up the subject of Lily, and then perhaps he'd learn something. Matthew would be the best bet: they knew each other by sight, and sometimes passed the time of day when they saw each other in the village. Years before Lily had introduced them when Matt had been locked out of the farmhouse. Peter had promised Matt that he'd take care of Lily. He'd only been a boy and it was a long time ago – he wondered if Matthew remembered.

'I won't let you do it! Leave me alone.'

The voice came from somewhere ahead. It was a man's voice: a sort of wail that ended in a sob.

'I'll do it whenever I want. You can't stop me, brother.'

'Please, Mo . . .'

Peter knew it was the Crow brothers even before he came upon them. They were in the cobbled yard in front of the farmhouse. Moses' huge frame towered over the smaller, shrunken figure of Matthew, who was kneeling in front of him. He didn't understand what was going on but it looked like some private ritual.

He stopped in his tracks, and tried to draw back into the shelter of the trees so as not to be seen. But he was too late. A big black dog who'd been dozing in the sun leapt to its feet, and barking loudly ran towards him.

'Here, boy!' Moses called, and the dog's ears flattened at the command in his master's voice. He slunk away from the visitor, tail between legs, to cower at the farmer's heels.

'Good afternoon, Mr Crow,' Peter said, and walked forward with his hand held out in greeting. 'I lost my way back there.' He pointed over his shoulder. 'I must have taken a wrong turning.'

'What do you want?'

'I don't want anything. I've just told you, I lost my way.'

'This is private property. No one comes on my land without my permission.' Moses was advancing on Peter, and his movements looked threatening. Peter wasn't going to let a bully frighten him so he stood his ground. 'Hey, I know you, don't I?'

'Peter Jackson, Mr Crow.' Peter held out his hand again with a friendly gesture.

'You're one of Thomas's cronies, aren't you? I've seen you with him.' Moses ignored the hand and thrust his red-veined face close to Peter's.

'I work for Mr Thomas at Ring House.'

'So he's sent you to spy on me?'

'No. He doesn't know I'm here.'

'Well, he soon will: I'll see to that. I'll get you the sack; and in the meantime get off my land.'

He gave Peter a push with his large hands. Peter knew he wasn't a match for him. He was strong, but Moses was built like a bull, and wasn't afraid to use brute strength when he was angry. He was angry now and out to fight all comers.

'I'm going now. Good afternoon to you.'

'Matt!' Moses roared.

'Yes, Mo?'

'See Mr Jackson off my land.'

Matthew Crow stumbled forward, bent almost double. He was a pathetic figure with his tattered clothes and uncut hair, and a stubble of greying beard under his loose mouth.

'There's no need,' Peter said. 'I know the way.'

'You see, brother!' Moses roared triumphantly. 'I said it was a plot, didn't I? You said you'd lost your bearings, and you were spying all the time. Get him out, Matt, and see he doesn't come back.'

'You'd better come,' Matthew said softly, and began to lead the way back up the path.

The dog started to follow but a piercing whistle brought him back to his master's heel. Moses grabbed the animal viciously around the neck and pushed him in front of him into the house. Peter stopped in the shelter of the trees and smiled at Matthew.

'Don't worry,' he said. 'I'm going. There's no need for you to come with me.'

Matthew looked back over his shoulder; his eyes were wide and fearful. 'I must do as he says – he's got a gun.'

'He wouldn't use it, would he?'

'Yes, he would. It's my gun: the one I used to pot rabbits with. He took it from me, and now he threatens me with it to make me do what he wants.'

'Is that what he meant when he said you couldn't stop him?' Peter waited but Matthew didn't answer, just shuffled unhappily and hung his head. 'I'm sorry, but I couldn't help overhearing. What did he want to do?'

'You wouldn't believe me.'

'Yes, I would. I promise. You can tell me – perhaps I can help.'

So Matthew told Peter. He told a chilling story about the years of abuse he'd suffered at his brother's hands, in the name of love. Peter could see he wasn't lying: he could see the truth shining in the pale tear-filled eyes, and the trembling voice. All the while Matthew spoke his hands worked nervously as if he couldn't control them. At last the pathetic voice ceased; Peter put out his hand as if to console the man.

'And you've never told anybody before?'

'There wasn't anyone to tell.' The admission of being so alone in the world seemed to be too much for Matthew: a tear ran down his cheek.

'But there's your brother's wife. Surely she could have put a stop to it?'

'Edie? Moses treats Edie like an animal. He claims to speak in the name of God – but I thought God protects animals.' The simplicity of his words moved Peter. 'And children.'

Suddenly a terrible thought struck Peter. This was where Lily had spent the first few years of her life. He'd heard the story of how she'd been found in the barn. A gipsy woman was supposed to have abandoned her when she was only a few hours old. He couldn't imagine a helpless child growing up in this dreadful place where a religious fanatic ruled, and whose sexual appetites dwelt on incest. Perhaps his victims also included children. If he'd molested Lily in any way he'd have to pay, and Peter swore silently to himself that the price would be high.

'Lily,' he said softly. 'Did he ever touch Lily?'

A smile lit Matthew's face: a tender smile at the mention of the name he loved. 'He wouldn't dare,' he said. 'Lily was mine.'

'You mean you cared for her? I know she loved you.'

'I know I'm slow,' Matthew said. 'But I have feelings, you know.'

'Of course you have.'

'Mo looked after me when I was a lad. The other boys would laugh at me and Mo would see them off. In return I did what he wanted. Edie was good to me too; but after she had the baby her brain went soft.'

'You mean the babies buried in the cemetery?'

'No. The one she had in the barn – my baby.'

'Your baby?'

Peter stared at the trembling figure in front of him. His brain had obviously gone as well. If Lily was the baby he was talking about, Edie wasn't her mother. She couldn't be or surely she would have claimed her. And Matthew couldn't be Lily's father – could he?

'I'd never had a woman – didn't know about things like that. Only knew about animals and what they did. But we'd been drinking, and Mo made me do it.'

'Moses made you make love to his wife?'

'Yes. It seemed all right at the time and Edie didn't care,' Matthew said wistfully. 'She hated Mo so much she'd go with anybody. She'd even gone with James Thomas, and Mo'd never forgiven her. He caught her creeping in late one night and beat her until she admitted who she'd been with.'

'Are you telling me that Mrs Crow let Mr Thomas of Ring House make love to her?' Peter couldn't believe what he was hearing.

'She must have done. That's why Mo hates being beholden to him. Mr Thomas wanted him to buy this farm; but Mo thinks it's his by right after what was done to his wife.'

'It's a terrible story,' Peter said. 'But you weren't to blame. No wonder Lily cares so much for you.'

'Lily doesn't know.' Another tear trickled down Matthew's cheek. 'But she was always kind to me, and I never let him hurt her. I didn't want her to go away – why did Lily go away?'

'Sometimes people have to,' Peter said gently. He couldn't explain to this troubled creature the real reason Lily had left. 'Haven't you heard from her? Hasn't she written to anyone?'

'No. Why should she? She won't come back – will she?'

'Listen,' Peter said. 'I'm Lily's friend, and I care about her as much as you do. The real reason I came here today was to find out if anyone had news of Lily's whereabouts. Haven't you any idea where she could have gone? After the things you've just told me I think it's even more important that she should be found. She needs to know that Mrs Crow's her mother – if it's true – perhaps there's a way the two of them could be reunited. I'm going to find her; and when I do I'm going to bring her back.'

Matthew's face lit up. He'd dreamed of his Lily coming home again, and he believed this young man would do what he said. There was an honest look about him; if anybody could find Lily – he could.

They parted then, and Peter left Matthew looking more cheerful. Peter knew what he had to do, and there was no time like the present. He retrieved his bicycle, and was just about to wheel it into the road when he heard a sound. He looked up curiously at the figure advancing towards him.

It was a woman: a tall, thin woman, wearing a strange old-fashioned dress with a dropped waistline and sailor collar.

Once it would have been smart and considered the height of fashion, but now, dirty and ragged and the collar awry, it hung on the bony frame like old clothes on a scarecrow. The woman's hair hung over her face in unwashed strands, and colourless eyes stared expressionlessly at Peter. The sound that came from the cracked lips was a travesty of singing; more a keening that drifted on the air like the cry of a wild animal.

She was almost upon him when Peter recognized the scarecrow as Edith, Moses Crow's wife. Wheeling his bicycle he walked to meet her. If this woman was Lily's mother she might know something.

'Good afternoon, Mrs Crow,' he said politely. 'How are you?'

Edith stopped She looked frightened, and glanced around as if searching for a way of escape. But the undergrowth was thick, and apart from retracing her steps there was no way but forward. The young man was standing directly in her path.

'Who are you?' she asked, peering short-sightedly into his face.

'I'm Peter Jackson. I've been talking to your husband.' Talking was an understatement but he couldn't tell her the truth.

'Moses! You've been talking to Moses?'

'Yes – and your brother-in-law, Matthew. I'm a friend of Lily's and wondered if you had her address. I want to write her a letter and don't know where to send it.'

'Lily.' A sly look came over Edith's face. 'Lily who?'

'Your daughter Lily.'

'I haven't any daughters – only sons – four dead sons.' She began wailing again like an animal in pain. She covered her face with her hands and rocked backwards and forwards.

'And one daughter,' Peter insisted. 'Lily.'

'Lily!' Edith froze. She stared at Peter as if she was seeing him for the first time. 'Lily's mother was a harlot.'

'Are you Lily's mother?' Peter asked gently.

'That's what I said: her mother was a harlot. Moses said so.' Suddenly coming to life Edith pushed past him and ran down the path towards the farmhouse, her tattered skirts flapping behind her.

Peter stared after her until she was out of sight. Then he pushed the bicycle out onto the road and mounted it. He wanted to find Lily now for two reasons. The first one was that she needed to know the information he'd discovered, although he wasn't sure if he believed it. Even if the revelation upset her it was better to know the worst and come to terms with it. The other reason was that he felt she might be in need of help. Only by discovering her whereabouts could he find out what sort of life she was leading. If she was happy he would go away quietly and never bother her again – but if she wasn't, she might turn to him now that Edward was safely married and out of the way of temptation.

As Peter pedalled his way along the country lanes his plan of action became clear. His first call was at Ring House.

He'd hoped to find Mr Thomas in the grounds but the gardens seemed to be deserted. He leaned the bicycle up against the wall of the house and knocked boldly at the front door. After a few minutes Elizabeth Thomas opened it herself and a look of disapproval passed over her face. Her gaze went immediately to Peter's working boots which were dusty although he'd polished them only that morning.

'What are you doing at the front door, Peter?' she asked sharply. 'You usually use the side entrance.'

'I'm in a hurry,' Peter explained. 'Is your husband in?'

'No. He's out visiting. Can I help you? I can't ask you in unless you take those dirty boots off.'

'I don't want to come in. I just want to give Mr Thomas a message. He told me I needed a holiday and I've decided to take one. Only a few days; I'm sure he'll understand.'

'When do you want to start this holiday?'

'Now. It's something important and I want to go now.'

Elizabeth looked at the young man standing in front of her with alarm. He was usually so quiet and polite, and she'd never heard this firm tone in his voice before. He sounded as if he knew what he wanted, and intended getting it.

'It might not be convenient,' she said.

'I'm sorry, Mrs Thomas. Tell your husband I'll explain later. I know he'll understand.' And Peter turned away, leaving a surprised Mrs Thomas staring after him.

He headed for home, and found his mother up to her elbows peeling vegetables at the kitchen sink. Billy was laying the table for supper. The appetizing aroma of stew and dumplings came from a black pot simmering on the stove.

'I want to borrow Billy's bike; and do you know where that old canvas haversack is?' he shouted as he headed for the stairs. 'I'm going away for a few days – to look for Lily.'

'You're not going anywhere, my lad, until you've had a good supper and a night's rest,' Emma said firmly. 'So you may as well sit down at the table and get on with it.'

She dried her hands, and commenced doling out the stew with a large ladle. Peter did as he was told. Between mouthfuls he told her what he had in mind.

'I'll make sure the bike's safe,' Billy said eagerly. 'The brakes want checking and I'll pump the tyres up really hard. You'd better take my puncture repair kit with you just in case.'

'And pack a waterproof,' Emma instructed. 'And at least one change of clothes. I'll make you some sandwiches. And money – don't forget to take enough money for emergencies.'

They packed him off to bed early but he was too excited to sleep. He was on the road by eight-thirty the following morning, the loaded haversack strapped to his shoulders and Billy's bicycle gleaming with polish.

His first destination was Lewes. It would take him at least half an hour to ride there, depending on the traffic. His intention was to seek out Edward Butler and try to get a lead from him. After all, Edward was the last person to see Lily, and although two years had passed it was at least a starting point. He had to start somewhere.

It was a beautiful morning, with a clear blue sky and plenty of warm sunshine. There was a fresh breeze, but it was behind him and helped him on his way.

Even so it took him longer than he'd anticipated because he missed his way a couple of times, and when he finally free-wheeled down a hill and over the River Ouse into the town it was well past nine. The shops were just opening their doors for the day. The town was built on the side of a hill, and the streets were so steep that Peter had to dismount and push his machine. Over his head loomed the remains of the castle, dark and mysterious against the skyline.

He found a workmen's café down a side-street and sat on a high stool at a shiny counter. He drank a cup of strong tea while he waited for a second breakfast.

The plate of bacon and eggs that was finally placed in front of him looked and smelt good, and tasted delicious. He ate quickly and then wiped the plate clean with a wad of bread before ordering a second cup of tea. Now his stomach was comfortably lined he was ready to make enquiries. The woman behind the counter was refilling the teapot from a steaming urn; as she turned to face him Peter caught her eye.

'Do you know of a doctor's surgery in this part of the town?' he asked. 'I'm looking for a Doctor Butler, and I've been told he has a practice in Lewes.'

'Sam!' the woman called into the back of the premises. 'What's the name of our doctor?'

'Charmian – no, Chapman. Something like that,' a man's voice replied.

'Not Butler?'

'No. You're thinking of that practice off the High Street. Castle Street, I think it's called. There's a Doctor Butler there and a son who's studying medicine.'

'That's the one I want,' Peter said, draining his cup and climbing down from the stool. 'Thanks very much. Which way is it?'

'Go up the hill, and then it is a turning on the left.'

Peter retrieved his bicycle, and following the directions he'd been given soon found himself outside a double-fronted house in Castle Street. The Georgian façade opened onto the pavement, and there were rows of small-paned windows, a large heavy door with a brass handle set in the centre, and a brass plate fixed to the wall with the doctor's name engraved on it. By the size of the place, and the opulence of the building, John Butler was doing well for himself.

Peter pressed a bell, pushed open the door, and found himself in a square hall which was obviously being used as a waiting room. It was lined with chairs, and a low table in the centre contained dog-eared magazines. Morning surgery was in progress. Peter took his place and tried to wait patiently.

An elderly man came out of an inner room clutching a prescription, and a woman who'd come in after Peter nudged him and spoke in a low voice.

'It's your turn. You just knock at the door and walk in.'

She watched as Peter followed her instructions. She thought he was an odd client in his rough clothes, and he obviously hadn't consulted Doctor Butler before because he left the door open behind him and she could hear part of the conversation.

'What do you want, young man? You're not one of my patients.' And then came the murmur of the answering voice as if the young man was explaining something. 'I don't think it's any of your business,' Doctor Butler then said angrily.

The reply was something about a person called Lily being very much the young man's business.

'Leave Edward alone,' she heard the doctor retort loudly. 'That girl's done enough harm.' Then he seemed to weaken and said in a different tone of voice. 'Try Pierhaven. That's where she was living two years ago.'

'Thank you, sir,' Peter said, and strode out of the house leaving all the doors swinging open behind him.

The woman was Doctor Butler's next patient, and she found him walking up and down his surgery with a disturbed expression on his face. She wondered what the young man's visit had been about.

Peter was pleased with his morning's work. Two years was a long time, but at least it was a start. He knew Pierhaven was somewhere on the coast, but he didn't know how to get there or how far it was from Lewes.

He pushed his machine further up the hill until he was in the shadow of the castle, and then wheeled it off the road and sank down on a grassy mound. The castle attracted many visitors although there wasn't much left to see, only a few ruins, and people passed Peter constantly.

There were six other bicycles leaning against a metal cannon so he wasn't the only person using that mode of transport. As he watched the owners of the other machines came to claim them. They were young men of about Peter's age, clad in knee-length cotton shorts and open-necked shirts. They were noisy, cheerful, and looked approachable.

'Have you heard of a town called Pierhaven?' he asked the nearest lad. 'Do you know where it is?'

'On the coast – Brighton way. We're going there later.'

Peter's spirits rose. 'Can I come with you?' he asked, grabbing his bike. 'My machine's old, but I'll keep up.' He saw the way they looked from his old-fashioned steed to their glossy sports models.

'We're not going straight there. We're going the long way via Uckfield and Mayfield. We want to explore Sussex thoroughly. We're on a touring holiday.'

'I don't mind,' Peter assured them.

So they agreed to take him along. He soon found himself sailing through the countryside, his legs going like pistons as he tried to keep up with his new friends.

It was mid-afternoon and the road stretched white before them. Peter was longing for a rest, but his companions only stopped every ten miles or so because they were timing themselves. He spotted a pub at the side of the road; its sign said it was called the Piltdown Man.

He longed to stop and order a long cool drink, but his companions urged him on and he had to keep up with them.

A few yards up the road they passed a row of cottages, but they were out of sight when Lily came to lean on the white fence with Timmy in her arms. Fate had intervened: Peter had missed her by a matter of minutes.

CHAPTER TWENTY-TWO

Piltdown Manor

'Let me give you a hand, Granny Langridge.'

'No, lass. I've been mangling all my life so I'm used to it.'

The wooden rollers creaked as the old woman turned the handle and water poured from the linen onto the cobbles of the yard. Lily sat on an upturned box and watched. She admired the strength in Mrs Langridge's arms, and the dedication she gave to her task. Her work was long and arduous but she enjoyed every minute of it. At least there was always a smile on her lined face and her voice was cheerful.

'I'm not earning my keep just sitting here,' Lily said.

It was nearly autumn and she'd been living at the cottage for over a month. Harry had only paid for two weeks' board and lodging before his sudden disappearance. Lily had been shaken, but not entirely surprised. She'd suspected all along that it was her voice he was interested in, and not her person; so when she couldn't sing any more her days were numbered. Even so, it was an unkind thing to abandon her in the depths of the country, without a penny to her name and only the clothes she stood up in.

Mrs Langridge had watched her, her wise old eyes taking in the girl's unhappiness. She'd grown fond of Lily, and when she'd discovered her crying in her bedroom one morning her heart had been moved. She'd sat down beside her on the bed, and taken her in her arms as if she'd been her own daughter. The story didn't take long to tell because she was a sympathetic listener and Lily needed to unburden herself to somebody.

'So you see,' Lily had ended, accepting a handkerchief and wiping her eyes, 'I can't afford to stay here any longer. I shall have to pack and move on – but the thing is I don't know where.'

Her eyes filled again and Mrs Langridge had patted her shoulder, as reassuringly as if she'd been Timmy.

'You're not going anywhere,' she'd said firmly. 'You're staying here with me.'

'But I can't pay you . . .'

'Who said anything about paying? You've got a pair of arms and a pair of legs, haven't you? And they're a good deal younger than mine. You've already been a help to me round the house and garden; and Timmy's taken to you. We're not short of freshly grown vegetables with a garden this size and I do all my own baking, so it'll be easy to fill another mouth. You can stay here as long as you want and give me a hand, especially with looking after Timmy while Grace is working at Piltdown Manor. It's a bit of a strain at my time of life caring for an active toddler, so you can take your turn with him. What do you say?'

Lily hadn't said anything; she'd just surprised Mrs Langridge by putting her arms around her neck and kissing her on the cheek. And she'd been so happy she hadn't missed Harry, or the singing. It was like being back at Valley Farm, only with friends instead of enemies.

Mrs Langridge folded the newly mangled clothes into a basket and stood upright. She stretched her back as if it ached.

'There's a good brisk wind. These things will dry in no time.'

'I'll do it.'

Before the older woman could argue Lily picked up the basket, and balancing it gracefully on her hip, walked down the path towards the clothes-line. She walked with a natural grace, almost like a dancer, and having regained her confidence in life held her head proudly so that she was a joy to see.

Mrs Langridge watched her, a smile on her face. She worried over her as if she was her own daughter. She knew little about the girl's background, and could only guess at the relationship she'd had with Harry Smith. Mrs Langridge had called Harry a slimy little toad and thought Lily was well rid of him. She sighed, and prayed softly to herself that all would go well with the girl.

But Lily herself wasn't worried. She was happy to be working in an environment she loved. Although her hair was untamed, and blowing free around her face and shoulders like a dark cloud, it suited her. The days of hairdressers were long past. Her pale skin had caught a healthy glow from the sun, and she never bothered now with make-up. She was wearing a faded cotton dress Grace had given her. It was white, with a pattern of tiny blue flowers like stars; and over it she wore a baggy cardigan. Her legs were bare, and on her feet were scuffed sandals.

Lily bent over the basket, and with one graceful movement selected a white sheet and flung it effortlessly over the line, securing it against the wind with two gipsy clothes-pegs. It blew around her slim figure like a sail, winding itself around her body. The rest of the washing was easier to manoeuvre, and the line was soon full of flapping towels and pillowcases.

Her job completed, Lily returned to the cottage. She stopped on the way to pick a sprig of mint to flavour the potatoes she'd peeled earlier.

Mrs Langridge was in the kitchen busy measuring out the ingredients for a cake. She'd baked so many cakes in her long life that she'd dispensed with scales, and spooned flour and currants into a mixing bowl using her eyes as a guide.

'Pass me two eggs,' she said with a smile.

Lily handed her two eggs from a bowl on the dresser. They'd been laid only that morning by her own hens, and had golden shells speckled with brown spots.

'What can I do now?' Lily asked.

'I can hear Timmy through the wall. He's just woken up from his nap. Would you go and get him for me?'

Lily hurried into the adjoining cottage. The doors were always left wide open unless the weather was bad. Burglary was only something the residents of Piltdown read about in the newspapers, so they never bothered to lock their doors. Anyway, they were poor folk and had nothing worth stealing.

Timmy was standing up in his cot shouting cheerfully for

attention. When he saw Lily he laughed and put out his arms to be picked up. She carried him downstairs and sat him on his potty while she found a flannel to wipe his face and hands. His brown curls stood on end, and his fat cheeks were rosy with health.

'Mummy,' he said seriously as Lily slipped his arms into the sleeves of a miniature jacket and pulled a knitted cap onto his head.

'We'll go and meet her,' Lily promised. 'Let's take your pushchair.'

She strapped the infant into the small wobbly baby carriage, and called to Mrs Langridge as she passed the open door.

'We're going up the road to meet Grace; and then we're going to the common to see if there are any tiddlers in the pond.'

'Mummy – 'iddlers,' Timmy agreed enthusiastically.

'Don't let him get wet then,' Mrs Langridge said. 'There's quite a chill in the air now.'

'I won't,' Lily promised.

She pushed the pram around the side of the house and out through the white gate into the roadway. She crossed over and walked along the grassy bank, bumping the pram over the rough ground to Timmy's delight. A peewit rose from the bracken ahead, and a robin sang to them from a nearby may tree.

They saw Grace coming towards them from a long way off. Her tall figure and long-legged stride were unmistakable. She was wearing a brown skirt and hand-knitted jumper, and a bag swung from one of her hands, bumping against her thigh as she walked towards them.

'Mummy!' Timmy shouted, bouncing up and down. 'Run, 'ily.'

So Lily ran, pushing the pram ahead of her. Grace ran too, so that they met breathless and laughing, their cheeks rosy and their hair wind blown.

'I've had such an afternoon,' Grace told them when she'd got her breath back. 'I polished all the silver, and cleaned out so many drawers I've lost count. They all had to be relined and everything put back in its place. There was a chest of drawers in Mrs Sayer's room that hadn't been touched for years.'

'Was there anything interesting in it?' Lily asked. She was

curious about her friend's afternoon job at Piltdown Manor and always asked questions.

'Some rolls of material that had been there since before the war. Silks and velvets such as you've never seen. Mrs Sayer had forgotten all about them. She's going to have some of them made up into dresses and skirts. Stop here a minute and I'll show you what she's given me.'

The ground was dry and the grass prickly and brown, so the two girls sat down side by side while Grace poked around in her bag. Under her overall and house-shoes was a parcel. She pulled it out excitedly and unrolled two lengths of cloth: one a grey wool and the other green and blue tartan.

'This tartan would make you a lovely skirt,' Lily said.

'That's what I thought. I might even manage a little jacket and trousers for Timmy. There's more than enough.'

'What about the grey?' Lily asked. She fingered the soft cloth greedily.

'That's for you.'

'Oh, no!' Lily's eyes lit up at her friend's generosity. 'I can't take it. It was given to you.'

'But I want you to have it. I'll make it up for you. I've got a pattern that will suit you down to the ground. A winter dress with three-quarter length sleeves and a panelled skirt. What do you think?'

'It sounds lovely,' Lily admitted. 'I'd love it if you're sure.' She only had summer clothes with her and had no money to buy new ones.

'That's settled then.' Grace reached over her head and picked a ripe blackberry from a tangle of brambles. She popped it into her mouth. Timmy put out his hand so she got to her feet to search for more. 'There are heaps of berries over here,' she called over her shoulder. 'If you've got a bag we can pick them.'

They hadn't got a bag, but there was a basket attached to the handles of the pram and they lined that with leaves. The ripe fruit fell easily into their hands and soon the basket was half-full. By the time they'd finished it felt heavy, and their mouths, as well as Timmy's, were stained purple.

'We must have pounds,' Lily said. 'What are you going to do with them? Make jam?'

'I've got enough to see me through the winter. That plum

jam we made is Jake's favourite. But I know Granny Langridge will like some to make a pie. Then I'll make the rest into bramble jelly for the harvest fair.'

'When is that?' Lily asked. She'd heard about harvest festivals but this was the first she'd heard of a harvest fair.

'On Saturday. Mr and Mrs Sayer are holding it in the gardens of the Manor. They hold one every year. There are stalls, and people from miles around bring all their extra produce and sell it cheap. There are cake stalls, and jams and chutneys as well, so bramble jelly will be just the thing.'

'Sounds wonderful,' Lily said. 'Can anyone go?'

'Of course. Why?'

'I'd like to have a look round. You've told me so much about Piltdown Manor; I'd like to see for myself what it's like.'

'The public's not allowed inside the house. Anyway, I was going to ask you to keep an eye on Timmy for me. Mrs Sayer has asked me to run a stall. I said I would.'

'Oh, I see. Of course I'll mind Timmy for you. It doesn't matter about the fair.' Lily looked disappointed and Grace felt sorry.

'But it does!' Grace brightened as an idea suddenly struck her. 'I know – you can bring him with you. There'll be lots of things for children because Mrs Sayer's grandchildren are staying with her while their parents are abroad. I know there's going to be a sand-pit and balloons, and last year they had donkey rides. I hope it keeps fine.'

The weather was perfect. Saturday morning dawned crisp and still, with a blue sky and a watery sun. Grace left early, loaded down with baskets of provisions; leaving Lily to follow with Timmy. He was wrapped up warmly in a knitted suit with a hood hiding his curly hair, and there was a blanket tucked around his legs in case it turned cold.

Mrs Langridge was on her hands and knees scrubbing the kitchen floor. 'You're off then,' she said, looking up at Lily with a smile.

'Yes. Why don't you come with us, Granny Langridge? I can finish the floor for you later.'

'No, dear. It's kind of you, but there are lots of jobs that need doing, and I can get on much faster if I have the house to myself. It's time you had a break; so you go and enjoy yourself.

Take that shilling on the dresser. It won't buy much but you can get yourself a drink and a balloon for Timmy.'

Lily picked up the money gratefully. In the financial state she was in a shilling was a fortune. She thanked the giver and slipped the coin into the pocket of her dress.

Although she'd never been to the manor, Grace had given her instructions so that she wouldn't get lost. Anyway, everybody else seemed to be going in the same direction, and soon she was part of a merry band all bent on having a good day out.

By the time they reached the gates Lily had become friendly with a chattering woman accompanied by two little girls. The children's names were Poppy and Daisy, and they were lively little things of five and seven. Their poor mother was constantly on the alert as to their whereabouts. On their arrival she relaxed as she watched them bound away across the grass.

'They can't do any harm,' she told Lily. And Mrs Sayer likes children. She doesn't seem to mind where they go or what they get up to.'

Lily looked around her with pleasure. Piltdown Manor looked more like a fortified castle than a house, with its long arched gothic windows and turreted roof. There were statues standing to attention in niches in the walls and tall chimneys towering up into the sky. The roof was of grey slate, and the ivy-covered walls were rust-red brick.

'You should just see the gardens in the spring,' her companion enthused. 'There are snowdrops, tulips and narcissus, and great drifts of daffodils. In the early summer Mrs Sayer opens the gardens to visitors. People come from miles away to see the cherry trees and the lilacs in flower. Do you like flowers?'

Lily admitted that she did. But she didn't enlighten her friend to her preference for the wild varieties rather than hothouse blooms.

'They've just opened the tea-tent, and my tongue's hanging out. I must go and find Poppy and Daisy. I expect they'll be thirsty after their long walk. Are you coming?'

'I want to find my friend,' Lily said, knowing that Timmy would want to see his mother. I think she'll be serving on a stall.'

'See you later then. If you see my girls you can tell them where to find me.'

They parted and Lily found herself alone in the crowd. But she wasn't lonely because there was plenty to see and Timmy kept up a babyish babble of conversation. They found a stall selling home-made confectionery. She spent a precious penny on sticky fudge that had congealed to the texture of toffee and stuck their teeth together.

There were so many stalls, selling such a variety of wares, that Lily was soon confused. Huge pumpkins nestled with marrows and apples, and heaps of colourful carrots and golden onions shared a table-top with cauliflowers and cabbages. The season's tight button sprouts were piled into nets and boxes, to be weighed out to customers on a giant pair of scales.

She found Grace manning a home-made produce stall. She could hardly be seen behind a mound of bread and buns. Golden loaves of all shapes and sizes, some smooth as honey and others speckled with seeds and nuts, shared the space with cakes and tarts. Fruit and jam, and jars of pickles and preserves were on the verge of toppling to the ground. Timmy shrieked excitedly at the sight of his mother's face peeping at him over the produce.

'Mum – Mum – Mum,' he shouted. ''ily – 'udge.'

'He's trying to tell you I bought him some fudge,' Lily explained. 'That's why he's so sticky.'

'I've sold all the bramble jelly,' Grace confided. 'Mrs Sayer bought a jar herself.'

Lily bought a loaf of fruit bread as a present for Mrs Langridge. She still had eightpence left in her pocket.

'Shall I buy some rolls?' she asked. 'We could have them for lunch.'

'No need.' Grace grinned. 'I've already paid for some. And I brought cheese with me so we can have a picnic.'

'It's time you had a break, Grace,' a woman's voice said behind them. 'Who's your friend?'

'This is Lily. She's looking after Timmy for me.'

'Hullo, Lily. I'm so pleased to meet you. I do hope you're enjoying yourself?'

Lily turned quickly. The speaker was a short, grey-haired woman, wearing a tweed suit in a mixture of brown and green, and sensible lace-up shoes. She had a brisk down-to-earth manner and a friendly smile.

'This is Mrs Sayer – my employer,' Grace said by way of introduction.

'Do you like children, Lily?' Nancy Sayer had noticed the competent way Lily was coping with the little boy.

'I like Timmy,' Lily said honestly. 'But that's because I'm used to him and he's so good; but I'm not sure how I'd find other children. I haven't had much to do with them.'

'That's because you're still young. But Timmy obviously likes you – and that's a good sign.' Mrs Sayer turned to Grace. 'Why don't you take him up to the nursery? Dorothy and Paul are up there with Nanny Grant. You can leave him with her while you take a break.'

'Thank you, Mrs Sayer.' Grace came round from behind the stall and took the pram from Lily. 'Come on.'

Mrs Sayer took Grace's place and soon had a queue of potential customers. Lily and Grace headed for the house.

They left the pram at the bottom of the front steps, and Grace gathered Timmy into her arms and led the way through the door into the hall. Lily had always thought Ring House was grand, but it was nothing compared to the interior of Piltdown Manor. The walls were covered with ornate paper embossed with a design of vines and chrysanthemums: it had a velvety texture, and the petal of each flower was outlined in gold leaf. A chandelier hung from a central rose, its crystal droplets reflecting the light as it spun slightly in the draught.

Grace knew her way around and telling Lily to follow close behind headed for the stairs. Lily wished she'd slow down so that she could have a good look about her.

Some of the inner doors were ajar and the glimpses of the interiors made her curious. The portraits hanging on the walls, gloomy in their heavy dark frames, looked interesting and she would have liked to study them more closely. The upper floor was carpeted in thick red pile, making their progress almost regal.

Grace stopped at a door at the end of a passage. They could hear a woman talking in a loud, sharp voice on the other side.

'I told you to pick it up, Paul. If you don't do as you're told I'll . . .'

'Oh, dear.' Grace put her hand over her mouth in mock alarm. 'Nanny's on the warpath.'

She pushed the door open without knocking; Lily found

herself in the nursery. It was a spacious room, the low ceiling making it look even larger. A cheerful fire burned in a deep fireplace, protected by a wire guard with a brass top. Various items of children's clothing were draped over it to air. There was a rocking-chair, a low table covered with a check cloth, and child-sized chairs. Shelves of well-worn books and toys, as well as a giant rocking-horse standing in the window, a doll's-house and piles of puzzles and games filled the room.

The nursery at Piltdown Manor looked like a children's heaven, and the two children standing in the middle of the room the luckiest on earth – until you saw Nanny Grant.

'For the last time – pick it up, Paul!'

Lily looked at the speaker in her blue and white striped uniform and immediately knew why the children appeared so frightened. Nanny Grant wasn't old or ugly: about thirty or thereabouts, with a handsome face and blue eyes. Her reddish hair was tucked neatly away under a cap, and her regulation black shoes were so highly polished you could see your face reflected in the toes. In fact she looked the picture of the perfect English nanny who would run a nursery with competence – until you looked into her eyes. They were like twin marbles of blue granite; and instead of love for her little charges they were full of dislike. Lily knew at once that Nanny Grant hated her job, and detested children.

But the children were sweet. The little boy, Paul, about four years old, looked like a child from a Pears soap advertisement, with his dimpled cheeks and chubby knees. His sister, Dorothy, a couple of years older, solemn and shy with eyes like pansies, stood on one leg and hugged a rag doll to her narrow chest for comfort.

Lily wanted to rush forward and put her arms around them. Anything to bring back smiles to their faces.

'And you can put down that stupid doll, Dorothy, and get your hairbrush. I'm not taking you for a walk looking like that. What would people think?'

The children came to life like puppets. Paul bent down and started to gather up the pieces of puzzle from the floor, and his sister walked primly across the room and sat the doll down carefully on a chair. She then reached up to a shelf for her hairbrush.

'Hullo, Nanny Grant,' Grace said, as if she was used to this behaviour. 'This is my friend, Lily.'

'What do you want in my nursery?'

Without so much as a glance in Lily's direction Nanny Grant snatched the brush out of Dorothy's hand and began to aim vicious strokes at the child's head. Obviously used to this treatment, Dorothy stood motionlessly, only her wide eyes showing her fear.

'Mrs Sayer sent us up. She said you'd look after Timmy for a while.' Grace put her son down on the carpet. He immediately headed for a pile of coloured bricks heaped in the corner.

'As if I haven't got enough to do,' Nanny Grant snapped. 'And he can leave Paul's toys alone. Hasn't he got any of his own?'

Grace ignored the unfriendly remark. 'We won't be long. We're just going to have a look round.'

'You'd better not be . . .' Nanny Grant started to say, but Grace had grabbed Lily's arm and pulled her back out into the corridor. They ran down the stairs side by side and out into the garden.

More visitors had arrived, and the lawns were packed with a colourful crowd, all enjoying themselves and spending their hard-earned money freely.

'What did you think of Nanny Grant?' Grace asked.

There were lavender bags on the nearest stall; she picked one up and admired it. It was made of muslin and lace and gathered with a ribbon bow; perfect for placing in drawers containing linen and underclothes.

'I didn't like her very much,' Lily admitted. 'The children looked scared of her. I'm surprised at your leaving Timmy with a woman like that. I wouldn't if he was mine.'

'I know what you mean.' Grace handed over a threepenny-piece and pocketed a lavender bag. 'But it's only for an hour. She was highly recommended. Mrs Sayer said her references were splendid and she used to work for a foreign royal family.'

'That wouldn't have influenced me,' Lily said. 'I thought she was a most unpleasant person.'

'Well, Mrs Sayer was desperate,' Grace said. 'Dorothy and Paul are her grandchildren. Her daughter and son-in-law are abroad and she's responsible for them. So she advertised, and although there were lots of people interested in the position,

Nanny Grant was the most qualified.'

'Even so, I wouldn't have employed her,' Lily said emphatically.

'It can't be much fun looking after other people's children. Come on, Lily, we're wasting time. Let's go and see what's in that tent over there.'

It was a fortune-teller according to the handwritten sign outside. After much giggling the two girls decided to spend the last of their money finding out what their futures held.

Bending their heads low they entered the tent together. A woman dressed in a gipsy costume was sitting in the shadows shuffling a pack of greasy tarot cards. On a table covered with a black velvet cloth stood a crystal ball. All the light in the tent seemed to have gathered in its depths, and it glowed like an opalescent eye.

They couldn't afford the cards, so the gipsy took Grace's hands, and turning them over studied the palms. She ran her brown fingers over the tell-tale lines almost as if she was reading braille.

'I see gold,' she said at last. 'Lots of gold. And a husband – his name begins with a J. And children.'

'How many children?' Grace asked breathlessly.

'Four . . . no, five. Five at least. Probably more. They all have brown curly hair.'

'Are they girls or boys?'

Grace had confessed to Lily that she wanted another baby, and didn't intend waiting too long. It would be nice to give Timmy a little sister.

'Girls,' the gipsy said firmly. 'You will only have girl children: it says so on your palm.'

Grace covered her face with her hand. So much for fortune-telling. But she was too kind-hearted to admit that she already had one healthy son.

'Your turn, Lily.' She pushed her friend into the chair she'd vacated.

'I'll consult the crystal ball for you, my dear.'

The gipsy took the ball into her hands and rolled it slowly backwards and forwards. Then she smoothed out the black cloth and placed the ball in the centre. It seemed to glow in the dim light and Lily wondered if it was a trick. She felt her hands taken and held tightly. The brown face with its long gold earrings bent over the shining globe. Its centre seemed streaked with coloured light.

'Can you see anything?' Lily asked impatiently.

'Sh!' came the reply. 'I have to concentrate.'

'Sorry.' After a pause. 'What can you see?'

'A house on the top of a hill. A big house with trees behind it. There's a little girl playing in the garden. A little girl with dark hair – it could be you, my dear.'

'I did once live in a house on a hill,' Lily said, thinking of Ring House. 'Can you see anything else?'

'A man is coming out of the front door: a big man with a gold watch chain. He's calling to the child and she's pleased to see him. She's running to meet him and he's opening his arms to her. I think – yes, I'm sure – the man is the child's father. What's the matter?'

Lily had jumped up from her seat and was staring at the gipsy. She felt odd: as if she'd just been transported down through the years. She was standing by a hospital bed and a fat old woman called Auntie had insisted on reading her palm. Auntie had read a similar story in the lines of her hand, and although she'd only been a child at the time she'd never forgotten it. If the house was her former home, Ring House, then the man with the gold watch chain was Mr Thomas without a doubt. Auntie had thought he was her father, and now this gipsy was saying the same thing Why were they both making such a terrible mistake? Because Lily wished – oh, how she wished – that it was true.

'I don't want to hear any more. Come on, Grace.' She left the tent hurriedly, pulling her friend behind her.

'Why were you so rude?' Grace asked, as they walked side by side across the grass. 'It was only a bit of fun.'

'Well, I didn't find it funny.'

'But you didn't believe it, did you? Nobody believes fortune-tellers. They tell you what they think you want to hear, and guess the rest. She said I'd be rich, with lots of gold, which is most unlikely.'

'She was right about your having a husband whose name begins with a J.'

'But five daughters!' Grace laughed. 'I hadn't the heart to tell her about Timmy.'

'I wish I hadn't wasted my money now,' Lily said wistfully.

'I could have bought a hot potato.'

'I'll treat you. We can have the cheese rolls later.' Grace headed for a cart where a wrinkled farmer was roasting potatoes on a charcoal brazier. 'We'll walk back to the house through the gardens and probably meet Nanny Grant and the children. She usually goes that way.'

The potatoes were so hot they had to wrap them in their handkerchiefs. But they were filling, and their soft floury centres were flavoured with the cloves of garlic pushed into the skins.

The gardens were peaceful and deserted and they strolled happily between clipped hedges, the soft turf under their feet like a velvet carpet. Suddenly they heard a sound nearby: someone crying out with pain.

'What was that?' Grace stood still and looked about her.

'It sounded like a child. Perhaps it's hurt itself.'

'It came from over there.' Grace pointed to a gap in the hedge.

Both girls headed for the spot. Before they reached it they heard a woman's voice, and recognized the tones of Mrs Sayer. She sounded angry.

'I saw you do that, Nanny Grant. How dare you!'

They came upon an unhappy scene. Nanny Grant, in her navy-blue coat and hat, was holding little Paul by the scruff of his neck. On his white cheek were red weals where someone had slapped him viciously. His sister was standing a few feet away, tears streaming down her cheeks, and her shoulders shaking with silent sobs. Only Timmy seemed undisturbed. He was crouched on the grass trying to pick up a beetle. Mrs Sayer was glaring at Nanny Grant who had obviously thought she was unobserved. The children's nurse spoke first.

'He deserved a smack. He never does what I tell him.'

'You had no right. What had he done?'

'He'd stolen a biscuit out of the tin in the nursery. I found it in his pocket.'

'Hardly a crime, Nanny Grant.'

'I believe children should be reprimanded.'

'But a smack like that – and on the face!'

'He'll soon forget. Children do.'

'He certainly will forget – if I have anything to do with it. Come here, Paul.' The little boy walked uncertainly across to his grandmother and looked up into her face. She bent down and put her arms around him. 'You are dismissed, Nanny Grant. You will go and pack your things now.'

Nanny Grant's face flushed an angry red. She was obviously trying to think of something to say to pacify her employer; but she could see by the expression on Mrs Sayer's face that this time she'd gone too far. She shrugged her shoulders and started to walk away, giving Dorothy an unpleasant look as she passed.

'I'll be pleased to go,' she said curtly. 'First thing in the morning.'

'I think this evening would be better. And don't ask for a reference because I have no intention of giving you one.'

When the nurse was out of earshot Mrs Sayer turned to the girls and sighed. 'I'm sorry you overheard that,' she said. 'I hope I've done the right thing.'

'Of course you have.' Grace bent down and picked up Timmy who'd given up his pursuit of the beetle. 'She's a most unpleasant woman.'

'But I don't know what I'm going to do with no one to care for the children. I don't suppose you know of anybody suitable?'

Lily stepped forward. 'I need a job, Mrs Sayer,' she said eagerly. 'I like children, although I haven't had much experience as I told you. But if you'll trust your grandchildren to me I promise to do my best.'

Nancy Sayer looked at the pretty dark-haired young woman and liked what she saw. She put out her hand and smiled.

It was settled – Lily had a new job.

CHAPTER TWENTY-THREE

A family affair

'Does Lily remind you of anyone, Noel?'

Mr Sayer put down his book and looked across the room at his wife. Nancy Sayer was standing by the drawing-room window watching the group on the lawn. At the centre a dark-haired girl stood, slim as a wand, her face full of laughter and smiles. Around her three children played. Dorothy ran on spindly legs, her white socks slipping down and her skirts bunched up, while her little brother struggled to keep up. Behind them Timmy toddled, thumb in mouth, occasionally losing his balance and crawling on hands and knees.

'Who were you thinking of?'

'Why, Victoria, of course. There's a striking resemblance: particularly at a distance.'

'I suppose so.' Noel joined his wife. He was a big untidy man and towered over her; but his hand was gentle when he placed it on her shoulder. 'But Victoria's eyes are blue; and why this sudden comparison? You haven't mentioned Vicky for days.'

'I know. But I miss her – and so do the children.'

'They don't at the moment. Look at them: they look happy enough to me.'

'I didn't mean that,' Nancy Sayer retorted. 'Children can be happy and still miss their parents.'

'I'm just glad you got Lily. That nanny might have come

with plenty of references but the children were scared of her.'

'I know. I didn't realize why they were always so quiet and subdued. The last person I blamed was Nanny Grant. Then when I caught her hitting Paul – well, I couldn't believe my eyes.'

'I'm glad it's all turned out so well. And Grace's little boy fits in so well. Is he going to be a permanent fixture?'

'No.' Mrs Sayer waved as her granddaughter suddenly spotted her at the window and turned a beaming face to them. 'Grace will be leaving us soon. She's expecting another baby, so she'll be able to stay at home with Timmy.'

'As long as we don't lose Lily.'

'I can't see any sign of that. I've never seen such a contented young woman. She was only telling me the other day how much she loves living here.'

'You'd better keep her out of sight then. If the village lads see those violet eyes their heads will turn. It's a good thing I'm not twenty years younger.'

Mrs Sayer laughed. 'I think I'll invite the children to have tea with us if you can stand the chatter. I've been saving that letter from Victoria and Robert to read to them.'

'Good idea. But don't ask for boiled eggs. Last time Paul insisted on sitting on my lap to eat his, and I couldn't get the stains out of my waistcoat.'

Dorothy and Paul were excited when they heard they were to have afternoon tea with their grandparents. Usually their meals were served in the day nursery and they felt very grown-up being allowed downstairs. Timmy was invited as well so that he wouldn't feel left out. Lily led them into the cloakroom first to wash their hands and tidy their clothes.

Nancy Sayer kissed each of the children in turn as they filed into the room. Then she smiled at Lily.

'The children seemed to be enjoying themselves outside,' she said. 'I hope I didn't break up their game?'

'No, Mrs Sayer. I was just about to bring them indoors anyway. I don't like them to get over-excited.'

'Sensible girl,' Mr Sayer said from the depths of his chair. 'Not like that damned Grant woman: they were always crotchety with her.'

'I'm not surprised,' his wife said. 'Now that I know how she treated them.'

'Is that damned Grant woman coming back?' Dorothy asked innocently.

'No, darling,' Mrs Sayer assured her. 'But you shouldn't say damned.'

'Why not? Grandpa just did.'

'Then your Grandpa's a naughty old bear.'

This made the children giggle. Paul immediately wanted to sit on the naughty old bear's lap. Then the tea trolley was wheeled in by Grace. Mr Sayer was relieved to see that the plates held neat little sandwiches with their crusts removed, and fairy-cakes in crinkly paper cases. The children had weak tea to drink as a special treat. Usually they had milk, or lemonade made with freshly squeezed lemons.

Lily sat Timmy on a little chair. She secured him with the strap of his walking-reins before handing him a sandwich. He immediately peeled the two slices of bread apart and peered suspiciously at the filling.

'Chis?' he asked, looking up at Lily questioningly.

'Yes, Timmy, it's cheese. Your favourite. Eat it up like a good boy.' He took a large mouthful and chewed contentedly.

'I'll come back for him later.'

Lily had turned to the door. She thought it was kind of Mr and Mrs Sayer to include Grace's son in the invitation. It was generous enough for him to be allowed to come to the Manor every day with his mother, and be cared for as if he was one of the family. He was going to miss the company of the other children when Grace's pregnancy stopped her coming.

'Sit down, Lily, and have some tea,' Mrs Sayer said. She filled another cup and passed it to Lily together with the plate of sandwiches. 'You don't want to eat upstairs all by yourself.'

So Lily joined the party around the trolley. She made herself useful passing plates, and making sure the children didn't scatter too many crumbs on the thick carpet.

In the daytime she wore a white dress with a navy-blue belt, black stockings and flat shoes. Mrs Sayer had chosen it for her. It wasn't a proper nanny's uniform, but it was easy to launder and kept her cool and tidy. Her hair was tied back from her face by a blue ribbon. She looked charming.

'I've finished,' Paul announced at last.

'So've I,' Dorothy chimed in. 'Can I get down?'

'Not yet.' Mrs Sayer was smiling at her grandchildren. 'I have a surprise for you.'

'What sort of surprise?' Dorothy looked wary. She knew from experience that surprises were not always welcome.

'A nice surprise. I've had a letter from your parents – and there was one inside especially for you two. What do you say to that?'

Nancy Sayer picked up an envelope with a foreign stamp stuck to the corner from a side-table. She extracted a sheet of thin paper covered with spidery handwriting.

Dorothy got down from her chair and slowly walked across to her grandmother. She put out her hand and gently stroked the paper. The look on her solemn little face showed her feelings.

'I can't read it,' she said sadly.

'I'll read it to you.' Mrs Sayer put her arm around the child, drawing her close. Paul looked interested, but his parents had been away for over six months; that was a long time for a four-year-old. '"To my darling babies . . ."'

'I'm not a baby,' Dorothy said indignantly. 'Lily says I'm a big girl.'

'So you are, my pet. But to a mother her children are always babies, however big they are.'

'Even when they're . . .' Dorothy looked around for a comparison, 'as big as Lily?'

'Yes. I'm sure Lily's parents love her just as much now as they did when she was a tiny baby – and think of her in the same way.'

'Do they, Lily?' the little girl demanded. 'Do your mummy and daddy still love you as much?'

Lily pretended not to hear and bent over Timmy, wiping the crumbs from his mouth with a napkin. She didn't want Mrs Sayer to see the tears swimming in her eyes at the mention of the parents she'd never known.

'Don't bother Lily,' Mr Sayer said quickly. He sensed something was wrong. 'Listen to what your mummy had to say.'

Nancy Sayer carried on. '"To my darling babies. It seems such a long time since you waved to me from the nursery window, but I'll never forget your dear little faces, and the way you both cried when I kissed you goodbye. You know I didn't want to leave you, but Daddy and the doctor insisted. They said I'd only be ill again if I stayed in England during the winter. It was cold in Switzerland, and there was so much snow that you could have built a snowman every day. But the air was so clear that I found I could breathe easily for the first time in months."'

'Will she bring us back a snowman?' Paul asked hopefully.

'Don't be silly,' Dorothy said. 'It would melt.'

'Be quiet, children, and listen,' Nancy Sayer said gently, turning the page. '"After Switzerland we travelled down to Italy and stayed for a few weeks in Venice. There were boats there called gondolas, and they floated down the canals right past our hotel window. Now we're in Spain; in a town overlooking the Mediterranean Sea. Grandpa will show you where it is in the atlas. When I'm feeling well enough Daddy and I go for walks. The sea is so blue, and the beaches are full of golden sand. You'd love it, my darlings. I am looking forward so much to coming back home and enjoying an English summer. We will be with you in about three weeks, so be good children until I can kiss you and hold you in my arms again. Love from Mummy."'

Dorothy's face had lit up as the letter was read aloud, but now her face dropped. 'Three weeks is a long time,' she said sadly.

'It will soon pass,' Mrs Sayer assured her.

Noel Sayer had picked up the envelope and was inspecting it. 'By the postmark this letter has taken over a week to get here, so it could be sooner than you expect.'

'I've forgotten what Mummy looks like,' Paul said dolefully. 'Was she the lady with the red hair and the nasty voice? The lady who used to hit me.'

'That was Nanny Grant, you silly,' Dorothy told him. 'She's not coming back. Grandma promised.'

'Nanny Grant was a witch,' Paul insisted. 'She flew away on a broomstick.'

'Don't tell fibs.'

'I'm not. I saw her.' Paul's face screwed up as if he was about to cry. 'I want to know what Mummy looks like.'

'She's got dark hair and she's beautiful,' Dorothy informed him. 'She looks like Lily – only her eyes are blue.'

'That's all right then.' The little boy seemed reassured by the comparison. His chubby face broke into a smile. 'If no one wants that last cake can I have it?'

'Of course.' His grandmother passed him the cake and he peeled the paper off and bit into the golden sponge. He'd already forgotten about his mother and Nanny Grant. The cake was more interesting.

Lily got up from her chair and unstrapped Timmy. 'I think I'd better take him upstairs,' she told Mrs Sayer. 'Grace will be looking for him.'

'All right, dear. Tell her that I'll do the clearing up so she can get along home. And Dorothy and Paul can stay down here with us until bedtime. We haven't seen much of them all day.'

'I'll fetch them later then.' Carrying Timmy straddled across her hip Lily left the room and climbed the stairs. She loved the old house with its spacious rooms and furniture dark with age and polish. But most of all she loved the nurseries on the upper floor, and her own room that adjoined them. After Nanny Grant's untimely exit she'd worried that the memories of the cruel woman would come back and haunt the place; but now that the rooms were full of kindness and laughter there was no room for remembering the sad past. Nanny Grant had gone – never to return.

Grace was sitting in the rocking-chair waiting for them. Her legs were splayed wide apart, and she'd slipped off her shoes to stretch her toes. The mound of her belly was more obvious as she relaxed and allowed the chair to sway gently backwards and forwards. Her hands caressed her stomach through the cotton stuff of her dress. She looked happy, lazy, and perfectly at ease. As Lily and Timmy entered the room she looked up and smiled.

'I'm sure I can feel her head,' she said. 'And her fingers feel as if she's playing cat's cradle. Do you think she can feel me stroking her?'

'I'm sure she can,' Lily said, putting Timmy down on the floor. He immediately headed in the direction of his mother. 'Leave Mummy alone now. I expect she's tired.'

'Hes all right; aren't you, my love?' Grace bent over and lifted the little boy onto her knee. 'The problem is I haven't got a proper lap any more.'

'You soon will have.' Lily laughed as she collected a row of vests and knickers from the fireguard and folded them neatly.

'Put your face there, Timmy. Can you feel your little sister moving?' Timmy laid his cheek against his mother's stomach as if he was concentrating.

'How do you know it's a girl anyway?' Lily asked as she put the clothes away. Then she started to gather up the toys that were scattered over the floor. 'You sound so sure.'

'Of course I'm sure. I want a daughter, and so does Jake. Timmy wants a sister; and anyway that fortune-teller predicted it.'

'She predicted that all your children would be girls – what about Timmy?'

'I don't expect she gets everything right. I'm still waiting for the gold,' Grace said with a grin. 'And what about you? The big house, and the man with the watch chain.'

Lily didn't want to be reminded of that puzzle so she changed the subject. 'Mrs Sayer says you can go home early.'

'She is kind; and I do get tired these days. Were the children good?'

'As good as gold. She read them a letter – from their mother.'

'I bet that pleased them.'

'Yes, it did. What's the matter with her?'

'Their mother? She's been poorly for as long as I've known her. Gets these spells of breathlessness when she can't do anything. I found her one day in the garden: her chest was making a terrible wheezing sound, and her lips were blue. I was terrified and ran for help. Her husband, Mr Robert, came and carried her indoors. Asthma, I think they said it was. She seems worse in the winter when the weather's damp – that's why they've gone abroad.'

'What's she like?' Lily asked.

'Victoria? Kind and gentle like her mother. She looks a bit like you.'

'That's what Dorothy said. She said in the letter that they were coming home soon.'

'That's good news.'

'Do you think it will change anything?' Lily sounded worried.

'Change what?'

'Well, me being here. Perhaps she'll want to care for the children herself.'

'Don't worry about that,' Grace hastened to reassure her friend. 'Families like theirs need someone to care for their little ones. Even if there was to be a change you could always replace me.'

'I wouldn't mind that,' Lily admitted. 'I love it here. I'd do almost anything so that I could stay.'

'Even scrubbing floors?' Grace groaned, remembering how she'd started. For the first few weeks she'd done nothing but the rough work, and then Mrs Sayer had promoted her.

'Even that,' Lily said sincerely.

After Grace had gone Lily went into her own bedroom to change her clothes. She was glad to peel off the black stockings that made her legs look thin, and change them for a more conventional pair. And her old sandals were more comfortable than the lace-up shoes.

She hung the white dress on a hanger and unhooked a pink and white striped one from inside the wardrobe, slipping it on. Pulling the blue ribbon from her head she shook out her hair, letting it fall in a dark curtain over her shoulders. Then she started to brush it with long, even strokes.

Sitting on the stool in front of the dressing-table Lily could see the room behind her reflected in the glass. The walls were papered in a design of cabbage roses, as were the curtains and bedcover. There were delicate china ornaments decorating the window ledge and mantelshelf. Although she didn't have many possessions Lily delighted in keeping everything tidy and in its place.

The last six months, since replacing Nanny Grant at Piltdown Manor, had been a revelation for her. Not only was she treated with kindness and understanding by Mr and Mrs Sayer, but she was earning her own living and doing a job she found she loved. And she didn't miss the singing at all. Although she was still hoping that her voice would correct itself, it was a relief to be away from the constant adulation of an audience and the stresses and problems it brought. But most of all she loved Piltdown Manor and the children.

Once, long ago, she'd dreamed of living in a house like this and being a lady. But they'd been the dreams of a child brought up in poverty and deprived of a normal family. Even at Ring House, Mrs Thomas and Betty had never let her forget her humble beginnings; although Mr Thomas had always been kindness itself. But now she'd come into her own. Her new life suited her down to the ground and she was determined not to look back. She'd also tried to resign herself to a life without Edward.

Lily leaned forward and studied her face in the mirror to see if she'd changed at all. Her cheeks were a little plumper even to her critical eyes, and her hair was certainly thicker and glossier. The fresh air, hard work and good food had left its mark. But it wasn't only that. The expression on her face was calmer, more placid, as if she was feeling contented with herself. Her body was still as slim as it had ever been, but it had a new maturity, and she stood straighter with her shoulders back.

Would Edward recognize her if he saw her now, Lily wondered? Or did he still think of her as the young impulsive girl she had been? If he ever thought of her at all. Lily's smile faded slightly as she thought of Edward, wondering if her beautiful golden boy had changed, if he was happy, or if he regretted the past.

She got up quickly from the stool and turned her back on the revealing mirror, shaking out her striped skirts. The past was over and the future yet to come. All she had was the present and that was enough.

She walked back into the nursery with a spring in her step as the children came running into the room.

'I was just coming down to fetch you.'

'Grandma sent us up,' Dorothy said. 'You do look pretty, Lily.'

'So do you.'

'Do I look pretty?' Paul asked, a cheeky grin on his face.

'Don't be silly,' his sister said. 'Boys shouldn't want to look pretty.'

'Well, I do. I want to look pretty because Mummy and Daddy are coming home and I want them to love me.'

'Your mummy and daddy will love you whatever you look like,' Lily assured him. 'It's not looks that count.'

'That's all right then. Grandpa says there's going to be a storm.'

Lily hadn't noticed how dark the nursery had grown. Now she looked out of the window and saw the threatening sky. The sun had gone down and been replaced by menacing clouds that had blotted out the last of the daylight.

A tremor of fear ran up her spine: she hated thunderstorms and it looked as if one was heading their way. But she mustn't show her anxiety in front of Dorothy and Paul: it would be all too easy for them to catch her feeling of dread.

'It's a long way off,' she said, deliberately keeping her voice calm. 'It's nearly your bedtime anyway, so you'll be safely tucked up in bed.'

'Will there be lightning?' Paul asked in an interested voice.

'Of course,' Dorothy said. 'And rain and winds and . . .'

'Gales and floods,' Paul finished.

'And tidal waves, and volcanos,' Dorothy added. She'd just read about them in a geography book although she didn't really understand what they were.

'And you're going to sleep through them all,' Lily laughed. 'Come on now, get ready for bed, and in the morning the sun will be shining again.'

She ran the bath and helped Paul out of his clothes. Dorothy could manage to undress on her own, but she was still childish enough to enjoy splashing in the bath with her younger brother. Once the children were out of the bath and rubbed dry, they looked contented and sleepy.

'Will Daddy be here in the morning when I wake up?' Paul asked, sitting cross-legged in the middle of his bed, his bare toes curling impressively. He was wearing pale blue pyjamas with a teddy bear embroidered on the pocket. His thumb was in his mouth, making the words come out oddly.

'No, but you must be a good boy so that he'll be pleased with you when he does get back,' Lily said, seeing the difficulty the little boy was having keeping his eyes open. 'Get under the covers now, and I'll read you a story.'

Tucked up in their beds they looked like a pair of angels. Dorothy was already holding out a book.

'Read this,' she commanded. 'It's a poem – my favourite one. It's called "Windy Nights".'

Paul grizzled around his thumb and screwed his eyes tightly shut. 'Not that one. It's about winds and storms and things. Read another one.'

So Lily chose something more appropriate. She read them a poem about cosy nurseries and parents watching over their babies, and another about a red and white cow who gave her milk to be turned into cream for children to eat with apple tart. It was all very safe and ordinary, and by the time she'd read the last line they were fast asleep.

Lily collected the discarded clothes and folded them neatly away. Then she returned to the day nursery to tidy up and leave everything ready for the morning.

It was so dark she could hardly see her way across the room so she switched on a table-lamp. It made a cheerful glow in the corner. Her duties finished, she crossed to the window to watch the progress of the storm. It was nearer, the angry grey clouds rolling towards the house and in the far distance an occasional flash of lightning. But it wasn't raining. The trees in the garden were standing ominously still, as if they were preparing themselves for an onslaught.

Lily sat down in a chair and propped her chin in her hands as she peered through the glass. She didn't hear the tap on the door, nor was she aware that she had company until she heard a sharp intake of breath behind her, and turned round.

'I'm sorry, Mrs Sayer,' she said, getting to her feet. 'I didn't hear you come in. Is something the matter?'

In the dim light Nancy Sayer looked pale and agitated. 'It was just seeing you sitting there, and in that chair,' she said.

Thinking she was being reprimanded for laziness Lily said, 'I've finished my duties, and the children are fast asleep.'

'Vicky used to sit in that chair looking out of the window.'

'Vicky?'

'My daughter Victoria, the children's mother. It was her favourite spot when she was a little girl; and even when she was grown-up she liked to sit there with a book. Seeing you there, in the dim light, I thought it was her.'

'I didn't know,' Lily said softly. 'Do you miss her?'

'Yes, of course. She's my only child.'

'But that letter – the one you read out at tea – she wrote that she's coming home soon.'

'Yes.'

'Does she and her husband live with you, Mrs Sayer?'

'They have their own home about ten miles away, but Victoria's never been very strong. She suffers badly with asthma; that's why Robert decided to close up the house and take her abroad. The dampness of an English winter aggravates her condition. This house is a second home to the children. I like to keep this nursery just as it was when Vicky was little.'

Lily moved the chair away from the window and pulled the curtains to hide the threatening sky. 'It's going to rain any minute,' she said. 'I thought I heard a rumble of thunder.'

'Let's put the radio on,' Mrs Sayer said. 'Then we won't hear it.'

There was a wireless standing on a corner shelf and she turned the switch. After a few seconds, music, and a woman's voice, filled the room. Lily was putting some books away, but the familiar melody of 'My Dearest Dear', and the sweet soprano voice of the singer, made her start to hum an accompaniment. It was one of the songs she'd sung when she was known as Lilith Fortune.

'Do you like the music of Ivor Novello?' Nancy Sayer asked innocently.

'No!' Suddenly startled, Lily surprised her employer by the unusual sharpness of her voice. 'At least, I did once, but it brings back unhappy memories.'

Nancy Sayer couldn't imagine what unhappy memories such a young pretty girl, like Lily, could be troubled by. But no doubt she would confide in her, she thought, when the time was right. She decided to change the subject.

'I came up because of the storm. I didn't know if you would be frightened.'

'It's still a long way off,' Lily said. 'And the children don't seem to be disturbed. Perhaps it will pass us by.'

'Well, if the little ones wake up, or if it gets too close, you must come downstairs. Noel – I mean Mr Sayer – is a very heavy sleeper, and so am I, so we'll probably sleep through it.'

They wished each other good-night and Lily heard Mrs Sayer's footsteps trotting away along the passage, muffled by the thickness of the carpet.

It seemed very quiet and lonely when she was on her own again. She could almost feel the night outside closing around the house. But it was safe inside: nothing could hurt her. Even if the storm struck, the walls were thick, and there were stout trees in the grounds to act as wind-breaks. She would be better to go to bed, and in the morning it would be all over and the sun would be shining again.

She checked on the children but they were both fast asleep.

Dorothy lay primly on her back, with her hands folded together like a marble statue on a tomb; while her brother was curled in a tangle of bedclothes, his face pressed into the pillow. She kissed each child lightly and then went to her own bed, leaving all the doors ajar so that she would be aware of every sound.

CHAPTER TWENTY-FOUR

The man who cried

The storm reached Piltdown at just after two in the morning. First the wind rose and whipped around the house, rattling the old tiles and flaying the trees, so that they had to dig their roots into the ground and hold fast with all their might. Then the rain came. No gentle introduction: just huge drops blowing against the window-panes and the roof, so that the gutters were soon full and overflowing. The heavens seemed to have split asunder and a second flood poured down on the sleepy Sussex village.

Lily had been sleeping dreamlessly. The first rumble of thunder woke her, and she sat up in bed clutching the bedclothes around her in alarm.

The room was in darkness, but the window-panes vibrated as if a banshee was trying to get in. There was nothing to be frightened of, Lily told herself firmly, it was only a storm. It would soon pass over, or blow itself out, and everything would be peaceful again. There was no sound from the night nursery so it hadn't disturbed Dorothy or Paul; so why was her heart beating fast in her chest as if she was on the verge of something terrible?

Perhaps the window wasn't secured properly. Now that she was wide awake she might as well go and see. The room felt cold after the warmth of her bed, and she pulled a quilt around her shoulders and shook back her hair before padding across the carpet.

The window was closed, but there was a gap where the frames met. Lily wedged a fold of paper in the space and it seemed to do the trick. Now she was up she thought it would be as well to check on the children. Perhaps their window needed securing too.

The twin nightlights beside the little beds were still alight but burning low, like tiny flickering stars. She could just make out the outlines of the small sleeping bodies, and hear the gentle rhythm of their breathing.

The window glass was streaming with water but even so the first flash of lightning caught her unawares. She put up her hands to protect her eyes, and lost her hold on the quilt so that it slithered to the ground around her feet. The rumble of thunder, like a roll on a drum, came only a few seconds later, indicating that the storm was almost overhead.

Lily had to open her eyes to make the curtains meet, so she was unable to avoid seeing the second flash. The garden below the window was illuminated as bright as day. Each tree stood like a waving silhouette; every hedge rippled in the passing wind; the bluebells that only the day before had been a sea of colour under the trees were beaten flat. From her position she could see everything. But it was all securely fastened to the ground, the sap running like a life-force up the stems and through the branches and boughs, allowing the living things to bend without breaking in the wind.

Except for one thing. At first Lily thought it was a bough that had become detached from one of the trees in the driveway. It was buffeted by the wind and blowing towards the house for all the world like the figure of a man. As it came closer she saw that it *was* a man. Head bent and arms and legs working wildly to keep himself upright, the man, for a man it certainly was, staggered to the middle of the lawn and then stood still, looking upwards.

Edward! Lily knew it was Edward Butler.

Although the man was soaked to the skin she could see the paleness of his hair plastered to his head. The tall, slim figure was the one she remembered, even though it was hunched forward against the elements. A third flash of lightning followed, and she strained forward to get a better look. Before darkness descended again the figure changed direction, and rather than continuing towards the house as had seemed at first to be his intention, he turned instead to the right, and staggered away towards a row of bushes that lined a path that led to a dilapidated summer-house.

Edward! Had she been dreaming, or was it really Edward? Surely her imagination must be working overtime, her eyes playing tricks. What could Edward be doing in the middle of the night, wandering around a private garden in a place like Piltdown?

But Lily had always believed that he would come for her. He was her fate, her destiny. Love was supposed to be strong: strong as a silver cord, drawing the prince and princess of the fairy-tale towards each other. Edward was her prince, and even if he'd willed it, he couldn't stay away.

She had to go to him now, to prove he was real. To touch him and know that he wasn't just a figment of her imagination. Lily forgot all about the sleeping children who were in her care; she forgot that it was the middle of the night and she was wearing only a thin night-gown; she even forgot the storm raging outside. Love could move mountains, and Lily was going to move a mountain to reach Edward before he disappeared.

She ran out of the nursery leaving the door wide open and swinging in the draught, down the stairs not caring about waking the sleepers, and along the passage past the gloomy portraits and the darkened clusters of the chandeliers, until she reached the front door.

This was the first mountain she had to conquer. It was bolted and barred nightly by Mr Sayer; not against intruders, but as a matter of habit. Lily's fingers were cold, and struggle as she would they couldn't master the heavy brass chain or the stiff bolt.

The garden door wouldn't be locked. That was Mrs Sayer's province, and she was less safety conscious than her husband, and not driven by habit. It was also nearer the summer-house.

'Edward – wait for me. I'm coming.'

Along the passage Lily ran like some pale ghost. There was the door in front of her, its handle in the shadows so that she had to grope for it. Now she had it in her hand, smooth and cold. It needed both of Lily's small hands to turn it, but turn it she did, and it was open and she was free – running across the wet grass on bare feet, the skirt of her gown blowing around her slim figure and the wind catching her and buffeting her about.

The rain was cold against her skin, plastering her hair to her forehead and neck, and making the thin material of her night-gown cling to her body. But she didn't feel the cold, or the pain when she stepped on a sharp stone. She was going to Edward.

The summer-house brought her to a halt. She stopped in her headlong flight and looked about her. There was now no sign of the figure, only the thrashing branches and the dancing raindrops. Then she heard a creak and saw that the summer-house door was swinging on its hinges. Edward must be inside sheltering from the rain.

Lily was too excited to feel the cold; she hurried forwards, pushed the door inwards and stepped over the sill. It was dark inside and quiet, the wooden walls muffling the sound of the storm. And then there came the rasp of a match, and the sudden glow as someone standing nearby lit a cigarette.

'Edward!' Lily said softly. 'Is it really you?'

She saw a familiar square jaw, and grey eyes fringed by pale lashes, a sensitive mouth and white-blond hair falling forward. The man before her had every distinctive quality that Edward had – but it wasn't Edward.

And the man, whose name was Robert Lovegrove, stared unbelievingly at the girl in the doorway – the girl with the delicate features and dark cascade of hair – and said, 'Vicky?'

'I'm sorry,' Lily said, feeling foolish. 'I thought you were somebody else – someone I knew a long time ago.'

'And I thought you were my wife, Victoria. But now I can see that you're not. Vicky's eyes were blue – and yours are violet.'

'I'm so sorry,' Lily said again. 'I'm Lily – the children's nanny.'

'Children?' Robert said. He'd forgotten about the children.

'Dorothy and Paul.'

'Oh – my children.'

'I know I shouldn't have left them, but they were fast asleep. I saw you crossing the lawn and thought you were Edward.'

'And I thought you were Vicky. But how could you be? Vicky's dead.'

To Lily's horror the man before her started to weep. At first she thought it was rain on his face, but then she saw the way he hunched his shoulders as sobs shook him, and realized that it was tears running down his cheeks. If this man was Dorothy and Paul's father, then he was Robert Lovegrove. He cried in exactly the same way Paul did when he was distressed: there wasn't much difference between the man and the boy. When Paul cried Lily tried to comfort him, and now, instinctively, she crossed to Robert's side and put her arms around him in the same gentle fashion, and the crying man rested his head on her shoulder and was comforted.

'Now it's my turn to say I'm sorry,' Robert Lovegrove said at last, when he'd regained a semblance of control. 'I don't usually cry on strangers' shoulders, you know. It's not a manly thing to do.'

'Crying is good for everyone,' Lily assured him. 'It helps people cope.'

'Vicky's dead, you see. My wife Victoria. My dear, dear wife is dead. And I've come home to tell the children and her parents.'

'Do you want to tell me about it?' Lily could tell by the expression on Robert's face that he needed to talk to someone. 'But not here – you're soaking wet.'

'So are you.'

Suddenly Lily wondered how she'd mistaken this man for Edward. He had fair hair it was true, and the same sensitive lips, but there the resemblance ended. Now that she was close to him she could see the differences. Robert was older – probably in his early thirties – and his eyes were set farther apart. In fact, she had to admit it, he was not at all good-looking – not compared to Edward.

'Why don't we go indoors,' she said. 'And then, while you get dry, I can go and wake Mr and Mrs Sayer.'

'No!'

'But they'll want to know you're here.'

'I know – but not tonight. I can't face them tonight.' His eyes were pleading with her. 'In the morning.'

'I'm sure they won't mind being disturbed.'

'But don't you see: I have to break the news to them that Vicky's dead. It's going to be a shock. She's their only child, you see, and they adore her. It will be easier to tell them tomorrow when I've had time to rest' The pleading gaze was suddenly replaced by a look of concern. 'You're shivering.'

All at once Lily realized how cold she was. Her teeth were chattering, and she couldn't feel her toes. Outside the wind had dropped and it seemed to have stopped raining. The moon had ventured out from behind a cloud and the garden was now bathed in silver light.

Holding the damp skirt of her nightgown away from her legs, Lily walked in front of Robert across the lawn. When she turned at the door to beckon him inside she reminded him of the picture he'd once seen of a fairy creature, who charmed, and then led innocent men to their doom.

But once they were inside the house reality set in. The kitchen was warm, and Lily put milk on to warm for cocoa, while she fetched dry clothes for herself and towels for Robert. Dressed in a red woollen dressing-gown, she sat at the table, rubbing her hair dry and waiting for Robert to tell his story. His coat was laid over a chair and his hair standing up in spikes; he looked like Paul did when he'd just come out of the bath. He still looked sad, but at least he'd stopped crying.

'Drink your cocoa,' Lily said, pushing the cup closer to his hand. 'Now tell me about Victoria.'

'She was ill, you see,' Robert started softly. 'She'd never been very strong, and then she developed asthma. First they thought it was a nervous condition because she became allergic to all sorts of things. Sometimes it was animal fur or certain plants. Then some foods would bring on an attack. One doctor said she was an hysteric and was imagining things.'

'And what did you think?'

'She was suffering. During the attacks she couldn't breathe and it was terrible to watch her. Sometimes the attacks would last for an hour, or even two, and nothing seemed to help. The doctors tried everything. They gave her skin injections and tablets of ephedrine sulphate; she inhaled amylnitrite and burned stramonium in a saucer, but it was no good. No one could invent that sort of thing.'

'And was it the asthma that killed her? Did she die during an attack?'

'I only wish she had. Then I might have been there holding her hand. Nobody knows exactly what happened.'

'Tell me,' Lily prompted gently.

'We were staying at this hotel on the Spanish coast. Vicky loved the sea, so we chose one where she would have a good view of it from our bedroom window. It was right on the headland. She'd seemed better; she'd even been talking about taking a walk along the shore. We were planning to come home soon, and she'd written to tell Dorothy and Paul.'

'Their grandmother read them the letter. They were so excited.'

'So was Vicky. She missed them. Her whole life revolved around the children.' Robert paused and Lily feared that he was going to break down again. But he shook his head, took a sip from the cup, and resumed his story. 'She always took a rest after lunch when it was hot, and I said I'd fetch her some fruit from the local market. I saw her into bed, and opened the windows so there was plenty of air. I kissed her goodbye. That was the last time I saw her alive.'

Lily waited but Robert seemed to have drifted far away. He was sunk in bitter memories. She put out her hand and covered his: it was cold and trembling.

'What happened?' she asked.

'No one knows for sure. When I came back from the market there were crowds of people around the hotel. Sightseers. Some people love a tragedy, and the Spanish are an excitable race at the best of times. They were just carrying her body up from the beach below her window. She'd fallen over thirty feet, and died instantly of a broken neck.'

'Did she do it deliberately, Robert? Or was it an accident?'

'Victoria would never have taken her own life,' Robert said emphatically. 'She loved life and had too much to live for. And she was looking forward to coming home – that's all she talked about. A passer-by saw her leaning out of the window only a few minutes before she fell. He said she looked distressed. He called out to her, but she didn't seem to hear him.'

'So he went away?'

'Yes. I don't blame him for what happened; there was nothing he could do. I think she had a bad asthma attack. Sometimes she would wake up from sleep struggling for breath and try to get into the fresh air. I'd left the window open, remember, and the sill was very low. If she was half-asleep it would have been all too easy for her to have leaned out too far and lost her balance. I blame myself.'

'You mustn't. It's a tragedy, Robert,' Lily said, squeezing his hand. 'But you did everything you could.'

'I should never have left her. But she seemed better. I didn't know what was going to happen.' He started to cry again; but this time there were no heart-breaking sobs, only tears of relief. The sort of tears that bring healing in their wake. Lily waited, and soon Robert seemed to recover and started to talk again. 'She looked so beautiful when they carried her up from the beach. She looked very like you; and when I saw you standing in the doorway of the summer-house I thought you were Victoria, come back to me from the dead.'

'So you've come home to tell her parents?'

'Yes. I boarded the first train, took the first boat, and then hired a car to get here as soon as I could. I wanted to be the one to tell them; I didn't want them to learn by any other means. But when I got here I couldn't face it. It was the middle of the night. I couldn't drag them from their beds to give them the news. And the children: how was I going to break it to Dorothy and Paul that they were never going to see their mother again?'

'So you hid in the summer-house?'

'Yes.' Robert smiled somewhat sheepishly. 'I wasn't acting sensibly, I know. I suppose I was planning to stay there until the morning – sort of delay things.'

'I'm glad I found you,' Lily said, and she smiled because she meant it. She liked this man, even if he wasn't Edward, and she wanted to help him and his family.

'I'm glad too.'

'Now you must get some sleep.' Lily got up from her chair and pulled Robert to his feet. 'There are no spare beds made up – but you can have mine.'

'I'll sleep anywhere,' Robert tried to insist. But he was so exhausted by emotion and travelling that he swayed on his feet. 'If you could get me a blanket I'll be quite comfortable in a chair.'

'You'll do no such thing.' Lily was already pulling him towards the door. 'Tomorrow will be hard enough for you, and you'll cope with it much better if you can sleep properly. You will have the bed and I'll take the chair in the nursery; then I'll hear if the children wake.'

Before giving way to sleep Robert wanted to see Dorothy and Paul, so Lily allowed him to creep quietly to their bedsides. She stayed inside the door in case he needed her. He bent over each sleeping figure in turn, and kissed their soft cheeks. They didn't wake; just stirred slightly as if they were dreaming. Then she led him away and saw him into her own bed, and watched his eyes quickly close in sleep. His face looked so sad that Lily felt close to tears; but when she sat down in the rocking chair and pulled a blanket around her shoulders she was too tired to cry. She fell asleep almost immediately.

The next few days were like living through a nightmare, and Lily was the rock on which the family kept themselves anchored.

Paul was the first one to discover that his father was home. He wandered into the bedroom early in the morning looking for Lily.

'I haven't any socks,' he announced to the sleeping form. 'You haven't left me any clean socks, Lily.'

But Lily was behind him, wrapped in a red dressing-gown and a blanket, her face pale. He looked again at the shape under the bedclothes.

'Who's that?' he demanded. The shrill voice aroused Robert, who turned on his back and stretched one arm out from under the covers before peering sleepily at the intruder. 'Daddy!' Paul's voice rose even higher, if that was possible, and in his excitement he flung himself onto the bed, pummelling his father with his tiny fists as if he was a punchball. 'Dorothy – Daddy's home.'

But his sister was already in the doorway, a cotton petticoat hanging in a lopsided fashion from her shoulders. Her mouth was open in a circle of disbelief, but her eyes were like stars.

'Where's Mummy?' she asked.

'I'll get your clean socks,' Lily said.

She left them, closing the door behind her. This was something Robert Lovegrove had to do by himself. She couldn't help him: she'd only be in the way. In the wake of a tragedy a family found its strength by closing ranks. All she could do to ease the pain was see to their material comforts, and try to make each day run smoothly.

But they needed her, all of them; and although she tried to

stay in the background they searched her out for advice. It was as if she'd suddenly grown an older, wiser head on her young shoulders.

'Do you think the children should be allowed to come to the funeral?' Nancy Sayer asked her. Her eyes were red with weeping and her grey hair was in an unusual state of disorder.

'I'm sure Dorothy would want to be there,' Lily said after careful thought. 'She's old enough to understand what it's all about. Naturally she'll be upset, but when she's older she'll be pleased you let her go. But Paul is a bit young.'

'You're probably right,' Nancy Sayer said with a sigh. 'I was talking to him about death the other day. Trying to explain. He listened very carefully and I thought he'd taken it in, and then, when I'd finished, he turned to me and said – I understand, Grandma, but when is Mummy really coming home?'

'He is only four, Mrs Sayer.'

'I know. Lily, would you take them in to Uckfield to buy them new clothes?'

Lily looked up from the sock she was mending. 'Do they need new clothes?'

'I was thinking of something black. A dress for Dorothy and a little suit for Paul.'

For the first time Lily's eyes filled with tears. The children were confused enough already, wandering around the house like miniature ghosts with pale faces and low voices. To dress them in identical black would depress them even more.

'Dorothy has a navy coat and dress. I'm sure she'd be more comfortable dressed in something she likes, and is used to. And if Paul isn't coming to the funeral he won't need much. Just a black tie, or an armband is the usual thing, I believe.'

'You're so sensible, Lily,' Mrs Sayer said. 'I don't know what we'd do without you.'

Later the same day Lily came upon Mr Sayer in the garden. His jacket was hanging over a nearby hedge, and his shirt-sleeves were rolled up to the elbows. He was wielding a spade and hacking away at the roots of a lavender bush. He'd already uprooted some hyacinth bulbs, and tulips that hadn't really finished flowering. They lay on the path beside him in a pale glistening heap.

'What are you doing?' Lily asked curiously.

Mr Sayer stood up, and stretched to ease his back. There

were beads of perspiration on his brow and he was panting with the unusual exertion.

'This was Vicky's garden,' he said. 'When she was not much bigger than Dorothy she came to me and asked for a bit of garden to grow things in. I said she could have this patch, and bought her the lavender myself. I remember the day I helped her plant it. She was so pleased she danced for joy.' He paused to wipe his face on a large handkerchief, and blow his nose. 'After that we always used to give her plants as presents. The bulbs reproduced themselves and came up year after year.'

'If she loved the garden so much why are you digging everything up?' Lily asked softly. She thought she knew the answer, but felt it would be good for Mr Sayer to talk about it.

'Because every time I come here I can smell the hyacinths. Later it'll be the lavender, and everything else flowering to remind me. I don't think I can bear it. I shall have paving stones put down instead, and perhaps a bench in her memory.'

Lily bent down and picked up a bulb. The petals of the flower were already wilting and drooped coldly in her hand. The scent was still powerful. She held the flower against her cheek, and when Noel Sayer turned to look at her he saw that it was the same colour as her eyes.

'I think your daughter would be unhappy if she knew what you were doing. You helped her make the garden and now you want to destroy it; almost as if you wished you hadn't given it to her in the first place.'

'Vicky would understand,' Noel Sayer said.

'Perhaps she would – but will Dorothy? She likes flowers too, you know. She's always bringing home posies she's gathered – daisies, and buttercups; and the other day violets she'd found under a hedge. She puts them in jars along the window-sill in the nursery, and no one else is allowed to touch them.'

'Does she? I didn't know.'

'I think you should tell Dorothy about her mother's garden. Just as you've told me. You should give her the choice. She could decide whether she'd like a garden seat in her mother' s memory, or whether she'd like to care for the garden herself.'

'Perhaps you're right.' Noel Sayer looked at the devastation he'd caused, and for the first time seemed to regret his hasty actions.

'We could replant the bulbs,' Lily suggested. 'They may recover. If not they'll flower again next spring. And lavender is a very hardy plant, difficult to kill. It will grow strong again in time. And there are lots of new things pushing their way up through the ground. It's difficult to kill a garden. Peter told me that.'

'Who is Peter?'

'Someone I knew once. He loved all plants, and after his father died he cared for the garden around his mother's cottage.'

'What is he doing now?' Noel had taken Lily's advice and had started to replace the bulbs and tidy up the ground. Lily bent down to help him.

'I don't know. The last I heard of him he was tending the garden of a house where I lived for a number of years.'

A picture of Peter Jackson sprang into Lily's mind. It was a comforting picture: a sturdy young man with rough rosy cheeks, and hair that stood up untidily. He'd been a dependable person all his life: calm, gentle, and always ready to give sensible advice. Lily had listened to him, but not heeded his opinions, particularly where Edward Butler had been concerned.

Mr Sayer was fumbling in his pocket for a pencil and paper. 'Write down his name and address. I could do with a good gardener. If I like him I might offer him a job.'

Lily wrote down the address of the Jacksons' cottage, and then returned to her job of planting without giving it a second thought.

The next few days passed slowly and had a dreamlike quality about them. Lily accompanied Mrs Sayer into town to help her choose a suitable outfit for the funeral. She settled on a black and grey tweed suit, and a hat with a brim to hide her face. She was glad of Lily's company and thanked her profusely.

Grace still came to the Manor every afternoon, but she would be leaving at the end of the month to prepare for her confinement. She always brought Timmy with her and the whole family welcomed him. He was too young to be aware of the tragic faces around him and demanded cheerful attention. Like a little ray of sunshine he toddled around the nursery, building castles out of bricks and knocking them down, asking for songs and stories and expecting smiles and cuddles.

Dorothy and Paul adored him. He brought a sense of normality into their lives for a few hours every day, and made them forget their sorrow for a short time and behave like normal children.

The night before the funeral the coffin was carried into the house. It was placed on trestles in the drawing-room for people to pay their respects. Robert sat with his dead wife all that night; and followed her coffin silently to the service in the country church and then to the graveside.

Lily watched from the nursery window as the procession of cars left the house. Dorothy, a small silent figure in her navy-blue coat and dress, climbed into the waiting car carrying a spray of white roses to place on the coffin lid.

Paul sat on Lily's lap playing with a toy dog. He seemed uninterested in what was going on outside. In fact he rarely talked about his mother; his short memory seemed to have already forgotten her. Lily was there every day and was more real to him.

After the funeral things slowly returned to normal. Grace stopped coming, so Lily had more work to do until the Sayers found a replacement.

One day in early June she was playing with the children on the lawn. They had a large ball made of coloured rubber and were practising kicking it to each other. Paul became excited and kicked so wildly that it bounced away into the bushes and both children raced after it.

Lily sat down on the grass, stretching her bare arms above her head and turned her face to the sun with half-closed eyes. When she opened them Robert Lovegrove was standing a few feet away with a blank expression on his face. Lily smiled, thinking that he wanted to talk to her about his children. But he turned away, and disappeared down a covered walk as quickly and quietly as he had come.

After that she was aware of him many times. Sometimes he'd be standing in an open doorway as she passed along a passage, or walking slowly past the nursery door as she prepared the children's tea. Once she saw him watching from an upper window as she ran with Dorothy and Paul across the grass. His gaze was always focused on her, earnest and unsmiling, making her feel slightly uncomfortable. What was the matter with him? What did he want of her?

One night Lily couldn't sleep. The weather was oppressive and she tossed and turned in her bed. At last she decided to go downstairs and find a book to read. Mr Sayer had given her permission to borrow books from his library. She didn't often have time for such luxuries, but it would pass the time until she felt sleepy.

As she walked along the corridor towards the stairs she heard an unusual sound. Someone nearby was crying. Stifled sobs reached her ears and made her heart turn over. She couldn't ignore such sorrow; she couldn't pass by and pretend she hadn't heard. It was coming from one of the bedrooms occupied by the family.

Lily knocked, but there was no answer; only a pause and then the continuation of the sobbing. She pushed the door open and entered the room. In the dim light she could see Robert Lovegrove stretched out on the bed. His fair head was buried in the pillow to stifle his grief. Silently Lily crossed the floor and put her hand on his heaving shoulders to let him know she was there.

He turned to her, a face wet with weeping, and the tragic expression turned into a smile of happiness. He took her hand in his and pressed it to his cheek.

'Vicky!' he said. 'My darling Vicky. I knew you'd come back.'

Lily tried to draw away but Robert was too strong for her. He pulled her down onto the bed beside him and put his arms around her. He seemed to draw comfort from her presence, and when he pressed his lips to hers she hadn't the heart to refuse him.

CHAPTER TWENTY-FIVE

The proposal

'What would you like for your birthday, Dorothy?' Noel Sayer asked.

The little girl looked up. In front of her were carefully positioned two orange marigolds in a jamjar; she was copying them onto a sheet of paper. The heads of the flowers were like bright suns and the stems as stiff as sticks. It was a good drawing for someone nearly seven.

'I'd like some new paints: the orange isn't right.' Dorothy held up her picture critically. 'I mixed the red with the yellow like Lily told me to, but it's still no good.'

'We'll get you paints and brushes – and how about a pad of paper?'

'With sheets I can tear off?'

'Yes. Like real artists use.'

Dorothy sighed happily. She'd grown over the last year so that her legs and arms were plumper, and her face was rosy with health. Her hair was cut in a straight fringe, with two short pigtails sticking out from behind her ears. Her eyes still looked at the world seriously, and her expression was solemn. She had the wary look of a wild animal who doesn't really trust life, and is always waiting for something unexpected to happen.

She picked up a brush and dunked it in the water jar and then sucked the bristles into a point. Noel Sayer made a silent note to make sure any paints he bought were not poisonous.

'There's something else I'd like, Grandpa.'

'I hope it's not too expensive – we don't want to break the bank, do we?' Mr Sayer said jokingly.

'It doesn't cost anything.' Dorothy rolled the brush around on the square of green paint so that she could colour in a leaf. 'I'd like a garden.'

Noel froze. He was transported back down the years to the time when another little girl had asked him for the same thing. A little girl called Victoria. He'd granted that child her wish, buying her bulbs and a lavender bush, and helping her tend her plot of earth. But that little girl was dead. He'd tried to kill her garden, as if by destroying it he would take away the memory and dull the pain.

'What sort of garden do you want, Dorothy?'

'One where I can grow flowers and things. Brightly coloured flowers that smell nice.' That was what Vicky had wanted: plants that pleased the eye and had a pleasant scent. That was why he'd bought her the lavender bush. 'Can I have a garden, Grandpa?'

Mr Sayer walked to the window and looked out. From where he stood he could see the patch of earth Vicky had tended. It had recovered from his vicious attack of the year before and was now colourful, but untidy and overgrown. At least he hadn't had it covered with paving stones as he'd threatened. The whole garden around the house had become run down and neglected since his old gardener, Tom, had died. Even the lawn was covered with a sprinkling of white daisies instead of the smooth green velvet he remembered.

'Of course you can have a garden,' he said. 'But you'll need someone to help you – show you what to do. What we need is a proper gardener to pull everything into shape. I found a name and address in my old jacket pocket the other day. Someone must have given it to me. Now, where did I put it?' After a search he found a crumpled piece of paper behind a vase on the mantelpiece. 'Peter Jackson,' he read slowly. 'Gardener. It's an address near Lenton: that's not so far away. Perhaps I'll drop him a line sometime.'

Of course he forgot, because other things took precedence. To start with he began to worry about his son-in-law. Robert's behaviour was first of all put down to his sorrow at the loss of his wife, and was completely understandable. But he'd become a recluse, shutting himself in his room and hardly ever venturing out, not even appearing for meals. He spoke to no one, and the children became upset because he ignored them.

Lily felt a personal responsibility for the man. After all, it was her he'd first confided in. It was her shoulder he'd wept on, and there can be nothing more personal than that.

At last Lily took her concerns to her employer. She tapped on the drawing-room door before entering. Nancy Sayer was writing letters at a table in the window. She looked up and smiled.

'What is it, Lily? You look worried.'

'I am. It's Mr Lovegrove.'

'Robert?' Mrs Sayer frowned slightly, folded a sheet of paper and slipped it into an envelope.

'Yes. I know it's not my place. Perhaps I shouldn't interfere; but he's not eating. Is he sick?'

'I don't think so,' Mrs Sayer replied. 'He doesn't come into the dining-room, but I thought perhaps he was asking for trays to be sent up to his room.'

'No. I asked him once if he wanted me to carry one up, but he said he wasn't hungry. Then I found someone had been raiding the pantry and taking biscuits.'

'That sounds more like Paul,' Mrs Sayer laughed.

'I asked Paul, but he said it wasn't him, and I believed him. No one can live on biscuits – he should have a proper meal occasionally.'

'What do you suggest, Lily?'

'I'll make him something special, and take it up to him if you want me to. I think I know how to handle him.'

'Then I'll leave it to you.' Mrs Sayer sighed, and picked up her pen to start another letter. 'You have a way with children, particularly when they're not well, so your charms might work with poor Robert.'

Lily hastened to the kitchen. When Grace popped in to see her later that morning, with her new baby strapped into its pram and Timmy trotting at her side, she was busy at the stove. The room was full of delicious smells.

'Whatever are you doing, Lily?' Grace parked the pram in a corner and tiptoed away from her sleeping daughter. 'Sally's been playing up, and now she's fast asleep. You go and look for

Paul,' she told Timmy, giving him a little push of encouragement. 'I want to talk to Lily.'

'I'm making Robert an omelette,' Lily said, shredding lettuce into a bowl for a salad. 'I was right, you know: he's not eating. Mrs Sayer's given me permission to try and tempt him.'

'Only with food, I hope,' Grace said with a wicked grin.

'Whatever do you mean?' Lily asked innocently, but her friend saw the way her cheeks turned pink, and changed the subject to save embarrassment.

'I only meant that you're becoming a really good cook.'

'I do try,' Lily said as she grated cheese into a bowl. 'I turn my hand to anything now you can't come so often. Cooking, cleaning and mending; as well as caring for Dorothy and Paul.'

'You're going to make some lucky man a good wife one of these days,' Grace said meaningfully.

'I don't know about that,' Lily said wistfully.

Nowadays Lily yearned, not for glamour or riches, but for a kind husband and children of her own. She loved Dorothy and little Paul, but they weren't hers; although she did everything for them and had almost taken the place of their dead mother. But when she saw Grace cuddling tiny Sally, or playing with Timmy, she envied her. There was something special about a mother tending the babies she'd given birth to. Lily shook herself because a shiver had run up her spine.

'What's the matter?' Grace asked, seeing the expression on Lily's face.

'Nothing. Just memories.' Before she could have those longed for babies Lily needed a husband. No one could take Edward's place, and he was in the past. 'I'd better take this up before it gets cold.' She picked up the tray and carried it to the stairs.

Outside Robert's door she paused. Should she knock and wait to be admitted, or just go in? He probably wouldn't answer anyway and she'd have to carry it away again, and then the carefully prepared meal would be wasted. Surprised at her own daring, Lily tapped gently, and then opened the door and entered.

The air inside felt stale, as if the window hadn't been opened for a long time. Robert Lovegrove, clad in a grey wool dressing-gown, was sitting at a desk in the corner and seemed to be studying a picture he held in his hand. He'd obviously been having a turn-out, because the desk-top was littered with bundles of letters, cards and photographs. He looked up at Lily's entrance, and his sad eyes lit up at the sight of her, as if he'd thought at first she was someone else. And then, seeing it was only Lily, the welcome faded.

'I hope I'm not disturbing you,' Lily said. 'Were you expecting someone?'

'No,' Robert said harshly. 'What do you want?'

'I've brought you something to eat.'

'I'm not hungry. Take it away.'

'No!'

'No?' Robert looked up at the dark-haired girl standing before him, and two dabs of colour flamed in his pale cheeks. Wallowing in grief and self-pity, he expected to be obeyed. He felt ashamed when he remembered how he'd weakened in front of this pretty young woman, who reminded him so much of Victoria; how he'd poured out his pain to her, and cried on her shoulder; and worse, how he'd held her in his arms and kissed her, pretending to himself that she was his dead wife come back to life. Lily was only a servant after all, and should obey orders.

'I've made you an omelette and a salad. At least you could show your thanks by eating it.'

'I told you – I'm not hungry.'

'Nonsense, you must be hungry. You haven't eaten properly for days.'

Lily spoke briskly, as she did to the children when they were being particularly awkward. In her eyes Robert Lovegrove was behaving like a spoiled schoolboy. However deep his grief, he wasn't helping himself; and her charges were suffering as a result.

'Well, perhaps I could try . . .'

But Lily had already swept the papers aside and set the tray in front of him. She didn't intend leaving until he'd at least started eating. While she waited she began to gather up the scattered papers.

Robert took a small mouthful and chewed absently. Suddenly he seemed to realize that he was hungry and began to eat with relish, watching Lily all the time. But Lily had found a black and white snapshot of a young couple with their arms about each others' waists. The man was easily recognizable as Robert although he sported a pencil moustache. His companion was gazing into his face adoringly.

'Is this a picture of you and Victoria?' she asked.

Robert glanced sideways. Lily noted with delight that he'd nearly cleared his plate.

'Yes. It was taken on our honeymoon. I'm going to burn it – and all the other things.'

Lily stared at him in horror. The pictures were all photographs and snapshots of his young wife. In some she was alone; in others with her husband, or holding one or other of her children. The letters were on scented paper, the writing feminine; obviously written by Victoria as well.

'But you can't . . .'

'I can – it's the only way I can bear it.' Robert placed his knife and fork carefully on the edge of his plate, and looked at Lily as if he was expecting sympathy.

'I've never heard anything more selfish in my whole life.' Lily spoke angrily, not caring if she upset him. 'What are you trying to do – destroy your children?'

'What do you mean?'

'Because that's what you're doing. So, Dorothy and Paul's mother is dead – but they still have a father. A father who should be keeping the memory of their mother alive – not trying to bury it. I never had a mother, and I didn't have a father either; but I'd rather have had nobody than a weakling like you.'

'You don't understand.'

'Shut up and listen. I do understand, so there.' Lily's eyes were glinting fiercely and her head was up. She didn't care what she said, who she hurt. Robert Lovegrove was going to hear the truth. 'I did feel sorry for you at first, we all did, but everybody's losing patience. You sit up here like a sulking schoolboy, while your children creep about the house like little ghosts, afraid of disturbing you. Even Mr and Mrs Sayer are getting on with their lives, and Victoria was their only daughter. If you keep this up much longer they'll all start to hate you. I do already.' And suddenly Lily burst into tears.

Robert was so shaken he was at her side at once. 'Don't, Lily,' he begged. 'Don't cry like that. I'm sorry.'

'No, you're not,' Lily said through her tears. 'You're not sorry at all.'

'But you are right,' Robert admitted. 'I've been selfish, only thinking about myself. Things are going to change. Where are the children?'

Lily wiped her eyes, and looked up hopefully. 'Downstairs. Dorothy has just learned to knit. I suggested she make you a tie, but she said you wouldn't wear it. So she's making it for her Grandpa instead.'

'I want to see the tie.' Robert grabbed Lily's hand and half dragged her towards the door.

'And Paul's just learned to read. He wants people to listen to him.'

'I want to hear him. Come on . . .'

From that moment things changed. Piltdown Manor turned from a house of mourning into a house of hope.

Robert was a constant visitor to the nursery, joining in the children's games and inventing new ones. Dorothy and Paul blossomed under their father's interest. He wore his knitted tie with pride, and helped his son to master the art of reading books. When he heard about Dorothy's longing for a garden of her own he wielded a spade himself, and helped her plant the first seeds. They chose the same plants Victoria had chosen so many years before; and were to be seen most mornings weeding, and watering, and watching the new seedlings grow.

When she had the time Lily helped them. She still remembered what she'd learned from Sister Clare at St Jude's. Their cheerful voices drifted across the overgrown lawns, reaching the ears of Mr and Mrs Sayer as they sat just inside the drawing-room window.

'Hark at them,' Nancy Sayer said one day, looking up from her sewing with a smile. 'They sound like a flock of starlings.'

'I never thought the children would smile again,' Noel said. 'Let alone Robert.'

'It's Lily's doing.'

'I know. That young woman has worked a miracle.'

'She talks to them about Victoria all the time, although she never knew her. She even rescued those pictures Robert wanted to burn. They keep a framed one in pride of place on the nursery mantelpiece.'

'I'm glad. She's keeping Vicky's memory alive.'

They sat in silent thought for a few minutes, but the laughter outside soon caught their attention again. Paul suddenly appeared, and ran past the window with his sister in hot pursuit. His legs were going like pistons and the tail of his shirt was hanging out. He looked the picture of health and energy: a small boy enjoying himself. Dorothy's longer legs soon caught up with him. They tumbled to the ground, rolling down the grassy slope and shrieking hysterically.

Lily and Robert came into view. They were walking side by side in deep conversation, their heads bent towards each other, his so fair and hers so dark. Robert's face was tanned golden above his white open-necked shirt, and his slacks were casually crumpled at the knees.

Lily was wearing a sleeveless dress the same colour as her eyes, with a gathered skirt and patch pockets. Her feet were bare, and her shoes swinging from one hand. The breeze lifted her hair from the nape of her neck, and swirled it outwards in a dark cloud. They made a charming picture.

'Does she still remind you of Vicky?' Nancy asked absently.

'More and more. Sometimes I have to remind myself that she's not.'

'I know. I caught myself yesterday, almost calling her by the wrong name.'

They sat in silence, deep in thought, watching until Lily and Robert disappeared into the shrubbery. It was Nancy who eventually voiced what they'd both been thinking.

'Robert is very fond of her.'

'So am I.' Noel put out his hand and patted his wife's shoulder. 'Does that bother you?'

'Of course not – but I don't want Robert to be hurt. I know it's a year since Vicky died, but he's still very vulnerable. He thinks he's in love.'

'Nonsense.' Noel laughed, and getting to his feet paced about the room. 'Lily's an attractive girl and she reminds him of Victoria, so it's natural that he's grateful to her for all she's doing for the children. But he's not such a fool as to fall in love.'

'Isn't he?' Nancy frowned, and got up to close the window. It had suddenly turned chilly. 'He follows her about like a lovesick boy, and she doesn't seem to mind. Didn't you see the way he was looking at her just now? Robert's in love – or he thinks he is.'

'Perhaps it wouldn't be such a bad thing,' Noel said thoughtfully. 'Lily's almost one of the family.'

'I'm glad you said almost. I'm as fond of Lily as you are, Noel, and the children. But what you seem to forget is that she works for us. She's Dorothy and Paul's nanny, and she cooks and helps me keep house. But we don't know anything about her. She didn't need references because Grace recommended her. And she never speaks about her past. I think she has something to hide.'

'Nonsense,' Noel said for the second time. 'How old is she: twenty-three, twenty-four? An orphan, probably, with a past she wants to forget. If it worries you, why don't you ask her?'

'What can I say?' Nancy laughed. 'Lily, we want you to tell us the story of your life, just in case Robert wants to marry you.'

'Marry?' That sobered Noel up. 'You don't think it'll come to that, do you?'

'I don't know. Perhaps it wouldn't be such a bad thing, for Robert's sake.'

'I think you're letting your imagination run away with you, my dear,' Noel said. 'There's probably nothing on those two young people's minds apart from the children's welfare, and what we're having for dinner tonight.'

Even so, Nancy wished she could have become invisible, so she could have followed Lily and Robert to hear what they were talking about so earnestly.

At that moment Paul chose to burst into the room carrying something carefully cupped in his hands.

'I need a jamjar – now!' he said grimly. 'Grandma, I need a jamjar.'

'What for, dear?' Nancy was used to these passionate demands. Only the day before he'd wanted a matchbox to keep a ladybird in.

'It's a butterfly. I want it to lay eggs so I can watch.' He opened his hands just wide enough to show a tattered cabbage white sitting forlornly on his palm. It shook its wings, leaving a cloud of powder on his skin.

'Poor little thing,' his grandmother said. 'If you put it in a jar it will only die.'

'Why will it? I'll feed it and look after it. It'll be my pet.'

'You can't keep a butterfly for a pet.' Dorothy had followed her brother into the room. 'It's cruel. Butterflies need to fly around.'

'I'll let it fly around the nursery then.'

'No, you won't. It'll get in my hair.' Dorothy grabbed Paul's hands, and the butterfly seized its opportunity and fluttered up into the air. It headed for the window where it beat its wings against the glass.

'Catch it! Catch it!' Paul shrieked, jumping up and down.

'No, my lad,' Mr Sayer said. He calmly opened the window and watched the butterfly flutter away. Paul screwed up his face as if he was going to cry, so his grandfather diverted him quickly. 'If you really want a pet I'll get you a proper one.'

'Will you?' Paul's mind raced through the possibilities, from ponies to crocodiles, as he looked up at his grandfather with wide eyes. 'What sort?'

'How about a puppy?'

'A puppy!' Paul shrieked excitedly, turning to his sister. 'Did you hear that? Grandpa's going to buy me a puppy.'

Dorothy's downcast expression showed her disappointment.

'And you shall have a bird in a cage. A canary, that will sing to you.'

'Oh, Grandpa!' was all the little girl could say, but her starry eyes spoke volumes.

At that moment Robert Lovegrove strode into the room. The children threw themselves at him, each wanting to be the first to impart the news.

'Where's Lily? I want to tell Lily.' Paul had exhausted the present company and needed a new audience.

'I'm here.'

Lily was standing in the doorway as if she didn't want to intrude on a family occasion. Her cheeks were glowing and her violet eyes sparkled. In fact, Nancy Sayer thought, she looked just like a girl who'd recently been kissed.

'Will you take them upstairs, Lily?' Robert said. 'Before they wear their grandparents out.'

'Of course.' Lily spoke with the tone of a dutiful nanny. 'Come on, children. Come and tell me all about it.'

At last Robert was alone with his parents-in-law. He wandered around the room nervously, picking up an ornament or turning the page of a book, but his attention seemed far away. Nancy Sayer suspected that it was directed upstairs to the nursery where a pretty, dark-haired girl was tending his children. At last she could bear the suspense no longer.

'Do stop wandering about, Robert,' she said. 'Sit down, for heaven's sake.'

'In a minute.' Robert crossed to the mantelpiece and picked up a photograph of his dead wife, tracing her face with his finger, before replacing it with care. Then he turned and faced Nancy and Noel as if he was facing a firing squad. 'Lily and I want to get married,' he said.

They'd expected a declaration of love; maybe even a request for permission for him to pay court to his children's nanny; but not this statement of their joint intent. It sounded as if they had no say in the matter. But what business was it of theirs, Noel thought? Robert was a widower and free to do whatever he wanted, without asking their permission. He had a house of his own, although it had been shut up for more than a year. He had two children who needed a mother. It sounded like an ideal arrangement.

'Lily's a charming girl,' Nancy began. 'But . . .'

'I know what you're going to say,' Robert butted in. 'Lily's just a servant, and I should be looking for someone of my own class.'

His parents-in-law were silent. They knew whatever they said would be misinterpreted. By his eyes, his voice, his words, he was showing his infatuation.

'Not at all,' Noel said, his calm tone soothing the other man's excitement. 'This is nineteen-fifty-five, you know; not the reign of Queen Victoria. You're a comparatively young man and are bound to marry again sooner or later. But there's plenty of time. No need to choose the first pretty face you set eyes upon.'

'It's not like that,' Robert insisted. 'I love Lily.'

'Because she looks like Victoria? Because she reminds you of your dead wife? It's Lily I'm thinking of now – it would be a dreadful cross for any woman to bear.'

'Lily understands.'

'I hope she does.'

'Whether you like it or not, Lily has agreed to become my wife,' Robert said. 'We just wanted your blessing, that's all.'

'You'll always have that, dear boy,' Nancy Sayer said, and to prove her words she kissed his cheeks fondly. 'We only want your happiness; and because we're so fond of Lily, we want hers as well.'

'I'll make her happy,' Robert promised.

'Then we wish you well,' Noel said. 'Don't we, Nancy? But take my advice and don't rush into things. You can both have a home here for as long as you want. The children are settled, and it's not fair to uproot them just yet. Get engaged to Lily by all means. We'll make the announcement ourselves so everyone knows we approve. It will prevent gossip. But wait a few months before you marry. You owe that to Victoria – and us.'

After Robert had gone, hastening to Lily with the news, Noel and Nancy sat for a long time talking things over. They went over the same ground again and again; and at last came to the conclusion that they'd done the right thing. Now they could only sit back and hope.

'He loves her,' Noel said. 'You can see that.'

'But only because she reminds him of Vicky.'

'It's not only that. I think he loves Lily for her own sake; and the fact that she reminds him of Victoria is an additional bonus.'

'But does Lily love him?'

'I've no idea – but she certainly looked as if she did just now.'

'Flushed cheeks and sparkling eyes can mean more than love,' Nancy said dryly. 'It could mean that she's got what she wanted.'

'You mean she's been planning this? She's not that sort of a girl, Nancy.'

'Lily's a woman – and so am I. I caught you years ago, Noel, so I wouldn't blame her for seeing a good thing and going for it.'

'You make it sound very cold-blooded,' Noel laughed.

'Not at all. It's just common sense.' Nancy smiled to take the sting out of her words. 'Anyway, you have to admit that things are much more comfortable around here since Lily came. And it's nice to see Robert smiling again, and taking an interest in life; and the children laughing.'

'Yes.' Noel stroked his chin thoughtfully. 'Now all I've got to do is ask around the village for puppies and canaries.'

'What about a party? Don't you think it's time we had a party?'

'Whatever for? It's nobody's birthday – and nowhere near Christmas.'

'Not that sort of party, Noel. A house party, to announce the engagement. Robert can ask his friends, and we can invite a few of the local people. It would be a way of showing that we approve of the match.'

'Good idea.'

'But we'll have to get things moving.' Nancy looked around. 'We'll need the painters in; with all the upset nothing's been done for ages. And we could do with new curtains in the dining-room, and loose covers in here. The spare bedrooms need the rugs cleaned, and new lampshades wouldn't come amiss.'

'Do whatever you want and I'll foot the bill.' Mr Sayer was pleased to see his wife looking so excited and cheerful. A party for the engagement would give her new things to think about. 'I really must do something about the garden, though. Since old Tom died it's been sadly neglected. It's not really enough to have the odd labourer giving their services when they can fit it in with everything else.'

'Perhaps you could advertise,' Nancy suggested.

'No need.' Noel crossed to the fireplace, and looked again for the crumpled piece of paper he'd pushed back behind a vase. 'I have a name and address here. A Peter Jackson. Someone recommended him to me, but I can't for the life of me remember who it was. He doesn't live locally, but he might come over and advise me. I'll write to him now, before I forget.'

Nancy left her husband to his letter writing. If they were going to open the house to visitors she'd have a lot to do. She'd have to count the linen and spring-clean the rooms. Perhaps Grace would be able to put in a few hours, and she might know of someone who needed a temporary job. Lily would help, too; she knew that. But as she was soon to be one of the family Nancy didn't want to take advantage.

Left to his own devices, Noel picked up his fountain pen and unscrewed the cap. He sat meditating for a few minutes before he began to write:

Dear Mr Jackson,

I have recently lost the services of my regular gardener, and am urgently in need of a replacement. As you were recommended by a friend I wondered if you would be interested. The garden in question is about two acres, and comprises mainly lawns and flower-beds. As I am planning a house party in a few weeks' time the matter is urgent. If you already have a regular position perhaps you could find the time to give me your advice, and then I may be able to find someone local to carry out the work. My wife and I would be pleased to put you up as I see that you have some way to come. I will make it worth your while. I hope we can come to some satisfactory arrangement, and in the meantime remain

Yours sincerely,
Noel Sayer

Lily posted the letter herself, but there was always such a pile of correspondence leaving Piltdown Manor that she didn't notice that one of the letters she carried was addressed to her old friend.

CHAPTER TWENTY-SIX

The new gardener

Peter was working hard on the flower borders at Ring House. He was stripped to the waist and his shoulders were tanned a dark brown. Every muscle under his skin rippled with strength.

He whistled softly under his breath as he studied the spaces of spare earth. There would still be time to plant afresh, between the white japonica and the metallic blue heads of the eryngiums, with their heads like thistles. He was just trying to decide whether an eau-de-Cologne mint would be suitable, when he noticed that the heads of the Michaelmas daisies had become so top-heavy that they were in danger of tumbling over. He was so busy tying them back with pea-sticks and a ball of twine that he didn't hear Elizabeth Thomas approaching.

'I've just been looking at the roses, Peter,' she said. 'That rain in the night has all but ruined them. I wanted some for a bowl in the dining-room.'

'I could pick you a mixed bunch from the border, Mrs Thomas. Everything's a bit blown, but there's still plenty of colour.'

'Just a small posy then. Enough to fill my Japanese bowl.' Mrs Thomas bent down and picked a sprig of rosemary, rubbing it between her fingers to release the scent.

'Shall I bring it up to the house?'

'Leave it on the kitchen table; and then go round to the terrace. My husband wants to have a word with you.'

The Michaelmas daisies now secured, Peter bent to the task of selecting suitable flowers to fill a shallow bowl. He chose for colour and perfume, resting the blossoms on leaves and surrounding the delicate stems with moss. When he was satisfied he delivered them as directed, and then clumped around the side of the house in his heavy boots in search of Mr Thomas.

He found him stretched out in a wicker chair in a sheltered spot away from the sun. He was wearing a baggy cardigan with the buttons undone, and a Panama hat on the back of his head. His eyes were closed as if he was asleep, and his nostrils quivered at every breath as though he was about to snore.

Peter looked sadly at his employer, noting how he'd aged in the last few months. He'd lost weight, so that the skin on his face hung in folds; and his body weight seemed to have slipped downwards so that, instead of the firm, rounded figure he'd once had, his belly protruded and wobbled loosely under his ill-fitting clothes. Looking at him, it was hard to remember the fine figure of a man he'd once been. But Peter was fond of him.

Thinking he was sleeping, the younger man turned to retrace his steps. But before he could move far James spoke, his voice as firm and strong as ever.

'Don't go, Peter.'

'I didn't mean to disturb you, Mr Thomas. Your wife said you wanted me – but I can come back some other time.'

'I wasn't asleep.' James pulled himself up in the chair and straightened his hat. 'Just having forty winks. Sit down, boy.' There was another chair close by, but it had a frilled cushion as well as Elizabeth's knitting on the seat. Peter sat down on the edge of a large stone tub containing sweet-scented geraniums. He waited patiently for his employer to put into words what was on his mind. At last James spoke, and Peter was surprised by his question. 'How old are you, Peter? Twenty-two – three?'

'Twenty-five, sir.'

'Are you indeed! Doesn't time fly? And how long have you been working for me?'

Peter thought: he needed time to work that one out. 'About

four years, I think,' he said at last.

'As long as that?' James Thomas rubbed his chin in surprise. 'And what are your plans?'

'Plans?' Peter stared at Mr Thomas. 'I don't think I have any plans.'

'You're a young man, Peter, you must have plans; these days I think they call them ambitions. You had ambitions once if I remember rightly. Something to do with a Miss Clark, wasn't it?'

Peter shuffled his feet in embarrassment, remembering his brief encounter with the schoolteacher. 'That didn't come to anything,' he said.

'But you bought the cottage with the idea of settling down, didn't you? Perhaps you have another young lady in mind?'

James winked, and tapped his nose knowingly. Peter Jackson was an attractive young man, if a bit on the rough side, and he'd heard gossip in the village about him being free and eligible. Surely it would only be a matter of time before one of the girls led him to the altar.

'No,' Peter said, with a firmness in his voice that surprised both of them. 'There's nobody at the moment.'

'I'm sorry to hear it,' James said. 'A man needs a wife. But on the other hand perhaps it's as well.' Peter looked at him questioningly. 'I'm not being nosy, lad. There's a purpose behind my questions. You see, if you haven't got a wife to support, it's not so bad being out of a job.'

'But I've got a job – here. I'm happy to stay here, Mr Thomas. I'm content with things as they are. I wouldn't want to better myself if it meant moving on.'

'I know. I can see you're a contented man, Peter. The thing is I might have to let you go.'

'Let me go! You mean, sack me? Why? What have I done?' Colour flooded Peter's face, showing his distress, as his mind ranged about, trying to discover the meaning and the reason for Mr Thomas's words.

'I'd never sack you, Peter. You're a good worker and the garden has never looked so good. If your father had lived he'd have been proud of you.' James's hands moved restlessly. 'I said – let you go. It's not the same thing. You know I've sold a lot of land over the years. Didn't want to, had no choice. Times are hard, and I'm not as young as I was. And the heart's playing up – I suppose you know that?'

'I guessed, Mr Thomas.'

'John Butler keeps an eye on me, but I know he's worried. Keeps warning me about doing too much. Might as well be dead if I can't enjoy life, that's what I told him. But he says I must think about Mrs Thomas; be fair to her. And then there's Betty and the children . . .'

'You must enjoy being a grandfather.'

James smiled proudly. 'Yes. First little Jennifer, and now the boy we all wanted so badly. The image of his mother, and just as bossy. Bit of an argument about the names. Betty wanted to call him after me, and Edward was set on naming him after his own father. In the end they decided on both. They put the names in a hat and drew them out in order. I lost.' Mr Thomas grinned happily. 'Baby christened John James, but everyone calls him Johnnie.'

'I'm pleased for you.'

'But back to what I was saying: if I sell up I'll have to let you go.'

'You mean you're going to sell Ring House?'

Peter looked at Mr Thomas in astonishment, and then around at the lovely garden. In all his wildest dreams he'd never imagined Lenton without the Thomas's at Ring House, or himself working for anybody else.

'Don't look like that, Peter,' James said kindly. The young fellow looked so devastated that he half wished he hadn't spoken. But he had to be fair. Peter had to be prepared for the worst. 'There's nothing settled, and it may not come to it. But if things don't improve, and my health deteriorates, I may be forced to make changes.'

'What sort of changes?'

'Well, selling this place would solve my money worries. I could buy a smaller house that's easier to run. Ring House is too big now that Betty's gone: all the empty rooms that have to be kept clean, and no help for my wife. She's always had domestics to do the heavy work, but you can't get them these days even if you can afford it. It's only commonsense really, although I should be sorry to go. We wouldn't move far, because of Betty and Edward. Now that I've got a grandson I want to see a lot of him – just in case . . .'

He didn't finish the sentence but Peter knew what he was thinking: in case he was going to die. Peter got to his feet and brushed the earth off the seat of his trousers, and then held out his hand.

'You're not to worry, Mr Thomas,' he said. 'You've been good to my family. My father thought the world of you, and so do I. If you do move into a smaller place you'll still have a garden. I can't see Mrs Thomas without her roses. I'll still look after it for you whether you pay me or not. I can't think of a better way of using my spare time.'

They shook hands. Peter's firm grip reassured the older man, who sat back with a sigh. 'Well, boy, it hasn't come to that yet. Just wanted to put you in the picture, just in case you get a better offer. Whatever you do you'll have my blessing.'

'Thank you, sir.'

Peter was saddened, but as he walked down the drive home he looked about him with fresh eyes. He couldn't imagine Ring House belonging to anybody but the Thomas family. When he was a boy he'd watched his father working on the estate: chauffeuring Mr Thomas, collecting rents from the farms, and overseeing a team of employees.

He'd sat on the wall over there with his elder brother Mike, as Betty Thomas had trotted past on her brown pony, the feather in her hat bobbing in the breeze, and her yellow curls dancing. They'd both longed for a ride on Bracken, but the nearest they'd got was to lead the little animal back to the stable and rub him down.

And then Lily had come to Ring House. Lily, with her dark hair and violet eyes. She was more Peter's kind than proud, bossy Betty Thomas. They'd played together, and walked to school side by side. He'd watched her in her purple dress and crushed straw hat on that day, so long ago, when the boys had chosen their May Queen. Lily should have been the winner, but Betty had threatened and cheated to get the honour, and Peter had felt anger at the unfairness of it. Edward had drawn a picture of Lily that day and Peter had been pushed into the background. But Lily from the Valley had always had a special place in his heart.

Peter reached home to find his mother sitting on a bench in the sun shelling peas. He squatted down on the grass at her side and helped himself from the basket, squeezing a pod between his fingers and dropping the raw peas one by one into his mouth.

'How's everything up at the house?' Emma asked.

'Not so good. Mr Thomas is poorly – he's got a bad heart – and he's talking about selling up.'

Mrs Jackson turned a surprised face towards her son. 'Never! The Thomas's have been at Ring House for as long as I've been in Lenton. It wouldn't be the same without them. Elizabeth's got a heart of gold even if she is a proud woman; although I never could abide that girl of hers.'

'Betty's all right,' Peter said generously. 'Mr Thomas is so pleased about his second grandchild, it's a pleasure to see. He was telling me, they've called him John James – Johnnie for short.'

'Good, no-nonsense names,' Emma said approvingly. 'Good luck to them, that's what I say.'

'The thing is, Mother, if they do sell up I could be out of a job.'

Emma didn't look worried. She put her hand over her son's big brown one and patted it reassuringly. 'You'd get something else, never fear. Everyone knows what a good worker you are. If things get too bad you can always put yourself forward for seasonal work on the farms. They always want labour.'

Peter counted off the local farms on his fingers. 'Crofts have got a full work-force, I know that. And Barnside have been putting men off. I could try Deans for the harvesting. The only other farm remaining is Valley Farm.'

Emma Jackson laughed. 'I shouldn't try there, son. That place is so run down there is not even enough work for the Crow brothers themselves.'

'I heard things were bad,' Peter said.

'Bad! It's a crying shame. It used to be a fine place; but now the fields are full of nettles and the house is falling down around their ears.'

'I know Mr Thomas wanted to be shot of it at one time. Offered it cheap to Moses, and had the offer thrown back in his face. I wouldn't mind a farm like that – even as it stands. I'd get it on its feet in no time.'

'You would, son; but you're not likely to get the opportunity. So you'll have to put up with our cottage and your poor old mother.'

'You're not old,' Peter said gallantly.

'Get away with you.' Emma turned back to the shelling,

judging the weight of the pan with an experienced hand. 'I was in Lenton yesterday, and Moses Crow was in the High Street with Edith. Spouting the bible at her, he was: all about the whore of Babylon, or some such thing. Off his head, I think he is. And she's not much better.'

'What happened?'

'The vicar was passing and tried to calm him down, but it didn't do much good. Told Mr Plummer not to interfere, Moses did. Threatened to get his old shotgun out, so he thought better of it.'

'There's going to be a tragedy there one of these days,' Peter said. 'Give me that: I'll carry it in for you.'

Emma was struggling to her feet, balancing the heavy pan. Her legs were still troubling her, particularly when she'd not been on them for some time.

'A letter came for you, Peter, by the second post. I put it on the dresser.'

'A letter!' A letter was an event in the Jackson household, and usually meant bad news. 'Who'd be writing to me then?'

'You'll find out if you open it.'

Peter picked up the envelope gingerly. It was made of thick white parchment, and his name and address were written boldly in blue ink. It was almost a pity to open it, but he did, fumbling with his fingers to extract the single sheet of paper it contained. He unfolded it curiously.

'Well, I never!' he exclaimed after reading it. 'Talk about coincidence. Someone's offering me a job.' He passed the letter over to his mother.

'Noel Sayer?' she said. 'Who's he?'

'No idea. He says here someone's recommended me, but I can't imagine who. The address is Piltdown.'

'Where's that, son?' Emma asked. She hadn't been more than five miles outside Lenton in her whole life, except for one train journey to London when she was courting Bert. She hadn't liked that very much.

'Not so far away. I passed through there a couple of years ago when I took that trip to the coast. I borrowed Billy's bike if you remember.'

'Of course I remember. You were looking for Lily.'

'Yes. But it was a waste of time, visiting all those seaside towns – Brighton, Pierhaven, Worthing – and finding that nobody had heard anything about her. It was just as if she'd vanished from the face of the earth.'

Emma passed the letter back to her son. 'What are you going to do about this then?'

'I'd be a fool not to look into it with things the way they are at Ring House. This Mr Sayer says he'll put me up, so it'll be worth a trip to Piltdown to see what he wants. Mr Thomas will give me the time off even if it means staying away for a week or so. In an emergency Billy can always stand in for me. He's still young, but he's good with his hands. What do you say, Mother?'

'You do whatever you think best,' Emma said, putting the pan on the stove and adding a pinch of salt. 'It's funny, though, this letter arriving today of all days, just when Mr Thomas warned you. But God works in mysterious ways as the saying goes.'

So Peter wrote to Noel Sayer, and it was arranged that he would travel to Piltdown the following week. He would be paid a wage, and given free board and lodging. In return he would be expected to pull the garden into shape in time for a house party the family were holding to celebrate an engagement, and give advice about future landscaping.

Peter arrived in Piltdown in the late afternoon. He was wearing his only suit and an uncomfortable collar and tie. He'd even tried to smooth his hair down, but tufts of it still sprang up like a badly mown lawn. In his hand he carried a cardboard suitcase containing his few belongings, and his cap was rolled up and pushed into his jacket pocket making an untidy bulge.

Billy had offered to lend him his bike again, but he'd decided against cycling there. This time he travelled on the country bus that stopped at all the small towns and villages along the route, giving a pleasant and leisurely ride. It took him as far as Uckfield; and then he had the choice of boarding a local run-about, or walking. A fellow traveller told him the distance was about two miles, and as the weather was fine Peter decided that the walk would do him good.

At the top of the main street he found a signpost indicating that a track through the woods would eventually lead him to Piltdown. He turned into it and strode along purposefully, swinging his case.

Trees in their summer glory almost met over his head, and the winding path was soft beneath his feet. It was so quiet that Peter clearly heard a blackbird singing its distinctive song close by, and the snap of a twig as a rabbit shot across his path.

When he came out into the sunlight he found himself on the edge of a common. In front of him was a pond on which a pair of stately swans were sailing, ignoring the squawks and quacks of a noisy family of ducks quarrelling in the shallows. Peter skirted the pond and found a public house called the Piltdown Man at the side of the road. He remembered it from his cycle ride two years before. He'd been thirsty that day but his companions had urged him on. Today he stopped, ordered a cool glass of beer, and while he enjoyed it asked directions from the landlord.

'Piltdown Manor? Mr Sayer's place. Down the road towards Mayfield and then first on the left. You can't miss it. It's a big house – looks a bit like a castle.'

Peter thanked him, finished his drink and set off again. Ten minutes later he found himself at the end of his journey. He stood in the open gateway under a cherry tree, and put his case down on the ground to rest his arm.

The house in front of him was impressive with its long windows catching the sun and its ivy clad walls. He only glanced at the white statues and tall chimneys. It was a nice enough house, but he preferred the cottage where he lived. It was the garden he was interested in, anyhow, and he saw at once how neglected it was. The once smooth gravel of the drive was broken here and there by clumps of weeds. The lawns needed trimming – their edges were ragged, and daisies dotted the long grass. The herbaceous borders were strangled with bindweed and the box hedges hadn't had a cut for ages. But there was nothing that a strong arm couldn't put right. Peter already had ideas about changing the shape of the lawn to make it more interesting. At the moment it was a rectangle; but if Mr Sayer could be persuaded to let him change it into a half-circle, it would soften the hard lines of the house as well as widening the drive.

'I'll carry your case if you'll give me a penny.'

Peter had been deep in thought but now he saw that he wasn't alone. A little face was peeping at him from around the gatepost. It was a boy of about five years old with a round chubby face, and a big grin that showed the gap in his front teeth. He certainly wasn't a village lad, Peter decided, because he was wearing a white shirt and grey shorts. His long socks were neatly gartered, and on his feet were black shoes with shiny toe-caps. He looked a perfectly turned out child, apart from the wicked grin and trailing shoelaces.

'I said, I'll carry your case up to the house for a penny.'

'Don't take any notice of Paul, mister,' another voice joined in from somewhere above Peter's head. 'He's not allowed to take money.'

Peter looked up into the cherry tree and saw two bright eyes set in a serious little face, and two pigtails with ribbons on the ends.

'And who might you be?' he asked.

'I'm Dorothy,' the little girl said, and she dropped to the ground at his feet. She was as neatly dressed as the boy, in a tartan dress with red piping, sandals, and spotless white ankle socks. 'This is my brother, Paul.'

'I'm Peter.'

'Have you got the curtains in there?' Paul asked, pointing to the suitcase.

'Curtains? What would I be doing with curtains?'

'Grandma's ordered new ones for the dining-room. She said a man would be bringing them. We thought it was you,' Dorothy explained.

'I'm sorry,' Peter said. 'I'm just the gardener.'

Paul looked disappointed but Dorothy's face lit up. She slipped her hand into Peter's and looked trustingly up into his face. 'I've got a garden,' she said.

'I hope you look after it.'

'I try to. It's got a lavender bush in it; my mummy planted it before she died.'

'I've got a puppy,' Paul butted in. 'It's a black poodle called Tuppence. Grandpa gave him to me.'

'Is your grandpa's name Mr Sayer?'

'Yes, and so is Grandma's. Daddy's name is Lovegrove – the same as ours. Robert Lovegrove.'

'It's your grandpa I've come to see then,' Peter said. 'Do you know where he is?'

'In the library – making lists. Come on, we'll take you.'

Dorothy pulled at Peter's hand and led him up the drive

towards the house. Paul followed, carrying the case. He'd brightened up, even if he wasn't going to get the requested penny.

As they entered the front door a grey-haired lady was passing through the hall. She introduced herself as Nancy Sayer, and pushed open a door on the right indicating that Peter should enter.

'My husband's in there with Robert,' she said. 'Come with me, children, you can see Mr Jackson again later.'

'I want to show Peter my canary,' Dorothy protested as she was led away.

'I told him about Tuppence,' Paul added.

The library at the manor looked out onto a terrace. Peter, who wasn't much of a reader, found the book-lined walls depressing. However, the room was well used and pleasantly lived in. Two men were sitting at a long table on which were strewn the lists Dorothy had talked about. The older man got up at Peter's entrance and held out his hand.

'I'm Noel Sayer, and this is Robert Lovegrove,' he said by way of introduction.

'How do you do,' Peter said, shaking hands. 'I'm Peter Jackson. I think you're expecting me.'

'The gardener. Splendid. You're just in time: let's get to work.'

Before he knew it Peter found himself deep in plans to renovate the garden. A house party was being held in three weeks' time to celebrate the engagement of Robert Lovegrove, and Mr Sayer wanted the garden to be smartened up for the occasion. It was a mammoth task to complete in such a short space of time, but Peter knew he could do it.

'Of course it will only be a general tidying up of what is already there,' he explained. 'But I can draw you up plans for suggested improvements that could be made at a later date. I noticed a hollow down by the trees as you come through the gate. An ornamental pond would look good there; with a little bridge over the water.'

'Will it be safe for Dorothy and Paul?' Robert asked, showing what a doting father he'd become. 'You've met my children?' Peter nodded. 'Their mother died a year ago, and I'm remarrying.' He felt he needed to explain the situation.

'They're not babies,' Noel Sayer said. 'If you're bothered we can always put a fence around it and make it out of bounds. What do you think, Mr Jackson?'

'It needn't be deep. Even a few inches of water can look attractive and be enough to attract wildlife.'

'Then we'll have a pond.' Mr Sayer made a note. 'Now, back to the matter in hand. I want to use the house as well as the garden for the party. I suppose you won't object to giving a hand indoors as well?'

'Not at all,' Peter said, wondering when he was going to find the time. The work on the garden was going to be a full-time occupation if it was to be ready in time. But he liked Noel Sayer and wanted to please him. It would be a change from Ring House, and would be good experience if James Thomas decided to sell up. Robert Lovegrove seemed a pleasant enough chap as well.

'Anything else you want to ask while we're about it?'

'The box hedges need reshaping – and there's a lot of dead wood around the honeysuckle. It would flower better if it was thinned out.'

'Do whatever you want. Now you'll need to settle in. We've given you a room at the tower end. I'm sure you'll be comfortable; and I hope you'll join us for dinner. We usually dine at seven-thirty so you've got plenty of time.'

The room Peter had been allotted was small but comfortable. He had a quick wash and unpacked his belongings, needing only one drawer and a corner of the wardrobe for his few possessions. Then he opened the window and leaned out, enjoying the view.

The Sussex countryside rolled away in front of him: a patchwork of fields and woods, and the thatched roofs of cottages and spires of churches. They looked so small and perfect that Peter felt he could stretch out his hand and pick them up as if they were doll-sized buildings.

He looked at his watch: it was only half past six. He had an hour before it would be time to go down to dinner, a meal he was dreading. At home they ate in the comfort of the kitchen; but he'd heard about country houses, and meals served on expensive china, with an assortment of cutlery he wouldn't be used to. He would just have to copy everyone else and hope for the best.

A walk in the garden would pass the time. Peter wanted to

have another look at the site he'd suggested for the pond. There didn't seem to be anybody about, but when he passed through the main door a little figure slipped forward and took his hand. It was Dorothy.

'I want to show you my garden,' she said insistently.

'This is Tuppence.' A second figure danced forward. It was Paul with a curly black puppy clutched against his chest.

Peter dutifully admired the little dog, who rolled his boot-button eyes in ecstasy at the attention, and unrolled an endless length of flapping pink tongue.

Dorothy led him to a patch of earth that was a tangle of sweet peas and marigolds. Paul put Tuppence down on the ground and the little animal started to scrabble with his miniature paws in the loose earth, his stumpy tail wagging furiously.

Peter dropped to his haunches to pick him up, so it was only when Dorothy shouted 'Over here' that he realized that they weren't alone.

He looked up and the sun was in his eyes. He had to put up his hand to shield them from the glare. A slim figure was walking towards him across the grass: a young woman wearing a dress of violet silk that clung to her figure like a glove. On her head she wore a straw hat with a nodding brim. Peter could just see a pale, delicate face underneath its shade, and a cloud of dark hair falling to her shoulders.

He'd seen a similar apparition once before in the classroom of the village school at Lenton. A little girl called Lily had paraded like a queen in front of her schoolmates. Although Lily's dress had then only been an old petticoat, it had shown off her figure in the same provocative way. Everyone, the boys, girls, and Miss Stringer the teacher, had caught a glimpse of the beauty Lily from the Valley would grow into.

Peter rubbed his eyes but the girl was still there. And then he saw that her eyes matched the violet of her dress, and she was smiling a familiar smile of welcome as Dorothy grabbed her hand and pulled her forward.

'This is Peter,' the little girl announced. 'He's going to help me with my garden.'

'I know,' the young woman said softly.

'And this is Lily,' Paul said, not to be outdone. 'She looks after us.'

So Lily had become a nanny: Peter couldn't believe his eyes and ears. After years of worrying and searching he'd found her, and she was just the same as he remembered – only if anything more beautiful. His face broke into a happy grin and he was at a loss for words.

And then there was an interruption. Robert Lovegrove came running across the grass in search of his children. He came to a halt in front of Peter and spoke proudly.

'I see you've met Lily. This is my intended bride, Mr Jackson – the woman who has promised to be my wife.'

CHAPTER TWENTY-SEVEN

The house party

'What do Dorothy and Paul think of their new nanny?' Grace asked.

'They love her,' Lily said. 'She's straight out of training school, and this is her first post so she's very enthusiastic.'

'What's her name?'

'Patsy March. She wears her uniform as proudly as a schoolgirl, and behaves just like a big sister to the children.'

The two young women were gossiping in Lily's new bedroom. Since her unofficial engagement to Robert Lovegrove, Mrs Sayer had thought it unsuitable for Lily to reside in the nursery. The room she was given was at the back of the house: a spacious apartment with its own bathroom. It would be the bridal chamber after the wedding; but in the meantime Robert was occupying his usual single room.

He was also in the process of selling the house he'd shared with his first wife. Noel and Nancy Sayer had persuaded him to make his permanent home with them. After all, there was plenty of room at the Manor, and his children were settled and happy.

'Don't you find this big bed a bit lonely at night?' Grace was bouncing up and down on the feather mattress. The bed was a huge four-poster, heavily draped and with carved pillars.

'I put the bolster down beside me,' Lily admitted. 'It fills up some of the space.'

'I thought you were going to say you try and pretend it's Robert.'

Lily didn't answer. She crossed to the walnut wardrobe and swung the door open. 'I've got a new dress,' she said by way of changing the subject.

'Another one?' Grace's eyebrows rose in amazement.

'This one's to wear at the house party. Robert insisted.'

'Let's see it then.'

Lily unhooked a garment, shaking out the folds before holding it against her slim figure. It was a pink dress with a flounced skirt and an off-the-shoulder neckline.

'What do you think?'

'I've never seen you in pink before,' Grace said doubtfully.

'I don't usually wear it. It's certainly not my favourite colour. But Robert suggested it.'

Lily's cheeks flushed slightly. The colour of the dress had nearly caused an argument – the first argument they'd had so far. In the end Lily had given in. After all, pink was as good a colour as any, and the dress had been very expensive.

'I suppose pink was Victoria's favourite colour?' Grace said softly.

'I think it was, as a matter of fact.'

'Oh, Lily! Can't you see what he's doing? He's trying to fool himself into believing that you're his first wife, just because you look a bit like her.'

'It's not doing anyone any harm.'

'Only you.' Grace looked worried. 'What sort of relationship will you have after you're married? It might work at first, but one day you're going to realize that you can't step into another woman's shoes. Then what will you do?'

'I don't know. Perhaps by then Robert will love me for myself.'

'Well, I think you're just storing up trouble.'

'That's my problem.'

Grace could see that her friend was determined, so she changed the subject. 'How many people are you expecting for the weekend?'

'About a dozen, I think. Mr Sayer has arranged it all with Robert. They did ask me if I wanted to invite anyone, or help write out the invitations, but there wasn't much point. They want the party – not me.'

Grace looked dumbfounded. 'Do you mean to say you haven't asked anybody?'

Lily smiled. 'Now who would I ask? There's no one. I have no family, and no friends who know where I am.' She thought back. 'Anyway, they wouldn't be the sort of people who would fit in here.'

Grace laughed. 'I do believe you're turning into a snob just because your fortune's changed for the better. I suppose you only tolerate me because you want me to wait on the guests.'

'Oh, Grace, I didn't mean that, and you know it. You're the best friend I've ever had; but I know you disapprove of my getting engaged to Robert. You think I'm making a mistake and I'm going to be miserable.' Grace nodded. 'Well, I know what I'm doing. I don't exactly love Robert, but I do feel sorry for him, and look what he's giving me in exchange.' Lily flung herself on the bed beside her friend and spread out her arms, indicating the beautiful room and all it contained.

'So you're going to sell your soul.'

'Don't be so dramatic. You're lucky: you and Jake married for love and you're going to live happily ever after. I was in love once . . .' her voice trailed off sadly.

'Do you want to tell me about it?'

'His name was Edward. He had fair hair and grey eyes and I'd have died for him.'

'What happened?'

'He went away: left me just like that.' Lily clicked her fingers and rolled onto her stomach. 'I thought he'd learn to love me given time, but time wasn't on our side. I don't know where he is now. I think I'm not the sort of woman that men fall in love with. So I'll have to settle for someone who's fallen in love with an illusion.'

'Well, you've got it all wrong,' Grace said firmly. 'I know one man who's in love with you – and he never knew Victoria.'

Lily looked up in surprise. 'Who's that then?'

'Look out of the window and you'll see who I mean.'

Lily crossed to the window and looked down into the garden. 'There's no one out there,' she said. 'Only the gardener.'

'That's who I meant.' Grace joined her friend, and they both watched the sturdy muscular figure of Peter Jackson as he pushed a barrow across the grass. 'He's a man in love, if ever I saw one.'

'Don't talk so silly,' Lily said, but her flushed cheeks gave her away. 'I hardly know him.'

'I've seen him looking at you before,' Grace said. 'You'd better watch out if I were you.'

After Grace left Lily returned to the window. There was no sign of Peter but she knew where she would find him. He'd been on his way to the shrubbery, and she'd heard Mr Sayer telling him earlier to trim the borders. She needed to talk to him, clear the air.

Her delight at seeing her old friend had been short-lived. She'd longed to run to him, see his gentle smile and hear his reassuring voice. But before she had been able to do any of those things Robert had come on the scene, introducing her as his future wife. She'd seen the smile fade from Peter's face as he'd turned away. Whenever she'd seen him since his face had been expressionless, and if he could, he avoided her. It was so silly. Just because she was engaged to Robert Lovegrove shouldn't change anything between them. He'd always been her comfort and security and she had to know what was wrong.

Throwing caution to the winds – after all, Robert might think it strange for his fiancée to be searching out a gardener's company – Lily ran down the stairs and out of the side door. She was wearing a simple cotton dress and her hair was untidy, so she was glad Robert couldn't see her. He insisted on her being neatly turned out at all times. As the weekend guests would be arriving soon she had to hurry if she wanted to avoid them.

Peter was working at the far end of the garden. A wisteria had come loose from its trellis and he was securing it with twine. His broad back was turned towards her. He looked so strong, so safe, that Lily had to stop herself from running forward and throwing her arms about him. She stopped a few feet away.

'Peter,' she said softly.

He looked over his shoulder and his face lit up briefly. Then he controlled himself and turned back to his work. 'Oh, it's you,' he said. 'What do you want?'

'To talk to you.'

'What about?' Peter cut the green twine with his pocket-knife and stepped back to admire his handiwork. 'What does the lady of the manor want to talk to the gardener about?'

There was such sarcasm in his voice that Lily wanted to cry. He'd never spoken to her like that before. 'Please, Peter . . .' She stretched out her hand to touch his sleeve, but he shook her off. 'We've always been friends: old friends. Don't treat me like this.'

'Why shouldn't I? If only you knew what I've been through because of you. Oh, what's the use!'

He started to walk away but Lily ran after him. Now he'd started talking she didn't want him to stop.

'I don't know what you're talking about. What do you mean, what you've been through?'

He stopped and turned to face her, and she saw the pain on his face. 'I've been worried sick about you, Lily. We all have. Mother's always asking if I've heard from you, but nobody had any news. You can't imagine what it's been like. You disappeared out of our lives and for all we knew you could have been dead. I even went looking for you a couple of years back. I traced you as far as Pierhaven, and then the trail went cold. Nobody knew anything about you so I had to turn around and go back home. It nearly broke my heart.'

'You went looking for me!' Lily stared into Peter's honest face in surprise. 'But why?'

'Because I love you.' The words came out as if they were being torn from him. 'I've always loved you, Lily, ever since you were a little girl living in Betty Thomas's shadow.'

'But why didn't you tell me?'

'How could I?' Peter shrugged his shoulders helplessly. 'It was Edward Butler you cared for. All through the years you never had time for anybody else. It was always Edward this, and Edward that. You never had any time for me.'

Lily knew that everything Peter was saying was the truth and she felt ashamed. Because Peter had always been there she'd used him unmercifully. Even if she'd known of his love it probably wouldn't have made any difference.

'I'm sorry,' was all she could say.

Peter carried on talking as though now he'd started he couldn't stop. 'The memory of you spoilt every other girl I met. Even when you ran away with Edward I waited. I knew it wouldn't last, and thought you'd come back to Lenton and I'd see you again. But Edward came back and married Betty.'

'Did he?' Lily found she wasn't surprised at this piece of news. Even so, her heart beat a rapid tattoo at the sound of Edward's name.

'They're very happy, everybody says so. And they've got two children. Edward's going to be a doctor after all. Why are you crying, Lily? You've got everything you wanted, haven't you? A fine home and a rich fiancé – all the things you dreamed about. So why are you crying?'

But Lily couldn't stop. The tears were streaming helplessly down her cheeks and she didn't bother to brush them away. All her life she'd been searching for something: the elusive bluebird of happiness. She'd thought Edward held the key; that he was the prince, and she was going to be his princess and they'd live happily ever after. Then she'd become Lilith Fortune and thought that fame and fortune would bring her contentment – but Harry Smith's promises had proved false and had only brought her unhappiness. And now Robert Lovegrove was offering her the sort of life she'd dreamed about. Not because he loved her – but because she reminded him of his dead wife.

'I've been a fool,' Lily admitted. 'I wanted love so badly – and you were there all the time.'

'And now it's too late.' Peter spoke harshly. Lily felt her heart would break. 'You've committed yourself to this Lovegrove fellow, and you can't go back on your word. But at least I found you. My work here is finished: Mr Sayer can get somebody else to do the landscaping. I can't work here day after day and see you, knowing that you belong to another man. Tomorrow I shall go home.'

He turned as if he was going to walk away. Lily said the first thing that came into her head to stop him.

'How are they? How are they all at home?'

Peter's natural politeness made him stop. 'They're well: Mike and his children. And Billy's as big as a man and can do a man's job. Mother's fine; apart from her legs.'

'Have you seen anyone from Valley Farm?'

Peter thought. If he told Lily the tale he'd heard from his mother, about Moses Crow threatening Edith, it would only upset her. Anyway, perhaps his mother had been mistaken and there was only a grain of truth in it.

'I haven't seen any of the Crows recently – but I think they're well.'

'And the Thomas's?'

'I still work at Ring House; but not for much longer. Mr Thomas has heart trouble and is talking about selling up.'

'Selling up!' Lily sounded shocked. The greatest shock was the news of James Thomas's ill health.

'Nothing's settled yet, but it's on the cards. Now I must be getting on: I want to leave everything in good order before I go.'

He left her then, and Lily didn't try to stop him. She had a lot to think about, and would have liked to creep away to her room to lick her wounds in private. But it wasn't to be.

When she reached the house the first guests were arriving. Robert and Mr Sayer were helping to unload suitcases from the smart cars standing in the drive, greeting the new arrivals, and leading them into the hall. There was much chattering and laughter, but it all rang false in Lily's ears. She tried to slip away and make her entrance by the side door, hoping not to be noticed. But Robert saw her and broke away from his friends to follow her around the side of the house.

'Where are you going?' he demanded, grabbing hold of her arm. 'Some of our guests have arrived. I want you to meet them.'

'Not now,' Lily said, trying to smile. 'Can't you introduce them to me at dinner? I'm not dressed properly at the moment, and I don't want you to be ashamed of me.'

'I did tell you what time they'd be arriving, darling. You could have made an effort. If anyone saw you creeping away like that they probably thought you were one of the servants.'

I only wish I was, Lily thought. But she said, 'I'm sorry, Robert. I'll just run upstairs and get ready. I'll be down in half an hour.'

'Promise?'

'I promise.' She kissed his cheek to keep him happy. 'Which dress do you want me to wear?'

'The pink one. I chose it for you specially.'

'I know you did. But I'm not sure if pink is my colour.'

'Of course it is. Vicky had your colouring, apart from her

eyes, and she looked wonderful in pink. Wear it to please me.'

'All right, Robert,' Lily said obediently.

She watched as he hurried back to his guests; but as she entered the house she heard Grace's words in her ear: *Robert's trying to fool himself that you're his first wife. Can't you see what he's doing?*

As if to pacify the gods Lily paid particular attention to her appearance. She brushed her hair until it was as sleek as the wing of a bird, falling smoothly to her bare shoulders and curling slightly at the ends. The pink skirt of her dress stood out as crisp as freshly made meringue, and the frill that held the tight bodice in place accentuated the slender column of her neck and the proud set of her head.

Leaving her bedroom Lily paused on the landing. Why was she feeling so nervous? The visitors were only Robert's friends, and acquaintances of Mr and Mrs Sayer – people she would have to meet sooner or later.

The hall below seemed to be deserted, and then a little maid, hired for the occasion, came out of the kitchen carrying a tray of glasses. She disappeared into the drawing-room. As the door swung open Lily heard laughter, and saw smartly suited men and the bright skirts of their female companions. She was as good as any of them: there was nothing to be frightened of.

When Lily entered the room she'd regained control over her emotions, and passed among the company as if she was completely at home.

She saw Mr Sayer standing in the window talking to a man in a black evening suit who had his back turned towards her. Noel smiled, and beckoned. Lily was just about to join him when Robert stepped forward and steered her away.

'I want you to meet my cousin,' he said. A large red-headed young woman smoking a cigarette grabbed her hand and shook it enthusiastically. 'Alice, this is Lily.'

'Pleased to meet you,' Alice said gushingly. 'Robert's told me all about you. I know you're going to make him as happy as Victoria did – oh!' She covered her mouth with her hand. 'What have I said?'

'It doesn't matter.' Lily tried to smile, but she was disturbed by the uncalled for remark. 'I shall try, of course.'

'And the darling children,' Alice went on. 'When are we going to see the darling children?'

'Not tonight,' Robert said firmly. 'But I've promised them that they can join us for a picnic tomorrow.'

'A picnic! How delightful. I haven't been on a picnic since I was at school.' Alice let out a whoop of delight.

Robert turned to speak to someone behind him; it gave Lily the opportunity to break away from Alice's clutches. She headed towards the window, and Mr Sayer's calming presence. He put out his hand to draw her forward, although he still kept talking to the dark-suited man.

Lily's heart turned a somersault. She saw a tall, upright figure: a young man with grey eyes fringed with fair lashes, and hair so pale that it was almost white. It was Edward Butler, four years older, but just as handsome.

He smiled and held out his hand, saying, 'Hullo, Lily, this is a surprise.'

Lily's world fell apart. She could hear Mr Sayer saying that the Butlers were old family friends. His voice came from a distance; the room swung around and she thought she was falling. After all this time it was too much to take in. Edward here! It was surely a dream, or at the most a coincidence. The spinning stopped and the room fell into focus again. She was still holding Edward's hand and no one seemed to be aware of her inner turmoil.

'Darling, come and meet Robert's fiancée.'

He pulled his hand gently away from hers and turned to someone standing at his elbow. Before she looked into the baby-blue eyes Lily knew who it was. Betty, and her old rival for Edward's affections.

She hadn't changed all that much. As plump and pretty as a pigeon, dressed, or rather poured into a black silk cocktail dress with a diamanté trim, much too old and matronly for a young woman of twenty-five. Her fair hair was carefully arranged into a pile of intricate curls, and there was a painted smile on her scarlet lips. In her ears she wore real pearl clips, and a similar row of pearls around her white throat. She held out a plump hand to Lily, and flashed the heavy rings on her fingers.

'If it isn't Lily,' she said in a loud, carrying voice. 'This is a surprise.'

'Do you two know each other?' Noel Sayer asked.

'We're old friends, aren't we, Lily?' Betty pinched Lily's

hand playfully. 'In fact you could almost call us sisters.'

Noel seemed pleased at this unexpected piece of information. It was good news to find that Robert's intended did seem to have a background after all.

'Lily has never mentioned you,' he said.

'Oh, we lost touch years ago, didn't we, Lily? When I married Edward.' Lily expected the remark to be barbed, but when she looked into the blue eyes they looked free from malice. 'I've so much to tell you,' she carried on. 'We've got two children, can you imagine it? A girl called Jennifer, she's two years old, and a baby boy. His name's Johnnie and he looks just like his father, doesn't he, darling?' She turned to Edward and slipped her arm through his, gazing up adoringly into his face.

'That's what your parents say,' Edward said gruffly.

'How are they?' Lily asked. 'Your parents.'

'Mummy's very well, but Daddy isn't. He has a bad heart and has to take care of himself. Mummy's worried about him.'

'I'm so sorry.'

The kindly figure of James Thomas flashed before Lily's eyes. The broad chest with the gold watch chain stretched across, and the kindly arms that had carried her away from Valley Farm when she was a little girl. He'd been more than a father to her over the years, protecting her from his watchful wife and jealous daughter. He'd always been there, like Peter – the two people she loved most.

But what about Edward? She'd always believed that he'd been destined to be her only love. She'd overlooked Peter. She'd left Lenton and run away with Edward, and tried to move the world because she'd been so sure of her love for him. But now she looked at the young man before her and didn't feel anything – neither love nor hate.

Betty and Edward looked so complete with their fair heads bent towards each other. Lily was glad there was no spite in Betty's eyes. She was gazing up at her husband with pride, as if she was truly contented with her marriage, and Edward's eyes were full of tenderness for the wife on his arm. They were like two pieces of a puzzle only complete when they were together. They didn't need outsiders.

Lily's eyes brimmed with sudden tears. Not for the couple before her, but for herself. She'd wasted years pursuing a dream. Now she had to face the world of bleak reality.

'Would you excuse me?' she said quickly, and turned away.

'Where are you going?' Betty asked. 'I want to hear all your news.'

'I'm sorry.' Lily's voice was muffled by emotion. 'I don't feel very well.'

She pushed through the crowd towards the door. All around her people were laughing, and Lily wondered if they were laughing at her. She wouldn't blame them if they were. She saw Robert's face through the crowd. He put out his hand and beckoned, mouthing her name; but it wasn't the name Lily on his lips, she was sure – it was Vicky.

Half-blinded by tears, Lily found herself in the hall. There was no one about and she stood helplessly with her face turned towards the panelled wall, holding her throbbing head in her hands.

'Here, drink this, it'll make you feel better.' A glass was thrust into her hand and she sipped the sweet sherry obediently.

'Thank you.' Lily looked up, expecting to see Robert or Mr Sayer. But it was Edward standing there: awkward and apologetic.

'Are you all right?'

'I think so.' Lily smiled a watery smile. Even now Edward still had the power to stir her to the depths of her being. Perhaps it wasn't too late. 'I want to talk to you,' she said.

'There's nothing to say – only that I'm sorry.'

'Surely you can spare me a few minutes.'

'Not here.' Edward was weakening. 'Betty might see us.'

'Later then. Meet me out on the terrace after dinner – please.'

'I'll try to get away.'

Lily grabbed Edward's arm and looked up into his face. 'Promise.'

Edward didn't answer, but Lily was reassured because he hadn't actually refused to meet her. He turned swiftly on his heel and joined the crowd just surging out of the drawing-room in search of dinner. Lily saw the way he put a tender arm around Betty's waist and guided her across the hall. But just at that moment Robert appeared at her side to claim his fiancée.

'Are you all right, Lily?'

'Yes. A bit tired, that's all. It's been a long day.'

Dinner was a nightmare. Lily had no appetite and picked at the four courses as they were placed in front of her. Robert seemed oblivious to her unhappiness. He ate heartily and kept up cheerful conversation with his guests.

He refilled Lily's glass and she drank thirstily. The wine was rich and dark and helped her through the meal, although it made her head ache. And then Mr Sayer was on his feet calling for silence.

'You all know why you're here,' he said heartily. 'To celebrate the engagement of Robert to Lily. Will you all please raise your glasses.'

The wine had been served at room temperature but the champagne was cold as ice. The shock of it made the room spin and Lily wondered if she was drunk. But when Robert pulled her to her feet to accept the congratulations of the company the ground felt firm beneath her feet and her head was clear.

Someone put a record on the gramophone and everyone moved back into the drawing-room. A space was cleared in the centre of the floor for the younger couples to dance to the music of an old-fashioned waltz.

Lily looked around. Betty was standing in a corner deep in conversation with Nancy Sayer, but there was no sign of Edward. Had he already made his excuses and slipped away? Was he already waiting for her outside on the terrace?

'Shall we lead the dancing?' It was Robert at her elbow.

'I have a headache. I think I'll go up to bed.'

'Good idea. The excitement's probably been too much for you. Alice will dance with me: she hasn't got a partner.'

Lily waited until the floor was full of revolving couples and then she slipped away. It was cold outside and she wished she had something to cover her bare shoulders. She stood shivering in her thin dress under a trellis of trailing honeysuckle, the honey-coloured trumpets giving off their sweet scent into the evening air. Edward wasn't coming and she was glad. It was better this way. She would creep upstairs to bed, and if she cried herself to sleep there would be no one to hear.

A figure detached itself from the wall and stepped forward. It swayed slightly, but that could have been Lily's imagination.

'I knew you'd come,' Lily said.

'What do you want?' Edward's grey eyes searched hers. A lock of pale hair fell over his forehead as it had in the old days. She had to stop herself from putting out her hand and smoothing it back. If she played her cards right perhaps Edward could still be the prince of her dreams, who would sweep her off her feet and carry her away to a place where she could be happy. Perhaps it wasn't too late. She forgot about Betty, she forgot about everything except her desperate need to love and be loved. She took his hand in hers and drew him towards her, turning up her face.

'Kiss me, Edward.'

'I can't.' He pulled his hand away and stepped back.

'Why? What's the matter?'

'Nothing's the matter. I just can't.'

'Don't you love me just a little bit?'

'Lily, listen to me.' Edward's face was flushed and he was trembling. 'Whatever happened between us ended a long time ago. I thought I loved you then; but we were so young and didn't know what love was.'

'I did,' Lily said softly.

'You thought you did – but it was all an illusion. I behaved badly, I know, leaving you all alone. But you were the strong one: I knew you'd cope. And then when I met Betty again I realized how much I loved her and what I'd nearly lost by running away with you. I'm not going to let it happen again.'

'Why did you come, then?' Lily asked bitterly.

'To explain. It's all over, Lily. I'm sorry – and you've got Robert now.' He turned on his heel and left her.

'I've got Robert now,' Lily said softly and her voice broke. She'd promised herself to a man who didn't love her, and Edward was gone for good. She couldn't go back to the house to face them. She had to get away, somewhere where she could hide her bruised spirit. She headed for the garden where no one would find her. She would hide in the summer-house, and when the party ended and her way was clear she would creep back into the house by the side door.

As she ran across the grass she was blinded by tears and didn't see the figure step out of the nearby bushes. It was Peter. He had changed out of his working clothes and was wearing a collar and tie, and in his hand he carried his suitcase. He saw her first, put down the case, and opened his arms as if to ward

Lily off. She couldn't stop in time and ran straight into him.

'Where are you going?' He looked down into Lily's tear-stained face.

'I don't know. Anywhere, as long as it's a long way from here. Where are *you* going?'

'Home. I can't wait until tomorrow: I wouldn't know how to explain. I'm leaving now.'

'Take me with you?'

They stood there: the gentle giant and the girl in the pink party dress, and they didn't need words.

'Come on then,' Peter said.

He picked up his case, and with his other hand under Lily's elbow led her away from Piltdown Manor towards the gate and the road home.

CHAPTER TWENTY-EIGHT

The homecoming

They had all the time in the world. The whole night was before them. The moon came out to light their way, but the direction they took didn't seem important. Any road would eventually lead them home.

'You're cold.'

Peter stopped to take off his jacket and place it around Lily's shoulders. His touch was tender and his voice caring. They came to a cross-roads where there was a sign indicating Uckfield to the right, and Mayfield to the left.

'Which way?' Peter asked. He guessed that Lily would know the area better than him.

'Uckfield's a town,' Lily said. 'Lets go left.'

So they turned left and passed through a country village. Houses hugged the edge of the road: cottages with thatched roofs and flower-filled gardens. A dog barked somewhere close by, and a cat stalked along a nearby fence looking for night prey. Nothing passed them on the road, and the lights went out one by one as the villagers retired to bed. But Lily was happy. The road was before her and the sky overhead, and Peter's arm was about her, keeping her safe.

Peter was happy too. This was what he'd been waiting for all his life. He looked down at Lily's dark head, and she turned up her face and smiled at him. Outlined in silver by the moon she looked like a fairy thing; he hoped she wouldn't vanish away when the dawn came. They didn't need words: his touch spoke for itself, and so did Lily's smile.

Peter would have been happy to walk all night, but after a few miles he suspected that Lily was tiring although she didn't complain. She stumbled on a piece of rough road, and if he hadn't put out a steadying hand she would have fallen.

'You're tired,' he said. 'We must find somewhere to rest.'

'It's these silly shoes,' Lily said ruefully, looking down at the dainty silver sandals she was wearing with the pink dress. 'They were comfortable in the shop but they're not much good for hiking. Shall I take them off?'

'You'll cut your feet. We'll find somewhere away from the road, and wait there until it's light. It'll be easier when you can see where you're walking. Perhaps we should have taken the other turning. There might have been a late train from Uckfield.'

'No,' Lily said firmly. 'It's better this way. Just you and me and the countryside at night.'

The way she said it moved Peter to the very centre of his being. He wanted to kiss her there and then: her hair, eyes, lips, and the dark triangle of shadow between her breasts. But he held back. He wasn't going to break the spell of this wonderful night by rushing things. He could wait a little longer.

A dark shadow loomed to their left, and they could hear the gentle lowing of cattle somewhere close by.

'There's a barn,' Peter said. 'It will be warm and give us a chance to rest.'

Lily nodded gratefully. As they stepped off the road she stumbled again, so Peter put down his case and picked her up in his arms. She was no weight at all, and when she wound her arms about his neck and her head drooped onto his shoulder he could feel her trembling.

Inside the barn Peter's eyes soon grew accustomed to the darkness. There was a heap of loose straw in one corner. He lowered Lily down onto it before going back outside to collect his suitcase. When he returned she was sitting up in the straw with her hair ruffled and his jacket still around her. She looked up and smiled.

'I love the smell of straw,' she said. 'It reminds me of Valley Farm. My earliest memories are of the barn there where I spent my early childhood. Do you want your jacket?'

'You keep it. I don't want you to catch cold.' He moved away as if he was going to leave her.

'Don't go!' Lily said quickly. 'Come and sit by me.'

Peter sat down in the straw by her side, and it seemed the most natural thing in the world to put his arm around her. She snuggled closer as if for reassurance.

'Comfortable?' he asked.

'Yes. I've been such a fool, Peter.'

'In what way?'

'Firstly with Edward. Did you know that he's one of Robert's oldest friends? It appears that they were at school together, so it was only natural that he would be invited to the party.'

'You mean he's at Piltdown Manor now?'

'Yes. And Betty Thomas – though of course she's Betty Butler now. It was a shock seeing them again after all these years. I really thought I loved Edward.'

'I know,' Peter said gently. 'That's why I almost gave up hoping that you'd ever come to love me.'

'He's changed, Peter.' Lily sounded tearful, and Peter waited patiently for her to recover and go on. 'He wasn't the Edward I remembered. Or perhaps he was and I'd been blinded by love.'

'So you decided to run away again?'

'Yes. But this time I was running away from Edward – not with him. He's happy with Betty, you know; I could see that. And she adores him.'

'What about Robert Lovegrove?' Peter prompted softly, wanting to know the worst.

'He thinks he loves me, but he doesn't really. I just remind him of his dead wife, and that's no foundation for a happy marriage. I'll write to him and explain. He'll be hurt, I know, but later on he'll understand.'

'Have you any more confessions to make before I kiss you?' Peter whispered into Lily's hair. 'Have you broken any other hearts?'

'Well, there was Harry.' Feeling Peter freeze Lily laughed. She told him about her life as Lilith Fortune, and the way Harry Smith had deserted her when she'd lost her voice. 'So you see, he didn't love me either,' she finished sadly.

'What happened to your voice? Has it come back?'

'I don't know. I'm frightened to test it. But it doesn't really matter because I never want to sing in public again.'

'What do you want, Lily?'

The words were soft, but Peter's happiness depended on her answer. Lily thought carefully before replying.

'I want to love someone,' she said in a low voice. 'And I want them to love me in return. I want a little house to look after, with a kitchen and a fireplace that's all my own. I want a garden in front full of flowers, and another at the back with vegetables. And I want a cradle with a baby in it.'

'I love you, Lily, and I always will.'

His arms tightened around her, drawing her into an embrace. He kissed her gently and it seemed so natural that she returned the kiss greedily. His arms felt so safe and strong, and she liked the smell of him. He reminded her of the freedom and wholesomeness of the fields, the fresh air, and the world she'd once belonged to. Suddenly all the romantic longings of her girlhood seemed childish. Reality was here and now, and Lily knew that she could easily love Peter Jackson more deeply than she'd ever loved Edward.

'Show me you love me,' she said softly. 'Now.'

Peter's inexperience was made up for by tenderness and passion. Lily thrilled to the touch of his rough hands as they fumbled with the buttons on her dress. In the end she had to help him. When their bodies came flesh to flesh on the mattress of straw neither felt the cold or the discomfort, just the wonder of finding each other.

Peter's lovemaking carried Lily to heights she'd never imagined. Finally she drooped in his arms with exhaustion, and he covered her gently with his coat and let her sleep.

She looked like a child in his arms: her hair a tangle of darkness against his chest, and her eyelids with their sooty lashes hiding her violet eyes. He bent over and kissed her: first her eyes and then her lips, and she stirred contentedly. He was frightened to sleep himself, in case he woke up to find it had all been a dream. But in the early hours of the morning he dozed. It was the dawn chorus of birds that woke them to a new day.

Rubbing their eyes and stretching, they struggled out into the sunlight to the surprise of the farmer who was leading his herd in for milking. He didn't seem to mind their using his barn for a temporary shelter without permission.

'That barn's seen many things,' he said cheerfully, picking his teeth with a piece of twig. 'Birthings and death, dancing and tears. You're not the first travellers it's welcomed. Go on up to the house now and the wife'll give you breakfast.'

What a breakfast they sat down to, and not a penny would the farmer's wife take in return. Toast like doorsteps, dripping with golden butter. Eggs and bacon, home-cured and fried to a crisp, and fat sausages bursting out of their skins.

They felt newly born when they set out on the road once more. Their cheeks were glowing from the icy water drawn up from a well and the roughness of the towel they'd been given to dry themselves. The first thing they discovered was that they'd been travelling in the wrong direction. But they were soon back on track, and when a country bus came into view Peter flagged it down.

'You've walked far enough,' he said when Lily tried to protest. 'You deserve to travel the rest of the way in comfort.'

So they found themselves in Lenton High Street on a summer's afternoon, and Lily looked around expecting to find changes. It was five years since her flight with Edward and she didn't know what sort of welcome she could expect to receive. Luckily there were not many people about, and those who were were too occupied with their own affairs to take much notice of Peter Jackson, the gardener and handyman from Ring House, and his female companion. Lily spotted a few familiar faces and smiled, but although her smiles were returned they were guarded, as if people weren't sure who she was.

'Have I changed much?' she asked at last, when a young woman passed who'd sat next to her in the village school. 'No one knows me.'

'Country people have short memories,' Peter said. 'You look like a smart town lady in that dress – not a bit like Lily from the Valley.'

Lily's spirits rose, and she laughed. 'Come on,' she said. 'I'll race you home.'

Peter liked the way she said home: as if she classed the Jackson cottage as her real home. Although his legs were longer than hers, she beat him; but after all, he was still carrying his suitcase while Lily was free as a bird. They fell panting into each other's arms at the gate, much to the surprise of young Billy who was pumping up his bicycle tyre. He looked up, but didn't smile a welcome as Peter expected him to.

'We're home. Where's Mother?'

'Inside,' Billy answered, unscrewing the pump and fixing it back in place. 'Hullo, Lily.'

'Hullo, Billy.' At least someone had recognized her, Lily thought with relief, so she couldn't have changed that much. Billy had altered more than her: he'd grown from a grubby schoolboy into a quite presentable young man. 'Haven't you grown?'

Billy blushed, and preceded them into the kitchen, which was the busiest room in the house where everybody congregated. Lily looked around with satisfaction at the blue and white china and the shining pans. There was a tabby cat curled up on the seat of a chair and a pot of scarlet geraniums on the window-sill, making everything look cosy and homelike. This was the sort of kitchen she yearned for.

Before they had time to get their breath back Peter's mother appeared in the doorway. She was carrying a hand-crocheted shawl over her arm and a glass in her hand. Her mouth was set in a grim line and there was a worried frown between her brows, but her face lit up at the sight of Lily.

'He's found you at last,' she said by way of welcome. 'I knew he would. Sit down and make yourself at home.'

Peter pulled a chair up to the table for Lily and seated himself next to her. 'We've so much to tell you,' he said. 'I don't know where to start.'

'I can guess most of it, son. But it'll have to wait. Things have been happening around here – and they're not good things.'

Peter stretched out his hand and took Lily's. Whatever they were going to hear they had to support each other. 'You'd better tell us, Mother, or we'll be imagining the worst.'

'Steel yourselves then,' Emma said. 'Firstly, Mr Thomas was taken bad last night. He'd gone out walking when he shouldn't have. Came back ashen-faced, so I hear, and collapsed.'

'He's not dead?' Lily was half out of her seat with alarm. Dear Mr Thomas, the saviour and protector of her childhood, ill – perhaps dying. She couldn't bear it. Peter pulled her back gently into her chair.

'No,' Emma assured them. 'But he had a bad attack, and Doctor Butler seemed to think that it was a near thing. Elizabeth Thomas wanted to send for Betty and Edward; it seems they're away on a visit. But he wouldn't let her. They're expected home in a few days anyway.'

'I must go to him,' Lily said firmly. 'As long as Mrs Thomas doesn't mind.'

'I'm sure she won't.' Emma paused before telling them her other piece of news. 'We've got a visitor.'

'A visitor?' Peter looked at his mother in surprise. 'Who's that then?'

'Matthew Crow.'

'Matt?' Lily was immediately alarmed. What on earth was her old friend doing here?

'Yes, Lily. He's upstairs in Peter's bed. Billy found him out on the road an hour ago. The poor old man was on the point of exhaustion, so he says.'

Billy took up the tale himself. 'I nearly ran him down. I was only riding slowly but he was staggering about all over the road. I thought at first he was drunk, so I called Mum and we brought him indoors.'

'He was babbling and crying, something about his brother. None of it made sense to me. Billy and I got him upstairs between us and put him to bed.' Emma looked at Lily. 'Do you think I should call the doctor?'

'Let me talk to him first.' Lily got up from her chair. 'He'll tell me what happened – he always used to tell me everything.'

Emma stayed downstairs, but Lily was glad when Peter offered to accompany her. She paused on the landing outside the bedroom door to steel herself. After all, she hadn't seen Matt for five years. Peter put his hand under her elbow and guided her into the room.

She looked at the man on the bed and her heart was filled with pity. Matthew looked so old, and although he'd never been a big man he now looked shrunken. His uncut hair fell to his rounded shoulders, and his gnarled hands trembled as they picked nervously at the bedcover. But his eyes were as blue as ever and they filled with tears at the sight of his visitor.

'Lily,' he mumbled. 'Is it really you?'

'Yes, Matt.' Lily ran across the room to the bed and took Matthew's hands in hers. 'I've come back. What's happened to you then?'

Matthew began to cry. Words tumbled out of his mouth so rapidly that it was difficult understanding what he was trying to say. The only word Lily could make out was 'Mo'.

'What about Moses?' she asked. 'Has he been hurting you again?'

'Gun,' Matthew babbled. 'Mo took my gun.'

'Did he threaten to shoot you; was that it, Matthew? So you were scared and ran away?'

'I ran away because he said he was going to shoot her.' Matthew put his hands over his face and rocked backwards and forwards.

'Who? Who was he going to shoot?'

'Edie, of course. So I ran away to get help. Do you think he's killed her?'

Lily and Peter stared at each other; and then they came to life simultaneously.

'You stay here, Lily,' Peter said. 'I'll go and find out what's happened. Try not to worry. I'll be back as soon as I can.'

After he'd gone Lily turned back to the man on the bed. 'Did they have an argument? Did something upset Moses?' she asked.

'*He* came last night. I told him to go away, but he wouldn't. I thought Mo was going to hit him.'

'Who are you talking about, Matthew? Who came to Valley Farm?'

'Mr Thomas. He came. Terribly sick, he looked – but he wanted to see Edie. Mo found them together – just like the last time.'

'The last time!' Lily stared at Matthew, her eyes wide. What was he trying to tell her? His feeble mind must be rambling, or he was imagining things. But he was talking clearly and didn't sound at all confused.

'Years ago Mo found Edie with James Thomas and he never forgave her. She was his wife, you see, and it says in the Bible that a wife must cleave to her husband. And Thomas had a wife as well. But they were young then and Edie'd had a hard time with Mo after all those baby boys died. He blamed her, but it wasn't Edie's fault. Mo's god was a god of anger and he took them away as a sort of punishment – it was his god Mo should have blamed.'

'Poor Edith,' Lily said.

'But she was a good-looking woman in those days. There was many a man she could have had after Mo refused to have anything to do with her. James Thomas was only one of them.'

Suddenly things clicked into place in Lily's brain. When she'd only been a little bit of a thing she'd found a photograph of a young woman in a box in the attic at Ring House. The face had looked familiar and she hadn't been able to place it; but it had been mixed with bills and papers belonging to Mr Thomas. She'd replaced it and forgotten all about it, until she'd discovered its duplicate in a drawer in Edith Crow's bedroom. It was a picture of the young Edith. She'd been an attractive young woman, looking out at the world with hope, and she'd ended up a drudge, at Moses' beck and call, lamenting her dead sons and her cruel husband. Who could blame her for snatching at happiness wherever it was offered? Lily didn't blame her: after all, she was a woman herself now, and had had her own share of unhappiness.

Matthew was tiring, but he seemed to have something else on his mind, so Lily prompted him. 'But why did Mr Thomas go to the farm last night, Matthew?'

'He's a sick man and afraid of dying before he's done the right thing. He's offered to sell us Valley Farm many times, but Mo always refuses. To his way of thinking, he's had it all these years and it belongs to him already. Mr Thomas thought Edie might persuade him to buy, and then he'd know she'd have a home for the rest of her life. If he dies as it stands, his wife would have to sell anyway, and we'd have to go.'

Matthew was talking so clearly and reasonably that Lily wondered why they'd all thought he was simple and dismissed his opinions. Perhaps it had been the overbearing influence of his elder brother that had robbed him of his natural confidence, and made him appear feeble-minded.

'And Moses thought Mr Thomas was with Edith for other reasons?'

'I suppose so.' Matthew rubbed his eyes as if the light hurt him, and Lily crossed to the window and pulled the curtains across. 'He refused to buy the farm again, and laughed in Mr Thomas's face. And him so sick-looking – it was cruel. But Mr

Thomas surprised him: he stood his ground and ignored the threats. Said Mo was a bully and he wasn't scared of him. Said he had to know Edie would be cared for and he was going home to change his will. If Mo wouldn't buy the farm he'd leave it to Edie.'

'That's the sort of kind thing Mr Thomas would do,' Lily said, sitting on the edge of the bed and taking Matthew's hand in hers. 'What happened then?'

'Mo went mad. He looked as if he was going to kill Mr Thomas so Edie and I tried to hold him off. Edie begged Mr Thomas to go home while he had the chance, so in the end he did.'

'And when he got home he had another attack,' Lily said sadly.

'I'm not surprised. He looked as if he wasn't long for this world.'

'Don't say that!' Lily held back the tears, but only just. She didn't know whether she wanted to cry for her old friend, or the man before her on the bed. She sat, deep in thought, and when she looked at Matthew she saw that his eyes were half-closed as if he was dozing. They sat like that, hand in hand, until the door opened and Peter burst into the room. He looked so wild and troubled that she dropped Matthew's hand and ran across the floor to meet him, enfolding him in her arms. 'What's happened?' she asked.

'Is Matthew awake?' A grunt from the bed reassured them that the old man had only been resting. 'I think he should hear what I found at Valley Farm.'

Two pairs of eyes stared at him: Matthew's faded blue, and Lily's violet. Matthew pulled himself up in the bed and Lily kept a firm hold of Peter's hand. They waited to hear the news.

'The first person I met was a policeman guarding the farm entrance. I said I was a friend of the family, but he wouldn't let me through or tell me anything.' Peter paused, and they waited. After a few seconds he carried on with his story. 'A police car arrived and distracted him, so I dodged inside the gate and hid behind a hedge. Then when I saw my opportunity I pushed my way through the bushes until I came out opposite the farmhouse. I'll never forget the sight that met my eyes . . .' He broke off and put his hand over his eyes, as if even the memory of what he had seen was painful.

'Take your time,' Lily said.

'I thought there was a sack, or rag doll, stretched across the cobbles. On its back, it was, with the top of its head blown away. The blood was already congealing and turning black. Someone had heard the shot from the road – you know how sounds travel on a quiet day – and reported it to the police.'

'So he did it,' Matthew said in a low voice. 'He called her a whore and a fallen woman, and said he'd kill her one day. Poor Edie.'

'Not Edith,' Peter said. 'The dead body was Moses.'

'Suicide?' Lily asked, trying to keep her voice even.

'No. It's almost impossible to shoot yourself with a shotgun,' Peter said. 'The barrel's too long. I believe Edith's story – and I think the police do too.'

'What did she say?'

'She was huddled in the porch in a terrible state. Just like a bag of bones covered with rags. A policewoman was asking her questions but she wouldn't say anything. Then she saw me and recognized me, and it seemed to loosen her tongue so they let me stay. It appears that seeing her with Mr Thomas last night had reopened all Moses' grudges. He said he was going to kill her. But he'd been drinking all night and he tripped. He set off the trigger when he stumbled.'

'So it was an accident?'

'Yes. Edith said he accused her of sleeping with any number of men – even you, Matthew.'

Matthew's pale face coloured and his hands twitched convulsively. 'It did happen once,' he said in a small, pained voice. 'But he got me drunk and forced me. Edie was past caring by then, and she never held it against me, even when I helped deliver her baby.'

'Which one was that?' Lily asked. 'There are four babies buried up in the churchyard.'

'Not those babies. The one that lived.'

Lily stared at Matthew. This was news to her: she'd never heard of Edith Crow giving birth to any babies that lived for any length of time. That was at the root of the poor woman's problems, and why she spent so much time in the graveyard.

'Which baby was that, Matthew?' she prompted.

'The one she had in the barn – the little girl.' Suddenly

realizing what he'd said, Matthew began to tremble.

'A little girl! Edith said she'd only ever had boys.'

'I made a mistake.' Matthew plucked at the bedcover again and wouldn't look at them.

'No, you didn't.' Lily sat on the edge of the bed and took Matthew's hand again. 'You knew what you were saying. Which little girl?'

Matthew began to weep. 'I promised not to say anything. I promised Edie. If Mo finds out he'll kill me.'

'No, he won't.' Peter walked forward to stand by Lily. 'I told you, Moses is dead. He can't hurt you or anyone else. He shot himself by accident.'

'So you can tell us everything,' Lily said gently. 'You said you helped Edith deliver her baby – and it was a little girl.'

'Thats right.' Matthew leaned back against the pillows. He was calmer now, and when he spoke again his voice seemed to come from a long way away. 'I'd guessed Edie was having another baby, although nothing was said about it. I went out looking for her that day and found her in the barn. I've seen animals in labour many times and helped them when their time came, so it was nothing new to me. She'd made herself a bed with some old sacks, and was laying there moaning something terrible. She begged me to help her, but I was scared in case Mo came.'

'He's telling the truth,' Peter said, seeing the expression on Lily's face. 'I've heard all this before, but last time I didn't believe it.'

But the story he was hearing shook him to the core. That any woman should have to hide herself away in a barn to give birth was beyond his comprehension. Although he'd only been a lad at the time, he remembered when his mother had given birth to Billy. His father had paced the kitchen floor while the midwife was upstairs doing her job. When he'd finally been told that it was all over, and mother and baby were fine, his pride and joy had been a thing to see.

'Could have been Mo's baby,' Matthew said, remembering their drunken orgy. 'Could have been mine too, I suppose. I liked to think it was mine.'

'So what happened? The baby was born; you helped to deliver it; and it was a girl.'

'I didn't know it was a girl. It all happened so suddenly. Edie left it in the straw and told me to come away, but I couldn't. She said it would die, but I could hear it mewing and I couldn't leave it. So I wrapped it in my shirt and carried it indoors and said I was going to keep it. I thought if it was a boy Mo might agree: he'd always wanted a son to take over when he was gone.'

'What did he say when he saw it was a girl?'

'He laughed and said I could keep it if I wanted, as long as he wasn't bothered. So I looked after it, kept it clean and fed it on milk warm from the cow. It was such a pretty little baby, with eyes the colour of violets. I called her Lily from the Valley.'

Lily was blinded by tears, but somehow they didn't matter. She wasn't ashamed of crying. This man, old before his time, could be her father. She'd be proud to admit it. After all, he'd behaved like a father towards her when everyone else would have let her die. All the tales she'd been told of a gipsy abandoning her were false. And yet she couldn't blame Edith. Her husband's behaviour, and the loss of four other babies, was enough to turn any woman's brain and kill all her maternal instincts.

'So Edith is really my mother?' Lily said softly.

'Yes, lass.' Matthew put out a trembling hand and pushed back a lock of hair that had fallen over her forehead. His touch was so tender that Lily took the lined hand and pressed it to her lips. 'Don't feel badly towards her: she couldn't help what happened.'

'I don't. And I'd be proud to have you for my father, Matt.'

'I'm proud of you too, Lily. I never thought you'd grow up into such a beauty.' But then Matthew pulled his hand away. 'Don't forget, Mo could have fathered you just as easily.'

'I suppose I shall never know,' Lily said. 'I mustn't let it matter.' But Peter could see by the expression on her face that it did.

'There's one person who could tell you,' he said, pulling Lily to her feet. 'And she's downstairs now with Mother. I brought her back with me because she needs looking after. They say a woman always knows; so go down and ask her. I think Edith will tell you the truth.'

Lily knew that it had to be now or never. She straightened her shoulders and walked towards the door.

'Do you want me to come with you?' Peter asked.

'No, you stay with Matthew.'

In the kitchen Emma Jackson had just made the inevitable pot of tea. Edith Crow, looking not much better than a scarecrow, was sitting at the table with a steaming cup in front of her. She looked up, but her haggard face didn't change its expression. Lily went to her and took her hand.

'Hullo, Mother,' she said simply.

'So, you know?'

'Matt told me.'

'After all these years.' Edith sighed. 'Now Moses is dead I suppose it's all for the best.'

'I'm sure it is. Who is my father, Edith?'

'Do you really want to know?'

'Yes. Is it Moses – or Matthew? You must suspect, even if you're not sure.'

'I am sure – it was neither of them. I suppose Matt told you how they used me. It didn't matter, though, because I was expecting already. I didn't dare tell Mo.'

'Who was it then?' Suddenly a great hope filled Lily.

'Jim Thomas, of course. I never told him, not even when he took you away. After all, I couldn't look after you. Matt tried, but it was no life for a little girl at Valley Farm. So I was glad. At Ring House at least you'd have a chance. And it pleased me to think you were being brought up with Jim's other daughter, Betty. I knew, you see – but nobody else did.'

There was nothing more for them to do but put their arms around each other. Their tears mingled as Lily held her mother in her arms. Edith Crow held her daughter tightly and wept as if a great weight had been lifted from her thin shoulders.

Emma Jackson crept silently away.

CHAPTER TWENTY-NINE

Peter

'Is your father coming to the wedding, Lily?' Emma asked.

Lily looked up from her sewing and smiled. She'd never dreamed that someone would be saying these words to her. She didn't know which pleased her most: father or wedding.

'No,' she said. 'I did ask him but he didn't think it a good idea. You see, his wife still doesn't know. Anyhow, he's not really well enough.'

'You mean to tell me that Elizabeth Thomas still doesn't know her husband fathered you?'

'No. She'd be terribly hurt, and she's got enough to cope with at the moment nursing him.'

'Even so, it doesn't seem right to me.' Emma set the wheel of her sewing-machine turning with her foot and guided the white silk under the needle. 'Surely now that you know the truth you want to put things right? I would.'

'Just knowing has put everything right as far as I'm concerned,' Lily answered. 'No good would come out of advertising the facts. I'm not ashamed of being illegitimate, and it doesn't bother Peter, so the fewer people who know the better as far as I'm concerned.'

Reaching the end of a seam, Emma Jackson cut the cotton and started on the next. The wheel hummed like a hive of bees, and the crisp silk rustled like water rolling across a sandy beach.

'You never did tell me what happened when you went up to Ring House and saw Mr Thomas.'

Lily stopped sewing and her eyes turned to the window. She could just see the beginning of the drive as it wound its way up the hill. She remembered how excited she'd been that day last year when she'd walked up to Ring House with the knowledge of her parenthood on the tip of her tongue. Elizabeth Thomas had met her silently, but not unkindly: after all, Betty was now safely married to Edward Butler so Lily had ceased to be a threat.

'My husband is resting,' she'd said. 'But I know he'll be pleased to see you. He's always had a soft spot for you – I can't think why.'

So Lily found herself standing by the armchair in the library where James was resting. She looked down at him and her eyes filled with tears. He'd always appeared such a big man, so strong, almost indestructible. But now he looked old and grey, his skin loose and lined. He opened his eyes and saw her, and his face was transformed by a smile so warm that the years fell away and he became, once more, the kind protector of her youth.

'Why, Lily,' he said, as if he couldn't believe his eyes. 'Is it really you?'

'Yes,' she said simply. 'I've come back.'

'I'm glad. If you'd left it much longer you might have been too late.'

'Don't say that.' Lily sat down on the footstool at James's feet and leaned against his knee. He reached down and stroked the top of her head with a hand that shook slightly with emotion. Without more ado she told him. Her soft voice unfolded the story Edith had told her, and her father sat silently listening, only the gentle motion of his fingers showing that he was still awake. 'So you really are my father,' she ended quietly – and waited.

'I should have guessed,' James said at last. 'My mother had eyes exactly the same colour as yours.'

'Did she?' Lily thought back to a grandmother she'd never known.

'Poor Edith.' James sighed deeply, and said again, 'Poor Edith. I know I did wrong, but we were both young and hot-blooded, and she was trapped by that cruel husband of hers.'

'Well, he's dead now,' Lily assured him. 'So he can't hurt her any more.'

'But Elizabeth isn't!' Suddenly James seemed to come to his senses and tried to struggle up in his chair. 'She mustn't know, Lily. It would kill her.'

'All right. If that's what you want.'

'Who else knows?'

'Only Peter and his mother – but they won't talk. Not if I ask them not to.'

'I kept trying to make Moses buy the farm, you know,' Mr Thomas said, sinking back in his chair. 'Partly because I needed the money, and partly for Edith's sake. Why, oh why didn't she tell me she was pregnant?'

'I suppose she thought there was nothing you could do, being married yourself. I suppose she was hoping it would be another boy – one that would live – and Moses would accept it as his own. Instead she had me.'

'All the more reason why I should change my will. I keep meaning to, you know. Then you and your mother would be safe. Of course Elizabeth would wonder.' James rested his head back and gazed out of the window thoughtfully. Lily reached out and took his hand.

'You don't have to leave us anything, Father,' she said. 'Just knowing that you acknowledge us is enough. We'll be all right. Peter and I will get married one day, and we'll make sure mother wants for nothing.'

They went on talking for a long time; but in the end Mrs Thomas came into the room and asked Lily to go. She said her husband must be tired.

'You'll come again, won't you?' James asked, not wanting to let go of Lily's hand.

'If you want me to – and if Mrs Thomas doesn't mind.'

'Well, you certainly seem to have done my husband good,' Elizabeth said. 'He's got much more colour in his face. Of course he always did spoil you. Sometimes I felt quite sorry for Betty. After all, she is our daughter.'

'Of course, Mrs Thomas,' Lily said respectfully. 'I quite understand. I'd like to come again, but only if you say so.'

'I'll send a message down when he's feeling up to it.'

Elizabeth ushered her guest to the door; but behind her

broad back Lily caught her father's eye, and they winked at each other.

But all that had happened months ago, and ever since Lily had been a frequent visitor to Ring House. Elizabeth welcomed her because she seemed to do James good, and it lightened her burden of care.

Lily would sit by his chair for hours at a time talking or reading to him. When he was feeling well enough she would walk with him in the garden, and it was on one of these walks that he told her he'd finally sold Valley Farm. A Kentish farmer, with many years' experience, wanted to start a dairy herd. He intended pulling down the outbuildings, modernizing the farmhouse, and starting from scratch. He was also a bachelor and needed labourers to work for him, so he would bring jobs to the village of Lenton. So while Lily was preparing for her spring wedding, alterations were going on all around her.

'You'd better try this on,' Emma Jackson said, holding up the wedding gown she'd been working on. 'It's nearly finished. You can tell me about Mr Thomas some other time.'

Stepping out of her blouse and skirt, Lily slipped the dress over her head. The silk felt warm as it slid down over her body: as soft as tissue paper, as crisp as meringue. It was a very simple dress, but after the pink creation Robert had made her wear she'd insisted on no frills or flounces.

'What does it look like?' Lily asked, twirling around on the floor among the snippets of silk and lengths of cotton.

'Lovely,' Emma said. 'You're going to be the prettiest bride Lenton has ever seen.'

Pretty was an understatement. Everyone agreed that Lily from the Valley looked radiant as she walked into St Patrick's church on Matthew Crow's arm.

The dress Emma had made for her fell softly from her shoulders to her slender waist, and then swirled gently outwards to her ankles. The bodice was embroidered with white silk and seed pearls, and the tiny coronet that held the veil on her dark head was set with pearls as well. In her hands she carried a posy: violets and freesias the same colour as her eyes, backed with sprays of delicate fern. Amongst the blossoms nestled a few of the flowers from which she was named – lily of the valley.

She'd insisted on Matthew giving her away, and the honour had turned him into a changed man. Wearing the first suit he'd ever owned, he escorted Lily with pride. Even if she wasn't his daughter he felt as proud as the true one would have been. With his hair trimmed and his face shining with soap and water, he beamed happily at the congregation as they walked down the aisle to where Peter was waiting.

Lily had expected a quiet wedding, but it was surprising how many people had turned out to wish them well. In the front pew Emma sat wearing a grey dress and a feathered hat, and a pair of new shoes that were killing her. She couldn't wait to get home and take them off. By her side sat Mike and Amy and their two children. Alec was now a sturdy five-year-old; and his little sister, two-year-old Sophie, was spruced up in sprigged muslin with an enormous ribbon bow in her curly hair. Next to them sat Billy, home for the day from college where he was studying agriculture.

Edith was there, weeping happily into a large handkerchief. Lily had helped her choose an outfit that was suitable for the bride's mother. They'd settled on a navy-blue and white suit and a matching pillbox hat, under which her thin hair was tucked neatly. But just like Matthew, a transformation had taken place in Lily's mother, and it wasn't only the new clothes.

Edith Crow had a job. When Dudley Oak bought Valley Farm he'd looked around for a housekeeper, and who better than the woman who knew the farm and dairy like the back of her hand, and who could milk cows and churn butter with the best of them?

And it wasn't a scarecrow who turned up for the interview either. Emma and Lily had seen to that. Lily's love for the woman who'd tried to disown her had softened Edith's bitter heart. The death of Moses had lifted a weight from her shoulders: the weight of years of cruelty and abuse. She'd stopped mourning for her dead sons, and no longer visited the churchyard to weep over their tiny graves. She wouldn't forget them, but her daughter Lily had drawn her out of the past, so that she could look forward to the future at last.

Emma Jackson had also done her bit, encouraging Edith to help around the cottage and take a pride in her appearance. And regular meals had played their part. Her emaciated body had filled out and she began to resemble a human being again.

Dudley Oak had been quite taken with her. His bachelor existence was lonely and he was on the lookout for a wife. He wanted a countrywoman who wouldn't be afraid of work, a companion, not a town floozy who would want new clothes every season, and holidays. Farm life wasn't like that. Edith Crow fitted the bill, and what was more, some of her former good looks had begun to return, shining through when she smiled, which she did quite often these days. In fact Lenton was awaiting an announcement – the news that there would soon be another wedding at St Patrick's Church.

Even Elizabeth Thomas came to the wedding, although she was late and had to slip into a back pew. James wasn't well enough to come, but his word still meant something at Ring House.. After all, he'd argued, Lily had almost been one of the family. One of them should attend. When he heard the church bells he smiled, knowing that now he could die happily. His Lily was safe, in the the arms of a good man. Then James shook himself. He mustn't think about dying: he had so much to look forward to. Elizabeth would be home soon to report on the wedding. He wanted to hear all about it. Did Lily look lovely? Did Peter look proud? But he already knew the answers to both these questions.

Mr Plummer, the vicar, was asked back to join the family for a celebratory tea – and what a tea Emma provided. Not for her the dainty fare usually served at wedding receptions. Emma knew the size of country-folk's appetites, and no one was going to leave her table hungry.

There was a ham, and sausages, hard-boiled eggs and salad. Scones oozing with strawberry jam and rich yellow cream. Tarts and pastries, and gingerbread men and trifle for the children. But of course in pride of place was the cake: two tiers of iced confection decorated with silver slippers and horseshoes, and on the top a miniature bride and groom.

The top tier was traditionally removed to be stored away for the first christening, as Emma informed the blushing bride. Everyone applauded as the newlyweds cut the cake between them, their hands entwined over the handle of the knife.

During a lull in the proceedings Matthew rose to his feet. 'I want to make a speech,' he said solemnly, picking nervously at his bottom lip. He'd learnt his speech by heart, rehearsing it in front of a mirror until he was word perfect, and now the moment had come. He looked around at the friendly faces smiling at him and waiting for him to begin. Suddenly he knew that it didn't matter if he made a fool of himself: he loved all of them and they loved him, so he had no need for words. He wiped his forehead with the handkerchief Emma Jackson had tucked into his top pocket, beamed around at the waiting company, and forgot what he'd intended saying. The short sentence he uttered went straight to everybody's heart. All he could manage was, 'To Lily and Peter – God bless them.'

Everyone in the room raised their glasses of elderberry wine and echoed Matthew's words, 'Lily and Peter – God bless them.'

Life soon settled into an easy rhythm. Spring crept into summer with its long, sunny days. Lily gloried in home-making and found she had a talent for it.

Most of her wishes had come true. She had a loving husband, a garden to grow things in, and a home of her own. Matthew was living with them and proved very useful around the cottage doing odd jobs; he also did seasonal labouring on the nearby farms. He was no problem.

But much as Lily loved Peter's mother she did find it difficult sharing a kitchen. Emma Jackson looked on it as her own domain, and although she tried to make allowances for her daughter-in-law, it didn't always work. They had different ideas about the most simple things: baking cakes, oven temperatures, and even the Sunday roast. But they both liked a quiet life and so usually ended up laughing over their differences.

Soon after the wedding Lily wrote to Grace and very quickly received a reply.

'Dearest Lily,' Grace wrote in her careful copy-book handwriting. 'Thank you for your letter. I shouldn't say, I told you so – but, I did tell you so, didn't I? I think you and Peter are made for each other. A real love match, like Jake and me. I never saw you as the lady of the manor; it wouldn't have suited you. I work for Mrs Sayer occasionally so find out what's going on. Dorothy and Paul are very happy with their new nanny, although they still talk about you. But they're not sad, so you don't have to worry about them. You asked about Robert. He was, of course, completely devastated at losing you, and everyone worried for a while that he was going to be ill again. He went away for a holiday, to the South of France I think, and when he returned he looked a lot happier. He'd made friends with a young woman he met there who'd recently lost her husband in an accident. She has a two-year-old daughter as well, so they have a lot in common. Anyway, she came to Piltdown Manor on a visit, and do you know – she looks a lot like you. She has the same hair and skin, and the same graceful way of walking. She could be you, only her eyes are green and her laugh is much louder. She laughs a lot, and Robert laughs too, and I don't think it will be very long before Mr and Mrs Sayer start to arrange a house party to celebrate another engagement. So you see you don't have to worry about Robert either. Timmy and Sally send their love, and you'll be pleased to know that I'm pregnant again. It'll be another girl, I suppose, if that gipsy's right. Jake sends his love, and so does your friend – Grace.'

In the September Lily suspected that she also was pregnant. Her delight knew no bounds, and Peter's radiant face when she told him showed just how happy he was at the news.

Emma immediately produced the wooden cradle on rockers that her husband, Bert, had carved so many years before for Peter and his brothers. The two women cleaned and polished it until it looked like new. Emma lined it with padded silk while Lily embroidered pillowcases and hemmed tiny sheets.

Before the baby was born James Thomas died. Lily had become a regular visitor to Ring House, at Elizabeth's invitation. James was excited at the idea of becoming a grandfather, even if his involvement with this baby had to be kept secret. During Lily's visits they would talk about many things. James always wanted news of Edith, and was pleased to hear that she was making a life for herself. They talked of the past, and Lily amused him by telling him about the predictions made by the gipsy and the old woman in the hospital bed. They had foreseen that a man resembling James Thomas was indeed Lily's father. He liked to hear about the plans she and Peter had for adding to their family. She assured him that they wanted more than one child.

He died on a cold January day. It had snowed in the night, and the trees outside his bedroom window were hanging with a frill of white lace, like the icing on a cake. Although it was cold there was no wind and the view was like an old-fashioned Christmas card. He asked Elizabeth to open the window, and when she argued with him he became quite distressed.

'Do as you're told, woman,' he commanded in the sort of voice that, although weak, had to be obeyed. 'I shall never see a view like this again, so do as you're told.'

Mrs Thomas stoked up the fire, and tucked a shawl around her husband's shoulders before opening the window. 'You're not cold, dear?' she asked.

'No. The air smells of pine needles. Can you smell it, Elizabeth?'

Mrs Thomas couldn't, but she nodded anyway. 'Would you like some tea?'

'That sounds nice. And biscuits – digestive biscuits.'

In the old days Elizabeth would have instructed the maid, but now she had to leave the room to make the tea herself. She was as quick as she could be – not more than a quarter of an hour – but when she hurried back with the tray James was dead. It had just begun to snow again and he was staring out of the window with his eyes open, but she knew he was dead. There was a smile on his face and he looked peaceful and contented.

They buried him in St Patrick's churchyard the following week. The weather had turned milder and melted the snow, softening the frozen ground so that the grave was easy to dig. A long procession of villagers followed the coffin to its resting place. Heads were lowered and caps doffed. James Thomas of Ring House had been a respected member of the community, and many had him to thank for their homes as well as their livelihoods.

As friends of the family, Lily and Peter stood by the graveside. They were sad but not distressed. Mr Thomas had been a dear companion and would be missed, but he'd had a full life and the end had come quickly. Doctor Butler had diagnosed a massive heart attack: James wouldn't have known anything about it.

Betty and Edward were there. They were both dressed in black, and Betty's eyes were puffed red with weeping. Lily caught her eye and smiled compassionately. After a moment Betty smiled back, and then turning to her husband reached for his hand. Edward didn't look at Lily at all. She noticed the way he slipped his arms around his wife's shoulders, and whispered in her ear as if he was trying to comfort her. Lily was glad. Edward belonged to Betty now, and they were so obviously happy.

Pregnancy suited Lily and she was proud of her swelling belly. She made herself pretty maternity smocks, and knitted tiny outfits for the baby. She was always busy. One day, when she was in her sixth month, Mrs Jackson came into the kitchen where she was making bread. Peter was washing his hands at the sink. They looked up at Emma's entrance: she'd left the cottage only an hour before and was still wearing her everyday coat and hat.

'I want to talk to you both,' she said, stripping off her gloves and unpinning her hat. 'Come and sit down.'

Peter wiped his hands on a rough piece of towel, and Lily abandoned her kneading. They sat down at the table and looked at Emma expectantly. Although there was a determined air about her she was smiling, so it didn't look as if it was bad news she had to impart.

'I've just come from Ring House,' she said. 'Elizabeth Thomas and I have just been having a good gossip.'

'What about?' Peter asked. Lily just folded her hands in her lap and waited.

'Our future – Elizabeth's and mine.' Emma looked from Lily to Peter, but she had their full attention. 'She's sold Ring House and I don't blame her. Even if she could afford to keep it it's much too big for one person. She's bought a nice little place in Lenton. One of those new houses they've just built behind the old church. There's six rooms and a nice little patch of garden front and back. I'm going to live there with her – as her housekeeper.'

'No!' Lily and Peter spoke together.

'I promised Dad I'd look after you,' Peter said. 'Your home is here with us for the rest of your life.'

'You talk as if I'm on my last legs.' Emma's eyes flashed with amusement. 'I may be getting on in years but there's still a lot of work left in me. Matthew needs a home here more than I do, and it'll be too crowded when the baby comes. You both need more privacy, and Lily needs her own kitchen. You should see the one at the new house: all modern, with shiny taps and hot water. I shall have sole charge – Elizabeth promised.'

Lily looked at Peter and he nodded. 'We'll only let you go if you promise us one thing.'

'What's that?'

'That you'll visit often, and still think of this as home.'

'I promise,' Emma assured them. 'And Mrs Thomas says the new owners of Ring House will be needing a gardener and she's recommended you, Peter, of course. They're a young couple with three children. They've just sold their house in London because they want to live in the country. So it's going to be pretty lively.'

Lily smiled: it all sounded perfect. The baby in her womb kicked and she stroked her stomach. 'Violet approves,' she said.

'Violet?' her mother-in-law queried.

'That's what we're going to call her. Peter wants a little girl with eyes the same colour as mine. And we're going to call her Violet'

'I hope you get what you want,' Emma said sincerely. 'You deserve it.'

*

Violet Edith Jackson was born on the first day of June. She weighed seven pounds five ounces, had a fringe of dark hair around her tiny head, skin the colour of rose petals, and when she opened her eyes they were the colour of newly washed violets.

It was the easiest birth the village midwife had ever attended, and at the age of sixty she'd seen most of the young people of Lenton into the world. When Lily told her that she herself had been born in the locality the midwife shook her head and decided that her memory must be going. She didn't recall any of her mothers calling their babies Lily. But there – she must have forgotten.

Lily was alone in the cottage when the first contraction came. She was baking a special cake for Peter's tea. As she guessed there was no hurry she poured the batter into a greased tin and popped it into the oven before going to the window to call Matthew who was outside chopping wood.

'I'll be there in a minute, Lily,' he answered. 'Can you make a cup of tea?'

Lily laughed. 'I'll put the kettle on. It'll be ready by the time you get back with the midwife. And you'll have to take the cake out of the oven for me because I don't think the baby wants to wait.'

One glance at her face assured Matthew that she wasn't joking. He dropped his axe and set off down the path towards Lenton, his heavy boots sparking on the flint-lined road.

Lily called after him. 'And you'd better stop on your way and alert Peter's mother. She'll be upset if she's the last to know.'

'Don't you worry, girl,' Matthew shouted over his shoulder without slowing down. 'I'll bring her back with me – I promise.'

Lily smiled. The house was tidy and everything prepared. All she had to do was climb the stairs to the room she shared with Peter, get into the big bed and wait. But first she crossed to the window and threw it open. The scents from the garden were overwhelming: a mixture of pinks, lavender, mint and honeysuckle, all the wild varieties that she loved. No formal beds of regimented flowers for her.

Under the window stood the cradle. Lily put out her foot and rocked it experimentally. Her baby would have everything she'd never had. A mother and a father, a proper home, and a cradle to sleep in. No bed of straw for Violet Jackson. She was the most wanted baby in the whole wide world; as would be the brothers and sisters Lily hoped she'd be able to give her.

She undressed and climbed into the high bed, turning her face towards the window. The baby made itself known, as if now that its time had come it was in a hurry to be born.

'Hush,' Lily said, stroking the tight skin of her stomach. 'There's no hurry – there's plenty of time.'

She found that she was humming a tune to calm the baby: communicating with the unborn child with her voice. The baby seemed to hear and was pacified.

When it came the birth was quick and easy, and Matthew was sent post-haste to find Peter and tell him the good news. He found him mowing the newly laid lawn at Ring House for the new owners. Following him across the grass were three children: two boys and a little girl, chattering and laughing like baby sparrows. Peter hushed them as Matthew stumbled towards him.

'What is it?'

'The baby's born, Peter! You're a father! It's a little girl – it's Violet!'

Without a word Peter dropped everything and headed for home. He knew Matthew would put away his tools and explain to his employers. Head flung back and feet pounding on the path, he raced towards the cottage, vaulted over the gate, and ran through the kitchen where his mother was making a pot of tea. On the table was the cooling cake that Lily had promised him. Lily always kept her promises and somehow the cake seemed more than just a cake. The baking of it had taken on a new meaning.

Peter paused halfway up the stairs. He could hear someone singing. The bedroom door was half-open and he could hear a sweet voice crooning a lullaby. He stood in the doorway to take in the picture of mother and child. The pretty young woman – his wife – with the wing of dark hair falling over her shoulder, and the tiny baby nestled safely in her arms.

Lily looked up at him and smiled. She stretched out her free hand towards her husband. Then she looked down again at the sleeping child and started to sing. In the voice that had been silent far too long she started to sing the beautiful strains of the Ave Maria.